Praise for
Once a Hero

Michael A. Stackpole's exciting fantasy debut!

"Magic, action, adventure, romance, political intrigue—this book has it all!" —Jennifer Roberson

"*Once a Hero* is a richly imagined tapestry, woven of sword-steel and sparked with threads of magic."
—Diana Gabaldon

"Michael A. Stackpole breaks out onto new ground with *Once a Hero*. Threaded through a big, exciting adventure story are the joys and sorrows of characters whose heart-break and triumph will stay with you long after you've finished reading." —Kate Elliott

"A great story! The legendary Neal and his Elven sweet-heart Gena come so alive on these pages that the bank or supermarket down the block are the *un*realities. Spell-binding in its color and action, this is a tale that draws you deep into its wild, wonderful world and makes you wish you were actually a part of it."
—Hugh B. Cave

Don't miss any of these exciting titles from Bantam Spectra!

Once a Hero

A Novel

Michael A. Stackpole

TM

BANTAM BOOKS
NEW YORK • TORONTO • LONDON • SYDNEY • AUCKLAND

ONCE A HERO

A Bantam Spectra Book / May 1994

SPECTRA and the portrayal of a boxed "s" are trademarks of Bantam Books, a division of Bantam Doubleday Dell Publishing Group, Inc.

ISBN 0-553-56112-X

Published simultaneously in the United States and Canada

Bantam Books are published by Bantam Books, a division of Bantam Doubleday Dell Publishing Group, Inc. Its trademark, consisting of the words "Bantam Books" and the portrayal of a rooster, is Registered in U.S. Patent and Trademark Office and in other countries. Marca Registrada. Bantam Books, 1540 Broadway, New York, New York 10036.

PRINTED IN THE UNITED STATES OF AMERICA

RAD 0 9 8 7 6 5 4 3 2 1

This book is dedicated to

Jim Fitzpatrick

As an artist, the pictures he paints are worth far more than a thousand words, and as an author, his understanding of heroes and heroism laid the foundation for much of this work.

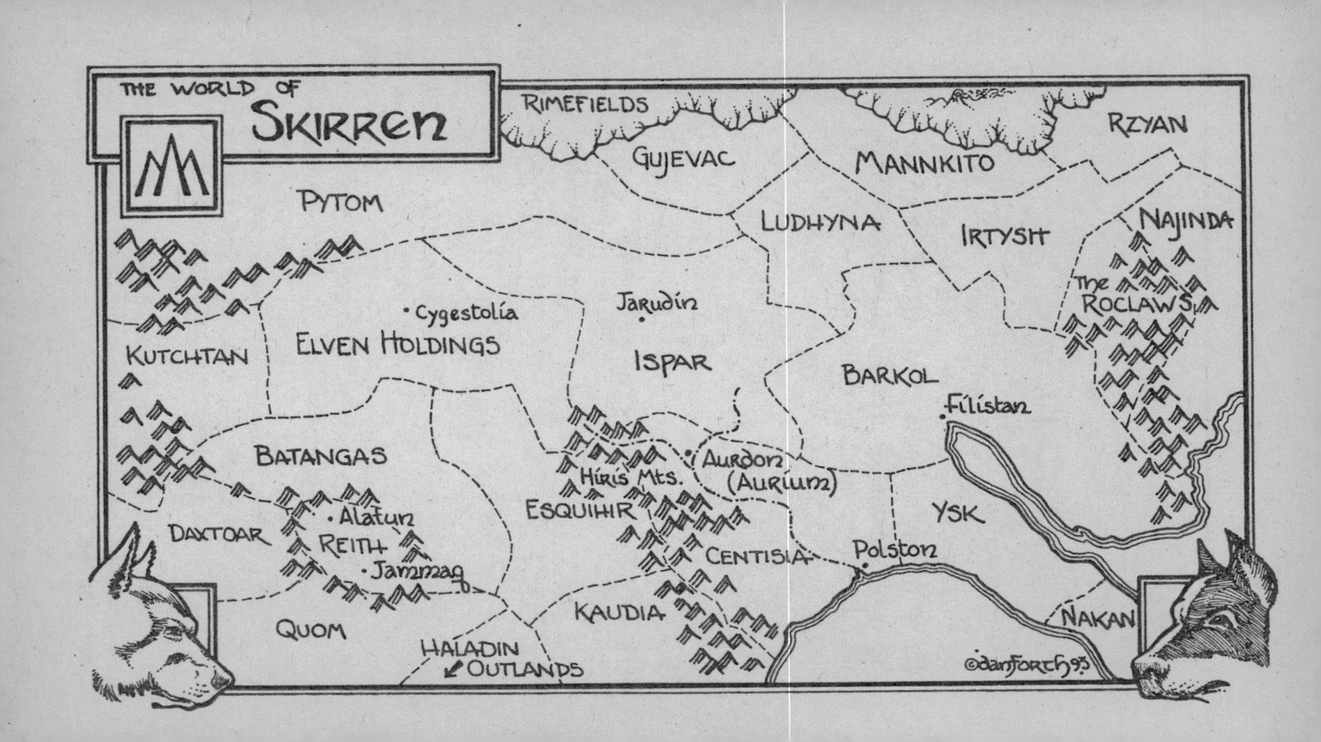
THE WORLD OF
SKIRREN
RIMEFIELDS
GUJEVAC
MANNKITO
RZYAN
PYTOM
LUDHYNA
IRTYSH
NAJINDA
The ROCLAWS
Jarudín
Cygestolía
ELVEN HOLDINGS
KUTCHTAN
ISPAR
BARKOL
Fílistan
BATANGAS
Híris Mts.
Aurdon
(Aurium)
ESQUIHIR
YSK
DAXTOAR
Alatun
REITH
Jammag
CENTISIA
Polston
KAUDIA
QUOM
HALADIN
OUTLANDS
NAKAN
©danforth95

Acknowledgments

This work could not have been completed without the help or influence of the following individuals:

Janna Silverstein, Ricia Mainhardt, Jennifer Roberson, and Liz Danforth, who, as the Four Horsewomen of the Apocalypse, promised me disaster if I didn't get this book right. All four of them endured the telling of chunks of this tale while I worked on it, and their forbearance was greatly appreciated.

Dennis L. McKiernan, Alis Rasmussen, and Kate Elliot, who provided insights into fantasy and character that enabled me to pick out key points for emphasis. All three of them, in addition to Jennifer Roberson, are great storytellers, and if you've not read them, you are missing a bet.

Ron Wolfley, Brian and Frances Gross, and Bob and Patty Vardeman, who asked questions and made me defend points that helped determine the direction and content of this book.

Chris Harvey who went above and beyond the call of duty in locating a Maltese/English English/Maltese dictionary for me.

Sam Lewis and Brian Fargo who were patient in allowing me to indulge myself in writing the book.

And, as always, my parents, Jim and Janet; my brother, Patrick, and his wife Joy; my sister, Kerin, and again Liz, who supplied the support and encouragement that made it possible for me to finish the job.

Prologue

A Night's Adventure in Jammaq

Midsummer's Eve
Five Centuries Ago
My Twenty-second Birthday

The high-mountain night breezes whipped through the dark canyons of the Reithrese charnel town and greeted me with cold razor kisses on my eyes. The chill thin air whistled and moaned as it broke around corners and over the myriad gargoyles decorating Jammaq. Not for the first time I wondered why I had traveled so far to put myself in the heart of a city sacred to a people who, as a race, had sworn to kill me.

As always, the same answer came to my question: *the sword.* And that answer satisfied me. Though I had seen it only once, and on that occasion had felt its steely caress a number of times, I knew the blade was meant to be mine. And if possessing it required me to chase it to the gates of the Cold Goddess's Realm or beyond, I was prepared to go that far.

I shivered in my stolen clothes and let a steamy sigh get whipped away by the wind. Obsession breeds foolishness the way stale water breeds mosquitoes, and folks would describe our efforts as foolishness if my Elven companion and I failed in our quest. Still and all, no one else had ever done what Aarundel and I had accomplished so far in our mission, and I took some delight in that fact even if he did not.

I winked at Aarundel. "Don't go thinking of it as grave robbing, Aarundel, think of it as . . . as mining ore for bards to refine into golden song."

"I never thought it my destiny to be lauded before inebriates in a song titled, 'The True Death of the Dun Wolf.' " Aarundel tugged the red scarf away from his mouth and hunched his shoulders. That trimmed four inches off his height, making him shorter than I am. The loose-fitting black *natari* cassocks we wore added enough bulk to his slender build to let him pass for a Reithrese, though both of us were too tall to fool anyone with one eye open and enough sense to recognize Aarundel's pointed ears poking up through his black hair.

Of course, anyone with that much sense was well away from here.

The Elf's dark eyes glittered in the wan moonlight. "I have half a mind to leave now."

"If you had half a mind, you'd not have come here at all."

The Elf shook his head ruefully. "Clearly my faculties have been atrophied by five years of association with you."

"I'm thinking it's our dying that has befuddled you."

"Ah, yes, to be dead in the city of the dead. The concept amused, but the reality has failed to satisfy expectation." He spat at the nearest building. "This is a foul place."

"Foul it is, and fairly we will quit it, when we are done." Looking about through the dark-shrouded streets, I thought "foul" a rather mild adjective, for death haunted the city of Jammaq. The wind kept it cold, even in high summer, though I had no complaint about that. Growing up in the Roclaws, I had been born in an unseasonable blizzard and had spent more time walking on snow and ice than in spring-green meadows.

With ourselves being the exception, not a living creature walked the cobbled streets in the Reithrese city of the dead that night. The swirling wind brought with it the rot-scent of decaying meat, and that made taking every step toward the center of the city a battle. I pulled the *natari* scarf up over my nose again and let the wet-wool scent mask the death stench so I could go forward.

I had no idea what the Reithrese envisioned when they created Jammaq, but I could see what it had become over the centuries and centuries. Streets ran haphazard through the city, like cracks in ice, without rhyme and certainly with little reason. The outlying buildings, none over a single story tall, sprouted corners as a bird would feathers. Odd blocks jutted out, studding the walls with stone thorns so thick that even a rat would be hard pressed to find shadowed space large enough in which to hide. That fact had caused my friend and I no end of anxiety, until we both discovered that all but a few of the buildings were empty, and those that were not, advertised their condition with loud music and thin slivers of light limning tight-closed shutters and doors.

If it weren't enough that all the buildings had been blackwashed, each had been decorated in a most horrible manner. Gargoyles big and small, ancient and new-carved, perched on lintels and hung from eaves. They grew like warts from the buildings, snarling outward with fearsome fangs bared. Moving through the night, I could feel a thousand eyes watching us, but nary a one connected to a brain that could think or a mouth that could raise an alarm.

The inhabited houses in Jammaq were not that different from their silent, dark companions. Music, likely intended to keep out the ghostly howl of the wind, pinpointed them even before we saw light. We snuck past them like spectres ourselves, but the risk of discovery remained low. There was a chance that someone might look out if we accidently made a noise, but we had taken precautions against discovery in that event as well.

Our dark trousers and robes, colorful scarf and sash, and the beaded-leather *quitawi* dangling from our right wrists, marked us as members of the *natari*. Perhaps more feared among the Reithrese than the ghosts lost in the city's street-maze, the militant guardians of Reithrese religious tradition had a reputation for brutal, cold cruelty in the prosecution of their duties. They were inviolate, and no one was immune from their judgment, so everyone avoided them. So arrogant and confident in their roles were they that the two we waylaid to obtain our disguises had been shocked that we dared strike them.

We came to a crossroad, and I lashed the quirt against my left palm as I looked around for directions. To the southwest I could see the tower complex for which we were bound. Towers of all heights and thicknesses stabbed into the air like a multifingered hand clawing stars from the night sky. The flickering orange glow from the center of the tower-circle pulsed out enough light to mold the towers themselves into grasping silhouettes.

"Do you think the *natari* have no street signs here to confuse the ghosts, or to earn money guiding families to their lodgings here and back out again?"

"More the latter than the former, I would imagine, but not having seen a ghost so far, I think their efforts in that direction are at least partially successful." Resting his war ax across his knees, Aarundel crouched down and reached out with a long-fingered hand to push at a couple of cobblestones. "None are loose, Neal."

I frowned. The city of the dead had no street signs and few enough landmarks beyond the tower silhouettes. So far, operating on the idea that the gargoyles were all meant to scare ghosts from the tower back into it, we had been keeping the stone faces at our back. Here, though, the gargoyles faced us from one alley and looked away down two roads. The broader street curved off and away, while the narrower one seemed to continue dead west. Loose stones might have marked which way others had gone before, but Aarundel's report dashed that hope.

I dropped to my haunches beside him. "Being as how the Reithrese and Elves are both Elder races, how would you mark them as balancing ceremony with practicality?"

Aarundel's head came up, and scorn echoed through his harsh whisper. "They are a vulgar and ostentatious race, given to frivolous display."

"And probably not very pleased with the prospect of spending much time here at their grisly doings, eh?" I glanced at the weathering of the gargoyles in both the wide and skinny roads. "We'll take this one, then, my friend. There's enough of a difference that says the wide is new and not for us."

The Elf nodded and headed off down the narrow roadway, with me quick at his heels. Neither one of us had much scholarship in the ways of the Reithrese—though Aarundel could manage their angular tongue—but we knew just enough about their religious fetishes for me to hatch my plot and for Aarundel to imagine it might succeed. What was born as an "I wonder" teamed up with a couple of "we really shoulds," and before reason could rear her fair head and dissuade us, we rode for the mountains and invaded Jammaq in search of a sword.

The Reithrese, being bound to the goddess of the underworld—called Reithra by those of us who had no need or desire to know her true name—have some peculiar rites when it comes to the treatment of the dead. Being like men in all ways except the length of their life, the power they command, and their hateful nature toward outsiders, the Reithrese bring their dead to Jammaq. They entomb them in the tower, with lesser folk being stored higher up—further distant from their goddess—and the great and mighty lying in the bosom of the earth herself.

A year or so later, weather willing and bandits bribed, the relatives of the deceased return to open the tomb. They clean the bones and put them in a box to be carried back to Alatun or one of the other Reithrese cities to be kept in family shrines. Finally, as part of the funeral, the dead's possessions, which were stored with him in that first year, are auctioned off to the person who can make the best case for why he should inherit the item in question.

"And no one can make a better case for owning my sword than I," I mumbled as we wound our way down a snake-twist road.

Despite my words being muffled in the scarf, Aarundel's sharp ears heard my remark. "Your sword? *Khlephnaft* was never your sword, my friend."

"It's a fated blade, Aarundel, you've said so yourself. It *has* to be mine."

"I must have missed seeing the name Neal Roclawzi in reading the various prophecies concerning the sword."

"It's there, unless someone like Finndali has been revising texts, and you know that for the truth." I turned left onto a broad boulevard that arced on down toward the towers. "Besides, you know Tashayul wanted me to have it. Cleaveheart is mine; he declared it so during his speech dedicating Jarudin to Reithra."

Aarundel's dark eyes flashed from above his scarf. "That would be a rather broad interpretation of, 'Neal is the last person in the world I want to have this sword!' would it not?"

"It loses something in the translation." I smiled devilishly. "In the original I'd wager he was more eloquent in describing how I should get the blade."

"This I believe sincerely."

Tashayul had no reason to want me to have anything but his undying enmity. The Reithrese people had once possessed a vast empire that had extended from ocean to deserts and back again. Over the centuries it had begun to shrink, as nations of men split off and proclaimed their own independence. The Reithrese contented themselves with a commonwealth for a while, then let a Human empire nibble away at their borders. Five hundred years ago they even accepted Elven intervention in the affairs of what had been their empire. The days of Reithrese glory had faded for all time.

At least it seemed that way to all but the Reithrese. Being long-lived—both because of their nature and the chaotic, elemental magicks they had mastered—they took an almost Elven view of mayfly Humanity. In addition to their perspective, they had another thing that made waiting and tolerating all possible for them. Like a dagger hidden in a boot, they had a prophecy, and this prophecy said their empire would be born anew.

Tashayul and his brother, Takrakor, determined through the former's cunning and the latter's magicks, that they were the individuals fated to reunify the old empire under their leadership. They started a crusade in which their troops committed atrocities that almost served to eclipse the excesses of the *Eldsaga* in their ferocity. The brothers let it be known that they intended to slay or enslave all Men within the borders of what had once been their empire. Humanity, politically fractured and without leadership, had no way to oppose them.

What Men needed was a hero. Having been proclaimed a hero by sayers of sooth since my birth, I came to see the Reithrese war as the crucible in which I would be tested. We Roclawzi had long prided ourselves in our warrior tradition, and the Reithrese had never beaten us before in a fight. Because I had been born on Midsummer's Eve—in a blizzard and beneath a triangle of full moons—great things were expected of me. The storm, the Triangle, and even one event hiding the other were all omens that could be taken for good or ill as appropriate and caused me to feel I had been born to be the sort of hero who could stop the Reithrese. In answering my call to duty, I forged a sword, mounted a horse, and headed down out of the mountains to lay claim to a legend or to lie still in an anonymous grave.

It was a time of chaos in which the whole of the world was filled with as many horrors as Jammaq itself. To the Reithrese, men were not really much more than demi-oxen who could guide their bigger brethren at the plow. While this did place us a bit higher in the scheme of things than in the average Elven view, it didn't spare many lives. As I rode west, I heard refugee tales of villages being burned, babies being drowned like kittens in rivers, and all resistance being crushed wherever a defense was raised.

It took no alchemist to see one thing about the Reithrese probes: they ranged far out and away from the main battle lines in Ispar. The only good thing about being pointed out as a heroborn among a warrior people is that my training involved heavy doses of military strategy and tactics. To be truthful, among my people a frightening war cry counts for more than either strategy or tactics, but I enjoyed the study of both, so I was given as much as I wanted.

It struck me that while the fight for Ispar raged on, the Reithrese were spending an inordinate amount of time in the mountains of Esquihir. Not having wanted to head into the world utterly ignorant, I had read of Reithrese history and tactics. From my reading I recalled a previous and painfully short-lived campaign by another Reithrese general that had ended in those mountains. His effort had been unremarkable—and it failed because internal Reithrese politics eroded his support—but he was supposed to have borne a magical sword said to confer immortality upon the warrior who wielded it and to guarantee that warrior the winning of an empire.

Tashayul clearly wanted that sword.

That meant I wanted it as well.

Khlephnaft had been lost to common knowledge, but Tashayul's torturers turned up some clues to its location. Full of the innocent enthusiasm of youth, I killed horses in my mad dash across Barkol's grassy oceans, and killed Reithrese in Ispar's southern reaches. Fearful humans gave me shelter and supplies on my trek. When I let them know that I had come from the mountains with a sword I meant to use to kill Tashayul, tongues loosened and directions flowed freely.

Hoping against hope that the foolish youth from the Roclaws might do what no other human had managed—the Triangle birth working to inspire hope—folks pointed me toward a small Jistani convent in the Esquihir mountains. They claimed Cleaveheart had been kept by the nuns as a weapon meant for a champion sworn to Jistan to use in destroying his enemies. I'd never been very religious—the gods are perverse and like torturing Men with dire predicaments—but I was willing to offer an oath to Jistan if he'd lend me the blade.

Of course, I was not alone in wanting to get my hands on that blade. What people told me freely, and the Reithrese had to torture out of folks, had almost been forgotten by the Elves. For reasons of their own, they wanted this blade that they called *Divisator*. Aarundel said that meant "Sunderer," but that was long after we first met. So, while Tashayul and I raced for it, coming from the east and the west, the Elves came in from the north.

I arrived on the site first, and the nuns welcomed me as

if I were indeed the champion for whom they waited. I asked to take possession of Cleaveheart immediately, but the abbess avowed that Jistan had specified a number of rituals before the blade could be given over to my keeping.

I pressed her on this point. "I'm thinking, good Sister Constance, that Most High Jistan would understand about the urgency of the situation."

"Were that true, Neal Roclawzi, he would have given us a sign." Her face closed up in all the sign I needed to know I was doomed to wait.

Tashayul and his Skull-riders arrived as I was sleeping off a long ride and a full meal. The nuns, given the choice between death or surrender of the sword and my person, found themselves divinely inspired to declare me a heretic. This they did while I slumbered. I awoke from a dream about wrestling a snake to find myself bound hand and foot.

Standing beside the abbess, I watched from a balcony as a trio of nuns bore Cleaveheart to Tashayul. "No rituals, Sister?"

"We have had our sign, Neal Snaketongue." The nun eyed me sternly. "If you are truly Jistan's champion, He, in His divine wisdom, will find a way to unite you with the blade."

Watching Tashayul take practice cuts down in the courtyard, I had a feeling *he*, too, had a way to unite me with the blade, causing me to wonder if what I had taken as good omens were not so good after all. With the dawn's rose light glowing from the long serpentine blade's single razor edge, and the sword whistling as it sliced the air, wondering became knowing and I knew I'd seen my last dawn.

Two of Tashayul's guards accepted custody of me from the nuns and brought me down into the convent's courtyard. I towered over both my warders, but that was to be expected, as Reithrese tend to be slightly shorter than the average man. Even so their stocky Reithrese builds mocked my gangling limbs. In the few combats I had fought against their kind, my quickness and reach had made up for what I surrendered to them in strength. Hobbled by a short length of rope and with my arms bound behind me, those advantages went the way of my faith in Jistan.

Coming into the courtyard, perspective on, Tashayal changed and with it changed my assessment of him. Unlike his fellows, Tashayul and I could see eye to eye, which made him quite remarkable among the Reithrese. Stripped to the waist, Tashayul moved quickly and smoothly, with thick muscles sliding effortlessly beneath sweat-sheened skin that had been darkened by long exposure to the sun. His black hair had been pulled back into a ponytail that fell midway down his spine. Successful cuts at imaginary foes brought a smile to his face, peeling his lips back to reveal a mouth full of emerald teeth.

A booted foot applied to the back of my legs drove me to my knees in front of Tashayul. The Reithrese slashed the blade within a hair's-breadth of my nose, then sheathed Cleaveheart in one fluid, practiced motion. He took my straight, double-edged sword from one of his human slaves and bared it. He flipped it over and back, then tested the weight of it in his sword hand. He sighted down the edges of the blade, then leaned on the sword as if it were a cane and he a Kaudian dandy on a seaside promenade.

"You meant to kill me with this?" His voice came as hard as his dark-eyed stare, but I caught in both a theatricality meant to frighten me mightily.

"You should not be thinking that, m'lord. 'Tis a mountain tradition to be inscribing the name of a warrior one wishes to honor on a blade." I tried to smile up at him, but one of the guards crashed a backhanded cuff over my right ear.

Tashayul frowned at the soldier and shook his head. "I take it the telling of tall tales is another Roclawzi tradition? Or are you not this Neal of which my spies have told me?" He opened his arms, pointing my sword skyward, and took in the whole of the aging monastery with his gesture "Is this not the place where you said you would kill me?"

"I said nothing of the kind, m'lord." I answered him truthfully, for I'd never specified a place for us to meet. I had been too intent on discovering the resting place of

Cleaveheart to make those kinds of boasts. I had assumed I'd have enough time to make them after I found the blade.

Tashayul laughed aloud, and I saw the Reithrese lounging around the courtyard smile in response. "Foolish little Neal, you gave these wretched people hope. They told you where to find *Khlephnaft* because they dearly wanted you to destroy me. And then they told my spies where I would find you to speed the process. Before that, I knew not where to find this wondrous blade. I am in your debt."

I returned his gracious nod. "Well met, then. As you have no further need for my service, we can speak of repayment at another time." I started to get to my feet, but rough hands pressed me back down to the ground.

"I may yet have need of your service, Neal." Tashayul handed my sword to a slave. "How old are you, boy?"

I squinted at the horizon and searched the sky for constellations before the dawn's rosy glow could devour them, all the while carefully choosing the words for my lie. "This being midsummer and a bit south of my home, I'd admit to twenty summers." In my travels I'd heard of an augury that a foe a score summers in age would be his death, so I decided to pitch some fear back at him.

The Reithrese general shook his head and pinched the pale, hairless flesh over my heart. "If I were to believe that, I would believe you carry Elven blood, for you have matured very slowly. . . ."

An offended voice from behind me cut the general off. "Beware who you slander with your musings, Tashayul."

I pulled away from the Reithrese and twisted around to look at the company of Men standing in the courtyard gateway. At least at first I took them for Men because, from my perspective, their height was not particularly noticeable. The edge of the sun backed them with yellow-fire, so all I could see were silhouettes. Only when one moved so I could see the odd curve to his bow and another doffed his huntsman's hood to let me see pointed ears did I realize the interlopers were Elves, not Men.

From the forge to the anvil, I groaned to myself. At least with the Reithrese I had a chance of being made a slave. With the Elves, well, the *Eldsaga* gave me a legion of fates to choose from with the Elves. Still and all, the Elves and the Reithrese were never known for their cordial relations.

Tashayul folded his arms across his broad chest. "Imperator Finndali, to what do I owe this dubious honor? Has this Man been threatening to end your life as well?"

The Elven leader dismissed me with a shake of his head. "Were he worthy of notice—say your speculation about his blood had veracity—he would be rapeget, and I would terminate his life. The Consilliarii have taken an interest in this *Khlephnaft*. I was sent to obtain it for them."

Tashayul's eyes narrowed. "I see. I have a pressing need for it. Do you want it now?" As he asked his question, his soldiers became more alert. They shifted positions to supply cover from Elven arrows or to bring weapons to hand easily.

The Elf shook his head with a motion that dropped his green leather hunting-hood back, freeing his fine black hair. "How long do you need it?"

The Reithrese shrugged. "Fifty years, I think. By then our rule will be restored."

"An ambitious schedule."

Tashayul glanced down at me. "Once we destroy their breeding stock, we expect resistance to crumble. We learned that from you, in fact."

Finndali smiled in a way that sent a rime asp wriggling through my entrails. "Fifty years, then. I will have it from you at that time."

I forced myself to laugh. "You're supposing, of course, the good general will have it at that time. Fifty years will a lot of battles bring."

"But battles waged against your kind, Man."

I nodded over at the slave holding my broadsword. "Those edges opened Reithrese veins easy enough. Lest you're mindful of a way to use arrogance as armor, I'd wager he's not got two score ten years left to him." I did some quick math in my head. "I'm thinking he'll sup at death's table in less than four."

Tashayul chuckled as he shook his head and let mock

surprise wash over his face. "Only four years? How did you arrive at that number?"

I decided not to tell him that were the prophecy about his death true, I'd need those years to prepare. I lied instead. "A year each for the conquest of Ispar, Barkol, and Irtysh, which brings you to the Roclaws four years hence."

"The Roclaws? Do you truly think your mountain tribesmen can defeat me?"

I shrugged. "If they saw you as a serious threat, don't you think they would have sent more than me to kill you?"

I heard a couple of the Elves laugh at my question, though a stern glance from their leader silenced them. I looked at Finndali. "Were I you, m'lord, I would take the blade now. You would find its price dear if you were to require Cleaveheart from the hand of a Roclawzi."

The Elf ignored me. "I find these younglings quite dolorous in general, but this one is a particular annoyance. Too moronic to be properly terrified."

"Pathetic." Tashayul drew *Khlephnaft* and presented it hilt first to Finndali. "I had thought to vet the blade's abilities by slaying him myself, but I will grant you this honor."

"Your offer is appreciated and laced with temptation, but it is *your* blade."

"And you dishonor it," I spat at the both of them. "Turning that fine piece of war-steel into a butcher's hatchet. Blades are what they learn, and you can't teach warring with an execution."

"Youngling superstition," scoffed the Elf.

Tashayul agreed with a nod. "Silly mountain nonsense."

"Mayhap be, but my sword learned well the drinking of Reithrese blood." Summoning a contemptuous scowl to my face, I looked from Elf to Reithrese, then raised my chin to expose my throat. "Kill me. I'll have no more of the company of cowards who dare not examine the lessons my blade has mastered."

The Reithrese conqueror threw his head back in a hearty laugh. "Is that what you want, Mad Neal? You want a chance to fight me?"

"I was thinking I wanted to kill you, but I'll settle for

the latter." I shrugged. "Of course, I'm not so close to newborn that I'd expect a fair fight."

That brought the general around and even appeared to spark some interest in Finndali's eyes. "The fight has not even begun, yet you already accuse me of treachery?"

"I'd be more charitable were I not wearing these ropes. I'll be facing a battle veteran with a special sword."

"Ah, but you were bragging that you had slain a number of my kinsmen."

I frowned. "True. Still, there is the matter of the blade *and* this fine company you have gathered around you."

The Reithrese watched me closely. "You have a compromise to suggest?"

"Since I'm just *fighting* you, not *killing* you, I'm thinking that if I pink you with my blade, I should be allowed my life and a day's ride."

"Else you might be forced to kill me and my warriors?"

I let Tashayul's sarcastic tone pass unnoticed. "I might take pity on them and only wound them, but I'm thinking that's the likely result, m'lord."

The Reithrese eyed me up and down, then nodded slowly. "Blood me with your blade and I will give you four years. Four years to prepare the Roclaws for my wrath."

I swallowed hard and nodded. "Done."

"Good."

"One more thing."

A pained look passed over Tashayul's face. "What is it?"

I nodded toward the Elven leader. "If my pinking should kill you, *Khlephnaft* is mine. I want it from his lips."

Tashayul shrugged. "For the sake of the fight, m'lord?"

The Elf nodded. "Aarundel, his bonds."

Another Elf left the company of his fellows and approached me. Holding his bow and a nocked arrow in his right hand, and a bared dagger in his left, he dropped to one knee beside me. The knife's edge made short work of the ropes. I slapped him on the shoulder, prompting a shudder in his captain that this Aarundel did not echo. "My thanks."

Aarundel nodded. "Success in your sanguineous devoir."

"Enough, Aarundel, return to your place." Finndali opened his hands apologetically to Tashayul. "Youth and their perception of the world . . ."

"No matter." Tashayul held out his right arm, and two slaves slid onto it a mailed dueling sleeve. It covered him from the back of his hand to shoulder, then over his right breast and shoulderblade. A black leather strap bound it to him across his chest and beneath his left armpit. He moved his arm around, the rings rustling as he did so, to test how much it restricted his movement. If it did at all, I was thinking, it was not near enough to comfort me.

I held my right arm out for similar sheathing, but a slave just shoved my sword's hilt into my right hand. "Not even a gauntlet?"

The Reithrese shook his head. "You delay the inevitable."

"Here, Mad Neal." Aarundel plucked a green glove from his belt and tossed it to me. "So M'Lord Tashayul does not disarm him in the first pass. A lesson quickly learned is one quickly forgotten."

I caught the glove in my left hand and pulled it on. The supple leather felt tight on my hand at first, but that eased. My fingers had not filled their sheaths fully at first, yet by the time I had worked my sword back into my hand, the slack had vanished. The glove molded itself to my hand and to the blade's grip.

I saluted the Elf, then struck an *en garde* position facing the Reithrese warrior. If I had reach on him, I was thinking, it would be only an inch or two. In a duel to first blood, the back of the arm is a likely target. A quick cut, a riposte, or a coupé, and a steelkiss would bring blood. With his armored sleeve in place, it would take more than a lovetap to win me the fight, and I tried to plan a strategy accordingly.

The Reithrese gave me no chance to plan. He came at me hard, starting single-handed, then shifting around to put both hands on the hilt of the blade. His first slash, coming from right to left, mirrored the one he'd shown me when I knelt before him. I jumped back from it, but felt the blade's sharp caress on my right shoulder.

A flesh wound only, it left a flap of skin flopping like an epaulet on my shoulder. The blood it brought dripped off my arm at the elbow, and the cry it summoned from his men echoed through the courtyard. I felt the pain and likened it to the sting of a bee, then dismissed it because Tashayul, having stung once, would sting again and again until I lay dead.

Another fighter, saluted by the cheers of his subordinates, might have backed off and accepted their applause. Not Tashayul. He pressed me, sweeping *Khlephnaft* around in a grand circle that brought it back down and toward my head. I raised my sword and blocked his cut, then sprang backward, tugging at my blade to free it. It came after a second's delay that choreographed the rest of our battle.

Khlephnaft had notched my blade. Roclawzi bladesmiths have no equal on the face of Skirren—which I can say as the Dwarves dwell beneath the earth—but *Khlephnaft* cut into it with the ease of a sharp knife hacking cheese. We both came to the same realization, and I saw what it meant to Tashayul reflected in his eyes. First he would whittle my blade, then he would pare me down to foolsplinters.

Double sure I was to die that day, my choices for the rest of my life narrowed considerably. I could die short or die long. The latter seemed the likelier choice, but it came with pain, which brought it into question again. Of course, I was thinking, I could share some pain with Tashayul and tarnish his victory. After all, at sixteen summers I was not the one fated to kill him, but I'd heard of no prophecy concerning suffering on his part.

I attacked. Scuttling forward, I slashed low at his forward leg and actually caught him in the ankle. My blade scarred the leather of his boots, but did not get through to his flesh. Snapping my wrist down and around, I disengaged from his parry and came up in a circular slash that reached toward his flat belly. He gave a step, then batted my blade aside with his armored sleeve.

His blade came up on a wrist-twist cut that had no power, but still looked to slice me from navel to nose. Ducking my left shoulder, I went down and over in a roll that brought me halfway 'round him. By the time I came to my feet and backhanded a slash at his legs, he'd spun and parried me hard wide. That gnawed my blade again and won him back the initiative in our fight.

With his back to the Elves, he drove hard at me. Twice he came high right, forcing me to take his cuts on the forte of my blade. Like a woodsman's ax on an old tree, his sword sent chips flying from my blade. When he came in the third time, I lunged in a stop-thrust that should have spitted him, but he had anticipated me. He came up short and brought *Khlephnaft* around in a sweeping cut that trimmed two inches from the end of my sword.

I recall hearing that piece of steel clatter, ringing like a bell, on the courtyard floor. I shifted my sword to my left hand as I recovered, stamp-feinted with my right foot, then advanced with my left and angled a thrust at his groin. My thrust came slow and clumsy, a final act of desperation.

Tashayul's parry came hard and quick. He trapped my sword against the courtyard stones, then a final push with bunched muscles shattered my worried blade. The strength of the parry tore the hilt from my hand, smashing it down against the stone. It bounced and cartwheeled away, back behind him, toward the waiting Elves.

As I had intended from the moment I switched my grip, I pivoted on my left foot and brought my right foot up and around. The ball of my foot caught Tashayul on the left temple. The blow twisted his head around and sent him reeling in retreat. He tried to steady himself, but dropped to one knee a half-dozen paces distant.

A heavy blow to the small of my back sent me to the ground and all fours. I looked up and heard an arrow whiz past my ear. It thunked into something behind me that sighed and gurgled and thumped. Tashayul shook his head and stood, turning to face the Elves behind him. Finndali had already begun to dress Aarundel down, but the undaunted Elf nocked another arrow with cool dispatch.

The fingers of my right hand closed on a flat piece of steel maybe two inches square. I dropped my index finger into a notch between a sharp burr and the old edge of my sword, holding the fragment as I might a flat skipping stone. I hauled it back, then whipped it forward, not caring if I hit Reithrese or Elf, but hoping for the best.

My missile bit Tashayul over his spine. Small though it was, it might well as been the full blade, because the lower half of his body died as quick as dry wood in a hot fire. The Reithrese reached back toward the wound, unbalancing himself. He fell onto his spine, dropping *Khlephnaft,* and just lay there. His peaceful legs contrasted with the fury on his face and the angry thrashing of his fists.

"Arrest yourselves, or I shall arrest your lives," Aarundel commanded the Reithrese at my back. Without waiting for orders from Finndali, I saw three more of the Elves likewise bring their bows to full draw.

"Foul! Base treachery!" Tashayul shrieked from the ground. "He used sorcery on me! I demand you slay him."

Still on my knees, I turned and freed a scimitar from the Reithrese body behind me. "I'm thinking that if there was treachery, it struck me full before it reached you, m'lord." I looked up at Finndali. "Mark you that it was my blade that blooded him. It was only a small piece of it, mind you, but my blade and his blood. The fight is ended."

As much as Finndali might not have liked me, I could see he had no loyalty to the Reithrese general lying on the ground. Had I not deferred to Finndali, he might have ordered me slain, but because I appealed to him as the arbiter of the battle, he rose to the responsibility and the superior position it assigned him. I waited humbly for his judgment.

"The veracity of the Man's statement is beyond inquiry." Finndali shook his head as he looked down at Tashayul. "In your generosity you gave him four years. He shall have them."

I walked over to Tashayul and kicked *Khlephnaft* into his reach. "Take good care of the blade, m'lord, for I'll be coming for it after I kill you. Four years. When I reach my twentieth summer."

I started off toward the convent's stables, but Finndali stopped me. "Roclawzi, how come you to be so bold, so young?"

I frowned at the Elf as my stockpile of fear flowed into anger. "I'm thinking, m'lord, that is a question that can only be asked by a someone who has been *watching* life for a long time. I'm *living* my life, I am, and it's a life that needs bold living. At dawn I had four minutes to live it, and now I have four years, so I'm not seeing any reason to be rationing my boldness."

The Elf laughed silently, clearly amused by something I had said. "Hrothdel, come and heal this youngling so more boldness does not leak out of him."

An Elven magicker stepped from that company to help me, but I shook my head. "Thanks, but I'll be seeing if one of the nuns is a tailoress to take a stitch or two in my wounds."

"But you will scar. There is no reason you should be marred."

"Ah, but there is—without a scar, I might forget. I'm not thinking I suffer hurts so lightly that I'll be wanting to be unmindful of them." I tossed the Elven leader a salute. "Come fifty years from now, I'm thinking the price you will pay to get Cleaveheart from my hand is to listen to the recounting of how I got this scar and that."

"If your life lasts that long, Neal, the recitation might be diverting." The Elven lord raised his right hand to shoulder height and waved one of his company forward. "Aarundel, you will travel with this Neal. Tashayul has given him four years, and I mean that he should have them."

"I'll not be wanting an Elf dogging my steps." I pulled Aarundel's glove off and tossed it to him. "Many thanks, *virsylvani,* for the loan of your glove."

Aarundel deftly plucked it out of the air. "I will not be a hound to your hare, but if you desire it, I can teach you more of the Sylvan tongue and make the Reithrese remember the oath their leader made."

More the smile on Aarundel's face than the look of disgust on Finndali's decided me to accept his company.

Truth be told, and not often enough it is, nights on the road had been lonely, and having an Elf as a boon companion would be an adventure in and of itself. I also gathered, from the whispers and glances of the other Elves, that more of that company would have loathed the duty than have welcomed it.

"And in return I can teach you how your blade and your arrows can learn, eh?" I smiled and offered him my hand. "Neal Roclawzi, honored to meet you."

"And I am Aarundel."

Much dust had settled on backtrails since that day, leading us from Esquihir to Ispar and Barkol and on to the Roclaws and all the way back to Jammaq in just a handful of years. Aarundel's presence had saved me more than once from danger, and I'd done the same for him. More important than that, though, was the friendship we built. If the foundation laid down over the first five years were any indication of durability of what would come after, all the gods themselves would have to combine to rip the two of us from the world, because no lesser power could do it.

Rounding a ghoul-backed corner, we saw the tower. As mausoleums go, I had to admit it was an impressive structure, if a bit ghastly garish for my tastes. The Reithrese architects had indulged their passion for pillars and arches, though all of the former looked like bones, and the latter had skulls as keystones. The rest of the walls had been carved to give the impression that they had been thatched with ribs, with any gaps patched by boneknobs, odd shoulder blades, and eyeless skulls. Given the necrotic design of the building, the horrified expressions on the faces of the gargoyles staring at it did not surprise me overmuch.

Aarundel straightened up to his full height and pulled his scarf away from his mouth. "Seeing this *mortuarium*, I do not begrudge any Reithrese termination."

"I'm thinking," I agreed as I tugged my scarf down, "it's not the sort of place I'd be wanting to lay about, even if for only a year."

The Elf pointed to a tortuous script carved into the lintel above the massive doors. "Granting you dispute my translation of Tashayul's supposed inaugural remarks, but that indicates that only the dead or faithful may pass into this place at night."

"It's a good thing we are dead, then, I'm thinking, because my madness has not extended far enough for me to be begging favors from the Cold Goddess." I slapped him on the shoulder and ran across the roadway to the tower. "Come on, it says we're welcome."

"Living or dead, I think the Reithrese would find little to welcome about us."

Aarundel had a point. After Tashayul's death in the Roclaws, the Reithrese focused their attention on completing the Imperial capital of Jarudin and did not expand the Empire at all. But instead of thanking us for the chance to consolidate their gains, they charged Tashayul's Skull-riders with the task of seeing to it that I was slain. For the purpose of maintaining cordial relations with the Elves, Aarundel's name was not on any death warrant, but the Skull-riders were not terribly inclined to using methods that would spare him while killing me.

Realizing we would not be shed of them—worshipers of a death goddess being rather focused in their beliefs—on this side of life, we lured a whole pack of them into the Roclaws. With them in hot pursuit, in the midst of winter and with a blizzard howling around them, we set a trap for them. An avalanche—quite common in the Roclaws at that time of year—wiped the lot of them out.

It was assumed the two of us had died as well. The Reithrese failed to realize that the people of the Roclaws had long before learned how to trigger avalanches and avoid being trapped in them. With the aid of Roclawzi nobles who hoped to use my status as a hero to their own ends, Aarundel and I escaped a frozen death and rode from the Roclaws free of hostile pursuit.

Newly dead—and thereby freed of normal, sane concerns—we set out on our pilgrimage to the city of the dead.

Taking a leg up from a shinbone carved into the stone, I peeked up into the death house through an arched window. Seeing no movement, I hooked a leg over the windowsill, jamming my heel behind a skull or two, then reached up and used a death's-head's open mouth for a handhold. Hauling myself into the tower and landing on solid stone on the inside, I helped Aarundel in.

The inside of the tower stood in marked contrast to the outside in terms of decoration—in a manner of speaking, anyway. A fair riot of columns and vaulted ceilings made the place a forest of stone. We had come in on a walkway that ran around three sides of the chamber. Steps came down from the center of the wall opposite us to the sunken floor of the chamber, and heading back up them would doubtless take us to the tower's main corridor. In the east wall I saw another narrower door that had a ramp leading up to it. It stood open and led back into the center of the complex. Enough light from the furnaces came through that opening to provide us with flickering illumination within the death chamber. Voices came to us through the doorway, but I understood nothing, and Aarundel apparently decided none of it warranted translation.

The chamber we were in had a frieze with selected scenes from the history of the Reithrese race. It started with their creation by the gods, then showed how they had proved victorious over the forces of the ancient gods in the long war that supplanted the parents with their children. It continued with a number of other events that had significance for the Reithrese, then ended with a newly carved piece nearly a full rod in length.

"Look at the frieze."

The Elf frowned. "Vulgar blasphemy. Look at how the . . . *artist* has placed the Reithrese above Elves in creation."

"Not that, my friend, the last piece." I pointed to the newly added section. "The banner there, lying under the bulky figure's feet. That's the Green Viper banner of Duke Harsian of Irtysh."

The Elf smiled. "Tashayul's last victory. That piece looks movable, too."

"They just rent this space, not own it." I moved to the right and threaded my way through the pillars. In the center of the room, with its back to us, a huge stone throne faced the newest piece of the frieze. "I'm thinking that either we've stumbled onto the right place . . ."

". . . Or another of the generals who perished in the

Roclaws is here." Aarundel followed in my footsteps, though being an Elf, he moved more quietly and had less trouble picking out the path through the half light.

I came around the corner of the throne. "No, this is Tashayul."

I shivered as the light from outside flared and I got a good look at what my old enemy had become. Seated in the stone chair, a skeleton stared at us with empty eye sockets. Wisps of his black hair decorated his bare shoulders and rib cage, yet barely a scrap of flesh and no trace of muscle remained on him. Only his jaw had dropped away from the skeleton—it had landed on his lap. A few lost emerald teeth decorated the bare stone seat between his femurs.

I glanced at Aarundel. "This explains it, then."

"Remarkable."

Outlining his skeleton in bronze, a metal framework of long and short, straight and curved pieces had been created for him by Reithrese artisans. Metal posts ran from each and every piece and attached themselves to his bones at the points where metal bands had been fitted. His femurs each had four attachment points, the shins and arm bones three, and each vertebra had one. A series of articulated joints connected the metal bones and allowed them to ape normal movements. It all ended at the back of his neck and, as nearly as I could tell, the last five vertebrae had been entirely replaced by metal substitutes.

"The metal lay close to his flesh except where it pierced it." Aarundel pointed at Tashayul's skeletal forearm. "I cannot imagine that did not hurt."

I nodded. "Constantly, I'd wager."

"Constantly, I would hope."

"Indeed." I smiled. "This explains a great deal."

"So it does."

After my escape from the monastery, the Reithrese conquests had slowed for a season. Aarundel and I both thought having his spine cut had taken the fight out of Tashayul, but then he was back. It was rumored that he was bigger and stronger. The two of us even scouted his forces during a battle in Barkol, nearly two years before he reached the mountains, and again in Irtysh. In both places he did seem much more massive than before. The two of us knew his being up and able to fight could not be possible, but the Reithrese were masters of vile magicks that might bring dead limbs new life, so we could not really even guess at what had healed him.

Aarundel dropped to his haunches and peered up through the rib cage. "You will be unable to see it, Neal, but a piece of your blade is still lodged in his spine. A blow struck four years before caused his expiration when you saw a score summers."

"Better it be believed I killed him in a duel than the real story çome out."

The Elf shook his head. "Roclawzi vanity. You killed him."

"I did, but expediently, not heroically."

"Heroism is the judgment of ages."

"Then remember me kindly, my friend."

Aarundel nodded, then froze with his head cocked toward the doorway. "If I have not misheard, your entrance will have the desired effect right about now."

Together, our faces bared, we mounted the ramp and entered the larger chamber without attracting any notice. Referring to the space as a chamber is only half-correct, because it made up the central courtyard for the tower complex. While at the center it was open to the sky, extending up for five levels from the ground concentric disks, each smaller than the one above it, formed terraces overlooking the courtyard.

At the courtyard's center, a huge stone ring surrounded what I can only describe as a firewell. Incandescent gases burned there in pulsed jets that filled the area with the heat of a forge. The ghoulish architecture had been used in this area with the terraces being bone-thatch, and the blocks making up the ring looking like compacted skeletons, where skull rested on knees with arms holding leg bones tight to the chest.

Opposite us, across an audience of fifty Reithrese individuals, a High Priest of the Dark Goddess stood resplendent in a cloth of gold robe hemmed to look as if his garment were made from flame. The fiery glow behind him softened his thick outline and, no doubt, revealed us to him, but either he did not notice us or took no concern over our presence.

In his two hands he held aloft a scabbarded sword. I did not understand his words, but I recognized the motions of an auctioneer offering something for inspection and bids. To me, after five years and twenty yards distant, the sword looked different, but I *knew* the blade he presented was Cleaveheart and that it would be mine before the night was out.

Aarundel leaned toward me and kept his voice low. "He says this is *Khlephnaft* and offers it for bid."

In the center of the crowd a Reithrese stood up. He turned this way and that to nod at the others present, and gave me a good look at his profile. Though more slender than his brother, he had the same hungry look in his eyes. His smile, from where I stood, appeared a sparkling black gash on the lower end of his face, but that was because, as a magicker, his teeth were diamonds. He pointed to the sword and began to speak.

I stepped forward before Aarundel could grab me and drop a hand over my mouth. "Begging your pardon, Takrakor, but would you mind speaking in Mantongue? My Reithrese is not that good, and I'll be bidding against you."

Only the fire's roar answered my request. The Reithrese and Reithressas present all turned to look at me, with their jeweled teeth not nearly as pretty displayed in shock as they were when flashed in a smile. Then, all of a sudden, everyone spoke at once in a riot of angry, angular words.

Aarundel stepped up beside me and shouted in guttural tones to the high priest. The priest considered the words, while Reithrese gesticulated at me furiously. He then looked down at the crowd and shouted one word that brought silence. When his head came up, the priest looked directly at me.

"The Elf has said you wish to invoke *wirt kalma*."

I nodded. "I understood that the determination of inheritance brought with it a truce, else I'd not have been mad enough to come here."

"It does, but only for those who are meant to be here."

The priest stared sternly at someone who grumbled from the front row. "*If* your suit for possession of the sword is successful, then we will know you were meant to be here and you will be granted *wirt kalma.*"

The murderous stares of the others in the room told me what would happen if I was not given possession of the blade. "I understand."

"Very well. Takrakor, you were stating the reasons why *Khlephnaft* should pass to you."

The Reithrese sorcerer nodded slowly. "My brother was not alone in his desire to reestablish our empire. This was a dream we had together, and together we realized it. In the time it took me to devise and implement the plan that put my brother back into the field, our efforts became welded together as had our dreams. He meant the blade, which is the catalyst for realizing our dream, to fall to me. It is upon this that I base my suit."

The priest looked up at me. "You, Manchild, state your case."

I smiled easily to hide the snake crawling around in my belly. "I found the blade for Tashayul because without my efforts, he never would have located it. I fought against the blade, and it drank my blood. And I cut Tashayul down and when Cleaveheart fell from his grasp, I returned it to him. A year ago I killed Tashayul and would have taken the blade then, as befitting the spoils of war, but his Skull-riders—may their frozen bodies one day molder here—brought him and my sword to Jammaq."

I pointed at the sword. "In other words, the blade should be mine—*is* mine—and I'll be taking delivery of it now."

Takrakor shook his head. "My brother did not intend for you ever to gain possession of *Khlephnaft*. His thoughts on this matter were quite clear."

"That's because he knew it was meant to be mine." I glanced at Aarundel, and the Elf nodded back. "He knew it, you know it, I know it, and the blade itself can prove it."

Takrakor's hands flexed. "More treachery from the mountains?"

"Just proof." I looked at the priest. "Unsheath the blade." I dropped my hand to the hilt of the scimitar I had borrowed from the *natari* I'd slain and took no comfort from the fact that Aarundel did not see fit to bring his ax to a guard position. "This better work, Aarundel."

"It will. The priest already knows it will."

The older Reithrese slowly stripped the scabbard from Cleaveheart's blade. As the leather sheath flaccidly slipped from the point, I saw a blade decidedly different from the one I expected. Whereas Cleaveheart had originally been the type of single-edged, serpentine blade the Reithrese upper crust favored, the blade had straightened. Now a broadsword, I saw orange highlights skitter across two razored edges, not just one. The hilt had changed slightly as well, and as far away from it as I was, I knew it would be balanced better than the broadsword I'd left back with the *natari* bodies and our horses.

I didn't know how the sword had changed, but the transformation had not been lost upon the assembled Reithrese. "You see, when it was meant for a Reithrese hand, it appeared as a Reithrese sword. Now it is meant for the hand of Man." I walked down the short set of steps and through an aisle to the dais upon which the high priest stood. Heat pulsing out from the firewell tried to drive me back, but I would not be denied. "My sword, if you please."

His flesh ashen, he gave me the sword. I turned to leave and found myself staring down the length of the blade at Takrakor's pale throat. "But for the *wirt kalma,* Takrakor . . ."

"One day, youngling, I will have that sword from your hand and Mankind will scream in pain."

"Will you, now?" I winked at him and tipped the blade toward the sky. "I'm to give this sword to an Elf in forty-five years, so you'd best be quick in getting it while it is still mine."

I stepped around him and rejoined Aarundel. "Before I leave, for I've no desire to tax your *wirt kalma,* one last thing: I also lay claim to this empire of yours. Give it to whomever you want, but remember it's just a loan. Someday I'll collect it."

Aarundel and I walked back into the tower complex and out through two cold bronze doors. Behind us angry voices rose and fell in time with the hot glow from within the towers. "I gather *wirt kalma* is breaking down?"

"As with their magicks, 'chaotic' and 'elemental' can be used to describe their interpersonal relationships. As much as they would delight in your termination, they revel in their internecine battles. Even now Takrakor is defending his right to destroy you."

"With luck that argument will last for a decade or two." I whipped Cleaveheart's bare blade up into a salute and felt its cold forte pressed to the flesh of my brow. I brought it down slowly after Aarundel acknowledged my salute with a nod. "Tell me, my friend, why does Finndali want this sword?"

"The Consilliarii have asked him to obtain it."

I bowed my head to him. "And why do the High Lords of Cygestolia want this sword?"

I saw reflected in his dark eyes the war being waged between his brain and his soul. He had his loyalties to me, but they were of recent vintage and might well be unreliable. He also did as he had been commanded by the Consilliarii and their agent, Finndali. In all the time we had been together, he had never once returned to his homeland for new instructions. Whether he could or would answer my question depended upon his assessment of me and, I supposed, my perceived threat to him and Elvendom.

A curt nod prefaced his answer. "*Divisator* is a blade of fate. It has many prophecies concerning it. It earned its name because of a black event in our history, proving the veracity of one prediction made of it. It is because of that prophecy being true that we have an interest in how the sword is used in case the others also come true."

I frowned. "Such as."

His dark eyes narrowed. "The blade will win an empire, but bring tragedy to the Man who wields it."

"Came true for Tashayul." I spun the blade in my hand.

"It was not necessarily meant to apply to Tashayul." The Elf looked back at the Reithrese towers. "That prophecy could possibly pertain to you, Neal. The Reithrese soothsayers were working from that same prophecy, but their translation may have been different from ours."

"I don't understand."

Aarundel shrugged. "Words can be chameleons, and translators can be magicians. 'Empire,' for example, could be read as 'immortality' or as a confluence of both terms."

"That's not so bad." I spun the blade again. "Immortality or an empire or both? Certainly the fare for a hero, I'm thinking."

"Yes, and more likely *your* get than any Reithrese. They read the word 'man' as a synonym for 'individual.' We believe it means Man."

That sobered me for a moment. "So the Consilliarii want the blade to prevent the winning of a human empire?"

"The infamy of the *Eldsaga* has not escaped us." The Elf opened his hands slowly. "A war with humanity sparked by a desire for vengeance is not something we wish to see initiated."

My head came up. "But Finndali was willing to give the Reithrese fifty years to destroy us."

"Ah, but Finndali knew Tashayul was wrong about the sword. After all, he did assign you a bodyguard to keep you alive until you reached your twentieth summer, did he not?"

Aarundel had a point, and it made me think of Finndali as being far more shrewd than I had thought before. "Is there any alternate interpretation to the word 'tragedy' in this prophecy, then?"

Aarundel shook his head.

I shook off the chill cutting at my spine. "Then I'll declare it a tragedy if I'm not able to bore Finndali to death with the tales of my scars in two score five years."

"It *would* be the height of tragedy indeed, my friend."

I threw him a wink. "And this 'immortality,' might it not be in tale and song rather than in a physical sense?"

"It could be indeed."

"Then, I'm thinking, in deed I'll win it." I rounded the corner of the alley in which we had hobbled our horses and killed the *natari.* "Do you think we can ride from Reith before they've stopped their squabbling?"

"Even if we were to carry our horses from here and not vice versa, yes."

"Dead men do not carry horses."

"Nor dead Elves."

I laughed and swung up onto my horse's back. "Now that we have *that* settled, let us be away from this place. It's time for us to come back from the dead and give bards plenty of fodder for insuring we never die again."

Chapter 1

An Encounter on the Way to Aurdon

Early Spring
A.R. 499
The Present

The bandits swarmed over the broken caravan like hyenas tearing at a carcass. Their howls of glee and yipped calls of triumph echoed through the vale, filling a placid dusk with the promise of a haunting night. Bright blades flashed red —tinted more by the sun's dying red light than by the blood they spilled—and left bodies scattered haphazardly on the road. Reduced to black silhouettes as they passed in front of a burning wagon, the bandits used their horses to herd crying women and terrified children into the grassy field on the downhill side of the road to Aurdon.

Exalted in their victory and masters of the chaos they had created, the bandits did not notice the two riders watching them from the crest of a hill above their kill. Even if they had, Genevera suspected they would have dismissed her and her companion. No one, assuming sanity and a choice, would be foolish enough to do more than ride away, and ride away swiftly at that. There were other ways to commit suicide, and most all of them promised an easier passage into death than attacking a superior force of bandits.

She looked at her companion, and Durriken smiled at her. "Only a dozen, m'love." He took the reins in his mouth and drew his two flashdrakes from the leather scabbard plate on his stomach. Holding one flashdrake in each hand, he cocked the spark-talons with his thumbs, then winked at her. The brown-haired man dug his heels into his horse's ribs and rode down into the tiny valley.

Genevera reached out toward him for a final touch, but her slender fingers just missed her lover's shoulder. *Would you have waited were it two dozen, Rik?* From their three years together she knew, had she asked or urged caution upon him he would have remained there with her, but she also knew she could never have made such a request. She accepted that as easily as she accepted the differences in their races, and drank in the fearful excitement rippling through her.

She followed him into the valley as quickly as she could. Her horse, a roan gelding named Spirit, was not as game as Rik's mountain pony in traversing a steep slope in the twilight. When Spirit reached the level grassland that ran from the road to the hills, his long strides regained much of the lead the pony had built up. Even so, Durriken reached the bandits first, giving Genevera time to begin her spell.

Durriken thrust his right hand forward as if his flashdrake were a lance. She saw a small spark as the talon fell, then heard an earsplitting crack as the handcannon vomited out a gout of flame that reached halfway to the nearest bandit. Durriken jerked his head to the right, pulling the pony back away from the caravan, then pointed his left hand at another bandit and triggered the second flashdrake.

As she had seen before, the flashdrakes worked as well as a spell to shift the nature of the battle. The first bandit Rik had shot slipped from the saddle and fell into the dust without much drama. The sound of that first shot had a strong effect and prompted half the bandit horses to shy, rear, or run. Rik's second target sat astride one of the bucking beasts, so when the lead ball from the flashdrake hit him, he catapulted into the air. Already dead, his limp body did a slow backward somersault, then landed with a thump on the rutted roadway.

Rik dropped his flashdrakes and drew the rapier from his saddle scabbard. He brandished the blade as if he meant to slay the rest of the bandits by himself; then he pulled his pony away and invited pursuit. He moved off diagonally, heading away from the road, and drawing four of the bandits near the burning wagon as they came after him.

Genevera smiled and concentrated for a second. She thrust her left fist toward the wagon, cocked her hand back, and opened it palm-first toward the fire. She felt a tingle as a bluish spark leaped from her flesh; then the burning pinprick streaked all but invisible through the air to its target. *Yes, it will hit!*

The wagon exploded as everything that could burn, that would eventually burn, ignited all at once. The ravenous fireball engulfed the four bandits, consuming their flesh and swallowing their screams in its golden sphere. The thunderous detonation dwarfed the flashdrake's noise, and the hot wind from the hell it spawned had her long golden hair snapping behind her like ship's canvas in a fiery gale.

Two other bandits fell from their saddles as their horses reared up in panic. Her eyes adjusted quickly to the fireball's brightness, allowing her to see shadow-wreathed refugees descend on the fallen men. Another bandit chose to cross swords with Durriken while the last three galloped out into the night, each heading for a different point on the compass.

Durriken's pony stopped and turned quickly as the small man tugged on the reins. As his right-handed foe bore down on him, Rik shifted his rapier to his left hand and nudged his pony back to the right and across the line of the bandit's charge. He parried the bandit's awkward cross-body saber slash, then took him through the chest with a riposte.

The rapier came away wet as the bandit spurred his horse out into the night. Durriken turned to watch him run, but did not pursue him. He smiled as he trotted the pony back toward the glowing circle of coals in the middle of the road. "Lungstuck. Needs to staunch the wound. Someone spells it, he might live."

Genevera acknowledged his comment with a nod and dismounted. She moved slowly and deliberately as she slung the canteen over her shoulder and rummaged in her saddlebags for her healing bag. "Were you injured, Rik?"

Swinging his right leg up and over his pony's head, he kicked free of the left stirrup and slid to the ground. "Nay, nary a scratch, love." He slapped his pony affectionately on the neck. "Benison here got his tail toasted." Durriken leaned forward, bringing his ear near the horse's mouth. "He says if the Elven princess will give his master a kiss, she will be forgiven."

"I will, will I?" She tucked a strand of golden hair behind her pointed left ear. "Were his master a proper equestrian, Benison would not have been so close to the fire."

"Don't listen to her, Benison, she's a sorceress." The slender man led his horse to the edge of the road and dropped the reins. "Bewitch you, Gena will, as she has me."

Gena caught Rik's smile and returned it, then flicked her head toward the huddled shadows on the downslope. Her violet eyes saw through the gathering darkness as if it were but a thin fog. For all she knew of Rik being sharp-eyed for a Man, she knew he would see only crouching silhouettes. She envied him as he could not see the stark terror in the caravan refugees' eyes, nor read the fatigue in their drawn, pale faces.

Rik looked past her toward the figures and broadened his smile. He stabbed the rapier into the ground, then waved his right hand in a big welcoming gesture. "You're safe now, people. Come up, come up. Nothing here to hurt you. The bandits are running to the end of the world." He punctuated his comment with a hearty laugh that brought a smile to Gena's lips in spite of the grim tableau before her.

In describing the motley collection of wagons scattered along the road, "caravan" was an extravagant term to use. Four wagons remained more or less intact. One had overturned going off the road, while the others stood scattered on the hard dirt surface. The oxen that had been pulling them were dead, pinned to the ground by bandit lances.

The wagons themselves were all of different design and crude manufacture. A pair were two-wheeled affairs with a small bed ringed by crooked ribs of old wood. Sticks had been woven between them to provide some solidity around the base, and torn canvas stretched taut across the heavy load piled in them.

The third, like the one that Gena's spell had consumed, had been built like a box and mounted on four wheels. It required a pair of oxen to draw it and had wooden walls and a flat roof, which even provided an overhang to ward the driver from the sun. Ropes tied down a lumpy, canvas-swathed load on the top of it, and a water barrel mounted on the side bled moisture through a cracked stave.

The last one showed the most work and had four wheels rimmed with iron. Its long, flat bed nearly overflowed with filled grain sacks. Above them, swinging like gallows-rested highwaymen, crudely built cages containing chickens and a pair of geese hung from a latticework of stout poles.

Around each of the wagons, or lying bloody and slumped over the dead oxen, Gena saw the bodies of the men who fought and died defending the caravan. The pitchforks and scythes they had used in their efforts lay bloodless on the dusty roadway.

Gena looked over at Rik. "Farmers heading for Aurdon. That grain should be in the ground, not heading to market."

Rik crouched next to the first man he had shot. "And these men should be burning in the Outlands."

"Haladina?"

Rik nodded and peeled the dead man's upper lip back. Gena easily saw the filed front teeth and the dark dots on the canines that meant each tooth had been drilled and fitted with a small gemstone. "Haladina they are, or I'm a Centisian noble out hunting marmosets."

"Haladina raiding this deeply into Centisia? Perhaps now we have an answer to the question of why Count Berengar Fisher sent for us." Gena turned away from the body as Rik ripped open the tunic and used a dirk plucked from the bandit's belt to probe the hole his flashdrake had made in the man's chest. She understood Durriken's fascination with his Dwarven weapons and the destruction they caused. She even applauded the determined and methodical way he experimented with them; but his willingness to poke, prod, and even cut corpses left her uneasy.

It is a strange Man you have chosen to love, Gena. She smiled unconsciously as she recalled fond moments of their time together, then looked up as the first of the refugees came up onto the roadway. Gena slowly squatted down and focused her smile on a young girl clinging to her mother's hand. The Elf held her arms open and nodded to the child.

The little girl ran forward a few steps, her bare feet slapping against the ground, then stopped and looked back toward her mother. The woman did not look down at her daughter, but continued to stare at where ashes and embers smoked, hoping perhaps the wagon that had been destroyed by magic would magically reappear. The dark-haired little girl ran toward Gena again, slowing and stopping shyly before she got within arm's reach.

"Hello," Gena whispered in a gentle tone. "I am Gena. What is your name?"

The little girl folded her arms and looked down. She smiled, but refused to look up or speak. Then, quick as a bird on the wing, her head tipped up and her brown-eyed gaze flicked over Gena's face seconds before the girl hid her face behind her hands. She mumbled something, and Gena caught enough of it to puzzle out what had been said.

"Andra? Is your name Andra?"

Peering out from between splayed fingers, the girl nodded silently.

"I am pleased to meet you, Andra." Gena held her left hand out, and the child took it. Slowly straightening up, the Elf lifted the girl up in her arms and perched Andra on her left hip. The little girl giggled, making the first happy sound in the vale for what, Gena would have guessed, had seemed like a very long time to the refugees.

As they came in, Gena saw them segregate themselves. The male children, the eldest standing as tall as Durriken but appearing barely past puberty, and the youngest no more than a year older than Andra, walked over toward Durriken. They approached him cautiously, clearly curious about what he was doing and likely a bit afraid of him because of his flashdrakes. As they crowded around him, he looked up and smiled, then stood and nodded at them.

"Greetings, lads." He flicked the borrowed dirk down, sticking it quivering into the ground near the bandit's head. The boys jumped back startled, then stared at the dirk and the man who had so casually flung it down. "Are any of you hurt?"

Most remained quiet, but the oldest nodded his head. He turned, and Durriken reached up, taking the boy's head in both his hands. He spread apart blood-matted hair above the boy's left ear. "Evil gash that, but closing." Rik glanced at Gena and shook his head, then released the boy and parted his own hair to reveal a small crescent-shaped scar. "I've one like it, but mine's not a relic of surviving a Haladin raid."

Andra's mother came away from the glowing coals that had been her wagon and curtsied before Genevera. "That is my daughter, M'Lady Sylvanii. I will take her so she will not offend you."

Gena shook her head and tickled the child beneath her dirty chin. "Your child is lovely and could not offend me. I thank you for letting me enjoy her."

Gena chose her words carefully and fought to keep her tone light. The woman's comment to her had been full of fear, and her careful pronunciation of the Elven name for themselves told Gena that the woman only knew of Elves through the *old* tales. She was used enough to being considered exotic in the larger cities, but the reverent terror displayed by the Men of the countryside sent a shiver running down her spine.

"Goodwife, are you injured?" Gena held Andra out to her, and the woman hugged her child close.

The woman shook her head and swiped at tears. "No, m'lady, I am not hurt in blood or bone, but . . ." She looked at where her wagon had stood. "Our wagon is gone, my husband is dead. . . ."

Gena grabbed ahold of the woman before she could fall down. She lowered her to the ground and freed Andra from her arms. "Here, have some water. I am Gena, my friend is Durriken." Gena unstoppered the canteen and let the woman drink long and deep. "How is it that you are here? Where did you come from?"

The woman lowered the canteen, and a droplet of water lingered on the lower edge of her lip. "We are all from Beech Hollow. It is . . . it *was* a small village in the mountains on the border with Kaudia. You would not have heard of it, but it was a good place until people started coming through. They told us of raiders, Haladin raiders. We decided to come north to Aurdon. We wanted to be safe."

Gena sat back on her haunches. "Durriken and I are bound for Aurdon. It is not far, barely a day's ride."

The woman shook her head. "We can never make it. Our oxen are dead, our menfolk are dead. I have nothing now. . . ." Her lower lip trembled, and the water droplet washed a clean line down her dust-coated chin. She drew her knees up to her chest and lowered her face onto them; then her shoulders began to heave as she wept silently.

Gena left her there and moved on to the other groups of people at the other wagons. She checked the unmoving men and boys for any signs of life, but found none. Stories told of how the Haladina pressed a dirk into the hands of every male child at birth. Haladin men were the product of years of warring against each other. Killing was their livelihood, and were the dead men here to be taken as a sample of their work, they knew their trade well.

Once she had determined she could do nothing for the men, she turned her attention to the women and children. Aside from being badly frightened and road weary, most of the children appeared healthy, if not a little too skinny for their height. The women did their best to hold their terror and sadness in. They wanted to mourn their fallen husbands, fathers, and sons, but they seemed to know that to lose control would lead to even more disaster.

Gena agreed with the thought expressed by a number of the women that they had been spared the sword or lance because the Haladina were planning to take them back and sell them into the seraglios of the Wastelands. She had her doubts about that, however, as only two of the women—

girls, really—were soft and pretty enough for that sort of life. The other women looked tired and well-worn. Even allowing for her cultural bias, Gena felt certain that the women had been saved because they had not offered much in the way of resistance to the raiders.

Despite the urgency of their reaching Aurdon, Gena and Durriken both agreed in a whispered consultation that they could not leave the farmers alone. One Haladin band might have been driven off, but the possibility that another might be nearby and try to finish the job could not be dismissed. Moreover, they both knew that people who had been raised in a closed and close community like a farming village were utterly out of their element on the road in the Centisian heartland.

"What we need is organization." Rik smiled and gave Gena a quick kiss. "I think we can take some steps toward that at this very moment."

Durriken whistled, and his pony trotted over to him. He boosted the oldest boy into the saddle and pointed out a circular route. "Take Benison out and around so you come up on the bandits' strays from the north there. Approach them slowly, and they'll trot in toward us. Let the pony do all the work, he knows how it is done."

As the pony trudged off, Durriken pointed to the rest of the boys. "Quick, now, gather up some firewood. Make a big pile right over here." Walking away from them, he dug the heel of his boot into the ground and scuffed out a cross. "Right here, now. Those what bring the most can help me feed my flashdrakes."

Durriken stooped and recovered the weapons from where he had dropped them. Blowing dust from them, he inserted each into the holding straps and crossed to where Gena crouched near Andra's mother. Kneeling at the sobbing woman's feet, he settled his hands on hers. "Have no fear, goodwife, we will get you to Aurdon." He stood as the other refugees began to drift in toward the reddish glow and warmth of the burned wagon. "All we need is a plan, but that is why I am here."

Gena watched Durriken as he began to pace back and forth. She knew him well enough to know he was putting on an act, assuming a role of brave importance and leadership—a role he hated when he saw it in others. He was a curious man, in that, when needed, he would slip into roles that he disdained. He became what he had to become, to do what had to be done.

"Now we have one bold lad out there on my pony—is he *your* son?" Durriken gave a plump woman a smile when she glanced off at the boy on the pony. "A fine youth. He will bring the bandits' horses back here. That will give us four."

Another woman, with twin daughters clutching her thighs through thick homespun skirts, shook her head. "Four horses will not pull our wagons to Aurdon."

"No, they won't, my good woman." Durriken paced over near the Haladin body he had studied earlier. As he turned back to face the women, he raised his left hand and pointed off behind them into the night. "Is that a light? Are the Aurdon Rangers this far out?"

When everyone turned to look back into the night, Durriken brought his heel down on the raider's mouth in a quick, sharp blow. He squatted down, using his crouched body to shield the corpse's ruined face from the women and shrugged as they all looked back at him. "It was nothing, a twinkling star mayhap."

He pried the raider's broken mouth open with his right hand and worked one of the canine teeth loose. "Now, as you were thinking, four horses are not enough to get your wagons to Aurdon. Luckily for you, these Haladina like to decorate themselves." He stood and held up a tooth set with a small sapphire. "Unless oxflesh is valued beyond good conscience and fair reason in Aurdon, a bandit smile will buy you a whole herd."

In silent agreement Genevera and Durriken split the work that needed to be done between benign and grim. Durriken dragged the bandit bodies off and harvested their valuables in the evening darkness. Gena encouraged the women to set their daughters to preparing food while she helped wives and mothers clean their dead and dress them for burial. They laid them out in the grassland beside the road, each family in turn bidding a tearful and private farewell to their loved ones.

With a borrowed shovel on his shoulder, Durriken

looked at the eight bodies and shook his head. "I have been glad, over these three years with you, to know your schooling in magick came in the areas of combat and healing. I have benefited from both, but there are times I could wish for your having other knowledge."

Gena shook her head. "If I knew the earth magicks, I would tear a hole open for you."

Rik caressed her right arm. "Not that, love. I was thinking necromancy. It would be a just thing for the Haladina to dig the graves for their victims."

"That it would." She glanced back beyond Durriken, toward the fire on the road and the people grouped around it. She saw one silhouette standing away from the others. "The boy who rode your pony . . ."

"Keif."

"Yes, Keif. He is looking this way. I think, if you ask, he will help you dig graves."

Durriken nodded. "I know. He's a brave lad. I will take him with me for the ride to Aurdon, but I will not have him dig." He gave Gena the half smile that she knew covered a hurt within him. "No boy should have to dig his own father's grave. I'll spare him."

She reached out and squeezed his shoulder. "It will be a night's work. I do not think many will be sleeping, but it might help . . ."

Rik's smile broadened. "Yes, love, I will come to the fire from time to time to let them know I am still here." He winked at her. "You should tell them one of your stories, one that will banish the terrors. Seems to me, last night, you told me about a battle waged against the Haladina by that hero . . ."

"Neal." The hair on her arms rose as she remembered the story, and her smile blossomed as she remembered how the night was spent after its telling. "Neal Custos Sylvanii."

"Aye, the Dun Wolf." He jerked his head at the refugees. "I doubt they know much about him—before I met you, I thought of him as the tragic hero of some dirges—but he's hero enough the way you tell things to keep the night frights away."

Gena bent down and kissed Durriken lightly on the lips. "Thank you, Rik, for doing all you have."

"I have the easy part. Killing and burying take no effort. The dead don't weep." He smiled at her and walked away from the fire. "You have to heal the living. Fortune smiles on them, because you are quite skilled in that way."

Gena returned to the fire and gratefully drank in its warmth. She gently refused a wooden bowl of steaming gruel, then looked up when she saw Keif hefting a piece of wood from the pile that had been collected and testing it for weight. The other little boys looked ready to follow his example.

She smiled. "That is a good piece, Keif, it will burn well."

The boy shook his head. "No, m'lady, I want it in case they return."

"The Haladina?" Gena forced a laugh that caught everyone's attention. "They will not be back."

A woman's head came up. "How can you say that?"

Gena sat down, pulling her crossed ankles in. "The Haladina are a fearsome yet fearful people. You know, of course, that they had not raided this far north in many, many years—centuries, in fact. Do you know why?"

Keif shook his head, as did others in the circle of the firelight.

Gena nodded and raised her voice enough to cover the cough of spade turning earth. "Five centuries ago, when the Red Tiger fought to rid Centisia of the Reithrese armies and their Haladin mercenaries, he had a hero leading a company of mercenaries. That hero was Neal Elfward, the Dun Wolf." She pointed back up into the dark hills. "Very near here it was that Neal destroyed a Haladin army and scattered them. He won through an ambush and even saved Aurdon itself from destruction. That is a tale for a night like this, and no Haladina will brave its telling to harm us. . . ."

Chapter 2

An Encounter on the Way to Aurium

Late Summer
Reign of the Red Tiger Year 1
Five Centuries Ago
My Thirty-fifth Year

I was thinking, as I flew through the air, that being unhorsed by an ambush was not a good thing. The wisdom of it ranked with my thinking that Haladin plainsmen would have no use for the thick-forested hills of Centisia. Clearly they did, the main use being to set ambushes for fog-brained warriors riding hell-bent through the night.

My weighing more than a bird and having neither wing nor feather to aid me meant my nocturnal flight ended in a tooth-rattling crash. The ground did its best to swap my spine for my breastbone, but I heard nothing snap and only a few things creak. The gods, taking perverse delight in complicating the lives of mortals, let me live with the pain and embarrassment instead of killing me outright. Being ever so appreciative of their efforts on my behalf, I let the gods carry my somersault into a poor tree and use my armored bulk to punish it for whatever offense it had given them.

My hauberk lost no rings in its war with the tree, but it graciously passed all the impact right on to me through my padded jerkin. Growling out an oath against the sharp stab in my ribs, I pulled in my feet, rolled back onto my haunches and stood. It surprised me that I managed it, and threw a quick scare in the Haladina coming out of the trees to dispatch me with a little finger-knife. The fact that I towered over him made him reconsider and step back.

I used the time it took him to draw his scimitar to raise my fingers to my mouth and blast out a whistle. I had been riding point, albeit too fast for being tired and night-blind, so I felt a duty to warn my friends of the ambush. I had no quarrel with my stupidity being the death of *me*, but I wanted a place in Fool's Hell, not False-Friend's Perdition.

The Haladin warrior came in at me with the fearless abandon I'd seen in his people throughout the war with their masters, the Reithrese. Curved sword slashing in at hip height, he clearly expected to cut me quick, then scarper off to help his allies kill my companions.

His blade hit solid and would have cut clean through my hauberk, excepting my mail had been pounded out of ore by Roclawzi craftsmen who prided themselves on doing proper work. The scimitar skittered across my belly with a raspy hiss like a snake slithering across a bed of gold coins. I felt the blow and even grunted as it doubled the aching in my ribs, but I didn't feel the need to die or even let my knees kiss the ground because of it.

The Haladina's smile slacked as I lunged forward. He tried a backhanded stroke at me, but I had already moved inside his range. I let his right forearm smack into my right flank, then I slammed my right hand into his throat. He gurgled and, spittle flecked his lips while his face turned dark; then he went over backward.

Coming down, his head met my left knee. I felt nothing through the knee-cop I wore, but the impact jarred him hard enough that his little steel helmet bounced off into the night. Soundlessly, his body went slack. I dropped his body, then took a step back and ground my right heel down onto his wrist, both to free the sword and to see if he was truly unconscious or feigning it.

He was out, and just as well, as his shattered wrist

would have hurt him far worse than my bruised ribs did me. I scooped up his scimitar and started running back up the hill. Even though I could not see well in the dark, the sound of battle provided me all the guidance I needed to tell where I was going.

The tripline the Haladina had used to bring my horse down had been placed on a good little downhill run. Had we all been running tight-packed, they would have had the lot of us all in a tangle. Their man at the line would have cut it, then their horsemen would have fallen on us and we would have been able to offer little in the way of a fight. The slaughter wouldn't have been worth a bard's chorus, much less a song all for itself.

Because I had been running the point a good hundred yards in front of my squad, my whistle gave them time to slow and time to stop before they fell to the same trick that got me. The Haladina, having learned to cut with a knife before they cut their teeth, decided to take a run at my people anyway, to see what they would see.

What they would see was blood and lots of it.

Cresting on foot the hill I'd descended in air, I hefted the Haladin scimitar. It wasn't my Cleaveheart, but it was a hard ribbon of war-steel. I'd seen more than enough men and boys who hadn't survived opening with a Haladin blade to denigrate it. The scimitar's broad sweep robbed me of a lunge, but fighting cavalry from foot meant the finer points of dueling were denied me in any event.

The Haladin horsemen had descended on my men thicker than wing-maggots on meat. I had been traveling with a small, handpicked squad that included a number of my officers. Though they were battle-hardened veterans all, being caught in an ambush still presented problems. Nighttime and fatigue likewise contributed to the confusion that greeted me at the top of the hill.

The ambush, which any leader would have seen as a nightmare, split the night with the ringing of steel on steel and the cries and shouts of men angry, desperate, and dying. Horses screamed and hooves pounded the ground, sending tremors up through the bottoms of my feet. The swirling martial maelstrom made it impossible for me to judge which side was getting the better of the other.

At my whistle Aarundel had immediately assumed command of the Pack. There were those who, mindful of the *Eldsaga,* would have mistrusted an Elf, but not my warriors. They'd too many times seen him as I did now, giving his Dwarf-made war ax a twist and jerk to free it from a Haladin corpse. Looking at him, none of us doubted the truth of the *Eldsaga,* and all were glad he fought with us rather than against us.

Being stupid enough to fall to an ambush infuriated me, and I wanted to vent my anger on the Haladina. I howled out my war cry and settled both hands around the scimitar's hilt. The wolfish call brought a Haladina around, and he drove at me. With his scimitar pulled back for a running-slash, he'd already figured where he'd weave my hair into his scalp-coat.

I raised the scimitar to my high left guard and blocked the slash all but hilt to hilt. The stout blow sent a shiver through my arms, but the blade stayed locked in my grip. Turning toward him as he rode past, I cut down with the scimitar. He had already begun to pull his arm back for another slash, so had no way to parry when I chopped into and through his knee.

I ducked beneath his weak return slash while his scream drowned out all but the last of Aarundel's shouted warning. I looked up to see another Haladina bearing down on me. He had a lance centered on my chest. Off balance as I was, I could have barely managed a weak parry, and my mail wouldn't stop a horse-lance.

From my right, moving like a scrap of shadow given life by a nightmare godling, the Dreel crossed from forest to horseman in an eye blink. A humanoid mountain of muscle and fury, Shijef hit the gelding on its shoulder with one paw, and its haunch with the other. The Dreel's charge lifted the horse from its hooves, and still driving his legs, Shijef slammed rider and beast into a thick pine on the road's far side.

Bones broke and metal groaned. A quick slash with the left paw's talons opened the horse's neck, ending its screams and almost severing the head. The rider likewise screamed, though more from terror than pain, and earned the Dreel's quick attention. Shijef reached up and closed his right paw over the raider's head. I turned away before he could do it, but Shijef took great delight in discarding the Haladin head so it bounced across my line of sight.

The rest of the band, made up of all my captains save Drogo, and two each of their own company's men, fed the forest blood, bone, and meat. It worked out to be not so much a battle as a slaughter, given that the ambush was not that much of a surprise and that the forest eliminated the Haladina ability to ride fast and make quick attacks. With our superior armor and heavier weapons, a close-in fight left them nearer to us, and to the goddess the Reithrese revered, than they had wanted.

After they broke and the half dozen that escaped us rode away, it also appeared that these Haladina had been hiding in the hills since before the Haladin defeat on the Central Plains. Aarundel and Senan found their camp back up in the hills and reported they had nothing in the way of supplies. The Elf suggested and I agreed that they had probably looked to harvest us for our provisions, not realizing until too late we were a fruit with a thick husk and sharp thorns.

Another long and loud whistle brought my horse back to me. Blackstar got his name because of the black blaze on his white face. Aside from face and white stockings, the monstrous beast is the color of midnight all over, and his disposition is not much lighter. He eyed me with a cold anger for having ridden him into a tripline, but he did not seem hurt by the mishap. It took a low growl from the Dreel to remind him that worse fates were possible before he allowed me to remount him.

Blackstar, as warhorses go, did not weigh as much as some of those my company rode, but he made up in strength and cunning what he lacked in bulk. The fact that he had been trained by Elven masters still made him a bit skittish of me, but we had reached an accommodation over the two years he had been mine. If he pleased me, I would keep the Dreel away from him.

Senan led our squad back to the Haladin camp, which had good water and a meadow where our horses could crop some grass. As the men made up camp and started boiling dried meat, millet, and wild onions into something edible, Aarundel and I inspected the detritus of the Haladin camp.

I poked some very dirty, lice-ridden rags with a stick. "They had been here for a long time, no doubt about it. They must have been deserters. I know the Haladina do not hold with cowardice, but they would have welcomed anyone back before the battle on the central plains."

"I cannot dispute that assessment, but I wonder if these were not more than ordinary brigands." The Elf concentrated for a moment, bringing his dark brows together as he did so. "I seem to recall having heard a rumor about one cavalry company having run off with a payroll for the rest of the mercenaries. This could have been them."

I frowned as I tried to remember details of that story. "That was Dijjal's unit wasn't it? I'm thinking I'm not missing their departure. If this was them, they fell on very hard times."

"Traitors are seldom welcome anywhere, and the Haladina have their tradition of death by Eight Cuts for traitors."

"True enough." I nodded. "In Dijjal's case I'd not mind seeing him roped to his saddle with his own entrails, but that's the only time I've not thought Eight Cuts extreme. Your point about traitors is well-taken, for the Reithrese would not welcome them back, and none of the Mantowns we've liberated would invite them in."

Aarundel shook his head. "Save, perhaps, Aurium. Market centers always have a need for gold and jewels."

"I suppose we will find that out, won't we?"

The whole of the Man-war against the Reithrese had been full of odd alliances, great heroics, and brilliant strategies on the part of the Red Tiger. A couple of years after Tashayul's death he led a slave revolt in south Centisia and took his men into the Kaudian mountains, where they became a bandit band that harried the southern trade routes. The first I heard of him, in fact, came when a bard added a verse to a song about me suggesting I'd be heading off to end the Bandit's career.

I had no such intention because I was spending most of my time with Aarundel, Drogo, and a few others who formed the core of the Steel Pack riding through the border provinces of Tashayul's empire causing trouble for the Reithrese. In Irtysh I picked up the Dreel—embarrassing Duke Sture, Harsian's son and heir, in the process. During that time I heard about how the Red Tiger was becoming bolder in his war with the Reithrese, but I stayed away because Sture created his Exile Legion and rode off to help the Red Tiger.

Of course, with Sture forming up his own military unit, I felt a need to do the same. The Steel Pack was born on my twenty-seventh birthday, and a year later the Red Tiger sent an envoy to me to ask us to join his war of liberation. I took a vote among the men, and we'd fought for the Red Tiger for the last seven years.

The Red Tiger showed a keen sense of strategy in planning out his war. Sture, who constantly agitated for the liberation of Irtysh, did not understand that Centisia and Ispar were the keys to destroying the Reithrese Empire. The Red Tiger did, and worked hard to deprive the Reithrese of their two richest provinces, because in doing so he crippled them *and* provided himself with the resources he needed to defeat them.

This year we had finally become strong enough to fend off all the assaults on the mountain freestate we had created, and ventured forth into Centisia. The strategy was to split Centisia in half and trim off the southern end of it. Toward that end we sent Sture's Legion driving down toward Polston, then had it turn north at the Aur River while the Red Tiger and I, with the main body of our troops, punched straight east across the Central Plains.

Polston revolted against the Reithrese, and they responded by sending Haladin units to lay siege to the city. Their cavalry units got there quickly on the eastern side of the river, missing Sture's Legion. The Reithrese and Haladin reinforcements, moving slowly with their supply trains and siege engines, hit Sture head-on and stopped. Then we slammed into them from the west and broke them.

The Red Tiger, having crushed the reinforcements for the southern Centisian garrison force, had sent on three quarters of his army under Sture to lift the Haladin siege of Polston. Sture accepted the assignment despite its taking his troops further from Irtysh. As much of a patriot as Sture was, he did tend to enjoy his time in cities, and Polston had all sorts of things to offer a man with such broad tastes as our Sture.

The Steel Pack had been sent north along the Aur River toward the little town of Aurium. The town itself was less important than its location, which was at the confluence of the two rivers that made the Aur. It was possible that the Reithrese might ship Imperial troops from Ispar down the river to attack Polston, and if they were going to do that, the Red Tiger wanted us in Aurium to slow them down. He himself was bringing the remainder of his army up in our wake, so if we could not hold the Reithrese at Aurium, he would stop them elsewhere along the river.

Our primary fear had been—and still was, for that matter—that part of the Haladin force operating in the Central Plains had retreated north and occupied Aurium. If they had done that, our job would be very complicated. By pulling a scouting detail from the Steel Pack and running along ahead with it, we hoped to be able to spot signs of Haladin movement. Still two days' ride out from Aurium, the ambush was the only hostile force we had run into.

I worked my left arm around and grimaced at the ache in my ribs. Hunched down in the shadows, Shijef watched me, his mouth open in a canine grin. He clearly took pleasure in the fact that I hurt, but in him I sensed some pride that the man who had bested him and had become his master had proven very difficult to kill. I smiled understanding at him, which disgusted him, and he shambled off into the darkness.

"Aarundel, if the Haladina get to Aurium first, do you think they will sack the town?"

"Their behavior will depend on a number of factors. I largely believe their conduct will be determined by whether or not they know you are coming after them."

"What difference will that make?"

The Elf smiled. "Were the Haladina raiding at their leisure, they would raze the town after looting."

"Raze it?" I frowned. "It's a trading town. Why destroy it when you can raid it over and over again? The Haladina are shrewd, they'll see the wisdom in that."

"They are quite intelligent, Neal, of that there is no question. The trick of it is this, though—if you are not following them, they will destroy it as a sign of contempt for the Red Tiger and for you."

"And if they know we're coming."

"You said it yourself, it's a trading town." Aarundel shrugged easily and fished a whetstone from a belt-pouch so he could apply it to the blade of his ax. "The Haladina will hold the town so they'll have something for which you'll be willing to trade."

Chapter 3

Received by the Lords of Aurdon

Early Spring
A.R. 499
The Present

The little girl's scream brought Gena running through the camp. Darting around small family knots gathered for the noontime meal, she saw Andra standing in the grasses by the edge of the road. Picked wildflowers lay scattered around the screaming child, and blood dripped from twin puncture wounds on her right wrist.

Gena scooped the child up and saw a black serpentine shape slipping off through green grass. She'd not caught enough of a glimpse of the snake to be able to identify it, but the swelling around the wounds already told her it was likely venomous. She carried Andra to the roadway and lay her down just as the girl's mother came running.

"My baby, my baby . . ."

The woman teetered on the brink of hysterics, and Gena knew she could not let the woman break down. Having Andra's mother wailing and crying in her ear would shatter Gena's concentration and distract her so she could not weave the spells that could save the girl. Knowing she had to act quickly, she put an edge into her voice and turned on the woman. "I need you to fetch me bandages, clean bandages, now!"

Her command sent Andra's mother scurrying off, so Gena turned her attention to her patient. The child thrashed on the ground and cried loudly, and both things threatened to disrupt Gena's concentration as much as the mother had. Knowing she would get no useful information from the girl, Gena brushed her fingers over Andra's clammy forehead, casting a spell that dropped the child into a temporary sleep.

Taking Andra's arm, she triggered a simple diagnostic spell. Aside from reporting puncture trauma to the muscles, the spell provided Gena with an impression of corruption spreading through the area. She knew that came from the necrotic processes started by the venom, and acted fast to limit and heal the damage.

Instead of wasting energy on a spell that would cut off blood flow from the arm to the rest of Andra's body, Gena picked a round stone from the roadway and forced it up into Andra's armpit. She enlisted one of the girls gawking down at her to hold the stone tight against Andra's arm, knowing the stone would compress the arteries and veins, temporarily isolating the arm from blood flow.

Had she known exactly what type of snake had bitten Andra, Gena could have chosen a spell specifically created to deal with that snake's bite. Instead she had to rely on a spell designed to counteract most hemotoxic venoms. Pressing her palms against the wound, she invoked the spell, and warmth passed, from her hands to Andra's arm.

The diagnostic spell reported the immediate neutralization of the venom, bringing a smile to Gena's face. "Good, good. You can drop the rock now." She looked up at the people who had gathered around. "She'll live, and with a bit more work here, she'll be fine."

Repairing the damage to Andra's arm should not be difficult at all. Healing spells worked to speed up the body's normal healing processes. With a child Andra's age, the magick had no trouble augmenting her healing rate, and when Gena finally pulled her hands away from the snake bite, smeared blood gave the only clue that Andra had been bitten.

Gena stood slowly and fought off a wave of dizziness. Though the spells had been simple, they had taken something out of her. After a moment or two the dizziness passed, and Gena wiped her hands off with one of the rags the girl's mother had started to tear into bandages.

As Gena moved away from the crowd—leaving Andra in her mother's care—one of the boys Durriken had charged with guard duty came running over to her. "You should see this, m'lady." He jumped up and pointed northeast past one of the wagons.

Walking around the wagons, Genevera saw distant dun hints of the dust cloud long before she heard trumpets or caught the scarlet pennants snapping in the breeze. Unable to identify them at first, she muttered a prayer in hopes they were not Haladina. She had the spells and experience necessary to raise a defense of the camp, but after treating Andra she needed rest before she could be at her best in combat.

The approach to the camp took the riders up a slight incline, which she knew would take the edge off a charge. That hardly mattered, though, as Haladina seldom fought in unison and would attack from many points at once. The grasslands, baked golden-brown by the sun, offered her magicks fodder for a fire, but it would rage out of control and kill her and the people she meant to save as well as their tormentors. Her defense would have to be more careful, making it that much tougher on her, and she wasn't certain she was fully up to the task.

Shenan, Keif's younger brother, stood beside her, shifting throwing stones from left hand to right. "What do you mark them to be, m'lady?"

Gena glanced down at the towheaded boy beside her. "How much can you see?"

"Cloud, all whispylike. Has to be riders." The boy lowered his voice. "If Neal was here, we'd learn them."

She gently rested her right hand on his left shoulder and felt tense muscles loosen beneath rough homespun. She narrowed her eyes and watched carefully, then smiled with relief. "I see banners of red, with black piping and devices."

"Flash of gold from the top of one standard, too, eh?"

The Elven female nodded. "You have the eyes of an eagle, Shenan. Just so you know, those are likely Aurdon Rangers."

"How likely?"

Gena squatted down and pointed at a rider at their head. "I believe that is Durriken riding beside their captain, so I do not fear another Haladin raid."

The boy's smile broadened, piling up dimples at the corners of his mouth. "Can I tell my ma?"

Gena nodded, and quite quickly the whole camp had its attention drawn to the approaching riders. She joined the refugees in smiling at the riders, but she neither shouted nor waved until Durriken cut abruptly to the right for a slow-count of three, then rode back to the line. With that signal she knew he had come without coercion or under duress, so she raised her left hand and shouted a welcome.

Durriken rode a bit ahead of the Rangers and reined up short. Cupping her jaw gently in his long-fingered hands, he bent down from the saddle and kissed Gena, then winked at her and turned back toward the others. "Lady Genevera Sylvanii, may I present Captain Floris Fisher of the Aurdon Rangers, Seventh Regiment."

Gena curtsied as the Rangers' leader reined his chestnut stallion to a halt before her. Floris rode very tall in the saddle, with the wings and horsehair plume on his helmet accentuating his height. He glanced at her, then quickly surveyed the area before returning his brown-eyed gaze to her. He smiled, bowing his head, but refrained from doffing the steel helm that capped his skull and protected the back and sides of his neck.

"I am honored, M'Lady Sylvanii, and very pleased your company has remained unmolested in the time it took us to get here." Again he looked up and away from her, and Gena smiled as she realized he was checking to make certain his men had taken up positions to surround the camp. "I detached a company to go back to Aurdon with the boy to see to the oxen, then asked Durriken to lead us back to you."

Durriken chuckled lightly, and she saw Floris shoot him a hooded glance. Something passed between them that she could not decipher, though she assumed it was more because it was a gender-bond than a secret to be shared only among Men. "The Three-Seventh had been sent out to deal with the raiders we encountered, specifically because Count Berengar did not want us inconvenienced as we rode to Aurdon. They caught the main body of Haladina earlier in the day, and those we found were a group who fled from the battle."

Gena looked at the black-and-red device painted on Floris's buckler and embroidered on the red tunic he wore over his gambeson. The downward-pointed equilateral triangular symbol had been split into three parts, in keeping with the style for most military units. In the upper right section she saw the crossed arrow and sword that marked the wearer as a Ranger, and the numerals 3/7 decorating the area next to it clearly indicated this was the Third Battalion of the Seventh Regiment. In the diamond at the bottom she saw two sleeves knotted above a crossed sword and dagger, which she knew from legend was part of Aurdon's crest.

Above it all she saw a red-and-black tiger with a striking bird perched on its back. She knew the bird to be a Fisher and the symbol of Count Berengar's family, but the tiger puzzled her for a moment. It normally appeared only on Isparian crests, for Ispar alone could rightly claim imperial traditions. Because of its position on the device Gena knew it stood for the unit's supreme commander, which she already knew to be Count Berengar.

She smiled sweetly. "Count Berengar is of imperial blood?"

Floris nodded proudly. "He is. The emperor acknowledged the count's mother as a legitimate member of his family, though she had not been born of a first wife."

"Ah, that is most beneficent and doubtless pleasing to the count." Genevera recalled that five years before, when she met then Lord Berengar in Filistan, he had not worn a tiger on his crest. "This honor must have been bestowed recently."

"A year hence, m'lady." Floris held his head up a bit

higher. "The Seventh accompanied him to Ispar for the ceremony."

Durriken gave Floris a wry grin.

"And doubtless he needed the Seventh to fight his way to the capital."

"It was an interesting journey to Jarudin, Durriken, but we were not hard-pressed despite some unpleasantries." Floris smiled and wiped sweat from the side of his face. "Once we arrived in Blackoak, we traveled with the earl's household troops, so the Seventh was able to relax somewhat."

"The Earl of Blackoak is known for his appreciation of discipline and martial order." His saddle creaking, Rik dropped to the roadway and stamped the dust from his boots. "Gena, the count would like us in Aurdon as soon as possible, so the good captain here has offered us some fresh horses and a company to ride back to the city. It's really not that far now, barely six hours at a fast ride."

Floris nodded in agreement. "We would have been here sooner, but when Durriken found me, I was reuniting my squads after they had been chasing Haladina through the hills. We took the night to get some sleep and repair our equipment in case of fighting this morning."

"The offer of an escort back to Aurdon is most welcome, Captain Floris, but I find myself reluctant to leave these good people behind here." Gena looked back at the ragged camp and took heart in noting the smiles and laughter from the refugees. "Though they appear to be happy now, we just had a scare with a snake, and they see Haladina in every shadow. I wonder if their joy will last into the night."

Floris looked the camp over, then nodded. "I understand your feelings, m'lady. I will send a company back with you, but keep the other two companies here. The oxen and my last company should be here in a day; then I will bring all back to Aurdon. No Haladina would dare attack a force of over one hundred fifty men. The welfare of the refugees is now my duty."

"Then I know their safety is assured. If you will excuse me, Captain, I will prepare my kit and we will be on our way." Gena smiled, curtsied, and turned away. Rik followed her, leading Benison by the reins, as she circled around the main camp to the small area she had set up for herself. One of the wagons largely screened it from the main encampment, affording both her and the Men a polite degree of privacy.

Rik took advantage of it by catching her arm and turning her around, then enfolding her in a warm embrace. She lowered her lips to his, once, gently, then again more passionately. She normally would have been more reserved and would have held back when others could watch them. While no prohibition on relations between Men and Elves existed, conservative Men often had as much difficulty welcoming Elven/Human relations as the Consilliarii did. Feeling Rik's arms around her and tasting his lips almost made her giddy with relief and neatly banished her concerns over other's reactions to their relationship. While she had been alone in camp, her sense of duty had overridden the anxiety she had felt concerning Durriken's safety away from her. With the troops taking responsibility for the refugees from her, she luxuriated in the cessation of pressure and felt happy that her silent prayers to Kyori to bring Rik back to her safely had been answered.

Rik broke the embrace and smiled. "As much as I hate being parted from you, I must admit returning almost makes going away seem worth it."

Gena reached down and plucked her blue woolen blanket from the ground. "I suspect you had the more interesting time." She handed the end with the broad red stripe to Rik, then took the green-striped end for herself. Together they shook the dust out of it, then began to fold it in quarters, making it a narrow strip. "The children asked for another story, so I told them of another of Neal's adventures—the one where he bested the Dreel king and made him his slave. Many of the mothers seemed to disapprove, though."

Rik nodded as he began to roll the blanket up and move toward Gena. "You must remember, my love, that Neal's not the greatest of human heroes."

Genevera blinked her violet eyes. "How can you say that? What he did to the Reithrese alone . . ."

"Love, I've come to see him through your eyes, so I

know what Elves think of Neal. True enough, he was a hero, but to Men weaned on the *Eldsaga,* well, his alliance with your kind is viewed with suspicion." Rik held the bundled blanket tight while Gena wrapped a heavy canvas ground cloth around it and tied it with leather thongs. "The stories you tell of Neal are grand, and I love the way you tell them, but to many a Man who actually knows them, the tales of Neal Elfward are tragedies to make tears flow into beer on a long tavern night."

Gena nodded distractedly. She'd seen the gulf between her image of Neal and the standard Human image of Neal —if the Humans to whom she spoke knew of him at all. There had been but five Elven generations born since the time Neal walked the earth and fought his battles, but among Men there had been at least ten more than that. Here in Centisia, near Aurdon, or up in Ispar, Neal was remembered by Men, but elsewhere he was as much a myth as the Reithrese or the Dreel.

Count Berengar Fisher had been one of the few Men she had ever met with a keen interest in Neal. He had confided in her, when they met, that the standard stories told of Neal Elfward in Aurdon had only whetted his appetite to know more. She had obliged him by relating a couple of her more favorite tales and even went so far as to tell him that she had heard them from the lips of her grandfather, the Elf known to men as Aarundel—a confidence she had not yet shared with Rik.

"You are correct, of course, Rik." Gena shrugged her shoulders, highlights slithering through her hair like gilded serpents. "Neal's tradition, among Elves, is tinged with that same tragedy, I think. I suppose my campaign to emphasize his heroism is doomed to failure."

Rik tapped the tip of her nose with his index finger. "Well, you have one convert, at least." He glanced slyly this way and that, his hands resting on the butts of his flashdrakes. "Any man that decides to weep at one of your stories will have to deal with me."

Gena laughed aloud, the overture of melancholy banished by Rik's antics. Though she had known him for only three years, he seemed to be almost prescient in his ability to make her laugh or change her mood. She had once thought, after a century and a half spent studiously learning her magick, that simple things could no longer delight her. In a drive to combat that diminution of her soul she had tried to recover much of the innocence of her childhood and had worked hard to study and gather together the stories of Neal Custos Sylvanii.

Yet even that, she reminded herself as she neatly packed her saddlebags, had not been sufficient to reawaken her sense of life. She petitioned the Consilliarii for permission to travel outside Cygestolia, and they had reluctantly granted it. At the same time they began a subtle campaign to blunt her wish to travel by telling her all manner of horror stories about the world outside the Elven Holdings —prime among them the danger that she might meet and believe she had fallen in love with a Man. Far from dissuading her, it only made her more interested in leaving Cygestolia, and in the dozen years since her departure, she had felt no desire to return to her home.

And having met Rik, she did not regret her decision to travel in the first place.

Unfolding her saddle blanket, she plucked a thistle from it, then draped the thick cloth over Spirit's spine. She wrested her saddle from the ground and settled it on the back of her horse. Rik cinched the saddle up tight while Gena coaxed the gelding into taking the bit and accepting the bridle. She fastened her bedroll behind the cantle, then laid her saddlebags over the horse's haunches.

Swinging up into the saddle, she reined the horse around and followed Rik back to the road. There they joined up with a company of soldiers under the command of a Man whom Floris introduced as Lieutenant Waldo Fisher. With him in the lead and the soldiers riding behind, they set off for Aurdon.

Gena found herself taking a slight dislike to Waldo, but she found it difficult to isolate the reason behind that feeling. He clearly knew his business because he had outriders on both sides of the column as well as a screen of scouts forward and a squad given to lagging back behind the main body. While short and a bit broad in the waist—almost built like the Reithrese were supposed to have been—he was not an unpleasant-looking man. The attention he paid to his surroundings marked him as intelligent, for he constantly looked around and once sent a rider to direct his scouts to investigate the fire-blackened ruins of a croft up off the road.

Then she saw it when Waldo glanced over at Rik and the soldier's face soured. It was a momentary thing, barely a heartbeat in duration, but the expression had carried with it a mixture of hatred and contempt. It was not the first time she had seen such an expression, but when she had, most often it had been directed at her—and then only by ignorant Men despising her because of her heritage.

She tickled Spirit's ribs with her heels and came in close beside Rik. "How much did you tell them about yourself last night?"

The small man shrugged nonchalantly. "Not that much, really. We were all sharing war stories. I mentioned an adventure or two, but nothing to reflect badly on you."

Gena nodded. She had met Rik through a Nakani dealer in antiquities. She had been invited to the merchant's estate to see if she could possibly determine the nature of some enchantments on two pieces of jewelry. She had been told these recent acquisitions were supposed to be Elven, but so seldom was Elven metalwork seen in the world of Men that the dealer needed her expert opinion on it.

As the merchant brought out the chest in which the items had rested, Gena had wondered about the small, silent man who stood behind the fat merchant's chair. His brown eyes seemed to take in everything and were bright with inquisitiveness, but his tension told in his crossed arms and in his swift attention to even the slightest wind-whisper or floor creak.

Genevera instantly recognized the style of the two pieces in the mahogany casket. The merchant lifted one from its black velvet bed and handed it to her. Hammered out of silver and set with an onyx oval, the metal bracer had two features that distinguished it for her. From the cuff a strong bit of chain connected it to a silver ring set with another piece of onyx. The other edge of the bracer, which came to a point almost four inches from the cuff at the midpoint where the onyx had been set, had silver mail decorating it. Its mate was smaller and more delicate and had been set with ovals of lapis and opal.

She considered for a moment how much she could tell them about it without compromising traditions and customs her people preferred to keep secret. "These two pieces are of Elven manufacture. They are wedding tokens. This one is for the groom, and the other, which you can see is smaller, is for the bride. The mail indicates the groom was a warrior. The ring was worn around his middle finger."

The merchant smiled. "And the magicks?"

She turned the bracer over and back again, and concentrated to pick up traces of the magick worked into it, even though she well knew what the spell would be. "It is an enchantment related to the marriage ceremony." She hesitated and the merchant missed it, but the small man caught it. "It roughly calls for the love between them to outlast the metal making up the tokens; then it prevents the silver from tarnishing." The magick really did much more and in the hands of an enemy the tokens could become very powerful weapons if used against those who had worn them; but Genevera felt the Men had no need for that information.

The smaller man spoke, prompting the merchant to frown. "Is there any way, my Lady, to determine for whom these have been made? I assume they'd not be abandoned lightly."

"No, they would normally be destroyed if the marriage was dissolved." She turned the bracelet over and up so she could see inside the cuff. "Ah, there are maker-marks here. Yes, I . . ." She stopped as her throat tightened. She recognized the marks instantly and bit her lower lip to stop it from trembling. "I know for whom these were fashioned. The pieces are nearly five centuries old. They belonged to my grandparents."

"Who are now dead?"

The ghoulishly hopeful note in the merchant's voice shocked her and clearly angered the smaller man. "They are still alive. I would like to know where you got these."

The merchant looked back at the small man, disappointment evident on his face. "You may tell her what you wish. I abide by our agreement."

The smaller man unfolded his arms, depositing the twin flashdrakes on the table, then bowed to her. "I am Durriken. I supply Frigyes here with things. We've agreed that he can sell anything we can't get back to the owner or an heir. These bracelets, as I understand it, were found about a hundred years ago by someone digging in the Dead Mountains. Various connoisseurs traded for them, and they recently came into my possession. But now they're yours. I hope your kin will be happy to get them back."

"If they do not want them," the merchant smiled solicitously, "I am certain the original owner would love to regain them."

Durriken snarled at the merchant, and the man sank back in his chair. "Her kin *are* the original owners. Sell Polus the imperial goblets I obtained a year ago to salve him, and let Avner console himself with getting the marble goddess that accompanied these beauties when they left Polus's vault."

Gena looked at the small man. "You're a thief?"

"Frigyes prefers to call me a Practical Antiquarian, but 'thief' sums it up nicely." He shrugged and pointed to the bracelets. "I've accepted as my life's duty preventing collectors from becoming too comfortable with their loot."

Gena came out of her reverie as one of the scouts rode back to the main body of troops. He reported to Waldo; then the soldier turned to face the two of them. "They found a dead Haladin bandit in the croft. He had been wounded in the chest. One of yours?"

"Likely." Durriken nodded curtly.

"More of the warrior in you than I would have imagined."

"I do my best to hide it, but there are times it slips out."

Waldo raised an eyebrow at that remark, then faced forward and kept riding.

Gena frowned at Rik. "In these stories you told, did you mention you were a thief?"

"How they'd have figured that, I don't know." A smug smile and playful wink put the lie to that statement. "You think that's a problem?"

"Rik, Aurdon is a city founded by and run by merchants!"

"And a bigger den of thieves we'll not likely find this side of Najinda. Merchants are just thieves who prefer robbing you while making you think you're getting a bargain."

"Rik!"

The thief smiled and patted her left knee. "Don't worry, Gena, I'll be on my best behavior, I promise."

"Promise?"

"My solemn oath." Durriken placed a hand over his heart for a second. "Besides, until *you* pass through the city gates, Aurdon has nothing I want."

The road itself followed the valley floors as it wound its way through the hills to Aurdon. Waldo, either impatient to get back to the city or complying with orders, took numerous shortcuts. At all times he kept his scouts and outriders in place even though their unorthodox route made the chance of ambush much smaller.

Riding up and over the hills provided Gena with breathtaking views of grasslands stretching as far as the eye could see. Farms dotted the landscape, their sod houses looking like warts raised on the bare hillsides. Gena shivered unconsciously when she looked at them and was thankful Waldo had not suggested stopping at one. She understood the necessity of sod houses in a land of so few trees, but growing up in Cygestolia had left her feeling as if dwelling in the mud were somehow blasphemous.

The sun had begun its descent into the underworld when she saw the first hint of Aurdon. She doubted the Fishers and Riverens would have enjoyed knowing what her first clue to the city's presence was. Even before the city itself came into view, she saw a brownish haze hanging at the lower end of the river valley toward which they rode. Recalling the cloud raised by the Seventh Regiment's approach, she wondered at first if it might be the oxen being driven back to meet the refugees. That speculation lasted only a minute longer, dying when a breeze brought to her the woody scent of thousands of cookstoves. Only then did she realize the haze had been created as the city devoured what were once proud forests to feed its hunger for building materials and fuel.

Riding in on the river road, Gena first caught sight of the city as they came around a bend. The moment she saw the metropolis, she shuddered. The ivory stone used to build the city's walls and largest buildings reminded her of aged bone. It appeared to her as if the earth's flesh had been gashed open and people had taken up residence in the wound, reshaping bone to suit their needs. It struck her that her revelation would have been better suited to a Dwarf, for the gods had used them to create the world—yet she knew her dismay came from the scarcity of green in the city before her.

Aurdon sprawled over a half-dozen hills, and three stone ribbons of wall surrounded the municipal core. The tallest buildings had been constructed within the second ring, and some more prosperous and ambitious dwellings lurked within the third. Outside the walls, smaller dwellings and various business establishments had spread across the valley, with a fair amount of the riverbanks near the tri-river confluence given over to warehouses and docks for servicing the barge trade.

A trumpet blast from the scouts parted traffic on the main road, so the company made quick time riding north to the first set of city gates. The guards up on the ramparts looked down at them, but did not challenge them, nor paid them overmuch attention. Waldo led them off on the first wide street that headed east and uphill around to the second gate.

The second gate had been placed facing north-northeast, requiring an army that breached the south gate to fight its way uphill to get to it. The Rangers, save Waldo and his scouts, rode off to their barracks while the lieutenant continued out and around, leading Gena and Rik to the third and final city gate. After riding down into a valley between two hills, they rode up again and around to the northwest to make another uphill approach to the gate.

Rik caught Gena's eye. "I've entered palaces at midnight with less difficulty than this."

Waldo shot Rik a sharp glance. "I have no doubt you

have, Master Durriken. We have built much here in Aurdon that others covet."

"I can see that, Lieutenant." Rik replied to the man respectfully, not rising to the bait of disdain in Waldo's voice.

The guards at the last gate snapped to attention as the group rode through. The pace of travel slowed, less, Gena thought, because the streets were crowded than because the people lining the streets here appeared to be a better class of denizen than those choking the avenues and courtyards outside the third ring. And she marked in Waldo's attitude a change that allowed her to think he was not so much concerned with riding even these people down as he was with being able to strut importantly before them.

As she had come to expect, she became the object of stares and whispers, much to Waldo's apparent consternation. While the inhabitants of an urban center such as Aurdon doubtlessly would scoff at the way the farmers had feared her on the road, they, too, would feel a trickle of terror if she met their gazes openly. Gena accepted that the novelty of seeing an Elf for the first—and perhaps *only*—time invited study, and she did not hold with other Elves who maintained this proved Men to be little better than the lowing bovines they tended in fields.

Curiously enough, Gena noticed a certain amount of deference being paid to Durriken. He seemed to have noticed it as well, because she caught him furtively glancing about, yet he accepted it and even nodded to one or two women who curtsied as he passed. His reception appeared to anger Waldo—if his scowl and stiff spine could be trusted to measure his mood—but the lieutenant did nothing to act on his feelings.

Waldo reined his mount to a halt before a stone building with the ivory patina of age in the stone walls and columns. Dismounting, he turned the reins of his horse over to one of his scouts, and two others came forward to care similarly for Spirit and Benison. Rik dismounted with a flourish, then patted Benison on the neck. He offered Gena his hand, and she took it less for assistance than the desire to touch him and be close.

Hand in hand they followed Waldo up broad steps, between two statues of perched Fishers and through cast-iron doors a full fifteen feet in height and half that in width. Without introduction or travelogue, he led them across the marble-inlaid foyer, around the decorative pond in which aurfish swam lazily, and on into a long hallway in which the spaces between the arched windows were covered by heavy tapestries. Though she recognized none of the scenes depicted, Gena assumed they came from Fisher family history because of the way the knotted sleeves played prominently across the top of each tableau, and because the tapestries themselves were fastened to the wall by iron hooks made to look like the talons of a Fisher.

Halfway down the corridor Gena began to hear the sounds of fighting, the ringing skirl of steel disengaging itself from steel. As no shouts of alarm accompanied it and Waldo did not react to it, she assumed the sound was not alien to the house this late in the day. Waldo turned right and pointed them through a doorway that opened onto a wide porch standing above a small courtyard surrounded by a splendid garden.

Despite all the combatants being covered in studded leather armor and wearing full helms, Gena recognized Count Berengar instantly. The locks of flame-red hair hanging down from beneath the helmet only provided confirmation of the conclusion she had based on his tall stature and heavily muscled body. Clad in black, using a rapier in each hand, he moved with a fluid grace she remembered well from the dance floor at the reception where they had met.

The two men he fought worked well as a team, yet remained unable to pierce his defenses. Berengar kept his blades wide, facing them straight on, waiting for them to choose an avenue for attack. Normally that would have resulted in his death, but Berengar's extended reach, fast parries, and swifter ripostes meant closing with him was to enter a sphere of death in which he held sway.

"M'lord, I have arrived with your guests." Waldo's announcement and a muffled "Hold," from Berengar brought the fight to a halt. As Berengar handed his blades to a servant and doffed his helmet, Waldo turned to Rik. "You will surrender your flashdrakes to me now, sirrah."

Gena felt a jolt through Rik's right hand, but her grip prevented his drawing one of the handcannons or punching Waldo. Rik shot Gena a sharp glance, then almost instantly let his anger go. "I beg your pardon, Lieutenant? Did you ask to examine one of my flashdrakes?"

"No, I demanded their surrender. It is the law here in Aurdon."

"Waldo! What is this?" Berengar rushed up the steps and stopped several short of the landing, keeping himself at eye level with Durriken. "These are my guests."

The soldier blinked with surprise. "But the law, it is clear. He . . ."

"He is *my* guest." Berengar shook his head and sighed, then looked up at Durriken. "Forgive this discourtesy, please. Waldo is correct in that it is a law here in Aurdon that only nobles may possess flashdrakes. I can clearly see these are of Dwarven manufacture, not the poorly constructed imitations that the Haladina occasionally circulate." The big man looked back at the people standing in the arena below. "While we have chosen to eschew flashdrakes in favor of more honorable weapons, the law was passed to prevent commoners and peasants from being harmed by the combustion of inferior examples of handcannons. If you will give me your parole that you will not use them except in most dire need, I believe we will have no difficulty with your continued possession of them."

Durriken nodded graciously. "You have my word on it, my lord."

"Splendid." Berengar stepped up to the landing and smiled at Gena. "My dear lady, it is once again an honor to bask in your radiance." He bowed, then took her right hand and kissed it gently, his moustache and beard tickling her flesh.

Gena looked up at him and smiled. "And I, we, are honored to be received in your home. You are looking well."

"And with you here, I am much, much better." He turned to face Durriken. "I understand from the men Captain Floris sent back that you are Durriken, a finder of items long lost."

Rik bowed his head. "I am."

"Fortune smiles, then, that you have come with Lady Genevera." Berengar's glance flicked past their joined hands, his bright blue eyes narrowing for a moment; then he pointed them past Waldo and back into the house. "I have arranged for adjoining suites for you. I would have used but one; however, my parsimonious forebears made the guest accommodations quite small. Please use one as your parlor and the other as your private chamber."

"My lord is most generous."

"I hope you will think so after we have a chance to speak more fully." A hint of urgency drifted into Berengar's voice. "As Lady Genevera can tell you, I tend to be more direct than other nobles, and I know you must be wondering why I asked for her to come here with all haste. I realize you are road weary and wish to rest, especially after having to deal with Haladina on the road, but I feel letting you know the reason I summoned you is quite important."

He looked at her quite solemnly. "You know, of course, that Neal Elfward played a key role in the history of Aurdon."

Gena nodded. "I do."

"Good." Berengar's eyes narrowed. "I've asked you here because I need your knowledge of him—and good Durriken's skills will likewise be valuable, I think. You see, I need to unmake what Neal created. If I do not, a city that has prospered over five centuries will cease to exist inside five years."

Chapter 4

Deceiving the Lords of Aurium

Late Summer
Reign of the Red Tiger Year 1
Five Centuries Ago
My Thirty-fifth Year

The final two hours of our journey to Aurium took the form of a nightride. We rode through dark woodlands and the northern foothills of the central mountains. Though we had seen no signs of Haladin mayhem since the ambush, I let Aarundel ride point and had Shijef ranging through the woods ahead of him. Aarundel's keen nightvision made him proof against the sort of trick that had gotten me, and Shijef's orders allowed him enough leeway to cause the sort of trouble that would raise an alarm for us.

The woods abruptly ended in a stump meadow that marked the source of the wood used to build most of Aurium. While the merchants who controlled the town dared name it "City of Gold" in the Elven tongue, truth was that the town had been built of tree-flesh and only recently had acquired a building of stone. It was supposed to have a palisade, which could help in defending it against the Haladina, but I knew of no local militia or native troops that called Aurium home.

We rode past some woodcutter camps, and that sparked some optimistic comments from my fellows. We had all feared that a Haladin force had somehow eluded our detection and laid siege to Aurium. Given the nature of the Man-town, a torch or two would have had it burning hotter than the firewell in Jammaq. Chances were, however, that the Haladina wouldn't burn it because of its control over river traffic.

Up ahead, on the crest of the last hill leading to the Aurium valley, Aarundel stopped his horse and whistled. I rode forward and drew abreast of his position. From our vantage point I could see little because the city lay a good half mile ahead of us in the darkness, but that did not bother my eagle-eyed companion. Where I saw dots of light in a pool of brooding darkness, he saw much more.

"The gates are open, Neal. There are no custodians on the walls."

I looked hard out into the darkness but saw nothing more nor less than I expected. The night's breeze came up from the river and into my face, but I smelled nothing to indicate the lights I saw were the embers of a fire that had consumed the town. "Does all else look normal?" I gave him a quick smile. "Excepting the fact it's a Man-town."

"Absent that consideration, I see a nimiety of normality." Aarundel's face remained impassive, but he let some amusement bleed into his words. Though we were good friends—brothers born of different races—Aarundel held himself tightly and seldom let down the fierce Elven facade that reminded others of the excesses ascribed to Elven Legions by the *Eldsaga*. When we were alone he would open up, but being soul-kin meant I understood the part he was playing and why he played it.

Blackstar shuddered and shied toward Aarundel's horse, which meant only one thing. I looked down to my left and a half-dozen paces forward. Crouched there sniffing the wind, Shijef turned his nose toward Aurium. "Lifeblack pools." He raised his head and let out a howl that echoed through the valley. "Lifeblack floods."

More than the howl, his words sent a shiver down my

spine. Over the dozen years through which I have suffered my Dreel slave, I learned one fact that was true. Like an old man whose bunions can foretell a gathering storm, Shijef just out and out knows when violence is building in an area. Given his choice, he would seek it out the way a lonely man hunts for a smile and a laugh.

He undoubtedly knew the ambush in the woods was coming, but he did not warn me because he knew the chances of my getting killed were—in his eyes—minimal. While my death would end his servitude to me, he was a creature of curious honor. As much as he hated me for enslaving him, he accepted that his servitude was the prize I won in our contest. As a result, he pledged himself to preserving my life. He left me to the Haladina on the trail because the man was not a threat, but killed the horseman because he could have killed me.

It had taken me a long time to see Shijef as more than a bear and a tiger mixed together with a lot of anger and a limited vocabulary. Not only was he intelligent, but he understood emotions and concepts like honor and friendship. I never imagined we would be friends because, unlike Aarundel and me, our partnership was not one of willing participation. Still, I had some admiration for the Dreel and trusted his reading of murky and complex situations under the right circumstances.

Circumstances such as these.

I glanced at the Dreel. "Shijef, are there Haladina in the town?"

"Not sandmen." The monster half hopped a bit down the hillside. "Denmen."

"Civil strife during a war?" Aarundel's saddle groaned as the Elf shifted his weight and reseated his feet in the stirrups. "Is intervention warranted?"

"It is, I'm thinking." I squeezed my knees together and urged Blackstar forward. Shijef's predictions of death coming to a place could be deflected or contradicted with proper action. If we could stop whatever was going on in Aurium, it would frustrate the Dreel, and that would be punishment enough for what he did to the Haladin warrior. "Being as how the Red Tiger is not wanting a whole

Reithrese navy descending on Polston, saving this inflated barter-post is likely within our duties."

The fifteen of us rode on into the valley and up to the gates. I put Senan in command and set him to closing the gates and seeing how secure the town was. The wooden palisade looked in fine repair, but the open gates bothered me. While I felt fair certain no Haladina had gotten this far north, I had no desire to have them inside Aurium when I learned I was wrong.

Aarundel, the Dreel, and I headed deeper into the town. It took neither the Elf's vision nor the Dreel's deathsight to direct us toward the center of the trouble in Aurium. Most of the town lay quiet and shut up tight against possible violence. Not a shutter opened as we rode through the muddy streets—the fear in the air clung like swampscent and smelled not nearly as sweet.

When we reached the stone building on the top of the hillock at the town's heart, I immediately knew what had to be going on. Two groups of Men stood on either side of the building's wooden doors. They had no weapons in hand, and were valiantly doing their best to ignore each other. Our arrival made that easy, though the eldest of each group stepped forward to give us orders—bringing the two groups of five into conflict again.

Without a word between us, Aarundel and I reined up just short of the men and dismounted in unison. Mirrors of each other, we flipped our reins to each of the groups' self-appointed legates. "Obliged, gentlemen. Now you'll be opening the doors for us."

"That is not possible," one Man blurted out quickly. His deep flush and hot words told me he was not in a good mood. He hastily signaled to one of the other Men in his group to take Blackstar's reins. "The doors are closed until the council makes a decision."

The sounds coming from beyond the doors sounded to me like those from a bloodpit duel, but I'd seen politics go malignant and become war before. "Good, then we are yet in time. They'll not be wanting to make a decision before they have had our counsel."

The Man in front of me moved to block my path. I could see from the emblem crudely embroidered on the breast of his tunic that he was bound to the Fisher Clan. A bird in flight, it had a fish in its beak and a purse clutched in its talons. I knew the Fishers to be one of the two clans that lived in and around Aurium.

Opposite him stood his equal in the employ of the Riveraven Clan. Like the Fishers, they took their name from that of a bird that frequented the tri-river valley. Common wisdom had it that Riveravens were rats with wings and that Fishers regularly placed their eggs in Riveraven nests to be tended. I'd also heard people wonder if the two clans wouldn't have gotten along well had their forebears been wiser in their totem-choices, because the two families seemed to everyone outside them to complement each other.

"Goodman, I do not doubt you've been given a duty to perform here tonight." I stepped in close to him, mounting the first of three steps to the level of the doorway. My right hand reached out quicker than he could see or block, and slipped my dagger, Wasp, from the sheath over my right hip. "Now, you're all guards, and that's a right proud job to be having."

Flicking the blade forward, I stuck it quivering in the right-side door to the squat and ugly *legislatorium.* I'd not expected the blade to stick really—Wasp has all the balance of a one-legged man hopping on wet ice—but the door's soft wood would have held the blade even if it had backed into place. Behind me the Dreel yipped appreciatively, and at my side Aarundel just narrowed his black eyes. "What you don't want to be are *dead* guards, I'm thinking."

The combined effect of action and words worked to open the doors faster than a latchkey. The two gangs of rowdies opened the building for us, bowing low and mumbling very polite greetings in what I believed they thought was Elven. Aarundel remained as silent and implacable as death, while the Dreel sniffed at one Man, then another, like a customer sorting fresh fish from spoiled. I recovered Wasp and rehomed it, then stepped through the threshold as if I were bound to see the Reithrese emperor in Jarudin.

The Hall of Laws had not risen very tall because of the cost of bringing stone in from the quarries upriver. To make the structure big, the people of Aurium had dug down into the hillock. Whereas outside, the building only rose a score feet above the ground, within the hall itself a good forty feet stood between floor and ceiling.

The excavated area had been paved with smooth river-stone. It seemed to me that what had been born of economy had turned out to be quite decorative. Three terraces surrounded the central floor. They had been finished in fancy woods of gold and rich mahogany, adding some warmth to the cold white of the hillock's stone carapace. Benches and tables provided seating for those who would enact laws. For such a small town, the Hall of Laws was a thing of which the people could be proud.

My earlier impressions of the sounds proved more correct than I would have imagined. The three of us arrived in the midst of what had to be a heated debate. Two young men circled each other in the center of the stone floor. Each had his left arm bared, as their tunic sleeves had been stripped off and knotted together to form a short tether. Each man held tight to the tether with his left hand. The loose cuffs stood up from the knot like rabbit ears and flopped this side and that as the two men pulled back and forth on the tether.

Each man held a dagger in his right hand. The blades more resembled filleting knives than they did Wasp, but each was long, sharp, and pointy enough to reach the heart through the ribs. Each also glistened with blood which, I gathered from the stains on each combatant's tattered tunic, came from a series of shallow wounds. Both the wounds and the way the two men moved listlessly told me any enthusiasm they'd had for the fight had been swallowed by exhaustion and excreted as mortal fear.

Surrounding them, standing on benches and sitting on desks, nearly the whole of the two clans hooted and hollered encouragement. I saw the mother of one lad sitting on the side, clinging to a daughter and crying silently. Uncles and cousins jerked and dodged in sympathy for their clan's fighter, but not a one of them had lifeleak splotches on their clothes. Older and wiser clan members hung back, occasionally shouting an obligatory bit of advice, but mostly watching and waiting and calculating what they would do in the event of whatever outcome seemed most likely.

Without breaking stride, I sailed down the open aisle dividing the *legislatorium* left from right. I drew Cleave-heart cleanly as I came and filled my left hand with Wasp. Before either of the young men even had a chance to notice me, the sword flashed down and the dagger up, split-shearing the knot. Each of the fighters spilled backward, flailing sleeve-half waving like the tail on a kite as they went down.

"Foul!" shouted a heavyset, florid-faced man of the Fisher Clan. "Edward was winning. You, Festus Riveraven, you cheated!" He pointed across the assembly at a slender white-haired man kneeling beside his family's champion. "These are your agents, but they shall not win Aurium for you."

Festus Riveraven raised his head and did not even look at me or Aarundel. "Nay, Childeric Fisher, these are not *my* agents. You are lucky they interfered when they did, for Rufus would have spitted your Edward in a minute." He turned to me and kept a snarl out of all but his eyes and voice. "Who are you that dares . . ."

Finding as I have in the past that my tolerance for politicians is inverse to their degree of liveliness, I spoke over him. "I am Neal Roclawzi and this is Aarundel." I looked back over my shoulder at where Shijef had taken up a post guarding the room's only exit. "He is a Dreel and my command is his will."

Childeric straightened up—no easy task for as corpulent a bulk as I'd ever seen on a man—and eyed me up and down. "You are the Dun Wolf? You command the Steel Pack?"

Aarundel gently hefted his war ax. "Sound not incredulous when you address Neal Custos Sylvanii. Treat him as a lack-honor and *I* will choose the manner of your punishment."

"I meant no disrespect, Lansor Honorari," Childeric offered in badly accented Elven.

"And I am near certain Aarundel *Imperator* did not take it as such, Fisher." I gave him a nasty glare, but saved half of it for Festus. "Yes, I command the Steel Pack. We have been sent here to prevent Aurium from falling into

Reithrese hands, but it appears there are other troubles here."

Festus waved my concern away. "No troubles that demand your attention."

I raised an eyebrow at his statement. "Mayhap, then, you can explain why you were about turning this place into a . . . a . . ."

Aarundel smiled easily. "An abattoir, Custos Sylvanii?"

"Thank you, Aarundel Imperator. An abattoir?"

"It is the business of merchants, mercenary." Festus dismissed me with a more vehement wave. "What happens here is not your concern. It is not your business."

"No?" I used Cleaveheart to link the two bleeding boys with an arc. "Tell me, then, what was it I saw? Were you trying to show the sharpness of the blades you sell, or was that a prelude to showing how a poultice you trade in will heal cuts?"

"You would not understand!" Festus looked to Childeric for a confirmatory nod and got one quickly. "You are not a merchant, you cannot understand."

"That may be, but were I a merchant, I know I'd trade in common sense. Here in Aurium it's in sad supply, and there is a sore need for it." I took a step toward Festus, and he pulled back to where his seated son formed a barrier between us. "I do know some things, though, and one of them is this: you're all, the lot of you, trading long in hostility, and that means war, which is my concern."

I shook my head and saw Aarundel give me wide berth. "Now I know, from what you've said, you're not wanting me to start gathering wool from your sheep, as it were. You want me to stay out of your business, and I respect that. I have no doubt you merchants have all sorts of your own rules and laws for dealing with this and that. Well, now, I know there are rules of warfare that I abide by, and I would be offended if anyone came in from the outside and started breaking them."

I sank my face into that touch-brow kind of expression that marks long thought with short success. "And I gather there is another likeness between our professions. Competition is at the heart of it, really. Like the two of your families competing one against the other. That's the soul of it, and if one side wins, the other is driven out of business."

Childeric gave me a patronizing nod. "There, Neal, you have the right of it. We are alike but different. Leave us, and let us settle our differences."

"Differences, true enough," I said, aping as much of his statement as served my purpose. "Of course, the difference between being a soldier and being a merchant is that *my* competition ends up dead. Makes a right fair mess, too, sometimes." My brow still furrowed, I looked down at the floor. "Pity, I don't think this will drain well."

Festus shook with anger at my antics. "Prithee, what are you prattering on about?"

The Elf answered for me. "Even a lackwit could figure it out, Festus: by introducing killing into your competition here in Aurium, you have become *our* competition."

"And our competitors end up *dead*." I smiled as benignly as I could and nodded at the Dreel. "Shijef, none shall pass you."

A low, rumbling growl rolled from his throat as his triangular ears came up to attention and he flexed talon-shot paws. He displayed his fangs for all, and his tail beat a happy tattoo against the door.

I shrugged as I turned to Childeric. "You understand, of course, why we have to do this. I mean, if you set to warring by yourself, without our help, why then everyone could just start slaughtering their neighbors. They wouldn't need us and I'd be obsolete. I would be out of business. My men would go hungry and their families would starve. No, no, we can't have that."

Aarundel brought his war ax up and rested it on his right shoulder. "Was I to terminate the Riveravens or the Fishers?"

"I was thinking that I was to do the young, and you were to start with the old."

"We cannot do that, Neal, for parents might see their children die, and I would spare them that." The Elf looked at the two men still seated on the floor. "Then again, that prospect appears to spawn no dolor here."

Childeric's jaw dropped open. "You cannot do that!"

"Have I a choice?" I smiled benignly at him. "I cannot

expect you to understand, for this is the business of mercenaries, not merchants."

Festus proved a mite sharper than his competition. "You are mercenaries, I have money. I will purchase your services. We will work together, we will unite."

I sighed deeply. "Oh, now, disaster! Why did you have to do that?"

Festus, for the first time, looked puzzled and just a touch afraid. "Do what?"

Aarundel looked down at the smaller man and slowly shook his head. "You have violated the Codex Mercenarius." The Elf's voice, kept low and sinking lower, paused long enough to make each of the Elven words clear, crisp, and razor-sharp to the ears.

My nod confirmed the worst fears anyone in the room could have had. "You see, neither one of you controls the government here in Centisia, so—as the Codex Mercenarius makes very clear—you cannot hire mercenaries. By offering us money you reduce us to alley-bashers and footpads who hurt others for the purpose of making money."

Childeric shook his head. "But that is what mercenaries *do*!" He saw me stiffen and hastily added, "Isn't it?"

"Common misconception, actually. Mercenaries are *warriors* who fight beneath the banner of a nation, or political subdivision thereof, for the purposes of furthering state policy." I looked at him. "Is a boy who finds wormy apples in an orchard and sells them to someone a merchant?"

"I should say not," both Festus and Childeric snapped indignantly. "We are professionals."

"Then don't be lumping cutpurses and rib-crushers with us *professionals*." I turned to Aarundel and smiled. "You have studied the Codex more recently than I, Imperator. I do not recall a way out of this."

The Elf shrugged and, looking up, studied the marble walls and ceiling. "This will make for an appropriate sepulchre. If everyone could lie down side by side, it would make the work easier." He casually reached down and plucked a hair from the red thatch on Rufus's head, then let it slide in twain down the edge of his ax. "Short of a total cessation of hostilities, our course is set."

I nodded. "Well, there is *that.*" I smiled at Childeric, then pointed Cleaveheart at the leonine woman and pretty young girl standing behind him. "Your wife and daughter? Good, families should die together."

"Wait, wait." Festus rose from behind his son. "What was this about stopping the fight?"

I looked at him as if he were a moron. "Clearly, if there is no war between you, you are not our competition. You would not try to engage our services, so no violation of the Codex Mercenarius would have occurred."

The slender man nodded curtly. "Then the fight is over. There is no war."

Childeric backed him up. "Indeed, total peace. You are not needed here anymore."

The two of them looked quite smug and self-satisfied with their solution to the problem—not the problem of their fighting, but of our objection to it. I shook my head. "I may be a mercenary, but I am *not* a fool. The instant I leave, you will return to your fighting. You will unite in the face of a common enemy, but then split apart again. You would play me false."

"No."

"Indeed, you would not." I slid Cleaveheart into its scabbard, then waved Childeric's daughter forward. "Come to me, child, do not be afraid." As I made my voice gentle for her, I took the anger I skimmed out of it and pumped it through my eyes into her father. "What is your name?"

"Ismere, Lord Custos Sylvanii." Her Elvish fell soft on my ear, and from the hint of a nod I saw Aarundel make, she pleased him as well. She took my hand, her pale flesh like snow on my darker, scarcrossed skin. Wearing a dress made of fabric spun and dyed sky-blue in the islands, the slender slip of a girl had been saved inheriting anything from her father with the exception of her clan affiliation and blue eyes.

I felt her tremble and smiled. "No need to be afraid, Ismere. I would slay all others before I would cause you hurt." With Wasp I cut at the seam of her left sleeve and sliced the stitching all the way up into the armpit. She let her arm hang limply at her side, bringing her right hand across her chest to clutch at her left elbow.

I pointed to Rufus. "Excepting the blood, he's not hard to look at, is he?"

"No, my Lord."

"Fancy him, do you?"

In her eyes I saw an instant recognition of what I was going to do. She hesitated for a heartbeat and started to look back at her father, then just looked at Rufus. She studied him for a moment, then nodded. With the conviction of someone realizing she was guaranteeing the future through her action, she chose her words carefully. "I believe him wise, couth, and pleasing."

I nodded at Rufus. "On your feet, lad." His father made to restrain him, but I shook my head. "Don't you think, Festus, a funeral would make this day very sad?"

Rufus stood, tugged at the hem of his nearly white homespun tunic and approached. "Yes, m'lord?" He was wise enough to know he couldn't pronounce my Elven title as well as Ismere, so he did not even try.

"Could you make Ismere happy?"

"I will."

I slit his right sleeve and knotted their sleeves together. "This is it, then. By the rights granted me in the Codex Mercenarius, I bind these two and their families together. You *will* work together until this knot is severed by Wasp and Cleaveheart. Anyone who tries to sunder this union will have me to deal with, whether I'm dead or alive. This I vow in the name of Herin."

My invocation of the warrior god's name in a merchant house brought some mild gasps and got everyone's attention. In doing that I'd reinforced the idea of lethal consequences if they fought my solution. "You'll be wanting to have your priests conduct their ceremonies to bless this marriage, but it's Neal Roclawzi, not the gods, who will harvest any who interfere with it."

I smiled as I turned to the two fathers. "And as for you, because old habits die hard, I want to give you a bit of a competition to occupy your efforts until this settlement has anchored in your hearts. This was a wedding. You'll be wanting to put on a feast to celebrate it. And, as I have the Steel Pack on the way here, you'll be wanting it to be a celebration remembered for generations because of the unflinching generosity of the hosts."

Chapter 5

The Reason for Coming

Early Spring
A.R. 499
The Present

Genevera bowed her head politely as Count Berengar Fisher ushered her into her suite. As he had suggested earlier, the suite itself barely deserved the name. Wider than it was deep, an archway that held up the roof nominally functioned to split the bedroom from the area nearest the door. Heavy curtains gathered at each side of the broad arch and, when drawn, would sever one half of the room from the other effectively, but would also shield the bed from the fireplace in the north wall.

Beyond the arch, in the sleeping area, Gena had two small arched lead-glass windows that looked out into one of the manor's gardens. Spring had not yet brought blossoms to the flowers, but the shrubs and plants had all begun to produce new growth, blending new green with older green in a display that pleased her. Since the windows faced east, she knew she would get the dawning sun, and it made her happy that she would start the day with the sun's warm caress.

Back in the northeast corner she saw a narrow door, which Count Berengar opened immediately. Durriken appeared through it and winked at her, then nodded. "Late Imperial furnishings. I am impressed, my lord, for such things are very expensive now."

The larger man scratched at the diagonal scar beneath his left eye. "I would accept your praises, Master Durriken, but we have these antiques because my penurious ancestors never even dreamed of buying anything new unless something old had fallen to pieces." His massive left hand stroked the carefully carved scrollwork on the corner of a chest of drawers. "These pieces have served well and would long since have fallen apart were they not housed in these seldomly used rooms."

Gena sensed weariness in the way Berengar spoke of his elders, as if he were well and truly sick of convincing them of one thing or another. She felt it somewhat odd that she could look at the wooden furnishings in the room and view them as serviceable yet less than appealing pieces, while the two Men recognized some value in them for their antiquity. She could not be certain, but she felt confident that she was actually older than most of the pieces in the room—and she hoped this was, in fact, the case with the straw in the canopy bed's mattress.

"My lord, your statement earlier suggests to me that these pieces might see no more service if we cannot help you." Gena moved away from the bed and back into the forward part of her room, then seated herself in a rough-hewn chair. "Can you tell us more of what you want of us?"

Berengar nodded easily and pulled a chair around so he could face her. He started to speak, then hesitated and pointed at the sideboard. "Would you like some wine? Something to eat, perhaps?"

"Wine, yes, thank you."

"I'll play the server." Durriken waved them back into their chairs. "I can listen while my hands work—makes my tasks go easier."

"I am in your debt." Berengar raked his red hair back into place with his fingers, then hunched forward with elbows on knees. "The union Neal forced on the Fishers and Riverens worked well for a generation or two. From the start, in memory of his friend, the Red Tiger made the Knott family the representatives for trade within the province of Centisia. They shared with their cousins and brought all of us the prosperity that built much of the inner city.

"The next couple of generations from the Knotts married back into the Fishers and Riverens, then the line died out when no more male heirs appeared. That's when one of the Riverens made the first attempt at severing the alliance. He set out to poison one of the Fishers, but ended up a *felos-de-se,* as I believe you put it in the Sylvanii."

Gena nodded, then looked up as Durriken frowned over at the sideboard. "*Felos-de-se* is a person who dies as a result of some nefarious enterprise of his own execution."

Rik nodded and handed Gena a silver goblet filled with a ruby vintage. "Stuck himself with his own fouled needle, did he?"

Berengar gratefully accepted a goblet from Rik, then shook his head. "Not exactly, Master Durriken, and that's where the tale begins to bear on why I asked you here. Apparently he had been drinking heavily to get his courage up and somehow managed to drink the poison he had prepared. Justice, no doubt, but when they found him, they also found the word 'Neal' traced in wine on the table."

Gena felt a shiver run down her spine. She sipped the wine, letting the hearty, dry liquid wash the road dust from her throat. "This was not an isolated incident?"

Berengar ruefully shook his head. "My ancestors immediately assumed the union had been broken by this attempt to kill them, so they plotted against the Riverens themselves. A Fisher out to assassinate one of the Riverens tripped and died when he fell down a broad staircase in the Riveren manor. A servant attracted by the noise thought he saw a shadowed figure moving at the head of the stairs, but when he rushed up there, all he found was a tapestry commemorating the union—complete with Neal's portrait—fallen from the hooks that held it up. It's believed the falling tapestry knocked the assassin down the stairs."

"Uncommon bad luck, or Neal's ghost is keeping his

promises for him." Rik shrugged and leaned against the back of Gena's chair. "I've no love for hauntings."

The count's chair creaked as he sat back in it. "Nor do I. Over the last three centuries or so various members of the Riveren or Fisher families have decided they knew how to sever the knot that binds us, but they have been considered quite daft. A few died as a result of their plots, while most of the rest abandoned their plans after particularly vivid nightmares in which Neal himself warned them off."

He opened his arms. "With that sort of history, I'd never even begin to consider repeating their folly were the situation not so dire. For years and years the two families have worked against each other, but only in very open and appropriate ways for merchants. Predatory pricing, yes, preying on each other's caravans or ships, no. It was a war, but one fought with coin, not sword.

"This changed four years ago, and I am forced to act."

Gena set her goblet down on the small table at her right hand. "What has transpired that could make you risk your life against a ghost?"

"The Riverens started trading with the Haladina. They claim they have done this to civilize the outlanders and earn protection for their own caravans. They neglect to mention that the riches with which they secured their alliance have led the Haladina again to raid through what was once the empire. As my family does virtually all of its trading here in the south, we fall prey to these raiders. We have protested to the Riverens that the Haladina they harbor in Aurdon here act as spies for the bandits in the countryside, but they ignore us."

Rik rested his hands on Gena's shoulders and gently kneaded her muscles. Her quiet groan as his strong fingers eroded the tightness half hid his comment to Berengar. "A strike at Riveren allies, you think, would run afoul of Neal's curse?"

"Especially if the Haladina were being housed on a Riveren estate, for example, yes." Berengar tossed off the last of his wine, then wiped his mouth on his sleeve. "I think, though, I have a way to bring the curse to an end. Neal said the union will remain until Wasp and Cleaveheart sever it. I have it in mind to mount an expedition to recover those two blades, then do the job as prescribed by Neal himself."

"Clever plan, that." Rik returned to the sideboard, then refilled Berengar's cup from an earthenware pitcher. He turned to Gena, but she deflected him by laying her hand over the mouth of her goblet.

Berengar drank, then leaned forward again, holding his silver goblet in both hands between his knees. "I have tried to learn as much as I can about Neal, but his legend is not well remembered here. I must have a dozen different versions of his actions here in Aurdon, but barely a whisper about him before or after. Tragedies do not play well here, and the Dun Wolf is mostly remembered as a comical character in the Red Tiger's cycle of folktales and songs. For this reason I need your expertise, Lady Genevera, and like as not will need your skills, Master Durriken."

He looked up at her, his blue eyes wary. "Do the blades still exist? Is my plan viable?"

Gena closed her eyes for a moment and wished Rik had returned to massaging her muscles. "You have asked two questions, and I have no favorable reply to either at the moment. It does seem logical that the blades could be used to sever the knot and break the oath, but only if the words have come down true and if Neal's *intent* is represented in them. I do believe most stories agree on his oath, so that is a beneficent omen. As to the other . . ." She shrugged helplessly. "The ending of Neal's life is overshadowed by his heroism and the tragedy. I will need time to remember details, but I recall at least one of the blades survived his last battle."

"The sword, Cleaveheart?"

She nodded to the Count. "That is my belief."

He nodded solemnly, drained his cup, and stood. "That is something, then, and easily enough for now. I will leave you. Servants will come to prepare for your baths and address other needs you have. This evening, in celebration of your victory, my father has prepared a formal banquet."

Gena's breath caught in her throat. "My lord, traveling on horseback does not permit me to bring much in the way of appropriate clothing with me."

"Of course not, no, it would not." He smiled easily,

and Gena knew her protest had been anticipated long before she could voice it. "As best I could, from my memory, I found a woman here who closely resembles you. My family's seamstresses have prepared a gown or two that can be fitted to you in an instant. They will come after you have rested and made your ablutions."

Fists planted on his hips, he looked over at Durriken. "As for you, my friend, I think you are nearly the size of my late brother. I will have someone select suitable items from his wardrobe, provided you do not mind wearing a dead man's clothing?"

"As long as the boots do not pinch and his shade is not as lively as Neal's, I would not refuse your generous offer." Durriken bowed toward his host.

"Ah, another idea occurs to me." Berengar smiled, then worked a silver and star sapphire ring off the smallest finger of his right hand. "The business with Waldo and your flashdrakes has been gnawing at the back of my brain. I would not doubt the story has been widely distributed, even this quickly, for Waldo is a notorious gossip when wounded. My brother Nilus held my title before his death, as well as many others. His love was a small holding that encompassed Lake Orvir. For your time here I will make you Lord Orvir, so no tongues will wag over your flashdrakes or your escorting Lady Genevera."

Rik smiled as Berengar presented him the ring. The small man fitted it on the middle finger of his left hand, then ran the cuff of his right sleeve over the star sapphire set in it. "I am in your debt."

"No, I am in yours." Berengar nodded curtly to Durriken. "If this venture is successful, perhaps I will make the appointment permanent. If you will excuse me." He bowed again, then retreated from the room.

Durriken closed the door behind the count, then turned to Gena. "I'm with you in this little task, though I'm not looking forward to bearding a ghost."

"Neal was clean shaven." Gena flicked her eyes up, then she smiled. "You could be ennobled by this."

Irritation and distaste flashed through Rik's brown eyes, then he shrugged. "From a slave to slavemaster? I don't think I will weather the transition well. Perhaps tonight will tell. At least tonight no one will be offended that one of the Fair Race is escorted by a base barrow bandit."

Gena rose from her chair and stroked her right hand softly against Rik's cheek. "There are nobles of the blood, then nobles of the heart. You are the latter, and it is my honor to appear anywhere on your arm."

The seamstresses Count Berengar had engaged to alter clothing to fit Gena worked quickly and well, clucking and cooing as they tucked the pale-blue satin gown at the waist, ribs, and bosom. Cut with a low neckline and a ribbon-laced front to draw it tight, the gown fit her like a second skin through the bodice. She noticed that the gown, aside from mildly restricting her ability to breathe, actually made her breasts seem somewhat larger, which was no mean feat, as Elven women tended away from the endowment of their human counterparts.

"That will assuredly please Rik," she muttered to herself. She smoothed the cool fabric down to the top of her hips with her hands, then let them brush against the satin as the full skirts flared out and down to the floor. She took a step forward, then turned quickly, pivoting around to nod at the seamstresses as the dress molded itself to her long legs. "It is magnificent. I just require one service more of you."

The older, dumpling-cheeked woman smiled nervously. "Yes, m'lady?"

"If you would be so kind, let the sleeves out?" Gena tightened her muscles, and the fabric pulled taut over her arms. "I fear my peregrinations have fostered more in the way of hard than soft."

"The model for your gown, M'Lady Martina Fisher—a distant cousin of the count's you see—rises at noon and bathes in mare's milk!" The seamstress's apprentice—Gena thought them enough alike to believe them mother and daughter—spoke of this Martina with a hushed reverence.

The seamstress did not share her daughter's view of the woman. "Softness comes from never having done a lick of work in her life. Better she spent her time milking mares than sitting in the milk of mares." She smiled up at Gena.

"I will have this gown ready before m'lady has finished her bath."

Once Gena had slipped out of the gown, the seamstress left her daughter, Phaelis, to draw a bath for her. That process ended up with Phaelis giving orders to other servants to roll a cask into the suite, then haul buckets of water in to fill it. The addition of hot water made the bath tepid, but after two weeks on the road it felt quite welcome. Had the water been any hotter, Gena knew, she might have slipped off to sleep.

Phaelis apparently saw it as her sacred duty to make sure that did not happen. At first she looked wounded when Gena told her that she was fully capable of washing herself, but she relented and allowed Phaelis to wash her back and hair. In return the young woman regaled Gena with stories about Lady Martina and the various swains she set off against each other, most recently Lord Waldo and Captain Floris.

"Which do you think she will ensnare?"

"Neither, m'lady, though the two of them won't know that for a long time. She's cousin to them all, but like tends to marry like in Aurdon, as long as they're not too close-blooded." Phaelis sighed as she lathered a washing cloth and applied it to Gena's shoulders. "I think she has herself set on winning the count's heart, though he barely knows she's alive."

Gena could understand how any woman would find Count Berengar desirable. Tall and handsome, even with the scar on his face, he had grace and intelligence in abundance. A ferocious warrior, he commanded the respect of other men, and that immediately set him apart from the rest of the male population. Combined with his title and fortune, it made him an attractive candidate for husband or lover, and the competition among women to win him made him yet that much more alluring.

She had seen it when they met five years before. They had been introduced at a reception, and Gena had immediately sensed the hostility of the other women when the count had asked her to join him in a dance. While she had found him handsome and witty, she had taken no steps to advance their relationship. A liaison between an Elven woman and a Human noble was almost expected, both by Humans and the Elven oracles who had warned her of the dangers of the world of Men. Because so many predicted their relationship deepening, Gena rejected the possibility out of hand, and Count Berengar had pressed no suit upon her.

It occurred to her, as Phaelis doused her with a bucket of water to rinse her hair, that her steadfast determination to avoid falling into the most common of traps had left her vulnerable to Durriken's charms. He had taken her off guard by giving her the jewelry—which she knew had to have been priceless—then asking for nothing in return. She had pursued him to learn where he had obtained the pieces, and his offer to help trace them back seemed natural given his avocation.

The *sylvanestii* who had tried to educate her about the outside world had been correct in pointing out that many would be attracted to her if for no other reason than her *difference* and exotic nature. Gena had discovered it was quite easy to tell, almost at the instant of meeting, whether or not she would ever allow a man into her bed. Few were the men who made the list of potential lovers, and fewer still were those she actually bedded. Berengar had made the former list, but not the latter.

Durriken had made yet another list altogether. She came to realize, as they traveled together, that he refrained from intruding upon her because he wanted to preserve the shell within which he lurked. Though she did not learn the details until later, she knew his initial distance had been born during the time he had spent as a mine slave in Ysk, a time in which even his own body had not belonged to him. That he was attracted to her cried out from every little kindness he performed for her and the harsh way in which he dealt with those who did not treat her with proper deference.

After two months as traveling companions, Gena found herself wanting to be *his* lover. They became lovers and had grown even closer through that experience. Rik opened up to her, sharing some of his life's experiences. She knew he kept many of the darker moments locked up inside himself, and even the bittersweet things he presented to her he softened with a laugh or an ironic comment. Despite his reluctance to let her in all the way, she knew she loved him, and that realization opened a whole other debate that she consciously ignored.

The seamstress returned with the gown just after Phaelis had toweled Gena dry and had begun to comb out her hair. After donning the various petticoats and underskirts that would help the gown retain its shape, Gena slipped into the gown itself and found the alterations perfect. She commented on the same to the delight of the seamstress.

Another servant, a woman of Phaelis's age yet more graceful and forceful of bearing, arrived and ushered the other two women out of the room. She brought with her a wooden case, which, when opened on a small table to the south side of the bedroom, was revealed to have a mirror on the underside of the lid and a wide range of cosmetics in the triple tier of trays contained below.

"Upon hearing of the foresight her son displayed in arranging for your gown, Duchess Beatrix thought you might require some additional aid in supplying yourself with cosmetics for this evening's festival. I am Noreen and have been serving the duchess for six years now." Slender and small, with long brown hair and quick brown eyes, the woman looked at Gena, then at the box, and back again. "Normally I do for her with my paints what nature itself has done for you. Pity we are still in the winter season, for the colors are too cold and severe for one as beautiful as you."

Noreen lifted the three trays out of the box and from the bottom drew a sheet. She draped it over Gena and the gown, then gently tucked it in, leaving her long neck and the upper half of her bosom exposed. Noreen selected a powder puff from the case, dusted it with white powder, then gently applied it to Gena's bare flesh. Once Noreen had moved it from the vicinity of her eyes, Gena looked at her reflection in the mirror and shivered as the golden color of her skin succumbed to the white powder.

"M'lady has lovely large eyes." Noreen carefully painted a black line around them, letting the curved lines from the lower lids arc up toward Gena's temples. She then applied a light blue powder to the lower half of Gena's cheekbones and brushed it back up to blend with her hairline. More blue dusted the hollow of her throat and her eyelids, then Noreen rouged her lips.

As the woman produced a brush from the bottom of the case and began to work on her hair, Gena smiled at her own reflection in the mirror. The cosmetics had sharpened her features, accentuating a natural difference between Men and Elves, and enough of her skin tone made it through the white to prevent her being taken for a walking corpse. She secretly wondered if the women of Aurdon chose to make themselves look Elven out of some hidden desire to be more than they were, or if changing styles had simply come around to the point where vulpine decoration just happened to be appropriate when she came to visit.

Noreen pulled Gena's hair back into a thick braid, then folded that up onto itself and secured it with two silver needles. "There you are, m'lady. I do not think my ministrations have dulled your beauty."

Gena smiled. "They have enhanced it."

"You are most kind." Noreen replaced her brush and the trays and shut the case. She carefully pulled the sheet free, then looked up behind Gena. "Evening, m'lord."

Gena turned, half expecting to see Count Berengar, and saw Durriken entering the room on the other side of the bed. He wore a long gray woolen tunic, edged with silver, that came down to his knees. Beneath that he wore a navy-blue hose and dark-grey slippers that had elaborately curled toes and a small bell set at each heel. On his head perched a blue beret with a silver feather in it that matched the silver belt tied around his waist.

She started to smile, then covered her mouth with her hand to stifle a laugh as Durriken glared at her. He looked miserable, and she knew he would have jumped at the suggestion of riding away from Aurdon or at least slipping out of their clothes and avoiding the festival entirely.

Noreen nodded. "My lord won't mind my saying he wears those clothes better than Count Nilus ever did. Quite handsome a figure you are, sir."

Rik smiled momentarily. "You are most kind, ma'am."

Noreen curtsied. "Evening, m'lady, m'lord."

When the door closed behind her, Rik scowled heavily. "Bells on the shoes?"

"I believe they are meant to remind people of the happy time when the winter will be no more." Gena shook her head. The bells on the shoes had to be especially galling to Rik, because his profession so relied on stealth for its successful practice. Given Waldo's animosity toward him, Rik had to be feeling persecuted by circumstance.

His scowl dissolved into a feral expression of forbidden delight. "If Waldo had these bells put on my shoes on purpose, what he owns, I will own."

"I do not think that is a very good idea, my Lord Orvir."

His head came up at the use of the title. "True, I would have to do something more befitting my station. Of course, that could be almost anything." He pulled off his ring and crossed the room to where she stood. "I don't know if Berengar knows about this, but it is an interesting trick. This is a genuine slapdeath ring."

"What is that?"

"Watch." Holding the ring between the thumb and forefinger of his right hand, he twisted the thin cylinder of scrollwork around the base of the sapphire to the left. Smiling, he flicked the gem up, exposing a small compartment in the ring. "Barely large enough to hold a pinch of gold dust, yes?"

Gena nodded. "Hardly useful for a hiding place, as a highway man would likely take the ring as well as a purse."

"Agreed. Now watch." He flipped the gem back into place and turned the cylinder back to the right. He continued twisting it after it had locked the gemstone down, and stopped when he apparently met resistance. "There."

"I don't see anything."

Rik winked. "You're not supposed to see anything—slapdeath." He rotated the ring so she could see the section that would lie hidden toward the palm of his hand. Extending upward at a shallow angle toward his thumb was the tip of a hollow needle barely an eighth of an inch long.

"That ring, if it held poison . . ."

"A pat on the back, a gentle caress, a slap across the

face, and someone dies." Rik retracted the needle with a twist on the scrollwork. "It looks as if Nilus had a reason to expect trouble. As this is a weapon well suited for use on one's familiars, he expected that trouble from someone close to him."

Gena nodded as she fastened a silver-leaf pendant around her neck. "I wonder if Berengar knows the secret of his brother's ring."

"And I wonder if Nilus had other secrets." Rik smiled wryly. "I think that is something I may try to find out."

"But not tonight."

"No?"

"No." Gena shook her head as she slipped her hand into the hollow of Rik's left elbow. "Tonight they are having a celebration in our honor. We will go and act as befits our station. And after that, provided you are willing to remove that ring, I will see if Lord Orvir is a better lover than a certain thief whose company I greatly enjoy."

Chapter 6

The Reason for Leaving

Late Summer
Reign of the Red Tiger Year 1
Five Centuries Ago
My Thirty-fifth Year

Though she stepped light as a cat bent on mischief, the faint crackle of straw being crushed underfoot betrayed Yelena's approach. Though I do not often wake quickly, I did so this time, with the faint tendrils of unease that had wracked my slumber evaporating slowly. Her steps lacked the furtive urgency of someone on a mission of mayhem, so I let my fists unknot beneath the woolen blanket, and I opened my eyes.

A warm smile brightened her heart-shaped face, and her black hair all but glowed from careful brushing. "I trust, my Lord, you slept well?"

"I have greatly enjoyed the hospitality of the Riveravens here, Lady Yelena."

"So I assumed when you slept away the day without snoring."

"I did?" I rubbed a hand over my face. I recalled having trouble getting to sleep because of all the dogs barking outside, but once they stopped, the weariness of the journey hammered me into unconsciousness.

I returned Yelena's smile politely, so as not to offend her, and to make amends for any offense I might have given the night before. She had been appointed by Festus to take me back to the River Raven longhouse and provide me suitable accommodations for the night, while Aarundel was made the Fishers' guest. Though fifteen years my junior by the most generous tally of her age, she had seemed willing to share the pallet to which I had been directed. My refusal, which I based on my being road weary, battle sore, and a notorious snorer, had been accepted even though I was thinking she had seen it as a lie.

"You did indeed, my lord Neal." She half turned back toward the center of the longhouse and, with a sharp, snapped twist of her hand, started two servants wrestling a heavy oaken cask over toward where I lay. "Your Steel Pack arrived two hours ago and is encamped down by the river. The Elf has seen to their care and ordered no one to disturb you. I only disobeyed because the sun is but an hour from slumber, and the festival that you ordered will then begin."

I worked my left arm around, bringing my elbow to my breastbone, and heard my shoulder pop. Yelena's eyebrows betrayed her surprise at the sound, but I had become well used to hearing it. The new twinge in my ribs reminded me of the Haladin ambush, but the pain was not as sharp as I would have expected. Though I would have preferred to have been awakened when the Steel Pack made Aurium, I was thinking that Aarundel had not been wrong in letting me sleep. Though I did not heal as swiftly as I had in my youth, I still did heal, and the sleep had helped a great deal.

Yelena smiled, her brown eyes lit with a devilish fire. "I thought my lord would wish to bathe before the festival. The Elf had things sent around from your personal train, in order that you be suitably attired for this evening." As the servants hauled buckets of steaming water from a cauldron near the central fire, Yelena drew the curtains that isolated the small area in which we stood from the rest of the building.

The longhouse itself looked to be four times as long as

it was wide, and two sets of pillars running the length of it split the width into thirds. On either side, up against the exterior wall, rough planking framed small stalls barely over nine yards square. The planking rose to six feet or so, which cut off most sight and filtered some sounds from one stall to the next, but hardly made an attempt at privacy. From the grunts and giggles, gawfaws and moans I could hear around me, the Riveraven Clan did not feel the lack, and to be honest, after months in the field, *I* felt closed in.

Yelena's closeness accentuated that feeling. In the dark of the night, when she had been my hostess, her invitation to enjoy the hospitality of the Ravens had been at her uncle Festus's behest. He had seen value in having me bed a woman of his clan and like as not thought it might win him some advantage or concession or a chance to renegotiate his son's position in the bargain struck the night before. Yelena had taken the rejection easily, likely pleased that her uncle's strategy had failed.

Her presence here now bespoke her coming on her own behalf, and it did not greatly surprise me. She did not seem the sort of woman who would pursue me to prove herself desirable—the intelligence in her eyes had me thinking she knew her beauty made her a prize. Even had her vanity been pinked by my refusal to let her share the straw-strewn pallet and thin woolen blanket, she would not have returned to salve her wound. Doing that would have conceded a battle to me, and in Yelena I sensed no concession and damned little compromise.

If she had come for herself, she had come to get what I represented. It wasn't the pleasure of bedding, I felt fair certain, because aside from one rather bawdy ballad about me and the nuns in the convent in Esquihir, I had no reputation for being a bold or romantic lover. While not above being flattered by a woman's appreciation for my meagre abilities at loveplay, I'm not a ram that wants to mount every available ewe in hopes she will sing my praises afterward.

To Yelena I represented what visitors to my father's court in the Roclaws had been for me: a window onto the rest of the world. I was what existed, what lived and breathed outside Aurium. I had defied the city's clan leaders, bearding them in their own den, and if I could do that, then I could certainly take her with me when I left. I did not think she saw me as a lover with whom she would remain for all time, but just someone with whom she could stay until she won her release from the city of her birth.

All the while I thought this out, Yelena busied herself with supervising the servants filling the wooden tub. She diligently tested the water for warmth and directed the servants to bring water in sufficient quantities of specific temperatures in accord with some arcane formula that at last produced a satisfactory smile on her face. Accepting a small unguent jar and a thick towel from the last servant, she drew the curtain completely shut.

Ignoring the mild laughter from the people in the center of the longhouse, she smiled and waved me toward the bath. Her husky whisper conveyed a multitude of messages. "Your bath awaits, my lord. As none of our servants would be satisfactory to you, I offer myself as your attendant."

Raising myself up on my elbows, I narrowed my eyes. "Do you know what you are offering, lass?"

She broadened her smile and nodded.

"And do you know why?" My question caught her unawares for a moment. Before she could reply, I pressed further. "Do you want to know why I'll be refusing you?"

Yelena hesitated, then her smile slackened. "It should have been obvious to me."

I shook my head and threw back the blanket. "There's no reason you could have known, so don't be thinking what you're thinking now." I stood, naked, with my joints popping and cracking like Dreel gnawbones. I saw her eyes widen, and looking down, I knew the purple bruise on the left side of my chest had been what caught her initial attention. As her focus opened up and she took a good look at me, one hand rose to cover her mouth.

"My lord, you . . . you . . ."

Aside from being a bit more furry than most flatlanders, as well as taller and more thickly muscled, the difference between me and the other males she'd likely seen in a similar state of nudity came in terms of my scars. Witch women and shamans, hedge-wizards and physickers, are all well able to close cuts and smooth gashes so as to leave no trace of a scar. Unlike me, the only thing most men took away from a fight was a tall tale.

I smiled to ease her distress and crossed to the tub. I sank myself into it, having to scrunch down a bit and bring my knees up out of the water, but it covered me to midchest and felt warm and inviting. "My compliments, Lady Yelena." I took a small cake of soap from a shelf near my toes and began to work it over my left arm.

"How is it, my lord, that the Dun Wolf is so worried and marked?"

I shrugged. "Well, now, this slice here, on my shoulder, I got from Tashayul when he meant to be killing me twenty years ago. And this one, the cross there above my left knee, that was a Haladin arrow I won near seven years past in the first battle I fought under the Red Tiger's banner." Lifting my left arm and leaning to the right, I exposed my hip. "See that tear there? That was from the Dreel."

"You have so many scars, my Lord, yet there are ways . . ."

"I've collected a tale with each one, my Lady, and in another thirty years I'll be delivering an accounting to one of the Consilliarii." I smiled. " 'Tis not much as ambition goes, but it is a goal worth striving for."

She kept the horror in her eyes out of her whispered question. "And these scars—they have left you . . . unable . . . which is why you refuse me?"

"No, lass, I am *able,* which is why I must refuse you." I rinsed my left hand, then gently cupped her jaw in it. The truth, I was thinking, would only pique her interest, not dispel it. That was good, because I'd never been inclined to share the truth with anyone. No one would have believed it of me, and I knew all the protests concerning its veracity would only cause folks to doubt it all the more. So, for her, a bit of a lie.

"How much of the *Eldsaga* do you know, lass?"

"I know some of the songs. 'The Rape of Lucenzia' and 'The Razing of Malchalach' are the most sung here. The songs are old and well remembered, which is why you are here and the Elf went with the Fishers." Irritation sent a tremor through her, and fear another after it. "Why do you ask, my lord?"

I soaped my face, then rinsed it off in a great spray of water before answering. "The songs you cite mark Elven crusades that destroyed cities and provinces, changing the very map of Skirren. The slaughter will never be forgotten, but the reason the Elves launched their crusade already has been." I leaned back and let her soap my knees. "You see, the reason the Elves left Cygestolia was because the people of the Roclaws had been bound together by a leader who started nibbling away at Barkol. His dreams went far beyond Barkol, of course, but to the *sylvanii* his dreams were night terrors."

Had Aarundel been there to hear me recount history, he might have objected to some characterizations, but he could have pronounced the rede of it true. "The Elven Legions rode into the Roclaws and scattered the tribes. I'm thinking they likely wanted us all dead, but the mountains have many valleys and dales, and territories that the Dwarvenfolk claim as their own. While they granted us no succor, nor did they let the Elves hunt in their domains, so the people of the Roclaws survived.

"But now, you see, that in the days when the tribes had been together, many a love affair had blossomed. When we fled, we fled as tribes, not knowing if lovers lived or died. So among our people there arose a custom of waiting a year and a month, a week and a day and an hour before considering ourselves well and truly separated from a lover.

"Over the years many have been the embellishments to this tradition—a married couple who remove themselves from each other's company for that time are divorced and free, and mourning for a lost love lasts that long."

"And you are in mourning?"

The sympathy in her voice made me regret the lie. "I am, fair Yelena. I had a message from my brother, and in it he told me the woman I loved had died. Was the falsethaw fever and not caught in time." I fell silent for as long as I thought right, then managed a weak smile. "The sting of it is mostly gone, but you remind me of her enough that . . ."

Yelena sat back on her heels. "Forgive me, my lord, if I had known . . ."

I shook my head. "You make me mindful of the good things, lass. Were I younger, and this summer next winter, I'd not be riding alone from Aurium."

That pleased her, and her reaction banished the kernel of regret taking root in my heart. "My lord, is one in mourning allowed to enjoy himself at a festival? Is he allowed to dance?"

I winked at her and smiled. "Oddly enough, the custom is he can only dance with a bath attendant."

"Ah, then it is well you keep to your customs, my Lord Neal, well indeed."

Yelena abandoned me when I emerged from the bath and dried myself off. I found the clothing that Aarundel had sent for me and recognized none of it, which meant he had bought it new in the Aurium bazaar. Aarundel prefers to avoid places with too many humans he does not know—the exception being his placement in the midst of an enemy formation. At the same time he has a sharp sense of what is appropriate in conduct and dress, and this he impresses upon me whenever the chance to do so comes about. The fact that we had acted the bloody-handed mercenaries the night before meant we would have to be equally gracious at the festival, and I assumed the red tunic he had supplied for me would help do that.

His willingness to brave the bazaar mirrored my own willingness to keep Yelena at arm's length. As I mentioned before, I am not a ram looking to mount a herd, but neither am I celibate or like-gender attracted. While I enjoy the company of women, I am also aware of Aarundel's isolation from *sylvanestii,* for they are more rare outside Cygestolia than mountain women are outside the Roclaws. Making matters more complicated is the Elven prohibition against coupling with women *or* Reithressa.

I dressed quickly despite the ache in my ribs. Though I had no intention of going armed to the festival, I did home Wasp and Cleaveheart in their respective scabbards and looped my weapons'-belt over my shoulder. Emerging from my stall, I found Lady Yelena dressed in a gown that flattered her slender figure and accentuated her bosom. She slipped her left hand through the crook of my right arm without saying a word.

I could tell from her smile that while she might respect the tale I had told her earlier, she would make my choice to honor tradition deliciously difficult. "My Lady, you are quite beautiful this evening, eclipsing your earlier beauty, I'm thinking." I let my voice carry enough to spawn giggles from others in the longhouse, and Yelena accepted the compliment with a gentle bow of her head.

The sun had not set by the time we emerged from the longhouse, so I got a chance to orient myself concerning the town's internal geography. The *legislatorium* stood on a hill above a green square with a statue raised in the center of it. East and west of that square stood two longhouses—one for the Fishers and the other for the Riveravens. Spreading back from them in a rough wedge were other, smaller houses and buildings of related clans and servants. To the south, in the direction of the rivers, other homes, shops, and warehouses bridged the gap between the clan sectors and the wharves. North of the *legislatorium* the buildings appeared more ramshackle and less permanent, and I had the feeling that somewhere in that transient sector was where I would find my company.

The square itself had been transformed from a muddy flat to something far more in keeping with a celebration. Brightly colored tents, well patched and road stained, had been set up in a haphazard pattern to form a rough perimeter around the square. I was thinking some traveling show had entered the town at a lucky moment, but given the Haladin activity in the area, it seemed likely they had been north of the *legislatorium*, waiting for a good time to travel.

Interior of the tents I saw carts and stalls of the sort I imagined would be found in the bazaar. Their hasty transplanting narrowed the area near the statue, but still left enough room for a good crowd. Musicians had set up at the base of the statue and looked to be a mix of the road minstrels and folks belonging to Aurium itself. In tuning their instruments they sounded like a herd of cats fighting on a bed made of bellowing walruses, but I was thinking the sound would resolve itself into something dance-spawning quite quickly.

I'd gotten a step and a half from the longhouse when the Dreel slid his shaggy red-gray body from a hollow beneath the building. He crawled up out of a hole around which he had placed fresh-killed dogs' skulls like merlons and paced beside me. Yelena started when she caught sight of him past my left shoulder, but forced a yawn. I casually handed him my swordbelt. "If I need this, you will fetch it to me. Meanwhile, try not to kill anything." Shijef flashed his fangs at me, so I added, "Be trying real hard not to kill anything."

Yelena shivered. "You have scars from a Dreel bite, yet you keep one with you as a pet?"

"Oh, the scars are from *that* Dreel's bite." I shrugged. "Besides, he's not a pet, he is a slave."

"Why would you want a Dreel as a slave?"

"I'm thinking you have a point—they're not good for much." I forced the image of the bouncing head from my mind. "I did not have much choice. His Dreelband was raiding a village one winter. We had a contest, he and I, and he lost, so he became my slave."

"Better that than the other way around."

I smiled. "I'm thinking I'd not have been a slave. Dinner, more likely."

Yelena took the lead as we entered the square and paraded me around like a groom leading a prize horse. I played my part, taking a bit of joy from the green-eyed glances shot in my direction by local men who doubtless had pondered ways to woo her. I wished the men no ill, but I was thinking one night of discomfort might spur them on to act. Part of me pitied any man who thought Yelena would become his chattel, but there had to be someone in Aurium who could be her match in spirit and mind.

As dusk passed into night, torches were lit and the orchestra had appointed a leader. Both Festus and Childeric made brief speeches about the union of their families. A priest, Jistani by the cut of his hair, said the words that needed saying; then the musicians struck up a tune, and the wedded couple engaged in a stately dance. I'd seen it performed more formally otherwhens, but seldom with more sincerity. It seemed as if both Rufus and Ismere had determined to defy their families by clinging together. If their offspring were as tough-minded, I was thinking, the union might well last a long time.

Yelena pressed me to dance when the music shifted to something more lively. Quick and light as she was, she managed to keep her tiny feet from beneath mine during the Centisian turn. The players then struck up a Kaudian reel, which I forced her through and showed her that speed in battle can translate elsewise into more pacifistic pursuits.

Our scores tied at a dance even, we agreed to let the third dance—a complicated Centisian walking step with twirls and bows and hop-skips—decide who was better. I kept up close to her level of performance until the spin right before the hop-skip then bow at the end of the dance. At that point the man next to me accidently smacked me in the chest with his hand, prompting my bruised ribs to report on their state of health.

I worked my way through the last two sets of the dance, then withdrew from the crowd as a young man whisked Yelena away into the swirl of an old quickstep. Keeping a smile on my face, and my left arm clamped down to protect my ribs, I headed to the outer edge of the crowd and started looking for Aarundel. Under normal circumstances finding him in a crowd was easy—both of us were tall enough to be visible over most other people.

I wandered halfway around the circle, then spotted him up at the top of the steps of the *legislatorium.* I joined him, plucking at the shoulder of my tunic as I did so. "A *red* tunic? I'm the Dun Wolf, not the Red Tiger, my friend."

"Red is heroic." The Elf shook his head. "Dun just looks dirty and is not festive at all."

"Your sartorial guidance is appreciated." I looked back down on the varicolored throng pulsing and weaving in time with the music. "Hard to believe Aurium almost tore itself apart last evening."

"Humans are quick to anger, yet quicker to distraction." Aarundel's dark eyes watched the crowd, then flicked toward me. "Our men have been told to be on their best behavior this evening. They were warned about everything from diseases to slapdeath rings. . . ."

I frowned. "I'm not thinking they have to worry about ringbites here. Polston, perhaps, but *this* place?"

"Neal, with the Fishers and Riveravens, the tools of treachery will soon be available here, if they are not already."

"You have a point."

Aarundel bowed his head in my direction. "Drogo brought word from the Red Tiger. The Haladin forces have abandoned the siege at Polston and seem to be withdrawing to behind the Kaudian mountains. Sture is pursuing them, but he is under orders to let them flee if they do not make war on the mountain freestate."

I arched an eyebrow. "So they are running in the direction of the Reithrese homeland?"

"Or their own deserts, affirmative. Beltran has decided to winter in Polston despite Sture's urging a strike north to liberate Irtysh."

"That explains why Sture is off chasing Haladina *away* from Beltran *and* Irtysh."

"I assumed you would notice that. The Red Tiger is going to use his armies to help bring in the harvests, which should endear him to the people. It will also prevent the Reithrese from sending their tax collectors in." The Elf grinned cautiously. "While there will be battles next summer to contest control of Centisia, there is no doubt who owns it for this year."

"Did Drogo bring orders for us?" As I asked the question, I sorted the likely missions to come with a positive answer. I put being allowed to raid far into Reithrese territory at the top of my list, and far below it I placed being called down to Polston for strategy sessions. While I admire and very much like Beltran, the Red Tiger, the thought of spending more than a month in a port city like Polston made me shiver. The fact that Sture was certain to return to Polston for the winter made me shiver as if *I* had falsethaw fever.

"Beltran desires us to remain here in Aurium and reconnoiter into Ispar, even advancing as far as the plains before

Jarudin. He wants the Reithrese to believe his next thrust will be to the heart of their empire and the capital."

I nodded because that made sense. The Man-force fighting the Reithrese relied on mobility and speed to defeat the Reithrese hosts. A feint at Jarudin would make the Reithrese reinforce it, expending supplies and trapping forces in the capital. If we struck elsewhere—preferably a place where they had only Haladina for defense—we could hurt them badly.

Beltran understood the problems of controlling an empire and was using them against the Reithrese. While Sture was probably correct that Irtysh was ready to revolt and come over, it was too far from the freestate to be able to have us defend it. And Sture's patriotic feelings notwithstanding, Irtysh was less valuable than even a town like Aurium.

I knew I might be a bit harsh in my dismissal of Irtysh, for Sture's troops fought well, but Sture and I did not get along at all. He found out, after I had formed the Steel Pack and joined the Red Tiger, that Aarundel and I had seen the battle in which his father, Duke Harsian, had fallen. He somehow decided that it was my fault that his father had died and his nation lay in thrall to the Reithrese.

Aside from the fact that the Roclawzi and Irtyshites had never been allies, with the Reithrese on the doorstep to the Roclaws, there was no way I could have convinced any Roclawzi to join me in fighting in Irtysh, even *if* I felt that was a good idea. The fact that I didn't think Irtysh was important enough to be liberated, and had no difficulty in voicing this opinion in front of Sture, meant that Takrakor and I would be good friends before Sture and I ever exchanged a civil word.

Down below I caught a flash of the blue gown Yelena was wearing. "So we will have to spend the winter here?" I frowned, trying to remember exactly what I had said to her. "I'm thinking that won't be a good thing."

Aarundel's face brightened as he picked up on the distress in my voice. "She is quite attractive, Neal. You could suffer worse than to have her warm your winter nights."

"Aye, my friend, but there are complications. Not being as glib as you, my lies do not allow me much room to run."

The Elf laughed. "Provide her a quote from the Codex Mercenarius that will remedy the situation."

"For a book you invented last night, I'm thinking we're working it hard." I shook my head. "I tried to match your wit by inventing a Roclawzi tradition that had me in mourning for a lost love. While celibate now, I could have taken her in the winter, I said."

"Arrange for your brother to send you a letter saying the lover who had been presumed lost has been found again."

"Ah, but I told Yelena my brother had sent a note saying the woman had died of fever."

"You terminated her? What a cruel thing to do." He gave me a look of Elven disdain, but overplayed it to the point of absurdity, then began to laugh.

I gave Aarundel a hard stare. "It's all well and good for you to laugh, my friend, but you've not got a woman setting her cap for you. While she is comely and smart, she is not the one for me."

"Not 'the one'?" Aarundel shook his head. "You listen to the bards who sing too much of romance, Neal. The idea of a True Love is not realistic."

"Emotions and reality combining—now there, I'm thinking, is an interesting idea." I folded my arms slowly. "So how is it that you can have your Marta, and I'm being denied *my* True Love?"

I could see he wanted to dismiss my riposte as something I couldn't possibly understand, but he conquered his reflex and opened his hands. "What we have is *vitamor*—it goes beyond any Man-thought of True Love. Moreover, Marta and I have known each other for over a century by your reckoning. We have seen each other in triumph and defeat, adulation and dejection. Even if examined in human terms, our courtship would have lasted a decade—a time in which most humans could have consummated and dissolved a half-dozen marriages, each with progeny as well."

I could have protested his example, but I saw no reason for punishing his attempt at explaining things to me. "Just so you know, my friend, I do not begrudge you your *vitamor*. I'm just hoping someday I will be as lucky as you.

Maybe after the Red Tiger wins his little war, I'll be free to find *my* Marta, and the Elven Councils will let you marry yours."

Aarundel's eyes focused distantly. I had seen that expression before, and I put it down to times when he was thinking on her and she on him likewise. Somehow they managed this momentary communion no matter the distance between them, and Aarundel always seemed the better in spirits and humor for the time spent enraptured.

A smile spread across his face. "When you find her, Neal, you will know it instantly. Your heart will beat faster, your stomach will clench. It is as absorbing as battle-madness, but in reverse, because it drives you toward *creation,* not destruction."

I shared his smile. "I envy you, Aarundel, and Marta as well. If ever the council lets you wed, I'd be proud to stand beside you."

"I shall demand it, Neal." We clasped hands and shook firmly, cementing more tightly a friendship unthinkable by anyone who had heard the *Eldsaga* sung.

A scream from down below killed the music. Releasing Aarundel's hand, I turned to face the square, but Shijef eclipsed my view of it. He thrust my swordbelt against my chest and let his talons tickle the bruise beneath my tunic. "This blade you will need."

The fact that he had presented me the sword in time with the scream came as no testament to his speed. The Dreel had doubtlessly smelled the trouble brewing below, but felt no reason to warn me. After all, I had not asked for warning, just the return of Cleaveheart when I would need it. In the little game we played, he had won a round.

Stepping aside, I took in the now-silent square and felt glacier-melt run through my insides. A dark wedge of armored riders moved slowly and deliberately to drive itself into the circle of people below. Their huge warhorses shouldered men and women aside as if they were stalks of grain in a wheat field. I saw Festus and Childeric impose themselves directly in the line of march, but the riders pressed on through them and their protests before executing a sharp turn toward the north.

Aarundel and I remained in place as they came toward

the *legislatorium*. Though I had never before seen the style of armor they wore, I knew from the riders' size and the strength of their mounts that they all were Elves. That fact had not been lost on Aarundel, which explained why his face tightened. It also explained why silence ruled the night, with the exception of some gentle sobbing.

I looped my swordbelt over my left shoulder, leaving Cleaveheart's hilt hanging breast-high from beneath my left arm. I tried to affect an air of bored indifference, but it was not easy. As much as I wanted to deny them the victory, the Elven riders were impressive. Memories of *Eldsaga* nightmares skittered icily up and down my spine.

The armor they wore, while clearly practical, had been designed for ceremony. It had been styled with hooks and barbs and horns that contributed to their fierce aspect. The decorations looked odd for the handful of heartbeats it took for me to identify the problem; then my sense of unease doubled. Instead of being modeled on an animal's antlers—the way most human warriors would want it—the armor's twists and curves had been taken from wind-warped tree limbs and gnarled roots capable of crushing stone through inexorable and inexhaustible pressure.

The Elves, their armor proclaimed, had the luxury of time with which to destroy their enemies. They needed not adopt the symbols of predators nor usurp the weapons animals shed to make themselves more powerful. Just as they had moved with careful and deliberate speed through the crowd below, so, too, could they leisurely slaughter their foes. The *Eldsaga* had made that very clear, and these Elves had no intention of letting anyone who saw them forget it.

The lead rider stopped at the base of the stairs, his eyes level with ours. Shijef started to creep forward, but I grabbed the scruff of his neck and restrained him. He grumbled and flashed fangs at me, but remained in place. He subvocalized something he knew irritated Blackstar, then followed it with a satisfied growl when the lead horse's nostril's flared.

The lead rider, his identity hidden by the full helm he wore, looked over at Aarundel through the cross-slit in his visor. "*Aarundel Imperator, salus!*"

Aarundel's head came up, his face implacable. "Speak

in the common tongue. Neal Custos Sylvanii knows some of our language, but he is not fluent."

"I am not come to converse with him, Imperator."

"But I will inform him of all you say, so I direct you to obviate the necessity of translation."

"As you will it, Imperator. I am to convey the felicitations of the Consilliarii. Your nuptial petition has been considered and approved. We are the Lansorii Honorari sent to conduct you to Cygestolia for the ceremony. We are to leave immediately."

As much as I knew that news had to have excited Aarundel, I marveled at his ability to keep his emotions hidden. "Neal and I, and the Dreel, will be ready to ride with you in the morning."

The lead horse shook its head as the rider's grip on the reins slackened momentarily. "We are to conduct you alone, Imperator. With all due respect to the Custos Sylvanii, his presence was not mentioned. And we were ordered to leave immediately."

Aarundel's slight shoulder shift was something I had seen many times and marked his absolute determination not to retreat from his position. "I am an Imperator; I travel when *I* will it. As the groom I have the right to bring to my wedding those companions with whom I enjoy fraternity. Forget any attempt at imposing your will on me, Lansor. Those who gave you this mission and promised rewards if I returned alone and quickly merely meant to make the impossible seem possible and defeat seem palatable."

His dark eyes narrowed as his chin came up. "Though I need not explain myself to you, Lansor, I have reason for wishing to delay my departure. You doubtless refused to mark the celebration through which you rode, but it is in honor of nuptials uniting the two largest clans in Aurium. I was invited to attend, and attend I shall."

Aarundel hesitated for a moment, then let a grin slowly twist his mouth up at the corners. I had no idea what he had in mind, but I cringed inside for the honor guard sent to fetch him home nonetheless. "As your arrival has disrupted this ceremony, I will require a service of you. I think it is fitting that we dance for the couple the way others will dance at my wedding."

The lead rider stiffened with a clatter-clang of epaulets on his armor. "Imperator, there are some things that should not be . . . made vulgar."

"The dance will be dishonored only if you do not perform honorably, Lansor." Aarundel waved the guards away. "Hobble your horses and remove your armor. You are guests and shall conduct yourselves as same. Your honor, *my* honor, depends upon it."

I remained silent as they reined themselves around to the rear of the *legislatorium* to dismount and shell themselves, though I did let Shijef skulk on behind them. When the Elves had disappeared from sight, I turned toward Aarundel. "Do you actually think they will let me ride with you tomorrow?"

He nodded solemnly. "After tonight they will be so anxious to be well rid of Aurium, they would let Takrakor ride with us. The Consilliarii's reaction to your arrival in Cygestolia will be something else entirely."

"No matter, my friend." I slapped him on the back. "You can't siege a city until you have arrived at it. To attend your wedding, I'd even brave another visit to Jammaq."

"Thank you for being willing to undertake the trek in the face of hostility." We both started down toward the square. "Let us just hope the reception you get does not make you think you *have* returned to Jammaq."

Chapter 7

The Short Ride

Early Spring
A.R. 499
The Present

The celebration in honor of their victory over the Haladina struck Genevera as less of a festival than a phenomenon. From the very start, when she appeared at the top of a grandiose sweep of marble stairs and was announced to the assembly, she felt detached from everything. The music rang in her ears, as did the applause from the people below, but both failed to reach inside her. She did not quite feel on display as much as she felt she had entered a contest, but it was a contest which she had no interest in winning.

She put part of the distance down to Rik's obvious discomfort over the whole situation. Though the chamberlain announced him as Lord Orvir, Waldo's wagging tongue had clearly been at work. The shock at hearing that title used quickly faded into clucking and whispers. Gena felt a tremor run through Rik's arm, then felt him relax as he let out a chuckle. "Fools ridicule what they should fear."

Gena recognized the tone in his voice immediately and gave his forearm a squeeze with her left hand. "Pity them,

Rik, for being creatures who allow themselves to be swayed by Waldo."

He looked up at her sideways, a feral light burning in his dark eyes; then he smiled and it died. "Punishing the flock for the shepherd's sin is unnecessary, agreed."

The staircase they descended worked all the way across the rectangular room's narrow southern wall, sloping down at a shallow angle. Halfway to the ballroom's floor it cut back toward the west and down again, depositing them in the southwest corner, twenty feet below the point where they had entered the room. Beneath the stairs a pair of doors centered in the wall led back out to the courtyard where they had seen Count Berengar fighting earlier in the day. A light breeze came into the room through the doors, bringing with it enough of a chill to keep most people from standing directly in front of them.

The north wall had three tall windows that reached from the floor to the ceiling nearly thirty feet above. The east wall had nine of those windows, but only the first six, those nearest the north wall, had been glazed with clear glass. The three near the southeast corner had huge stained glass tableaux in them. Because that section of the wall joined up to another part of the manor, the windows were illuminated artificially. In triptych they told a story from Aurdon's history, stressing, as would be expected, the Fisher family's contribution to the city's defense against raiders.

Three massive gold and crystal chandeliers, each with four smaller satellites, filled the room with a golden light. It reflected in kind from the gilt walls and the black marble floor. Tables grouped along the western wall held all manner of victuals and spirits, while smaller tables opposite provided places for people to sit and converse. A small orchestra had been arranged in the northwest corner of the room. Their music cut through the Man sounds in the room, pacing dancing guests as they spun and swirled across the center of the dance floor.

Gena spotted Count Berengar amidst the dancers with a tall woman who moved gracefully and sensuously in perfect time with the music. As Berengar spun her, the woman laughed and raised her free hand to her throat. The gown she wore closely resembled Gena's in design—though it did show off more bosom—and the skirts lapped like waves around Berengar's legs as they danced.

The dance ended by the time Rik and Gena reached the bottom of the stairs. Berengar bowed to his partner, then headed straight toward the two of them. That brought a flash of anger to the dark-haired woman's blue eyes. Gena immediately decided the woman had to be Lady Martina, so she gave her a politely patronizing smile intended to convince Martina that trailing after Berengar for an introduction would not be a good idea.

Berengar bowed deeply to the both of them. "Welcome, my friends, to this modest celebration. In an hour or so we will raise a toast in your honor—thoroughly embarrassing you, I am certain." A bright smile lit his face, and Gena saw a bead of sweat roll down his cheek from his temple. "Until then we have food and wine and the best music to be had in this region of Centisia. Please, enjoy yourselves."

Gena knew that even without resorting to magick, she could have predicted how the rest of the evening would proceed. When the music began playing again, Berengar waited for Rik to take Gena out onto the dance floor, but when he did not, the count asked Rik's permission to dance with Gena. Rik consented graciously, Berengar asked, she accepted, and the two of them moved into the crowd and into the music as if they had been partnered together for years.

In retrospect Gena realized that during the dance she came as close to slipping into the party as she would all night. Berengar's strong right hand at the small of her back provided just the right clues to tell her when and how and where they would move together. They wove through the throng, whirling in time to the music, barely avoiding collisions and tempting fate by darting back against the flow. They cut past the other couples like a ship's prow through light waves, laughing and smiling at the surprised and distressed expressions on those who parted before them.

Coming all the way around the dance floor, not unexpectedly did Gena see Lady Martina speaking closely with Rik. Gena laughed immediately at the idea that a woman barely a tenth of her age would attempt to show her up by flattering Rik. Elves were by no means above the common tricks used to embarrass and chasten rivals, but their longevity meant that their methods were often more subtle and would take decades to accomplish what Men might attempt in one turn on the dance floor. Gena's Elven perspective made Martina's flirtation with Rik transparent and, thereby, pathetic.

As Berengar spun her past the other two, Gena caught the quick flash of Rik's eyes. He, too, she saw, recognized Martina's game and indulged Martina for his own ends. Gena felt a moment of compassion for the woman because she knew Rik's contempt for pretense. Rik would play with Martina as a cat might play with a mouse. He would draw her out with smiles, nods and kind comments; encouraging her to reveal more of herself. Before she knew it, he would have gotten her to betray a secret held in the strictest confidence. In that moment she would find herself embarrassed at having spoken out of turn, and mortified over being outwitted by the man she had sought to use for her own purposes.

Her analysis of the games being played between Martina and Rik closed the window into the festivities that the dance had opened for her. For the rest of the evening she remained polite, but superficial. She marked people by their reaction to her. Those who were afraid because of *Eldsaga* tales she rewarded with a cold imperiousness that fulfilled their expectations. When someone showed signs of infatuation with her because of her race, she alluded to experiences that no Man could understand, heightening her alien standing.

She dealt most cruelly with those who deluded themselves enough to believe they were fluent in the Sylvan tongue. She made her replies to them in an older form of the language, then enlisted Rik as an interpreter. Though he knew much less Sylvan than the people speaking with her, Rik's glib tongue and quick wit often served to make plays on words. Many presumptuous people wandered away utterly confused, which brought Gena a perverse sense of satisfaction, yet one about which she felt embarrassed.

Soon enough Berengar offered the toast to the two of

them, and the assembly drank to their health. After that she danced again with Berengar, then she and Rik excused themselves and returned to their chambers. By agreement they met in her room for a final glass of wine, then had a celebration of their own. And unlike the ball they had left, in this celebration she felt no detachment at all, except for maybe once, just once, when Rik's hand rested against her back where Berengar had held her, and she wondered what it would have been like to have the count in Rik's place.

Gena awoke alone the next morning, but this neither surprised nor distressed her. The one true vice she had was a desire to sleep late. After a century and a half of rising with the sun as she studied the Arts from her grandaunt Larissa, she willfully indulged herself in waking up slowly. For her a perfect day began with quiet and reflection. She thought about the dream fragments she could remember, then planned out her day. In Cygestolia she often chose to sun herself in the upper reaches of her family's home, but she had not done that very often since her grandaunt went *excedere*.

In the Fisher mansion, which could not hope to rival Woodspire in antiquity or beauty, she contented herself basking in a sunbeam.

Rik, she had learned quickly, awoke with feline alertness and a boundless energy. He required noise in the morning. When they stayed in inns, he would be down in the common room at the crack of dawn, listening to gossip, trading stories, and offering opinions on whatever the latest news had been. When they were alone on the road, he would sing songs or whistle. Whereas she luxuriated in quiet to start the day, he reveled in chaos—seeking it out or creating it as circumstances required.

Rik had roused himself very early. Kissing her on the mouth, he smiled and whispered, "Last night we saw the birds that dwell in the top of the tree. Today I want to learn about the moles and voles."

Two hours later Gena finally swam clear of the sheets and thick comforter on the bed and pulled on the clothes she had worn on the road in coming to Aurdon. The faint trace of dampness in the blouse's cuffs told her the clothes had been laundered and, from the scent of them, dried in the kitchen. Her stomach rumbled once, tentatively, then quieted as she pulled a chair over and sat down in the rectangle of sunlight coming through one of the windows.

A gentle knocking on the door brought her head up. She could see by the shift in the sunbeam that she had drifted off to sleep again, but she reawakened more clearly and sharply than earlier. Brushing her golden tresses back from her face with her right hand, she stood and turned toward the door. "Enter."

Count Berengar bowed his head as he opened the door. He glanced up at her, smiled, then briefly looked around the room. "You are awake, good. Where is Durriken?"

Gena shrugged. "Out. He prefers cities and has gone exploring."

The count frowned for a moment. "When do you expect him to return?"

"I do not know. He did not say."

"I see."

"Is this a problem?"

"I suppose not, no." Berengar toyed with his beard. "Could you leave him a note telling him that you have gone riding with me?"

"I can do that, yes." Gena heard a restrained energy in Berengar's voice, and his movements betrayed an urgency that he was trying to keep hidden. "Our sojourn, it cannot wait his return?"

"Circumstances being what they are, no. It is but a day trip. I had hoped to leave immediately."

"I will write the note." Retreating to the bed, she opened the drawer in the night table and removed a sheet of paper, a quill, and a small capped bottle of ink. She wrote out a suitable message, then folded it and wrote Rik's name on the outside. Leaving it on the table, she followed Berengar out of the room and to the stables. There she found Spirit already saddled and standing beside a huge black stallion.

They mounted up and rode out through the gates. Berengar chatted politely, pointing out items of interest. What Gena noticed most about his conduct and tour was that everything he said and did dwelt on a superficial level—a level that they had always moved beyond when speaking with each other. She suspected Berengar would share the reason for his caution, and she found herself hoping his situation had not made him an irredeemable paranoid.

Once outside Aurdon, they headed east and picked up an escort of six riders. Two rode before them, two behind, and one wide on each wing. They were not clad as guards and appeared to be people just out on the road, with the pair bringing up the rear leading a heavily laden packhorse. Gena discerned their connection with Berengar because of their abnormal alertness and the fact that they varied their speed so that the count never left their sight.

Gena smiled as she turned to him. "I think this would be an excellent time to inform me about what is going on. We are not out for a simple ride, despite neither of us being armed, are we?"

The red-maned giant shook his head. "You are most perceptive, Lady Genevera. Captain Floris sent riders ahead of his column to report suspected Haladin riders in the area. We have pinpointed a number of Haladin camping grounds. I have a company going out to inspect the nearest of these, and I thought you would find it interesting to come along."

"And you wanted to verify what you told us about the Riverens and the Haladina."

Berengar nodded easily, acquiescing to Genevera's deduction. "I asked you here to undo what Neal did long ago. This will not be an easy task, and while it would please me for you to agree based on my reportage of facts, I think presenting you some evidence that I am telling the truth is important."

"What we saw with the caravan was quite convincing." Gena smiled up at Berengar. "The Haladina clearly are ranging far from their Outlands."

"True, but that is as much a symptom of the chaos born out of the empire's collapse into the commonwealth."

Gena realized that Berengar had thought deeply about the political situation in the remains of the Red Tiger's empire. In Cygestolia the news of the empire's division by the provinces into a commonwealth had not excited much attention. That had been predicted since the forming of the empire in her grandfather's time. The fact that the empire had survived nearly four hundred years was seen as a mark of maturation by Men, though the bloody fighting that resulted as Men fought for control of their own small domains eroded some of the gains the humans had made in Sylvan minds.

Berengar pointed at a large building set on the far shore of a small lake. "That is Lake Orvir. You can tell Durriken you have seen his holding."

"It looks quite beautiful, and I imagine it can be quite pleasant when the city becomes too hot in the summer." Gena saw a small thread of smoke rising from behind the manor house. "Does someone live there? I see smoke."

"Only a caretaker—an old servant who used to work for my brother in town. He was devoted to my late brother." Berengar shook his head. "I have suggested he be recalled to Aurdon because of Haladin raiding, but he refuses to come. He says he is too old for the Haladina to cause problems for him."

"Though the caretaker may not have sense enough to realize it, Haladin raiding is a problem. I will help you curb it, whether or not the recovery of Neal's weapons is required."

Berengar smiled broadly. "That is an offer I will gladly accept. I do have sorcerers among my Guard units, but they do not have the skill I understand you displayed in defeating the Haladina."

Gena glanced down at Spirit and picked a bit of straw from the gelding's mane. "I suspect the telling about my efforts exceeds the actual event. I also have no doubt that your sorcerers are quite skilled and efficacious in their magicks. If I have an advantage over them, it is that I have spent far more time learning what I must know to work the Art."

The tall man shrugged. "I will believe you because I understand nothing of magick." He sighed rather heavily. "Stratagems and tactics I understand perfectly, politics and mercantilism I have mastered, but magicks are color to a blind man."

"Nonsense. You are intelligent. You may not have the

talent for magick, but you certainly can understand its principles." Gena saw the disbelief on his face and took it as a challenge. "Have you a coin? Gold or copper, not silver."

Berengar fished in the pouch on his belt and produced a shiny gold piece large enough that his thumb and forefinger barely encircled it. "Will this do?"

"It will indeed." As he displayed it to her, she saw a man's profile on one side and a fisher taking wing on the other. "If you were to flip the coin into the air, as you might to make a choice or decide a contest, what are the chances of its coming up heads?"

The warrior frowned for a moment. "One in two, if I am not mistaken."

"Correct. So after flipping it ten times, what result would you expect?"

"Five heads and five tails."

"Good. Start flipping the coin."

Berengar laughed lightly and did as she bid him. As the coin first arced up into the air, Gena muttered the words to a simple enchantment, one of the first taught to all students of the Art. The coin fell back to Berengar's hand, apparently unaffected or unaltered in any way. It landed with the face up.

"One head."

Gena just smiled as he proceeded to flip the coin nine more times. Berengar did not appear to become disturbed until the sixth toss came up heads. For the seventh and eighth he increased the rotational rate and for the final two he sent the coin higher in an effort to make it land with the bird staring up at him. His efforts came to naught, and his fingers closed quickly over the coin.

"The Art allowed you to do that?"

Gena nodded as she wiped a trickle of sweat from her cheek. "One aspect of magick is the manipulation of chance. With a coin, where the chances of either result are even, the trick is simple and the effort is not terribly taxing."

Berengar frowned. "But you made a wagon explode. What do coins have to do with that?"

"The wagon's explosion was just an expansion of the

chance problem." She saw he had not made the connection. "What are the chances of a wagon catching fire?"

"Relatively high, I imagine."

"Correct. Getting it to ignite would have been very simple, but that wagon was already burning, so I had an advantage. The explosion came about because of the second factor in the Art. What I managed to do was compact the amount of time it would take for the wagon to burn completely. In effect, I made all of it combust at once, consuming it utterly. The heat and light it would have given off in the course of hours it gave off all at once, creating the explosion."

Berengar's brow wrinkled as he pondered what she had told him. "If you can manipulate time . . ."

"Saying it is much easier than doing it, I am afraid." Gena shook her head. "The difficulties of working magicks are legion. To work a spell I need to be able to concentrate on the casting. I need raw materials and I need to have enough personal strength to trigger the result I want. I could, I suppose, make horseshoes explode, but the amount of personal energy that would require would kill me."

"Personal energy? Anger, happiness?"

"No, physical strength and stamina." Gena felt a shiver run down her spine. "We do not allow emotions to become tied up in our magicks—speaking as an Elf now—except in very special ceremonies. Putting emotions into magick, using them to fuel magick, can lead to a loss of control that benefits no one. It could even kill the caster."

Gena shifted her shoulders to ease the uncomfortable feeling. "There are other factors involved in magick, of course. The Laws of Similarity, Contagion, and Holomorphism bend the laws of probability. For example, two things that look alike, or are similar, have a natural bond between them. Likewise, things that have been together are bonded, and an item that is but a piece of another item has a natural link to it."

"Hence the tales of witch women using a lock of hair or fingernail parings to fashion a love charm."

The Elf nodded. "Yes, those are the stories, and those things have a slight link, but not an important one. Hair and fingernails have no blood and no nerves, so their links to the body are very weak. A finger or an ear or a tooth would have a stronger bond to the person from which it came."

"That's a bit of a grisly example, but I understand it." Berengar smiled down at her. "Your skill at making the arcane transparent is impressive."

"But only possible with a receptive and intelligent listener as the audience."

Berengar laughed and spurred his horse forward as their ride took them out of the Aurdon valley. The outriders closed back up with the two of them, then they forded the Aurdon River and rode off toward the north and east. An hour later they stopped to water their horses in a tributary stream, then used that occasion to distribute the swords carried by the packhorse.

Armed and armored, they set off again at a gentle trot. Spirit found the gait comfortable and matched the pace set by Berengar's stallion with little trouble. They made good time, and the route they took seemed surprisingly well traveled, a fact Gena mentioned to Berengar.

"It is that. Logging teams created this road up into the mountains and down to the other side. Because the river curves far to the east, and farther yet east because of the way the floods three years ago moved its bed, using the mountain pass during the spring and summer makes the journey from Polston much quicker. The Haladina have been hitting caravans coming up through the mountains."

Their ride continued and brought them up into the foothills of the Central Mountains. The road carved a muddy brown track on through a high meadow, but halfway through the valley, the riders struck off southeast and slipped through grasses and into the dark precincts of a forest. As she rode toward it and the woods swallowed the first two riders, Gena strained for any sounds of ambush, but heard nothing.

The darker forest realm made her feel more comfortable than the trail and very much more than the city. She saw signs of a fire that must have swept through the area fifty or a hundred years earlier. For every fire-scarred giant still standing, she saw ten smaller, younger trees. Though most were evergreens, a few aspen and birch groves had carved out their own islands on the hillside. Dried orange pine needles carpeted the ground, but dark-green ferns and bushes sprouted up where sunlight pierced the verdant ceiling above.

The riders formed up in single file as they directed their horses onto a game trail. The young trees allowed for a fairly good field of vision, though the ravines and wrinkles in the landscape could have hidden dozens of Haladina. The guards kept a careful watch, with half of them resting their drawn swords across the pommel of their saddles. Their procession moved more quietly than Gena would have normally assumed Men could, and she knew, were these the ancient Cygestolian forests, the lot of them could have been taken by Elven Foresters before they realized they were under attack.

Her apprehension did not slacken as the troops crested a gentle rise and looked down on the campsite. The center of the small depression had been cleared of trees, which, in turn, had been used to make the crude lean-tos half dug into the hillside. A narrow footpath leading up and away on the opposite side of the depression suggested water could be found over in that direction, while another area on the north end of the gully looked to be where the Haladina picketed their horses. Down the center of the campsite ran a line of three firepits, bordered on all sides by logs or stones suitable for seating.

Berengar brought his horse back next to hers and leaned over. "As we thought, a campsite. From the smoke and ashes I would guess they heard Waldo and his men coming out here ahead of us and fled, probably off to the north."

The explanation made sense to Gena. If Waldo and his squad had followed the same trail, they would have entered the depression from the south, so heading out north would have made sense. "Do you think Waldo and his men have pursued them?"

Berengar nodded. "He's probably chased them halfway to Ispar by now." He pointed to the campsite. "Do you want to inspect it?"

"Please."

They rode on down into the bowl and dismounted. Gena crouched by one of the firepits and warmed her hands over the embers. "They must have left close to dawn, after banking the fire for the night. They made no attempt to extinguish the fires when they departed."

Berengar chuckled, hooking his thumbs in his swordbelt. "I have never known the Haladina to be fastidious or concerned with more than escape when pursued by Aurdon Rangers."

"You have a point there." Gena rose and crossed over to one of the lean-tos. Dark and damp, it smelled more of woodrot than Man-musk to her, but the worn blankets and scraps of cloth scattered around the enclosure suggested both human habitation and a quick departure. Everything looked appropriate, but still something did not feel quite right. She could not identify the incongruities, but they gnawed at her.

Her apprehension spiked when she turned back toward the firepits and saw the guards had spread themselves out through the camp. Dismounted, using their swords to stir ashes and poke lumps of leaves, they had abandoned their previous caution. Even Berengar seemed bored, his eyes unfocused as his mind drifted.

Across from her, where the footpath to water curved around a colossal pine, she saw the flash and heard the snap of a flashdrake's talon falling. As the puff of smoke curling up from the longgunne evaporated, she saw a swarthy Haladin face break into a fierce bejeweled grin. Even as she gestured in his direction and screamed a warning, keening Haladin war cries drowned her out, and a dozen of the Outland warriors broke through the brush to reclaim their camp from the count and his men.

Chapter 8

The Long Ride

Late Summer
Reign of the Red Tiger Year 1
Five Centuries Ago
My Thirty-fifth Year

It struck me, as I rode from Aurium in the company of the Lansorii Honorari, that a Haladin ambush was the least of my worries. In actuality I felt less in their *company* than in their *custody*. Had they been inclined to trust me, I'm certain they would have left me eating their dust for the whole of the journey. Because they did not, two lancers rode behind me, far enough back so they avoided my dust, but close enough to make me turn this way and that to keep track of them.

Aurium, being the size it was, was a mite small for supporting the Steel Pack for the time we would be away. While our fighting force numbered four hundred, grooms, armorers, quartermasters, and camp followers swelled the ranks to near double. Before I left, I struck a deal with Festus and Childeric that allowed my people to set up camp on the other side of the Aur River. The Steel Pack foraged for game, and all excess was sold to the merchants in exchange for grains and other staples. Aurium, in turn, paid for protection and advice on how to fortify the town against raiders, the net result of all this being suitable living conditions for my men and a slight profit for the merchants.

While Drogo gladly accepted promotion to acting commander in my absence, he tried to convince me that going with the Elves would be my death. He didn't trust them, and given history, I knew well his reasons. Part of me, deep down, shared his fear for my safety, but my friendship with Aarundel erased the past. The confrontation at the *legislatorium* made it clear he was not going to let the Elves sent to fetch him home give me trouble.

The journey itself would likely provide all the trouble any of us needed. The distance between Aurium and Cygestolia was near twelve hundred miles as the crow flies, but given that summer was slipping fast into the season of ice, not much was flying from the south up toward the north. More to the point, none of us had wings: as we were ground bound, the journey would take close to two months, and that only if we pushed the horses as hard as they would go.

The journey would also take us, albeit briefly, through Reithrese territory. While it struck me as unlikely that the Reithrese would actually attack an Elven troop, my presence might spur some ambitious Reithrese on to rash action. I was thinking, given the utter silence that greeted my presence as we rode off, that the honor guard would gladly give me over to any Reithrese we met. At the very least that would make me late for the wedding, so I was not looking forward to any confrontation that made my delivery to the enemy a viable solution.

Aarundel and I had decided during a late-night conversation that the permission for him to marry Marta had come because of the headway the Red Tiger was making in his war with the Reithrese. We both knew that the Consilliarii would love nothing better than having Men bleed the Reithrese while getting equally bled. Remaining neutral and watching both sides weaken each other meant that the Elves would not be challenged and not faced with the prospect of another crusade of the sort that spawned the *Eld-saga.*

Not that the Red Tiger's victory might not do just that, of course. Aarundel had pointed out a number of times that certain actions might invoke the wrath of the Elven nation, so the Red Tiger studiously avoided them. When Polston fell, for example, the Reithrese priests were allowed to deconsecrate their temples and withdraw from the city unmolested. Attention to Elven concerns meant that we waged a war which we kept civilized—no mean feat—and that, in turn, meant we remained in control and actually thought in terms of strategy and tactics before we hurled ourselves into battle. Even Sture avoided the elemental tactical mistakes that had cost his father his life and his realm.

The Consilliarii considered this shift in the way Men waged war to be the result of Aarundel's influence in our force. It is true that strategy and tactics were something that the longer-term Elven perspective made possible, but their introduction to our councils was not made by Aarundel alone. I had seen enough in watching the battles waged by and against Tashayul to see where victory had been snatched from the jaws of defeat by the Reithrese's superior planning. In doing so I realized that forethought, which brought with it an awareness of terrain, weather, supply, morale, and a host of other factors, could make a meagre force far more powerful than it had any right to be.

The Red Tiger himself came at tactics from an entirely different direction. Having been enslaved by the Reithrese, he saw their utter disregard for life, and human life especially. In losing friends to carelessness and cruelty, he saw no reason to win with blood what could be taken by stealth, surprise, and superior planning. While he saw the Reithrese nation as a giant scorpion preying on humanity, he knew the Reithrese army—filled out with Haladin warriors—was the scorpion's sting. Eliminating it or its ability to fight would force the scorpion to withdraw and win him the war more easily than anyone could imagine.

The Consilliarii's recalling of Aarundel was proof they could not imagine Men learning from past mistakes. By stripping us of his expertise, I assumed they thought we would collapse after having liberated Centisia. By withdrawing Aarundel they could claim to the Reithrese that they prevented the Red Tiger from overthrowing them. If we kept on winning, the lack of an Elf in our midst would free the Reithrese to use any means at their disposal to oppose and defeat us.

All of my thinking on this subject occurred in a vacuum. The Elves had decided to ignore me as best they could, but I'd probably not have discussed all this with them even under torture. Shijef might have offered interesting comments, but he opted to isolate me as well. He got along no better than I with the Elves, but he was used to a solitary existence and apparently had decided I should see what it felt like.

We had left Aurium early in the day and headed roughly northwest. We continued on for two hours, outstripping evidence of human habitation. The Elves and their mounts moved through the forest with a preternatural ability that included shadows' reluctance to surrender them to light. Even the slight clanking of their armor dulled in the forest, and as I looked around, I realized I could see only the two Elves directly in front of me. The rest had disappeared.

I knew the Elves meant to shock me and inspire fear in me. They succeeded, for I could easily imagine the terror of people in the *Eldsaga* when the Elven Legions materialized at the edge of a forest before riding down some tiny village. I also knew that Aarundel, up there at the head of the line, was allowing his compatriots' pranks because he would have been surprised if I showed fear. In his honor, and for the pride of Men everywhere, I relaxed in the saddle and started humming a little tune.

I resolved to smile as well because the day had dawned bright and even in the deep forest, the sun managed to warm the air. Slate-gray tree bark broke up the deep greens and bright rust of evergreen needles present and past. The trail on which we rode wound around, up and down, through various little hills and along streambeds. I was thinking it was a game trail because it tended to go around things instead of over them, but piles of mossless stones at certain points along the way told me Men had been using it recently.

Mud splashed up from our horses' hooves as we picked our way down a swampy streambed. Clouds of needle-flies rose up but ignored the Elves in favor of me. Slapping the little bloodsuckers distracted me enough that I missed the spot where the others had ridden up from the streambed. Blackstar, apparently likewise immune to the insects, plodded on and started up on the far side of the muddy track. I gave him his head, and though I saw nothing ahead of me, I assumed I was headed in the right direction.

Though I had lost sight of them for only a moment and had spent less than a minute in locating them again, the Elves surprised me when I found them. They had already shucked their armor, unsaddled their horses, and set up camp on a hilltop plateau. As I came through the circle of oaks that defined the perimeter of their camp, I wondered at how the trees would have taken root in such a precise pattern. Once inside, however, the answer to that question seemed unimportant, and I began to feel as if I were suffering from a morning-after without ever having enjoyed the night before.

A bit shaky, I swung out of the saddle, and a dizzy wave crested over me. I flailed at the saddle with my right hand, causing Blackstar to shy away from me when I needed the support. I kicked my left foot free of the stirrup and braced myself for the Elves' piercing ridicule. Before I could land flat on my back however, strong hands grasped me under the armpits and steadied me.

The dizziness vanished when my feet hit the ground. I felt energy pour up from the earth through the soles of my boots. My toes curled down into claws, and my spine arched back as millions of pinpricks raced up my body. I wanted to yelp from pain and surprise, but the power froze my throat. Old air burned in my lungs, but the urgency with which I felt I needed to breathe dissolved as the tingling bounced around inside my skull, then seemed to explode out through my forehead.

I dropped to my right knee, pressing my right hand to the ground to steady myself. I swiped with my left hand at the stinging sweat searing my eyes, then looked up at the

Elves gathered at the center of the circle. They regarded me closely, watching and waiting for something. I snarled at them, then forced myself erect. I repaid their curiosity with defiance and received surprise back again.

Aarundel clapped me on the back. "I had not realized we were so close to a *circus translatio*."

"A *what*?"

He crossed to where Blackstar stood and picked up the dangling reins. "This is a place of great magick. *Magii sylvani* wove great spells here eons ago. Had you not been with us, were the perimeter not disturbed by our recent passage, you would likely not have noticed this place existed. If you had, you would have most probably decided it was evil and have chosen to avoid it." He led the horse over to where the others were picketed, and I followed. "That is fortunate because the results could have been disastrous."

I frowned. "What are you talking about? What I felt here was not pleasant at all. If that wasn't a disaster, I'm thinking I don't want to know what would have been."

Aarundel gave me an open smile. "Among Men, the ability to cope with magickal energies is much akin to the tolerance for vital libations. With some, evidence your man Gathelus, even a weak drink profoundly impairs them."

I nodded. If Gathelus so much as stands downwind of an open bottle of wine, he falls fast asleep. Drogo and Fursey Nine-finger, by contrast, could use Nakanese brandy as blood and still remain sharp. "Entering here could have left me senseless?"

"It could have killed you—in theory—though I knew you would survive." He shrugged casually as he slipped the cinch strap on Blackstar's saddle. "I know you well enough to know that your ability to tolerate magicks is substantial."

"How?"

Aarundel tapped his left eye and smiled. "I have seen it. You have made oaths and they have been verified." He pointed back in the direction of Aurium. "When you joined those two families, you made an oath, and it will survive. Had you been educated in the Art, you would be, for a Man, a very powerful magician."

I shook my head, refusing to believe him. "I'm not saying you may not be right, but I'm thinking you're counting a lot on an oath not yet two days old."

"You vowed to kill Tashayul, and cited prophecies that came true."

"Luck, not power."

"Oh, you are Fortune's child, Neal—and your birth beneath the Triangle proves it—but you have power as well." He glanced back over his shoulder at the other Elves. "They expected you to faint and, if you had, would have used that as a reason you should not be taken with us."

"You will understand if I say that disappointing them does not cause me much pain." I slipped a halter over Blackstar's head, then attached the lead to the picket line. "Why are we stopping here? It is barely noon, and we've a long ride before us."

Aarundel smiled knowingly. "But not as long as you imagine, my friend. Rest here, and we will be off when it gets dark."

One of the other Elves called to him, and Aarundel answered quickly in the Sylvan tongue. I smiled and nodded toward the other Elves. "Go, speak with them. You've been apart from your people for a long time, and they *are* an honor guard. They're proud to be here, and we should respect that."

"Thank you for understanding."

I winked. "What are friends for?"

Aarundel walked off and squatted down at the base of one of the oaks. I leaned back and watched them jabbering away among themselves. Every so often, though I understood nothing they said, I laughed, japing them. That generally prompted their voices to sink to whispers until a speaker became excited enough that his voice rose, and I laughed again.

In their vanity—and their reaction to my laughter—I found Elves far nearer to Men than either side of the *Eldsaga* would ever like to admit. That set a great part of me at ease, which is why, seated there with over a dozen people who had once tried to exterminate my ancestors, I drifted off to sleep.

I awoke quite alert, which I put down to the power of

the magick circle instead of my distrust of my companions. Blinking the sleep from my eyes, I found Shijef crouched at my side. His fetid breath bathed me with the scent of long-deceased, recently devoured forest creatures. "Seek they steal Shijef." The Dreel pointed toward the Elves, then flexed his left paw, extending the claws. "Lifeblack pools."

I frowned as a semicircle of Elves approached us. Each of them wore a silver coronet, two silver bracelets, and a pair of anklets. The fire burning behind them flashed from the slender silver chain connecting bracelets up and over their shoulders. Two other looping chains hung from the coronet at their temples and linked into the shoulder chain. I suspected that similar chains ran up the backs of their legs and connected as well to the shoulder line, but I could not be certain because of the loose-legged black trousers they wore.

I grabbed a thick handful of the mane at the back of Shijef's neck and pulled myself erect. I knew it had to hurt him, but I wanted that to remind him who was master and who was slave. His appeal to me was not a request for rescue, but his asking permission to kill as many of them as he could. He knew I would not give it, but he asked in hopes I might make a mistake.

"Explain." Standing, I could see Aarundel seated back by the fire. He wore the same silver jewelry as the others, but had the faraway look on his face that I had come to associate with his communion with Marta. "I know we share a desire to leave the Imperator in peace at this time, so, please, do not make disturbing him necessary."

One of the Elves took a step forward and held out to me a set of the jewelry. "Required to continue the sojourn. You and it."

I accepted the jewelry and settled the coronet on my head. All I felt was cold metal against my brow and the backs of my ears. The catch-bracelets snapped over my wrists easily, which surprised me, as my wrists are thicker than those of an average Elf. With the anklets dangling down between my legs, I turned to the Dreel. "Secure them to my ankles."

Shijef snarled, but bent to the task. His huge paws closed the delicate loops gently even though I know he would have preferred to take my legs off at the knees. He remained seated on his haunches, refusing to look up, with his claws tracing odd patterns in the dirt.

I glanced over at the Elf holding the second set of chains. "Give them to me."

He did so, and I dropped to my knees in front of the Dreel. "Hold still." As I shut the bracelets and anklets, I made certain to clear all fur from the mechanism so Shijef would not have something more about which to complain. As it was, the bracelets were a fairly tight fit, and the coronet barely settled on the crown of Shijef's head. The chains had enough slack in them that I knew he could move normally, but he affected arm gestures suitable for a man thoroughly bound with chains of lead, not silver.

As I stood again and brushed the dirt from my knees, one Elf made a comment that prompted laughter from the others.

"He does not *serve* the beast, Siric, he prevents you from losing an arm while serving Shijef yourself." Aarundel's anger lashed out at the other Elves, and over half of them blushed.

I shrugged and looked beyond them at my friend. "I'd not be thinking Siric meant that comment harshly. Like as not he's thinking the Dreel is my pet—being as how, of course, only a Man would be dumb enough to keep a Dreel as a pet."

Aarundel nodded stiffly at first in acknowledging my point. "It would be like Siric to have forgotten to ask how a Man might have a Dreel traveling in his company. They might find the tale illuminating."

"Might be like they would, but enlightenment can wait." I held my hands up and shook the silvered chains. "Their explanation for our needing to wear these was a bit on the lean side."

Aarundel frowned at the other Elves. "The chains are attuned to the magick of the *circus translatio*. They allow you to use it. You'll see."

I smiled. "I can't wait. All dressed in our riding chains, should we be off?"

"Agreed."

Our horses had been similarly fitted with soft cloth of

silver bands around their fetlocks, with the chains running along their belly and connecting up into the saddle. A silver plate had been slipped over the part of the bridle resting on the horses' foreheads, and that had two chains hanging down to connect with the chain running along the horses' breastbones. Blackstar seemed a bit skittish as I mounted up, but I patted him on the neck and that settled him a bit.

One of the Elves—it could have been Siric, but they all look quite similar in the twilight—leaned down from his horse and set a torch afire in the fire burning at the center of the clearing. Two other Elves extinguished the fire as Siric moved out toward the perimeter of the trees. He stopped in front of the tree closest to the northwest, bowed, and muttered something in Sylvan. Then he started to ride to the left, smacking the torch against the boles of each tree excepting the one where he started.

As he did this, I noticed two things. The first was that an uneven number of trees circled the clearing. Like the signs at a crossroads, I learned later, each tree marked one end of a plumb line that pointed to another *circus translatio*. While I've not got a merchant's head for figures, I realized that the Elves had an interesting network of magickal pathways stretching out over the face of Skirren.

The second thing was that the sparks exploding from every touch of a tree started to trail after Siric as he made his circuit. His horse ran faster and faster, as if the burning sparks were a swarm of bees in pursuit. A second and a third time Siric rode the circuit of trees, each time fire-annointing each tree except the first. As he completed the final circuit, he cut his horse hard to the left, bringing it to the center of our company; then he turned it and rode at a gallop toward the tree where he had started the whole ritual.

The sparks swirled around us, then again followed in his wake. I felt a magickal tug impelling me to follow him. I hesitated, knowing he was going to dash out his brains when he hit the tree. The other Elves spurred their horses forward, and I saw the Dreel galloping ahead in the thick of the pack. Only Aarundel held back, clearly waiting for me, so I touched my heels to Blackstar's ribs, and like an arrow loosed by a war bow, he shot forward.

The sparks clustered and thickened ahead of me, hiding the tree behind a golden curtain. As I closed with it, each spark became a dot again in a black honeycomb that closed over me with the feathery touch of a cobweb. As I passed through it, each spark stretched out to the length of Cleaveheart and shifted color from red to blue as I rode past. They dragged at me like an ocean's undertow, then touched my chains and released me. Free, I felt a moment of nothing before the onset of a pressure against me.

I met resistance akin to that of a strong headwind, but I could not feel the wind. My clothes remained still, as if I were not moving at all, yet between my legs Blackstar ran for all he was worth and then more. I instinctively hunched down against his neck, and I could smell his sweat as he labored so. Even though I had no trouble remaining in the saddle, each heartbeat brought with it the fatigue that a minute on the road would have caused.

That sapping of vitality might have concerned me, but other things served to distract me completely. The world through which we rode had become the ghost of itself. Whereas we had begun our journey at night, the sky and the landscape were white. Black pinpricks dotted the sky, and a black ball hung where I expected to see the evening's first moon. Trees flashed past all whitewashed and spectral, and I felt a cold chill as their limbs tried to drag me from the saddle.

I looked forward and back at the Elves and saw them still in color. My flesh remained tan and my tunic still appeared blood-red. Whatever magicks had been invoked in the *circus translatio,* we were a company now set apart from the rest of the world.

As we rode, miles fell behind us like rain falling in a monsoon. Then, suddenly, the land dropped away from beneath Blackstar's hooves, but he did not descend to the earth. He pressed on, as did the riders before me, his hooves striking hard on an invisible roadway. The horse galloped onward, apparently unconcerned with the lack of visual clues to his location. It occurred to me then that the Elves and the horses and even Shijef might see things entirely differently from me. If that allowed them to navigate through this world of white-shadow and lead me out of it, then I'd thank the gods for my companions' special eyesight and hang on tightly.

It should have occurred to me—given that when we rode through a tree, no forest branches had stung me and the land lay well below where Blackstar galloped—that the real world and our passage had very little to do with each other. This idea finally came to me when Blackstar plunged into a mountain. Bone-freezing cold filled me, and a shudder even went through my horse. The stone layers flashed by like a gray rainbow, with cracks and fissures cutting through them like black lightning forks trapped immobile.

For the briefest of moments we burst through into a cavern. We rode a dozen feet above the floor and slashed through the cavern diagonally. While the stalactite that bisected me made me think the room was a normal formation, the afterimages of worked columns and a cowering dwarf told me otherwise. Having been in a Dwarven stronghold before, I turned to look back, as if my vision could penetrate stone as easily as we rode through it, but a stone shroud denied me another glimpse of the mountain's heart.

Flying out through the other side of the mountain, I saw what looked to be black bugs fleeing across a snowfield. Three wraiths chased after them, and though the whole sight grew smaller as we rode on, I was able to figure out what I had seen. A trio of shepherds were chasing down a flock that had been disturbed in the wee hours of the morning. If we looked to them the way they did to us, the shepherds would tell of ghost-riders raiding them, and I laughed soundlessly thinking that someday I would hear a bard singing a song inspired by our passage.

We sped straight across a mountain valley and again entered a forest. I reflexively dodged branches, but found myself getting sluggish. Lather covered Blackstar's neck and chest, and I felt thoroughly leeched of life. As Blackstar had come from Elven stocks, I had no doubt that he could go as long as any of the Elves' horses—I hoped, for my own sake, that I had as much stamina as the lancers themselves.

A vertical black line appeared impaled on the horizon. I expected it to widen as we pushed on, but it did not. Wider than a hair, yet barely broader than Cleaveheart, the line hung tantalizingly just beyond my reach. It did stretch out, above and below, but trees and rocks, streams and hills flew past on both sides without affecting it. Yet even though I caught no visual clues that we were getting any nearer to it, I *knew* we were.

Suddenly it engulfed us with the enthusiasm of a Dreel shoving food into its maw. An explosive wave of heat washed over me; then smoke swirled around me and I heard the sound of Blackstar's labored breathing. I cut the reins to the right, and as the dawn filled the grove with the first hints of color, I ran Blackstar around and clear of the Elven riders. I heard Aarundel come out from behind me, and a popping akin to that of a cork being pulled from a jug chased him from the magickal roadway.

I laughed aloud even though my chest ached from the effort of breathing. I felt as if I had ridden for a month, though it would turn out that we had only covered ten days' distance of normal hard riding. Blackstar stamped and I immediately swung off his back. "You've carried me far enough, friend."

My legs trembled but did not buckle, my spine crackled and muscles protested as I straightened up. Looking about, I saw very weary Elves clinging to saddles or already seated on the ground, but I resisted the urge to puff up my chest and carry on as if I were not weak as a kitten. Leading Blackstar back toward the middle of the clearing, I looked up as one of the horses emitted a little squeal and leaped sideways.

Shijef lay on the ground in the middle of the grassy circle, huddled over on his right flank. Blood, black-red at the dawn's first caress, covered his muzzle and paws. He clutched a fluffy ivory bundle to his chest and snapped and snarled at the Elves staring down at him. If not for the blood and the little black legs jutting out of the bundle, I would have thought it a pillow or a Dreel-sized toy, but I saw clearly it was a sheep, quite dead, and, for the Dreel, a prized possession.

Aarundel half fell from his saddle and landed beside me. "How did he procure that sheep?"

I shrugged and Shijef swallowed, then gave us a gory

smile. "Magick Elves have, magick Shijef is." He howled delightedly, and more horses shied away from him. He bit down through the sheep's skull and sucked noisily at the brains, which made me give him a wide berth. I led Blackstar over to where an Elf set up a picket line; then I stripped him of tack and rubbed him down with handfuls of grass.

Having fulfilled my duty to my horse, I stumbled off and collapsed into a heap. Sleep came swiftly, and mercifully did not bring with it a dream-recital of Dreel gustatory grunts, groans, and squeaks.

We remained in that *circus translatio* for three days, which still put us a week ahead of schedule had we not used so remarkable a method of travel. Discussion of how the Dreel managed to take a sheep on the ride brought me more into the company of the Elves, as Aarundel indicated I was the repository of all knowledge about the Dreel. I was not, but I offered a few interesting ideas. That, along with performing a little bit more than an equal share of all chores, made the Elves used to me and prompted tolerance from more than half their number.

The second and third legs of the journey pushed us deep into the vast forests claimed by the Elves as their gods-given holdings. Being as how I was from the Roclaw Mountains, where trees were wind-scourged, gnarly-branched bird-roosts, and that I'd only seen the forests in and around Manlands, the *Forests* of Cygestolia made me feel as small and insignificant as most of the Elves probably saw me. Where other forests were merely stands of growing trees, Cygestolia was a place where the forest *flourished.*

Before seeing the Elven wood, I was used to forests where one could look up and see a narrow river of blue sky coursing between treetops. In Cygestolia the trees grew on forever, rooted in the ground at one end and amidst the clouds at the other. In places, trees grew closely enough together that I could not see through them, and yet, at other times, wooded vistas extended for miles. The whole of the forest seemed almost quiltlike in how it shifted and changed—as if in the woodlands tended by the Elves, all the world's forests could be found.

With Aarundel or another of the Elves along, I was allowed to explore the areas outside the grove-circles. Dunlan and Reysawin seemed to detest my company the least, so we talked of all sorts of things while I rooted around looking for berries, roots, and herbs of various sorts—the Elves were feeding me, but I'm often as much a meat-gobbler as Shijef, so I laid claim to parts of his kills and cooked my own food from time to time.

The Elves all seemed initially reluctant to speak about themselves, so I drew them out by asking questions about the Reithrese. No love had been lost between those two elder races, so the Elves proved less guarded in speaking about them. I learned, for example, that the Reithrese have a similar system of *circii translatio*, but they base theirs around volcanoes and geysers. As Reysawin commented and I agreed, the Reithrese system was not very useful, because no one would want to go to those types of places in any event.

As we drew closer to the heart of Cygestolia, to the city that gives the whole region its name, Aarundel mostly and Dunlan a little bit began to instruct me on proper conduct. Dunlan treated me as if I were gutterkin utterly unschooled and uncomprehending about anything the least bit mannerly. He laid down absolute rules, which could be summed up as "Do nothing unless specifically invited to do it; and decline most of the invitations, because they will be offered out of politeness only."

As he knew nothing of my background, I expected him to give me such a simple system of strictures. I got some of the same from Aarundel, which surprised me, because he had been to the Roclaws and had dined at my brother's table. I put his occasional curtness down to nervousness concerning the reaction to my arrival. I knew he wanted me there as a friend, but doing something that might tweak the noses of the Consilliarii did cause him a little concern.

Aarundel laid out more carefully the things I could and could not do and explained some of the reasons behind the strictures, as well as *all* of the penalties I could incur if I broke them. Most things would be taken as my being ill-bred, which was a given because of my Humanity, but that would make Aarundel look bad. At the worst I could be whipped, though Aarundel allowed as how, given I was his guest, I would likely just be exiled from Cygestolia.

Only one crime bore a more severe penalty. "Under no condition, no matter the provocation, no matter the necessities of the moment, shall you touch one of the *sylvanesti.* Not a babe offered by a proud parent, not a lady falling faint, not a grandmother dead and in a shroud." Aarundel's dark eyes became slits. "You must remember this, Neal, for you will be slain and she will be disgraced. If things go too far, if there is issue, it will be slain and the defiled woman will be declared dead among her people."

I frowned and plucked a ripe blackberry from a thorny bush. "What if a big hole opens beneath her feet and only I can save her from falling into it?"

"No hole will open, but were one to open, you would let her go. She would want it that way." He grabbed me by the shoulders. "Promise me you will not touch a *sylvanesti.*"

I nodded and winked at him. "I promise. I'm thinking you're just afraid I'd steal your Marta away from you."

"No, I have no reason to think that. What I fear is that you, who know her through me, and she, who knows you through me, might be so pleased to meet each other that you would hug or touch in an innocent manner; then both of you would be lost to me forever."

"I comprehend the source of your anxiety." I frowned. "Now this poor *sylvanesti* who has fallen down this hole, I could toss her a rope."

Aarundel shook his head with resignation. "Yes, a rope would be fine. She cannot feel you touch her."

"So if I grabbed her by her belt to stop her from falling, but didn't actually touch her flesh . . ."

"Neal! This is not a game." Anger shot through his eyes, then vanished. "Forgive me. I know you and can trust you. Others do not, and therein lies the potential for difficulty."

"You will never have reason to regret that trust." I slapped him on the ribs, then tossed him a blackberry. "I will act so proper, your people will be thinking me a bob-eared Elf with an odd accent."

The final leg to Cygestolia proved as exhausting as all before it, yet our company arrived giddy and exalted to be at journey's end. Excitement coursed through us, and a couple of the Elves slapped me on the back in congratulations even after they realized who I was. Aarundel almost immediately sank into one of his contemplative fugues, so I dragged him from his saddle and put both of our horses up before lying down to sleep myself.

Being as close as we were to Cygestolia, it might have seemed a good idea just to ride out to the city immediately, but we did not for the same reason that using the *circii translatio* to mount an invasion was ineffective. The circles and the magical energy inherent in them allowed us to recover from the exertions of the journey much more swiftly than we could outside their precincts. An army moved in this manner would be unable to function in a battle shortly after their arrival, and any of us who had ridden out to the city would have fallen from the saddle asleep before we ever got there.

I awoke from my rest in midafternoon, which was a bit sooner than I had intended and a lot sooner than my body desired. Still, Aarundel's insistent demands that I wake up cut through the sleep cocoon in which my consciousness rested, so I sat up and rubbed sleepsand from my eyes. I had planned to ask him what could possibly be more important than sleep, but the raptured expression on his face answered me immediately.

"Come with me, Neal. Come, come." He pulled me to my feet, then waited impatiently as I stretched. "Neal!" he whispered emphatically and jerked his head toward the north.

I followed him as quickly as I could, and my eyes slowly focused on a form standing at the edge of the circle. Even my sluggish brain could determine that the dark-haired, gown-clad person had to be Marta. I smiled at that realization and picked up my pace, then raked fingers back through my hair to clear it away from my face.

At that point I knew Aarundel saw in me more of a friend than even he would have imagined. I had been riding for two days and a fortnight and looked it. Worse yet, I smelled like it. My beard had not been razor-slain since leaving Aurium, and while my tunic had been washed and wrung out twice since then, it looked more ready for burning than wearing. I had imagined washing up and preparing a proper image for when I met his Marta, but that chance had gone the way of the sheep Shijef had stolen.

None of my concerns would have mattered at all to Aarundel. His Marta had come out to see him, to welcome him, and he wanted her to meet me. I hoped, as I hurried along, that she loved him deeper than the hole I wished would swallow me up, because it would take a lot of love to excuse my pitiful appearance. Then again, if she didn't love him that much, scaring her off at this point would be the best thing I could do for him.

Slowing just a hair so I could pare the grime from beneath my fingernails, I approached the couple. I stopped short a good Man-length from them and shifted so I'd be more downwind than up. Holding hands together, they were lost in each other's eyes and didn't notice me until I cleared my throat.

Aarundel blinked, then blushed a bit and extended his left hand in my direction. "Doma Marta, this is Neal Roclawzi, the one I have named Custos Sylvanii. Neal, this is my heart-twin, my *vitamoresti,* Lady Marta."

I bowed deeply to her. "This is an honor I have long awaited."

"The honor is mine, Custos Sylvanii."

For the next two seconds we said nothing and appraised each other. I know I got the better of the exchange, for her exquisite beauty meant I could have watched her for a good long time without complaint. Tall enough to look me even in the eyes, she had a slender grace and noble bearing the equal of which I had never seen before. She wore her dark hair shorter even than Aarundel or me, and it molded itself to her head and the back of her neck with tight curls. Her blue eyes and bright smile made me feel welcome and told me she well understood how the hardships of the journey had left their mark on me.

I looked over at Aarundel. "My friend, until this day I have envied you nothing. Now I envy your tremendous fortune in sharing love with this *sylvanesti.*"

Aarundel laughed aloud and kissed Marta on the forehead. "I shall do all I am able to be worthy of your envy, my friend." He smiled at Marta, then looked beyond me toward the glade surrounding the circle. "You did not tell me she rode out with you."

Marta nodded. "While you slept, she decided to gather herbs and flowers."

Aarundel's smile grew and he waved his left hand. "Neal, it is also my pleasure to present to you my sister, Larissa."

I turned back toward the rustling in the brush with an easy smile on my face and laid my eyes on the most beautiful female the gods had ever blessed with life.

Chapter 9

The Magick of Battle

Early Spring
A.R. 499
The Present

The smile on the Haladina's face died when his flashdrake failed to fire. Gena concentrated for a second, then opened her hands in his direction. A burning spark sped at the man with the straight-line accuracy of a bee. It swerved once, at the end, darting down from his face to the powder horn dangling near his waist. The magickal ember pierced it, melting the Haladina's look of surprise into a mask of horror.

The powder horn's explosion launched the raider into the air. His longgunne fell one way, and, trailing thick white smoke, his limp body went another. From the corner of her eye Gena saw him hit the ground and bounce loose-limbed and bloody.

Knowing he was dead, she turned her attention to the four Haladina racing in at Berengar. A disorienting sensation passed through her as she turned her head. She recognized it as the aftereffects of casting two spells in haste, but that did not stop it from upsetting her balance and driving her to one knee. Her right hand closed on sand and pine needles as she caught herself.

Forcing nausea away, she prepared another spell.

Before she could cast it, the swiftest of the Haladina had reached Berengar. The smaller Haladina yipped his war cry, but Berengar drowned it out with a roar that would have pleased the tiger on his crest. The count caught the man's overhand saber cut on the forte of his rapier, then pivoted on his left foot and snapped a kick at the Haladina's leg. Berengar's right heel hit the man on the knee, snapping it straight, then carrying through to break it back in the other direction.

Taking a deep breath, Gena concentrated and felt power pulse down her arm and into the handful of dirt. She raised it up and threw it, releasing it in an arc going from high right to low left. Her arm fell leaden to her side. Exhausted, she shivered and watched as her sand spray hit two of the remaining Haladina bent on Berengar's destruction.

The ribbon of sand slashed at the men as if it were a stony whip. The very tip of it swept away the furthest man's ear and polished to shining the metal trinkets hanging on his vest. He found himself involuntarily twisted back to his right. His momentum carried him forward, but the broken rhythm of his steps caused him to falter and fall to his knees at the outer edge of Berengar's sword-arc.

Vertigo twisted her insides, but she saw the man closer to her stopped in midrun. Air exploded from his lungs as the sand-stream lashed his torso. The sand ate through his woolen vest, the tunic below it, and the flesh beneath that like strong acid. Gena thought she saw white ribs, then the man's legs flew out from beneath him, and he landed hard on his back, obscuring her view of his ruined chest.

The last Haladin raider rushing in at Berengar suddenly found himself alone instead of being the left flank of a united front. Berengar sidestepped to his right, then pivoted out of the way of the Haladina's weak cross-body slash. The second that blade passed, Berengar whipped his blade across the back of the Haladina's legs, slicing through muscles and dropping the man screaming to the sand.

A thrust through the throat finished the one-eared raider. Berengar looked up from him to the other man felled by magick, then jogged over to where Gena knelt huddled against the ground. She let her head drop down as he approached, heard the sound of his rapier being thrust into the sand, and felt his strong hands on her shoulders.

"Are you hurt, Lady Genevera?"

She coughed and wiped the sweat from her brow with her right hand. That smeared dirt across it, a fact that registered in her mind, but seemed decidedly trivial as Berengar's bodyguards finished the last of the Haladina. "Just tired. Combat casting is usually not difficult. *If* you have some preparation. Ambush means reacting without much forethought."

Berengar smiled and helped her sit upright. "If not for you, I would be dead. The Haladina with the flashdrake would have killed me." He glanced back over his shoulder at where the man's smoking body lay. "How did you save me?"

Gena smiled weakly. "The first spell taught to any student of the Art, for obvious reasons, involves extinguishing fires. Rik has explained to me and showed me that what happens in a flashdrake is fire building up behind the ball. Being familiar with the idea, and having discussed it before, I just put the fire out."

"Then you put fire in his fuel box."

Gena nodded and licked sweat from her upper lip. "That was easy. Making fire is the second spell most magicians learn."

Berengar laughed lightly. "And the sand?"

"I would have thought you too busy to notice that."

"I have forced myself to be aware of everything on a battlefield. Awareness is the key to winning." He gestured behind himself. "At this end of the field we have five men down, three dead, and two badly wounded. At the other end I have two wounded men and seven Haladina dead. Had I not been aware of what was happening, I would have helped my men finish off the raiders before coming to speak with you."

"I am impressed."

"As I am with you. Now, about the sand."

Gena sighed heavily. "I improvised with a spell used to enchant arrows to carry further from bows. It expands the time during which they accelerate from release to leaving the bow. My mistake came in that the spell is normally used on a dozen arrows or so, hence the requirement in energy is low. In my use, which was sloppy and hasty, each grain of sand became an arrow. While each required less energy than an arrow, there were far more of them." Looking down at her hands, she laughed. "If my hands were bigger, I could have killed myself."

"Can you ride? We can stay here if you need to rest."

"I will be fine after a moment." Gena shook her head. "Thank you."

"My duty, honor, and pleasure, Lady Genevera."

One of the bodyguards came over and stood beside Berengar. "Begging pardon, m'lord, but you left two alive. Do you want me to take care of them?"

"If you please, yes, Darrian."

Gena looked up. "I can still help heal, if you wish. I am getting my strength back."

Berengar shook his head. "Darrian will finish them, not patch them up."

"Kill them?"

"Yes. If I take them prisoner, I have to feed them. They will provide me with no useful information. If ransomed, their parole will be worthless because they will come back at me." Berengar frowned heavily. "I know it seems barbaric—something from the time of Neal, perhaps—but the only thing the Haladina understand is death. They are not civilized. If you are to be understood, you must speak to them in the manner which they will understand."

The count stood and walked over to where his men dragged the Haladin bodies into a rough line. Gena wondered at how the man could order their deaths so casually, then bother to kneel and straighten their limbs. Berengar saw to it that each dead man's hands clutched his sword hilt to his chest, after the usual manner of Haladin burial. He did not allow his men to take the gems from their teeth —both in burial and the lack of looting he paid the Haladina more respect than Rik had.

Gena shivered again, but not from fatigue. She had long

heard the argument about what the Haladina might or might not understand, but before, it had always been directed by members of the Consilliarii at Humanity as a whole, not just the Haladina. Though the discussion had raged for centuries before her birth—had raged since the time when the children of the gods saw fit to create Men—as she had grown up, Berengar's ideological counterparts among the Elves were seen as being trapped in the past. They made up the majority of Elves who had chosen to travel *excedere* and abandon the mortal world for the gods' paradise.

She had often tried to understand their arguments, but no one raised in her family could have agreed with them. Gena did concede that Humanity often acted without forethought and due consideration, but she argued often and long that what might be seen as a racial trait did not include each and every Man. Those she most often debated quickly learned to bait her by dismissing her points with the phrase, "Neal Custos Sylvanii aside . . ."

The shift in attitude among Elves concerning Men had been far simpler to accomplish than changing Berengar's mind would be. While it was true that since the time of Neal, Men had not encroached on Elven territory, Berengar saw the Haladina as an immediate danger to his family and his future. As one of her teachers had commented, "The theory of a thing is often easier to comprehend than the doing of it." The threat Berengar felt to family and home from the raiders meant that he reacted in the most direct and forceful way that he could to forestall and defeat that threat.

She hugged her arms around herself and rubbed some warmth into her upper arms. Berengar's concern for seeing that the Haladina were buried marked him as more complex than a man who hates solely on the basis of difference. He respected the Haladina and their traditions. He did not allow his men to defile their bodies. The graves they dug might not be as deep as they would be for his own men, nor would he raise a monument to mark them, but he would not just leave them for the wolves, either. He honored his foes in defeat.

Gena stood up and wandered out to where Berengar

examined the Haladin flashdrake. Though it had to have been quite heavy, the count handled it easily and studied it closely enough that he did not hear her approach. When she came into his circle of vision, he looked up and smiled, then frowned quickly and shook his head. "A horrible weapon, this."

He held it out for her inspection. It looked to be as long as Durriken was tall and had a pitted gray octagonal barrel with a silver bead mounted on the tip as a sight. The stock and foregrip had been made of the same type of wood, but were in two pieces. Silver straps bound the foregrip to the barrel nearly halfway along its length. The stock, which had been inlaid with bits of ivory and had a silver butt cap, joined the barrel at the last quarter of its length and housed the trigger and talon mechanism. The ramrod was missing, but a hole drilled lengthwise in the foregrip and another at the nose of the stock marked where it should have resided.

"I have witnessed the type of wounds they are capable of inflicting, my lord. I would agree that they are horrible. By the same measure, however, the wounds caused by an arrow or crossbow bolt or even a sword are likewise horrible."

"Yes, but their use requires skill and training." Berengar brandished the gunne. "This requires no skill. There is no honor in using it."

"I would imagine, my lord, that the first stick-wielding man hit by a thrown rock uttered the same refrain."

Berengar laughed aloud. "A point well made and deeply taken. I know Durriken uses flashdrakes, and I do not mean to imply he has no honor. His are Dwarven. His possession of them is a mark of respect of him by the Dwarves and, from what I understand, their respect takes a great deal of earning. This, on the other hand, is a poorly constructed Haladin imitation. Had you not quenched the fire in it, it likely would have exploded in the Haladina's face."

He looked ready to break it and bury it, but Gena stopped him. "I believe, my lord, if we bring it back to Durriken, he might be able to tell us something about it. It could be important, especially if more than one in a dozen Haladina are supplied with them."

"That is a good idea." Berengar dispatched two of his men to round up the Haladina horses while the others finished digging the graves with the steel caps taken from two of the dead raiders. Berengar took his turn digging, which surprised and pleased Gena.

The burying of the dead and the ride back to Aurdon proved quiet work, and Gena did nothing to prompt conversation. She let her body regain its strength on the ride back, and the leisurely pace the group adopted guaranteed the sun would set an hour or two before they made it back to the city. She suggested stopping for the night at Lake Orvir, but Berengar vetoed her idea, pointing out that stopping at the unused manor house would raise great alarm among those people expecting them back in Aurdon.

She quickly imagined Rik's reaction and bowed to Berengar's wisdom. He reassured her that despite the string of Haladin horses making them look like a caravan of horse traders bound for the city, he expected no more trouble. "We will be home soon enough, m'lady, hale, hearty, and for your part, I hope, rested."

As she rode, she watched Berengar and slowly integrated the different pieces and sides of him she had seen. From her earliest meeting with him, she knew him to be well mannered, gracious, handsome, and a student of folklore. Of his intelligence there was no doubt at all. His summons told her he was concerned for his family and for the people of Aurdon. The way he treated Rik marked his generosity, and his harshness in dealing with Waldo paralleled her own dislike for the little man.

In battle he was a worthy heir to the Red Tiger, matching the legendary leader in size, coloration, and demeanor. In the sparring match she had witnessed on her arrival in Aurdon, she had seen a man quite skilled in all the finer points of dueling. At the Haladin camp he had proved singularly efficient at killing—a remorseless and implacable foe. Even so he had shown respect for his enemies, honoring them as valiant combatants, not treating them as soon-to-be-carrion.

Fitting all the pieces together, Gena found herself comparing each against a standard she had not realized she held in her mind. At first she thought she might be judging him in comparison to Durriken, but were that so, she knew she would find stranger and greater differences than she did. She also knew that Durriken would appear, in many ways, to be the lesser of the two men, and she knew that was not true, for there was no real way to compare them.

But if she was not comparing Berengar to Durriken, who was she using to measure him? Not the Red Tiger. She knew next to nothing about him. He was a footnote to the adventures of her grandfather and Neal Custos Sylvanii. *Neal?* She knew that was the right answer to her question, but it struck her as wrong as well. She only knew Neal from legends and songs—no man could compare favorably with a legend.

Despite that impossibility, Berengar fought hard. He showed the same willingness to pitch in and help his men that had made so many loyal to Neal. They both were intelligent and fierce fighters, and they both had long careers fighting the Haladina. Each man thought about more than just himself, and did things to stabilize not only his time but the future.

They are much alike. Gena shook her head. *Is there anything Neal did that Berengar could not do?*

It took her a moment, but when she thought of it, she found she could not replace her mental image of Neal with that of Berengar in the same position. A little laugh escaped her, and she felt relieved that in the twilight no one could see her blush. "No," she whispered to herself, "no, you are far too proud, Count Berengar Fisher, to have survived admittance to Cygestolia."

Chapter 10

The Magick of Love

Late Summer
Reign of the Red Tiger Year 1
Five Centuries Ago
My Thirty-fifth Year

The first things I saw were her eyes. Larissa met my stare openly, yet not defiantly nor haughtily. She appeared as surprised at our meeting as I was. In that first unguarded moment I saw something flash through her hazel eyes, a light I expected to be covered quickly by a superior disdain or a frightened withdrawal.

The light blossomed in her large eyes to accompany the smile growing on her face. While her features were unmistakably and sharply Sylvan, from the pointed tips of ears jutting up from thick golden hair to her eyes, cheekbones, and jaw, the smile softened them. It made her more a vixen than a distant and cold *sylvanesti.* It would have been easy to read in her eyes and smile an invitation—an invitation I desperately wanted to see but knew she would not offer and one I could never presume to accept.

My mind echoed with the words Aarundel spoke in Aurium concerning how I would know I had met my True

Love. My heart pounded in my chest with the force of a giant's footfalls. My stomach did not so much clench as it felt as if Shijef had bitten half of it away. I wanted to speak, but words would not come to my mind, and breath stayed dead in my lungs. I wanted to turn away, to stop staring, but my muscles would not obey me. I could do nothing.

Nothing but return her smile.

She had stopped, Larissa had, a dozen feet in front of me. As tall as I am, she looked as lithe and slender as Marta, but she was to Marta as a woman is to a bare slip of a girl. While Marta had certainly been beautiful to look upon, there was something about Larissa that made me want to study her and memorize her. I wanted to possess her, not just physically, but mentally and emotionally and spiritually as well.

This realization collided directly with all the instruction I had been given in Elven custom. It collided with my memories of the *Eldsaga.* Part of me wanted to dismiss this longing as nothing more than lust. Though the blue-grey homespun gown she wore was meant for riding and woods-walking, it nonetheless flattered her. Broad shoulders tapered down to a narrow waist and flat stomach. Her hips curved into long legs, and as the breeze molded the skirts to her legs, I could see by her muscles that she was no soft palace creature.

Another part of me screamed that any thoughts, any wild fantasies I might construct around us, were sheer insanity. Though she appeared to be ten years my junior in age, she had to be centuries older than I was. I could be of no more interest to her than a child is to me. The fact that I was her brother's friend meant she noticed me. To expect anything beyond that, to dare interpret any sign as something significant, would lead to my death and her disgrace.

All the while these thoughts battled back and forth through my brain, my smile grew. I knew two things as absolute truths that I accepted as easily as I accepted the certainty of the dawn or of my bleeding when cut. The first was that I had met my *vitamoresti* and that I was doomed by our meeting. The second was that the only thing that could save me would be her turning away and rejecting me.

If she did that, I knew I would go mad, but madness I could handle.

Her smile grew in counterpart to mine, and I knew I was lost.

Aarundel slapped me on the shoulder. "Despite his lack of elocution, Larissa, Neal is a very intelligent and entertaining man. And a warrior without human equal."

"So I would expect of a warrior who succeeded in defeating death and wresting *Divisator* from Jammaq." She bowed her head respectfully, breaking eye contact for the first time. "I am honored to meet you, Custos Sylvanii."

Her looking down released me from whatever spell had paralyzed my brain, body, and tongue—and I marked her strength at having been able to look away. "The honor is mine, Doma Larissa." I clipped my words off as I killed the urge to step forward to take her hand and raise it to my lips. I wanted to say something else, to compliment her, but our races stood so far apart that even the most innocent comment, offered lightly as a jest, could be taken as a mortal insult.

While my restraint pleased me, it was made all that more difficult by the realization that Larissa had unconsciously freed her right hand from the basket she carried to permit me the common courtesy of kissing her hand. She shifted the half-filled basket from her left hand to right forearm and refused to look up at me. Instead she shifted her gaze to the side, then up and back to look at Aarundel.

"Our kith and kin await you at Woodspire, my brother." She smiled at him and nodded toward Marta. "Go, the two of you. Take my horse so you both may ride. I will conduct Neal to the city."

For all the caution Aarundel had shown in speaking to me of the consequences of contact with a *sylvanesti,* he abandoned his sister to me without a second thought. I could not blame him, for Marta's presence distracted him greatly. Moreover, he saw Larissa as his *sister,* making the mistake of placing her in a gender other than female. I had seen that problem with all manner of males, and I dearly wished Aarundel would not fall prey to it, because I was not certain I was worthy of the trust he was showing in me.

As Aarundel and Marta mounted up and rode off down

the road leading deeper into the woods of Cygestolia, I turned to watch them depart. "Your brother is very fortunate. He has a beautiful fiancée and a kind, considerate sister."

"Considerate?" She laughed lightly, likewise turning to watch them ride away from us. "You draw conclusions from very little evidence, Custos Sylvanii."

My eyes sharpened as I looked down. "I don't believe so, Lady Larissa. You spoke to your brother in Mantongue, even adopting words that are not derived from the Sylvan language, to send him off. You referred to your family home as Woodspire, when I know it is more properly rendered Conussilva. And you refer to me as Elfward, even though the title your brother conferred upon me has not been ratified by the Consilliarii."

"You are easily as intelligent as my brother has reported." Again she laughed throatily. "And as intelligent as Finndali has often complained you are."

"Not really intelligence, my Lady, just animal cunning." I smiled, not daring to face her. "If you wish, I will carry the basket for you on our walk."

"That is a kind offer."

She started to extend it toward me, but I shook my head. "It will be a pleasure to serve you, but I have been well warned about my conduct. Perhaps if you set the basket down and step away from it, I can save both of us difficulties."

Larissa did as I requested, moving away from the basket with a fluid elegance that threatened to birth fantasies about the two of us moving together so effortlessly. I reached down, scooped the woven basket up by its wooden handle, and smiled. "I'll try not to touch any of the plants you have gathered lest I make them unclean."

"Your grasp of our traditions is admirable."

I laughed. "Some things were made admirably clear to me on the journey here."

"Excellent." She paced beside me, easily matching her strides to mine. "Then you have a full understanding of why we, you and I, are doomed beyond any hope of redemption."

Her statement, made so conversationally as to have

been a remark about the sunny day, took my breath away. I stopped dead in my tracks and shook my head. I doubted that I had heard her words, deathly afraid that whatever she had actually said had been translated into what I had wanted to hear in my head. "I beg your pardon."

She walked on past me, then looked back over her shoulder. "When were you born, Neal Roclawzi?"

I blinked and started after her. "Thirty-five years ago."

"The date, what was the day?"

I shivered. "Midsummer's Eve, beneath the Triangle." At my birth all three moons had been full and arranged so the smallest stood midway between, and above, the other two. That omen, which occurred only once in every two and a half centuries, had been taken for ill or good depending upon which soothsayer had spoken last. Many, Aarundel included, had used it as a sign that I was marked for greatness, but I generally considered it a fell sign.

Larissa nodded slightly, sunlight riding the waves in her golden hair. "We share that, then, though my nativity came two hundred and fifty years before your own."

I arched an eyebrow at her back. "Is that why . . . ?"

She shrugged and waited for me. "It could well be the reason we are doomed, but I doubt it is the reason we have been brought together." Larissa smiled carefully, thoughtfully, and clasped her hands together over her stomach. "What you felt, Neal, when you saw me was but an echo of what I felt when I saw you."

"How? How is it possible?" I gestured wildly with my arms, spilling half the basket's contents. I squatted immediately and started to gather things up, and Larissa did the same. "I am a Man and you are *sylvanesti*! This cannot be."

She shook her head. "Even the *Eldsaga* tells of unions between Elf and Man."

"Rape and lust have nothing to do with love."

"True, but if those can exist, why not love?" She caught me with her eyes again, and I could not muster a counter to her argument. "And if love can exist, why not the greatest of love, why not *vitamor*?"

I broke away from her stare, then found myself watching her delicate, long-fingered hands plucking leaves and flowers from the road dust. I longed to reach out, to hold her hands in mine. Inside I found myself willing to die for that pleasure, but utterly unwilling to destroy her with my selfishness.

And in that I found the proof that she was absolutely correct in her reasoning.

"No, no, this cannot be happening." I stood, my fists clenched in frustration and disbelief. "You cannot feel anything for me. I am Man. I am Roclawzi!"

"Why can you, a Roclawzi, feel something for me, and not the reverse?" Larissa rose as well, leaving the basket on the ground between us. "My people rode yours down. You should hate me."

"You did not ride with them; you were not yet born at the time of the *Eldsaga*." I shook my head. "I have no reason to hate you."

She smiled triumphantly. "If you have no reason to hate me, then I have no reason to hate you." She raked her hair back and across, away from her face. "In you I find the greatest love."

Conflicting emotions raced back and forth through me. I felt the buoyant euphoria that comes with love, and part of me wanted to sweep her up in my arms regardless of the consequences. I realized I had begun to cycle through the same desire from which I had broken free moments before, so I ruthlessly overrode it. Even so, as when all the water is scooped from a muddy hole, bright and cheerful emotions slowly started filtering back into me. Before I filled again, I possessed a clarity of mind that I determined to employ immediately, before it was lost to me.

"Lady Larissa," I began slowly as I bent to retrieve the basket, "you must see how impossible this is. Even if I allow that what I feel is not some residue of the remarkable journey I have taken, and even if I allow that you feel what I do, that we, together, feel what your brother and Marta feel for each other, our situation is hopeless."

She nodded in agreement quite emotionlessly. "This I do see, Neal of the Roclaws. I also see I cannot deny what has passed between us."

I shook my head. Somehow we both moved into the eye of the emotional storm surrounding us. As we walked through the forest toward Cygestolia, the world around us melted away. I found myself aware of nothing save her words, her face, the rustle of her gown as she walked along. Even as those things enchanted me, I stripped away all but the cold logic of our conversation, and I wrestled with it as if grappling with some abstraction of Dreel fury.

"I want to know you, Larissa, learn about you. I want everything promised by your smile and the fire in your eyes. I want to know what makes you laugh and cry. I want to know how you can view this with such calm, and I want to know how your strength can keep me from going mad." I laughed briefly, forcing tension from me and into the sound. "I want the knowledge of you that I have of myself, and while the thought of succeeding in my quest to gain it pleases me, I dread that success."

"Because of the consequences imposed by Sylvan law?"

"No." I felt a chill run down my spine. "No, because I am afraid I would lose myself in you and our cultures would destroy us."

Larissa reached out and caught the handle of the basket. "Then you know my fear. And you know my hopes."

Though mere inches separated our hands, and our fingers could have touched without effort, almost by accident, neither one of us made that accident happen. I realized in that instant that what we were talking about was more than sexual. It was more than just lust or emotional hunger. Without knowing how I knew it, I recognized in Larissa another part of me. She was my complement. It felt as if the gods had torn us apart eons ago. They cast her into a *sylvanesti* body born beneath the Midsummer's Eve Triangle, and then, as an afterthought, they planted me in a Roclawzi body born under the same sign centuries later. Whether by malice to ensure our destruction, or by compassion, thinking we would never meet, they had kept us apart.

And now, united by chance, yet other things conspired to keep us apart.

The realization that I wanted more than mere physical union with her set aside carnal desires. I wanted all that she was, which meant that physical concerns amounted to only a small portion of what I meant to explore. Once I knew her emotionally, spiritually, and intellectually, then the other would and could be important. Indulging sexual urges would have parted us once again, and I determined, at that moment, that nothing and no one would ever do that while I had breath in my lungs and blood in my veins.

I glanced over at her and smiled. "I'm thinking we are in serious trouble."

"More so than you know." She returned my smile, and my heart felt ready to burst. "Until this day I have been sleepwalking through my life. Now I am awake and alive."

Nervous, giddy laughter exploded from me. "Exactly."

Her smile shrank a bit into a satisfied smirk, then she bowed her head and extended her left hand forward. "It is my pleasure, Neal Roclawzi, to present to you the city of Cygestolia."

I have no doubt, given the way my heart beat in my chest and my smile peaked up near my eyes, that anything she had shown me would have been magnificent. The Sylvan metropolis exceeded that by a league or three. As ugly and forbidding as was Jammaq, so did Cygestolia feel sacred enough to have been the womb of the world itself.

The city stretched down and out through a wooded, serpentine valley. Flashing like a quicksilver ribbon, a crystalline stream bisected the valley north and south, yet pooled into an azure lake in the center. Islands studded the lake and provided enough ground to support huge, ancient trees. While I did see stones of all sizes, shapes, and hues throughout the landscape, none had been used as building material. They were decoration, and rare was the rock that was not home to moss or a flowering plant growing from a crevasse or recess.

In the coastal jungles of Najinda I had seen villages built on stilts and others constructed high in the jungle bowers. Until I saw Cygestolia, I had thought of the Najindese as living in the trees. I immediately realized I had been far too generous in my thoughts, for the Najindese lived *among* the trees.

The Elves lived *in* the trees and *with* the trees. A dark-green canopy covered entirely the city precincts on either wall of the valley. The canopy broke over the stream and around the lake, allowing for enough sunlight to strike the lake shore and promote some agriculture. The island-based trees all grew together to form a green mushroom structure over the center of the lake. Long branches on the central trees grew out like spokes from the island hub and joined with similar branches from the trees on the valley walls.

From where I stood everything seemed normally proportioned; then I noticed people walking along the branches, passing high above the lake's mirror surface, from the island outward and vice versa. At that point I realized I had misjudged the whole city, for it was much larger and more titanic than I had first imagined. Whereas among the Najindese a tree would house a single family, the entire population of Aurium could have taken refuge in just one of the Cygestolian giants.

Larissa gestured toward the city casually, as if dismissing the vision, though I caught the way pride in it lifted her chin. "It may look a thicket to you, Neal, but it is simple to navigate. Trees, as you can see, are grouped in districts, as befits good growth, and are named after their most prominent feature. Conussilva, for example, is located in the Seven Pines district."

"Pinusseptem. Aarundel told me." I smiled. "The city is gorgeous."

I followed one branch as it led back into the trunk. Side branches provided a screen of foliage, but I saw where an Elf entered through a hole in the bark. Above and below that level I saw other openings and spied Elves moving through the trees like a line of ants. If each tree housed only a dozen Elves, there had to be hundreds of thousands of them, and that seemed all the more remarkable because they all gathered in this one spot instead of, as Men and the Reithrese had done, spreading out over the face of the world.

Larissa tugged on the basket. "We should go on to Woodspire. Your arrival was not expected, but it was not unanticipated. We have lodging for you and even for the Dreel."

I looked around to see if Shijef had been following us, but I did not see him. As I turned back to face the city, a half-dozen hooded Sylvan warriors slipped from the brush before us. Larissa did not seem concerned and did not release the basket, so I let it go. The Elves bore longbows and two had arrows nocked. One of the Elves stepped forward as the others spread out in a semicircle behind him. His face hidden by the hood, the leader said something in Elven, and I recognized it as a challenge from the tone, though the words meant nothing to me.

Larissa laughed and let the basket swing innocently in her right hand as she approached the leader. "Who am I? I would have thought the answer to that question would be obvious to you."

The leader nodded toward Larissa and allowed her to approach him as he turned and challenged me again. "What Man dares enter Cygestolia?"

I smiled, perhaps too broadly—like a newbeard-boy trying to impress his first love—and let a growl enter my voice. "I am Neal Roclawzi, Leader of the Steel Pack, Killer of Tashayul, Bearer of Divisator and named Custos Sylvanii by Aarundel Imperator. I have come as his guest for his marriage."

"Beneath the grime you are hard to recognize." The leader bowed his head. "You may pass, Neal Roclawzi."

Larissa, having reached the leader's side, frowned impatiently. "So formal? That's hardly like you." She reached up and tugged down his hood. Fine black hair framed a face I thought I recognized. "He is a guest, treat him as such."

I squinted at the Elven leader. "Imperator Finndali?"

He nodded and Larissa laughed. "Yes, Neal, this Sylvan warrior suddenly struck dumb is Finndali. Imperator and" —her eyes flashed dangerously at me—"he who is my husband."

Chapter 11

Intrigues in the City

Early Spring
A.R. 499
The Present

Though they arrived back in Aurdon near midnight, the Fisher estate appeared as active and alive as if it were midday. This struck Genevera as odd until Berengar pointed out that farmers had begun to bring in shipments of winter wheat that required warehousing, resale, and shipment to points downriver. "Commerce seldom allows one time to rest."

Gena nodded. "An idle merchant is a starving merchant."

"Bravo!" Berengar helped her down from Spirit. "You are recovered from the ordeal?"

"I am, my lord, thank you." She half curtsied to him. "Shall we take the gunne to Durriken?"

Berengar frowned for a moment. "I am certain Durriken would prefer, at this hour, after this absence, to greet you in private. I must report to my father and uncles what we have seen and done. If you wish, we can delay his examination of the weapon until morning."

"Can we afford the delay?"

"You are correct, of course. It might be unwise to take that liberty. An hour, then?" Berengar smiled encouragingly as they mounted the steps to the mansion entrance. "That would allow me to escape my kin after a short time, which I would prefer to do. Awakening them will not put them in a good humor, and I doubt the news will improve their disposition."

"An hour, then." Gena turned and worked her way through the building's maze of corridors to the door of her chamber. She knocked lightly, first twice, then once, then three times, in a signal pattern that Durriken had taught her. She waited a heartbeat or two after the end of the knocking, then opened the door.

Durriken sat in the bed, one candle burning, with a flashdrake propped on a sheet-shrouded knee and pointed at the door. As she entered, he tipped the weapon toward the ceiling. "It is good that you knocked, for I had fallen asleep waiting for you."

"I know better than to surprise you in your sleep."

"Especially here in Aurdon, for there are many, many surprises about." He set the flashdrake down on the bedside table and folded the sheet back on her half of the bed. "Was your ride of interest?"

"I believe you would consider it 'remarkable.'" Gena swung the door shut, then crossed to one of the chairs and leaned heavily on it. "Count Berengar will be here within the hour to show you a longgunne taken from a Haladin raider."

"Are you hurt?" Rik stood and swirled the sheet around himself, looping it around his body and up over his right shoulder. "One raider implies many more."

"A dozen, and, no, I am not hurt, though I am still a bit tired." She came around and sat down. She said nothing as Rik poured her a cup of wine, then pulled a chair up and sat facing her with their knees touching. Gena obligingly drank, then set the cup down on the table. "I cast spells in haste and suffered for it."

"From the beginning, Gena."

She sat back and drank again, then told Rik all about the journey and the ambush. She sensed an irritation in Rik whenever she mentioned Berengar, but she knew him better than to imagine it to be jealousy. Rik managed to remain near neutral as she described the elaborate lengths to which the Count had gone to keep the goal of their expedition secret. His attitude definitely soured as she described the ambush.

"Berengar should have been more watchful."

Gena shrugged. "This is true, but we were to link up with Waldo and his people at the camp. When we arrived, it appeared that Haladina had departed quickly when they discovered Waldo's men in the area."

"Only to double back and ambush you."

"Which is not Berengar's fault." Gena took Rik's hands in her own. "He was as much at risk as the rest of us—more, since they devoted nearly half their force to killing him."

"That does put a different complexion on things." Rik sat back, slipping his hands from her grasp. His left arm went around his chest and his right hand cupped his chin. "There is more going on here in Aurdon than Berengar has told us, I think. I had thought him the person orchestrating things, but this indicates he is but a pawn and expendable."

"What do you mean?"

Rik leaned forward again and dropped his voice to a conspiratorial whisper. "I went about in Aurdon today, into the lower rings. I wandered and listened a great deal. It seems, from what I heard bandied about among those who are not Fishers or Riverens, the battling between the two clans is cyclical. It usually begins as some sort of trade war, with each side undercutting the other until one begins to bleed gold. At that point the tactics escalate into sabotage. That means anything from arson to thievery. Everyone knows who is doing it and why it is being done, and the families are scrupulous in seeing to it that no one gets hurt physically."

Gena made no attempt to conceal her surprise. "I thought Men set great store in the saying, 'Cut off the head and the snake dies.' "

"Oh, we do, but both families greatly fear Neal's intervention. Berengar didn't tell us the half of the difficulties assassins have had over the years. Each one of the cycles eventually rises to the point where someone tries to kill someone else. The would-be murderer always runs afoul of his own plans, and Neal is always implicated. I think, now, that they look for Neal a bit too hard, hence they see his ghost in everything. If a bird flew over and a feather fell from a wing and caused the murderer to die of a sneezing fit, someone would note that some story had Neal possessing or shooting or admiring a bird like that."

"They find obscure facts to justify their fears."

"So it seems. These cycles tend to run one per generation and a half. In that time, enough people forget the consequences of the *last* one, and enough new people have come of age to imagine they can be just that one step smarter than any of their ancestors."

Gena frowned. "Do you think that is what Berengar is doing?"

"I don't know. I thought it possible, but two factors play against it. The first is the fact that he could have died in the ambush. He is no fool, and if he were as ambitious as those before him, he would never have put himself in the sort of danger he faced today. Moreover, he never would have allowed you, his key to success, to be risked."

Rik narrowed his eyes. "That line of thinking, of course, is new. What had made me think Berengar is being truthful is that the Riverens really *are* trading with the Haladina. There is a small Haladin section of town, and trade there is brisk. The Riverens hit upon a strategy that works perfectly for both the Haladina and themselves. The Riverens brought a number of Haladin artisans into the city and set them to the task of creating Haladin fabrics and jewelry with new fibers and materials. Whereas the Haladina had never seen silk before, their people are working with it now. As a result you can purchase a silk cloak woven and colored in traditional Haladin ways."

Gena smiled. "They have created a unique item that the Haladina themselves cannot produce on their own."

"And which Centisian artisans cannot easily match. The Riverens then gave a great deal of these products to their trading partners up and down the river. Because the items were rare and bestowed as gifts, they had an added value. They became very fashionable and highly sought after. The Riverens started selling these new wares and have a very hungry audience waiting for them.

"The net result is that the Riverens are slowly outstripping the Fishers. While the families were equal and united, Neal's vow helped maintain the balance. The alliance with the Haladina has given the Riverens an advantage. If the Riverens were to tell their trading partners that they will get no more Haladin wares unless they stop trading with the Fishers, the Fishers would be badly hurt."

"Why haven't the Riverens done this already?"

Rik spread both of his hands wide and shrugged. "I don't know. I believe Neal may be part of it—a couple of the Riveren elders are real metaphysicians, and they are arguing that cutting the Fishers off from trade would kill them, unleashing Neal's wrath upon the family. I suspect the Riverens will slowly start to cut off trade in small towns first and see what happens."

Gena finished the last of her wine, savoring the dryness. "If the Riverens are being that cautious with trade tactics, would they be pushing the Haladina to raid throughout Centisia?"

"That question assumes that the Riverens control the Haladina. The Haladina may be one people, but they spend more time fighting each other than they do fighting outsiders. The fact that Haladina are living in Aurdon may just have reminded others that the world does not end at the edge of their desert. While it is persuasive to suggest that the Haladina are raiding to help their kinsmen in the city, I have no evidence of that. Tomorrow, on the other hand, may change that whole situation."

"Tomorrow?"

"I'm going to look around in the Haladin district."

Dread coiled in her stomach. "Is that wise?"

"I am not worried." He jerked a thumb back over his shoulder at the bedside table. "The Haladin community is quite peaceful, and I have my flashdrakes to keep me out of trouble." He brought his hand down and tapped the ring Berengar had given him against the table. "And I even have the rank needed to keep them."

"I hope both keep you safe."

"I'd trust more in the flashdrakes than this rank." Rik smiled carefully. "Lord Orvir died in a riding accident four years ago. It happened about the time the Riverens had started trading with the Haladina. The Fishers claim he broke his neck when his horse didn't make it over a stone fence. They say he was being pursued by Haladin raiders. Others say he was riding away from Neal's ghost, an idea which carries with it a whole host of complications."

Gena reached out and caressed his cheek with her right hand. "You will be careful?"

Rik kissed her palm. "More so than you can even imagine."

A knock at the door interrupted what might otherwise have ended up in bed. As Gena rose to answer the door, Rik left through the passage into the adjoining suite. Swinging the door wide open, she invited Berengar in and waved him to a chair. "Wine?"

"No, thank you." The count looked around the room as he sat down, then rested the longgunne on the table. "Durriken is here, yes?"

Before she could reply, Rik returned from the other room wearing a pair of breeches and carrying a small cylindrical canvas parcel. "Good evening, my Lord." Rik set the parcel on the table and untied the string binding it shut. As he unrolled it, the weak candlelight reflected brightly from the silvery tools he revealed.

Gena lit and brought two candles to the table as Rik picked the gunne up and examined it. "There is a charge in the barrel, Rik. I quenched the fire with a spell."

"Ah, so it *did* work!" Setting the weapon down, Rik pulled a small flat-bladed screwdriver from one of the canvas pockets in his tool kit. Using it like a pry bar, he worked it under the strip of metal running over the barrel and around the stock. Warping the metal slightly, he managed to ease the band forward to where the stock narrowed; then it came off easily.

Rik asked Berengar to anchor the stock. Carefully jiggling the barrel, Rik loosened it and slid it from the groove cut into the stock. Keeping it tipped up so none of the powder would spill out, he freed it from the stock and indicated with a nod that the count could return the stock to the table. Rik lowered the barrel to the floor, muzzle first, and leaned it against the table.

He exchanged his screwdriver for a wooden probe that had been whittled flat at one end. He dug it into the breech end of the barrel and smiled. "Most of the charge is here. You worked very quickly, Gena."

"She saved my life."

"Possibly."

"I saw what happened. There is no question of it."

Rik nodded as he dug some of the unburned powder out of the barrel and placed it in the palm of his left hand. "Coarse ground and poorly mixed, with too much charcoal and not enough nitre." He flicked his hand toward one of the candles, and the mixture flashed as it flew through the flame. A white thread of smoke rolled up toward the ceiling while a few sparks landed on the other side of the candle. "At the range Gena described, the bullet would have hit you, but not terribly hard."

"You mean it might have gone halfway through, not all the way?"

"Exactly."

"Forgive me if I do not find that much comfort."

Rik laughed. "Forgive me for being so callous. I have undertaken a study of what effects flashdrakes have on their targets." He ran his thumbnail around inside the rim of the breech. "Just as well he had poor powder, the metal has started to fracture. One full charge or two and this gunne would have exploded."

Berengar smiled and looked up at Gena. "Is that not what I told you?"

"It is indeed, my lord."

"Which is precisely why we restrict these things here in Aurdon." The count tapped a finger against the gunne's silver butt-cap. "I gather you are not impressed with this weapon?"

"I believe you have archers who are more of a threat than anyone armed with one of these. It is poorly made and poorly supplied with powder. It is likely more a status symbol among the Haladina than anything else. Its being found in the possession of a Haladin raider would not alarm me, especially"—Rik nodded toward Gena—"with so able a mage as an ally."

The count smiled in agreement. "I already owe her my life. If things go as planned, my family and Aurdon will be in her debt as well."

Chapter 12

A City That Intrigues

Late Summer
Reign of the Red Tiger Year 1
Five Centuries Ago
My Thirty-fifth Year

Larissa's statement caught me by surprise and, in retrospect, should have sunk into my heart like a dagger. I am not entirely certain why it did not. I would have thought the giddy feeling in my chest would vanish, sucked down into a sinkhole of pain, but that did not happen. The good feeling lingered, blunted a bit, but still there, nourished by Larissa's smile and utter lack of deceptiveness.

A philosopher or poet would likely go on about his emotional turmoil, or agonize over the lack of same, were he in my position. I had already determined that we would never consummate our love. That physical union was unimportant to me and avoiding it the only way I could be certain that I would live and she would not be exiled by her own people. In light of such considerations, the fact that she was married made no difference at all. In fact, her marriage might even allow her greater freedom, since the idea that she would cuckold an Imperator with a Man had to be an outside possibility in the Sylvan mind.

I must also admit that the idea that Finndali's wife loved me was intriguing. Finndali and I lost no love upon each other, so any discomfort he felt when his wife was in my company would not bother me at all. If it ever turned out that I did not survive long enough to give Finndali an accounting of my scars, the scar that Larissa's love for me might leave on his heart would have to suffice as my revenge.

That sounds all cold and calculated. In fact all these thoughts flashed through my brain like ghosts through a haunted castle. Given my exhaustion and the fierce power of love for Larissa, the world had taken on an unreality that made me wonder if everything was a dream or a nightmare.

Larissa gave me no time for wondering. "Come along, Custos Sylvanii, you are awaited at Woodspire." She waved her left hand idly at the line of soldiers, and they parted like light drapes before a breeze. I smiled at Finndali, took away a scowl in the exchange, and followed Larissa.

A few steps beyond the line I caught up with her again. "I am surprised Finndali Imperator remembers me. We have met only a time or three, and the last meeting must have been a decade ago."

"The impression you created on those occasions has kept you fresh in his mind. In the same way, my brother's association with you—an obligation from which he was released after Tashayul's death—has caused a great deal of curiosity about you." She smiled easily as we moved into the towering groves that were Cygestolia. "There are those who believe you a powerful magus who has ensorcelled my brother into slavery."

"And what do you believe?"

"I believe my brother is shrewd in his judgments of Men and fortunate in his choice of friends."

Our conversation lapsed as we strolled into the city itself. Within its confines I learned the true immensity of the settlement. Trees bigger around than Man-castles predominated, and the city existed on a number of levels. Those whose occupations demanded easy access to the ground—farmers, herders, and soldiers, for example—were ensconced no more than thirty yards up. So the divisions progressed every thirty yards or so, with ascetics, philosophers, artists, and the mad dwelling so high up that their homes swayed in the breeze and brushed the moons at night.

When we reached Woodspire, it occurred to me that each of the massive trees was akin to a Man-lord's castle and the surrounding village, but instead of being spread out, it spread up and beyond. The other trees in that sector of the city were further holdings of the family who ruled the area, just as other villages within a fief were owned by the lord in charge of the county or barony.

We entered Woodspire at an opening between two roots. The narrow entrance belied the enormity of the hollow within the tree. Inside, in a wooden cavern that towered a good twenty feet above the ground, horses had been stabled and even some pigs had been penned. Elves moved to and fro from the tree's core. Around the edges of the cavern, where the floor had been dug down about ten feet below ground level outside, I saw tunnels into which grooms and swineherds were carting manure, presumably to help sustain Woodspire.

As we entered, I wondered how such a huge tree could survive with such a hollow at its base, but a moment's observation answered that question for me. The first thing I saw was that a central cylinder rose from the earth to support the heart of the tree. Since trees grow from the heart out, as long as the center had not been worked or worn away, the tree could continue living and growing. Given the size of Woodspire, the hollow's presence clearly had not hurt it.

The tree's exterior had the normal amount of bark one would expect on a titanic pine. The interior surface of the tree had developed a thinner, almost transparent bark that sealed and protected it. The faint stickiness I felt when I ran my hand over it made me mindful of sap or varnish, and the inner bark also reminded me of birch-bark because of how it curled up in a couple of spots.

Larissa noticed my interest in the tree's interior surface

as we walked toward the central core. "The trees are maintained by two groups: the woodwives and woodwrights. The former use their skills to heal damage done by pest, storm, or disease to the trees. With their skills and magicks they help the tree repair itself. The woodwrights shape the tree and coax it into all manner of shapes and configurations. Where a stonemason might carve a gargoyle from a block of stone, a woodwright facilitates growth into that same sort of pattern."

As she spoke, we drew closer to the central core of the tree. "Woodspire is two thousand years old and has been possessed by my family for all that time. It is not the eldest of holdings in Cygestolia, but it is one of the most elegant." She smiled carefully. "And the first to host a Man."

She stopped before one of many cylinders faintly visible through the crystal-bark. Where she touched the core, a dark circle began to spread out. It grew as wide as the cylinder, then extended up and down about half again that distance, forming a lozenge-shaped opening into the cylinder. Above and below, floor and ceiling, I saw amber disks. She stepped through the opening and onto a disk and I followed her example. Despite the cramped surroundings I managed to refrain from touching her.

Larissa caressed the interior of the cylinder, and it closed down. I immediately began to feel uncomfortable and cramped—though her presence did render the experience tolerable. When the opening closed completely, I felt a lurch, then we slowly began to move upward. Raising my right arm, I rapped a knuckle against the ceiling, then smiled at Larissa. "This is crystallized pitch."

She nodded, with a sly grin on her lips. "As your body has veins and arteries, so a tree has tubes through which sap moves up and down. Woodwife magick makes it possible to move within these tubes. We do have a stairway worked in the bark on the outside, but I thought you would find this more interesting."

"Indeed." I stood up again. "So are you a woodwife?"

"No, though there is nothing ignoble about that profession. My gifts are directed elsewhere—I am a healer."

"Of animals?"

"Of living creatures, though I prefer mammals to lizards and fish. Had I been there when you collected any of your wounds, you would not have scarred."

"Ah, but I collect scars the way others collect scalps or prizes. They are my *mementii bellicus.* When it takes time to heal, one has more to remember." I shrugged. "Besides, were you to touch me to heal me, I would be slain, so your handiwork would be wasted."

"Your point is well-taken." She laughed lightly. "I will then offer my skills only if your horse or the Dreel needs them."

"Your generosity is most kind and welcome."

Our ascent through the tree slowed and stopped. Another hole opened in the tube to allow us egress. When we left it, the cylinder in which we had traveled slowly dissolved. The ceiling liquefied and descended toward the floor. It melted away and rose up. Between them the twin liquid fronts expelled the air from the tube. The inner bark sealed itself over, and I found myself in a circular chamber with a slightly rounded floor and a towering dome vault above.

Lozenge doorways opened out of the two chamber walls, defined on either side by dark bands within the wood. I knew that they allowed access to other chambers within the flesh of the tree, because I would have to cross against growth-ring lines to reach the exterior, whereas moving with them as they curved through the wood would keep me on the same ring within the tree.

The woodwright's art is reflected in the two dominant features of Sylvan architecture. Curves are everywhere. While a Man would have created a room as a square, here they were shaped from circles and cylinders, ovoids and capsules. The same sort of twists and curves that gnarl trees are reflected in the curious branching of corridors or eccentric curves of alcoves and hideaways. As I followed Larissa from the entry chamber through the turns of the corridors, I marveled at the artistry of the woodwright who had shaped it, but I was thinking that I was being worked deep into a maze I could never unravel.

Woodwrights shape both the flesh of the tree in which they live and wood that is used for furnishings. Because of this it is possible to find in a white-pine chamber a full set of redwood furnishings. Woods are even fitted together so that a cherry panel provides trim, or oak defines a doorway in a cedar home. And, again, woodwrights are not limited to simple concerns of functionality: ebony and cedar might easily be combined to create a tiger stalking through a room. All those decorations for which men use paint, woodwrights accomplish with a rainbow of woods.

Nowhere did I see metal worked into the wood for utilitarian or decorative purposes. Shelving and hinges were grown in. Except where a polished silver mirror hung in an alcove or an object of antiquity stood on a pedestal grown up out of the floor, all the metal I saw came in the form of jewelry on the Elves.

Interior lighting came from small alcoves and channels at the upper reaches of the walls, where luminous mosses glowed and splashed their light across the ceiling. In larger chambers the same mosses were grown behind thin veneers of wood to illuminate designs or just to provide more light. While I did not feel any heat from the light, the whole dwelling place felt warm.

Larissa led me to a grand chamber easily ten yards high and half again that wide. Vaulting arches linked fluted columns grown out of the walls, providing an illusory strength that made me comfortable. I knew that the whole tree was quite solid, but seeing features that I easily recognized both put me at ease and made me wonder, somehow, if they had been produced for my benefit. Given the way they would have to have been created, I decided they were not created for me alone.

That thought collided with another immediately. Larissa said I was the first Man to set foot in Cygestolia. I had no doubt she had told the truth, which meant her family had planned, at some point, to create a room that a Man would find familiar. The only reason to do that would be to welcome a Man into their home. This made them unlike most Elves, but I knew that from my association with both Aarundel and Larissa.

A trio of Elves waited in the room to greet me. Larissa set her basket down on an oaken table, then curtsied formally. She spoke to them in Elven first, then turned toward me and smiled. "These are my parents: Thralan Consilliarii and my lady-mother Ashenah. And that is my grandfather, Lomthelgar."

I bowed to Ashenah first, then to the two Sylvans. I took a chance and bowed to Lomthelgar first, then Larissa's father. The older Sylvan chuckled and commented in Elven, but I could not understand him. Thralan returned my bow formally, then smiled at me.

"The respect you have shown my father reflects well upon you."

"It is but a fraction of the respect I hold for Aarundel."

It took both of them a moment to decipher what I said. Their not being used to Mantongue was less a problem than my using the name Aarundel to refer to their son and grandson. Because of the magick inherent in names, and the magickal trouble that can be wrought if one knows a person's name, Elves who travel the world, or who traffick with people outside their own family, adopt a new name for their journeys and affairs. That much Aarundel had told me, but he had not revealed to me his true name. In fact, I did not even know his family name.

Aarundel's parents looked to be only slightly older than Larissa and her brother. Their flesh appeared as seamless as Larissa's, and neither her father's golden hair nor the jet-black of her mother showed any hints of white creeping in. Their age, which I put at five centuries, only revealed itself in their calm grace and formality.

I would not have known even where to begin to look for signs of physical aging were it not for the presence of Lomthelgar. His skin had started to take on the consistency of crystal-bark. The lines in his face gathered around the corners of his eyes and stacked up on his forehead, though an unruly mop of iron-gray hair half hid many of them. His dark eyes remained bright and watched me carefully, but I sensed no suspicion or distrust in his attention.

Thralan nodded easily after a moment. "Our son is quite impressed with you—as evidenced by his bringing you here. This room will be yours to use during your stay here. The daybed there in the corner should serve you well. Behind the screen is the *lavabrium*, where you may attend to your personal needs."

"Thank you."

Ashenah smiled graciously at me. "We will leave you now so you may sleep. We know how tiring travel can be."

"You are most kind."

As they left the room, the weight of weariness crushed down upon me. I dragged myself over to the daybed and tugged my boots off. I lay down for just a moment, because I fully intended to wash before sleeping, but found I could not rise again. Sleep came swiftly, and I surrendered to it heart and soul.

His breath only slightly sweeter than when we left Aurium, Shijef awakened me. "They come." I heard no urgency in his voice, but his prodding me with Cleaveheart's hilt suggested trouble.

I shook my head to clear away the last of the sleep-dregs. "How did you get here?"

"Here you were, here I came. Climbed, did I." Suddenly self-conscious, he chewed at some sap matting fur between the pads of his left forepaw. "At the master's feet the slave is supposed to be. And bring things."

Concerned by the fact that in my half-awake state Dreel logic made sense, I sat up just in time for Ashenah and Lomthelgar to enter the room. The old Elf immediately dropped to his haunches to study the Dreel at eye level, while Ashenah looked at me above both of them. "You must prepare yourself. You are to appear before the Consilliarii." When I did not move immediately, she added, "My son needs you."

I vaulted over Shijef's shoulder and slipped behind the screen Thralan had indicated earlier. In the small cylindrical enclosure I found a pedestal topped with a basin of water, a larger wooden cistern suitable for bathing, and what looked to be an ingrown lidded bucket for collecting night soil. Lifting the lid, I saw the bucket had a bottom made of amber just as had the conveyance that brought us up from the ground. I made use of the device, then washed quickly in the basin.

Returning to my chamber, I found that Ashenah had gone away and the Dreel and Lomthelgar had reached enough of a rapprochement to allow the elder Elf an opportunity to pick through the luggage the Dreel had brought for me. Lomthelgar tossed me a blue tunic Aarundel had bought me in Polston and another pair of trousers.

"Appropriate."

I nodded and quickly dressed myself. "Why the urgency?"

"You are a Man." He shrugged. "And not a Man."

Lomthelgar's words came easily enough that I knew he could have spoken volumes, but preferred to keep his own counsel. "I'm ready. Are you leading the way?"

"Yes." He popped up to his feet and headed off into the corridor maze with a speed that belied what I would have expected from someone old enough to be Aarundel's grandfather. Lomthelgar had to be at least three quarters of a millennium old, yet he moved with the speed of someone much younger. Even knowing that Elves do not age as do Men, I did not expect to be led by an Elf who forced me to hurry.

Lomthelgar led me from Woodspire out along a huge branch to where it braided together with another tree. Elves shied from me as if I were a leper while we passed, but a certain number of them drifted in our wake as if unable to escape the current of our passage. I found it amusing, and I sensed the old Elf did as well. Shijef snarled, growled, and barked at those who followed us too closely, which put him in as happy a state as I had seen since he killed the Haladina in the forest.

We went from one tree to another toward the center of Cygestolia. In no time we passed over the lake to the trees grown together on the islands. Once through the initial outer foliage screen I could see a massive bowl-shaped depression in the heart of one tree. Branches led up and out from around it, and we traveled along one toward it. Other branches had been woven together above and around the circle to provide for a spectator's gallery, which appeared to be slowly filling.

Below us Elves crowded the bowl and argued loudly. Had I seen stalls and wares, I would have thought myself looking at a marketplace. Without evidence of mercantilism, I was left only one other guess. "The *legislatorium*?"

Lomthelgar nodded. "It is good that you are such a quick thinker."

"Why?"

"My grandson has announced to the Consilliarii that he has chosen you to be his *vindicator.* He would have you stand with him during the nuptial ceremonies."

I frowned. "And that has inspired such a heated debate?"

"No. You see, Neal Roclawzi, the *vindicator* must dance with the *vindicatrix*—in this case Larissa. The dance would require you to touch her." The elder Elf looked down at the assembly. "The debate is over whether or not they should wait for the crime to occur, or should just kill you now."

Chapter 13

A Sylvanesti amid the Councils of Aurdon

Early Spring
A.R. 499
The Present

Awakening alone for the second time in two days disappointed Gena. After Berengar had left them, she and Rik had made love. She had felt a desperate need to be with him and to share his strength. As always he had been kind and attentive and had focused far more on her needs than on meeting his own. Rik had purposely told her to lie back and ignore him, while making the latter half of that directive impossible.

Ecstasy had boiled up and over in her, leaving her flushed and exhausted. She remembered sleepily having told Rik that she would reciprocate in the morning. He had laughed and hugged her, and she realized now that he had known how truly tired she was. A glance over at the window showed her the sun already positioned for midmorning.

Groaning, she closed her eyes again, then pulled Rik's pillow to her. She crushed it to her chest, jamming her nose down into it to drink in his scent. Her groan shifted to a sigh and ended with a little laugh. "Good hunting, my hero, and hurry back," she whispered, "for I am in your debt and wish to discharge it promptly."

A timid knock at the door made Gena pull the sheet up around herself. "Come."

The seamstress's apprentice Phaelis pushed the door open with a hip as she hefted two steaming buckets of water into the room. "Begging your pardon, m'lady, but the count was hoping you would be joining him for a noontide audience with the Fisher Elders?"

Gena recalled Berengar saying he thought the entire Fisher family council would want to hear her story. "It would be my pleasure."

"I will inform the count of that, then. And would you be wanting some breakfast, yes?"

"I would."

Phaelis disappeared back out the door, having left the buckets in the middle of the floor, but Gena only laughed to herself. While waking up alone was not how she would have preferred to start the day, the residue of the previous night's lovemaking had left her in a giddy, goofy mood that had been utterly alien to her life within Cygestolia—and comfortably familiar since her association with Durriken. She knew many reactionary Elves would have thought her conduct demeaning to all the *sylvanesti,* and that just made it that much more attractive.

Gena labored under no illusions that Rik was somehow her *vitamora.* Finding a True Love was considered more of a miracle than anything else, and finding it among Men all but impossible. Having seen her grandparents together, she suspected that having a *vitamora* could come close to providing mood elevation on an almost constant basis. While she assumed she would find that almost intolerable, the closeness of her grandparents was something she very much hoped she would one day experience.

She also realized the chances of her dream coming true were small, so she took her pleasure where she could find it. Because of their long lives and the very real possibility of alienation between partners, Elven marriages were more for alliances between families than any enshrinement of sentiment. Liaisons between people who found themselves infatuated with each other were not forbidden, and with children coming by choice and not by accident, carnal pleasures became a gift to be shared, not property with restrictions placed upon it.

Gena knew her relationship with Rik would not last forever. At the very least she would outlive him by centuries, and that very fact frightened many *sylvanesti* away from even considering a human as lover. They saw as a tragedy the investment of emotions in any relationship that might be terminated after only twenty or thirty years. Gena knew, and Rik had reinforced the idea over and over again, that perspective might not make twenty years or twenty minutes seem very long, but existing in that place and that time could make it seem like forever. With Rik she had enjoyed enough "forever" moments to make the inevitable loss more than worth it.

Phaelis returned, rolling the bathing cask into the room. She wormed it between the two buckets without causing them to spill, then set it up in the corner. Emptying the two buckets into it, she nodded and headed out for more water. She came back quickly enough with more, and after a half-dozen more trips had filled the cask to a suitable bathing depth.

Genevera slipped into the bath and allowed the woman to wash her back. As Phaelis did this, she nattered on about all sorts of court gossip, including the latest news about Lady Martina. Gena made all the properly attentive noises, which kept Phaelis talking. Though Gena did not really know any of the people being talked about, she found it fascinating that news of liaisons that would have been treated matter-of-factly among her people were scandal-fodder among Men.

It is not surprising that some of us find them so venial, so easy to dismiss.

As Gena dressed, Phaelis went off and prepared her a breakfast. She brought back a small loaf of fresh bread, some cheese, and two apples that had been put up before the winter. The first apple proved a bit mealy, so Gena followed it with most of the bread. The second apple tasted better, and she used a bit of the cheese as spice for it.

Wearing black breeches and an emerald-green tunic

belted at her waist, Gena followed the servant sent for her by Count Berengar. The man led her through the mansion's hallways and to a large room nearly twice as long as it was wide. The ceiling, which had frescoes decorating it, rose up to the height of fifteen feet or so. False arches and marble pillars marked off the side walls in six separate groups, with paintings depicting mythological battles framed within the sections.

Four tables had been arranged in the room. Three, each eighteen feet in length and made of stout oak, had been arranged to form half a hexagon facing the door. The last table, which was smaller and made of darkly stained maple, faced the central table directly. Count Berengar sat at it while older men occupied places behind the other three.

Berengar stood as Gena entered and pointed her to the chair next to his. "Thank you for coming. I will need you to verify what I report about our encounter yesterday." He dropped his voice into an apologetic whisper. "My elders are all sticklers for detail. Last night I spoke with key members, but now everyone wants to hear what happened. They all *know,* but *all* must hear."

"I understand."

Berengar gave her a smile, then turned to face the man seated in the tallest chair. "If it pleases *all* my Lords, I have grave news."

The gray-haired, long-bearded man Gena remembered from the reception as being Berengar's granduncle Kellin nodded. "Proceed."

"Yesterday, not much past this time, I led Lady Genevera into a Haladin campsite. My cousin Waldo had preceded us with a patrol, and we found evidence at the campsite of a hasty retreat by the Haladina. We assumed that Waldo and the Seventh Rangers had scared the raiders off. Unbeknownst to us, the raiders doubled back and a dozen of them ambushed us. If not for the very powerful magicks Lady Genevera employed, I would be dead and my men would have died along with me. Because of her intervention, our forces suffered only minor injuries while slaying all of the Haladina."

As he spoke, Count Berengar moved in front of the table and imploringly put his case to his Elders. Gena heard passion in his voice and watched emotions knot his fists. While telling the Elders that she had saved his life, his tall, strong bearing and swift hand motions left no question that had she not been there, the Haladina would have paid a dear price for taking his life.

"There is no question, my Lords, that Haladin activity has continued to increase in Centisia. Lady Genevera and her companion drove Haladin raiders from a caravan, and we all know that such predation is more common than any of us would care to admit. We also know that the Riveren's harboring of Haladina here in Aurdon means that both our enemies have united. The Riveren are employing the Haladina to destroy us. This is a technique Neal Roclawzi did not anticipate—had he done so, the Haladina would be facing a foe more implacable than our Rangers."

Gena recalled Rik's explanation of local politics. While she admitted to herself that Berengar was probably correct in his assessment of the situation, she wanted to hear from Rik concerning the conditions and dispositions of people in the Haladin neighborhoods of Aurdon. Everything she had heard and seen so far did seem to indicate that the Riveren were working counter to what Neal had forced upon them back in the days of her grandfather's travels. If everything were as Berengar presented it, then Neal's vow was working against Neal's intentions.

One of the Elders, a man with only a little white distributed through his brown hair, frowned at Berengar. "You have dealt with the problem at the campsite, yes?"

"Yes, but that is dousing a spark when a fire rages."

The leader of the Elders held up a hand. "Berengar, Theobold, you both are racing toward a discussion that is, as yet, built on nothing." That quieted the two of them, so he turned his gaze on Gena. "Lady Genevera, did the events unfold as Berengar related them?"

"Yes, Duke Kellin. A dozen of the raiders ambushed us."

"Was there provocation?"

Gena frowned. "Aside from our being in their camp? No, unless you consider the apparent fact that they recognized and concentrated upon killing Count Berengar. This is not to say that they were sent specifically to assassinate him, but they did focus their efforts on him."

Berengar nodded quickly. "And just as they recognized me, they could recognize any of you, or your children, or servants. We are at war—there is no mistaking that."

Theobold shook his head. "If we are at war, then we must do as you have done and destroy those who attack us. In this case, that is the Haladina."

The count laughed. "You argue that killing the arrows is justified, but killing the archer is not?"

"You have yet to prove to me who the archer is!" Theobold looked over at Kellin. "My Lord, Berengar once again suggests that we are threatened with harm by the Riveren Clan when we do not know this is true. We have discussed all this before. Even if his argument is true, Neal will prevent us from striking back, so all of this is futile speculation."

"It was, until now!" Berengar turned back to look at Gena, and she saw triumph burning in his eyes. "Lady Genevera has indicated that it is possible to recover Cleaveheart and Wasp. With them, severing the knot and breaking the hollow vow is possible. I believe this is vital if we are to survive and prove victorious over Riveren perfidy. It is not a question of aggression, but of defending ourselves."

He pointed at Theobold. "As my uncle has so aptly noted, we have no proof that the Riveren are not working against us. I would suggest that giving me your blessing to undertake recovery of Neal's weapons will not precipitate problems. While I am gone, and I would expect to be gone for the summer at the very least, we can undertake a study of who is aiding the Haladina who prey upon us. If the Riveren are guilty, then we will deal with them. If not, Cleaveheart has drunk Haladin blood before, and I will not be averse to bringing Neal's brand of war to them in our defense."

Berengar had lowered his voice and strung the words together mellifluously. His audience, save one, clearly appreciated the way he had worked around Theobold's suggestion that he was out to precipitate trouble. Gena could see how the other merchants took to heart Berengar's point that his mission would benefit them no matter who proved to be behind the Haladin raids. Even Theobold seemed to consider the expedition seriously, though Gena thought that might be because it would remove Berengar from Aurdon for a time.

She smiled to herself. *Perhaps Theobold is the mastermind Rik is looking for.*

Kellin stroked his beard, then looked up at her. "Lady Genevera, is it possible to recover these weapons?"

"I believe it is, my Lord. I do not know where the sword actually *is,* but I know some of the places it is not. Count Berengar might be generous in suggesting he would have it by the summer, but by the end of the summer I believe we would know where it is."

Kellin nodded slowly. "I am inclined to send you off on your hunt, nephew, but there are details to be worked out amongst the elders here." The man broke off as the chamber door opened and a breathless servant ran in. "What is it?"

The servant fell to his knees before the duke. "Forgive me, sire, but there has been a murder."

"Who?"

"Lord Orvir."

Theobold shot from his chair. "Rattlebrain, Lord Orvir has been dead for years!"

"No, my Lords, not Berengar's brother, the new Lord Orvir." He turned and looked back at Gena, sending a jolt through her. "You know, the man what came with her. The thief. The Haladina have killed him dead."

Chapter 14

A Man amid the Councils of Cygestolia

Late Summer
Reign of the Red Tiger Year 1
Five Centuries Ago
My Thirty-fifth Year

The debate dulled a bit as Lomthelgar led me down into the heart of the bowl. I gravitated toward Aarundel, who flashed me a quick smile before anger recaptured his features. His father stood beside him wearing anger and parental concern in about equal amounts on his face. The Dreel padded behind me, but rose up on his rear feet to tower above and around me as if he were to me what a hood is to a cobra.

For my part, I felt a glacier moving through my guts. Save Aarundel, his family, and Shijef, I'd nary a friend in the *legislatorium* or the galleries above it. Finndali appeared to be a focal point for Aarundel, and the argument raged between them, sibilantly thrust and parried in the Sylvan tongue at a rate far faster than I could ever have understood. Hate-filled glances at me needed no translation, however, and Jammaq began to seem positively friendly in comparison to Cygestolia.

Lomthelgar's silver eyes narrowed; then he smiled in a world-weary way. "Finndali argues that, as a Man, you will dishonor his wife, so you must die now to save her. Ryslard and Stisel say that because you are a beast, you cannot be *vindicator*." He canted his head to the side. "My grandson is more a warrior than a politician."

And he is quicker than I am. Even as I thought that, the two lines of attack laid themselves out in my brain in very simple terms. The Beast argument simply wanted to block me from the nuptials. If successful it would embarrass Aarundel for his choice, and probably do some damage to Thralan's position as one of the Consilliarii. That attack, then, was directed more at him than at me.

Finndali's case bored in on me completely. If I were to touch Larissa, as one tradition demanded and another forbade, I would die and she would be exiled. Aside from the dislike that had sprung up between us so long ago, Finndali stood a good chance of losing his wife. As wars have been fought and murders plotted to prevent the same, his action here made a lot of sense. That it also fed his anti-Human hatreds made Finndali's stand that much more palatable to him.

The thing was, of course, that the two arguments tripped each other up. I raised a hand. "Might the target of this discussion speak?"

A *sylvanesti* in gold-cloth robes, seated in a throne grown up from the base of the floor, shook her head. "You have no standing here. You will be silent."

Lomthelgar stepped out of my shadow. "Calarianne, I would speak."

"I recognize . . . Lomthelgar Consilliarii emeratus."

The old Elf opened his mouth, but only a sharp, crow-like caw emerged. Clutching at his throat, he coughed, then whispered hoarsely, "My voice is gone. Neal Custos Sylvanii will speak for me." He slapped me on the shoulder with surprising strength and propelled me a step forward.

"Begging your pardons all, I'm gathering that there are two cases being raised against me. The first is that I'm a beast—no better than the horse I rode in on or the Dreel standing aback of me. I figure I could ask you all to examine the record of my dealings with Aarundel or with other Sylvan warriors, and we could start with Finndali Imperator and work on through the honor guard you sent to bring Aarundel here for his wedding. What they said, though, would be argued as opinion, having no weight, and therefore, I'm thinking, would be dismissed out of hand."

I tried to keep my voice low, and I purposely picked words that came more from Mantongue than had been brought over from the Elven. I wanted them thinking me simple so they could underestimate me. From Aarundel I had learned that Elves are fiercely proud but intellectually honest, and the latter trait overrides the first when they collide. I admired that, sought to do the same, and to make it save me in this instance.

"There is a more simple proof, however, and you all know of it. The fact is that Lady Larissa, being a healer as she is, could minister to my horse, the Dreel, a bull, or a ram and not suffer for it at all. Were she to touch me, even by accident in the course of her duties, I would be slain and she would be exiled. So, while there is no penalty for treating a male animal, a male Man is a different thing. In fact, that is the core of Finndali's very argument, so you cannot endorse his argument without disallowing the beast argument."

I saw a number of heads being nodded and whispers being exchanged, which I took as a good sign. Aarundel's face had brightened considerably, which helped buoy my spirits. A glance back over my shoulder showed me both Lomthelgar and the Dreel had crouched to their haunches and were chattering back and forth—the idea of their plotting anything together bothered me—but neither of them appeared to be displeased with my performance so far.

I looked over at Finndali. "The problem is, of course, that you also cannot endorse Finndali Imperator's argument without endorsing the animal argument. It assumes that while I am more than an animal—in accord with your laws—that I cannot think on a level higher than that of an animal. I know that to touch any *sylvanesti* will cost me my life, and despite being here, I'm not looking forward to the day I stop breathing. Moreover, I've promised Finndali to turn my sword over to him in thirty years, and that's a promise I mean to keep.

"I am *not* an animal, so I can understand your laws and I can abide by them." I pointed off vaguely in the direction of the setting sun. "There are lands out there in which I have observed and lived within all number of laws and traditions. Among the Najindese, for example, I did not eat *atalatha* fish despite having grown up fishing for and eating them in the Roclaws. According to the Najindese the fish will cause your soul to wander the rivers upon death, so they don't eat it. Though I did not share that belief, I respected it."

Finndali shook his head. "Your sensitivity to the mores and laws of other Men does you credit, Neal Roclawzi, but it does not change the fact that our mores and traditions require the *vindicator* to dance with the *vindicatrix* or the nuptials are invalid. If you touch her, you will harm her, and our law allows us to take action to prevent the willful harming of one party by another."

"So you will kill me?" I shook my head. "I'm thinking sending me out of Cygestolia would be an easier solution."

Larissa's husband shrugged his shoulders. "Ah, within our traditions a wedding is a time for all strife to be put aside, so exiling a guest is not permitted."

"But killing him is?"

"The law is the law."

"As it is in other places." I glanced furtively at Aarundel and kept a smile on my face. "In the Roclaws, as Aarundel Imperator can attest, we, too, can be circumspect concerning contact between men and women. For example, we have a dance, the kerchief dance, in which men and women are allowed only one link: a kerchief stretched taut between them. It is a dance that requires skill, for any slackening of the kerchief is considered bad form. Even so, it is a powerful dance and one that would honor your nuptial ceremony."

Our years of association allowed Aarundel to pick up on the fact that I had just lied through my teeth. "I have seen it. Neal is quite good at it, in fact."

Finndali shook his head. "Man-dances mean nothing. At your wedding the *torris* will be danced. The *torris* includes touching, therefore Neal will harm Larissa, therefore he must die."

My head came up. "The dance *includes* touching? What if we were to dance it *without* touching?"

Finndali's eyes widened at my suggestion. "You might slip."

"But I tell you that I will not. I tell you that I have no *intention* of slipping."

"If you touch her, you will harm her."

I smiled. "But you may slay me beforehand only *if* you know I *intend* to do Larissa harm. I have told you that I do not intend to do her harm. I know my place. I understand your laws. I would not hurt her because it would hurt my friend and his family to have her exiled." I thumped my right fist against my chest. "I'd sooner rip my own heart out than harm her."

Finndali's eyes smoldered. "If you touch her, *I* will rip your heart out."

"And I will bare my breast to you to do so." I pulled myself up to my full height. "That is all immaterial, however, because you cannot kill me for intentions I do not harbor. *That* is your law."

The *legislatorium* erupted in a legion of Sylvan voices. I heard a lot of things, including Lomthelgar's chuckling, but above them I heard Aarundel's voice as he shouted down the opposition to his wedding plans. "There, you have all heard it from Neal's own lips. He is a Man and he knows his place. Yes, he is my friend, and I have proclaimed him Custos Sylvanii, but he is not so unwise as to arrogate himself. He would never think himself worthy of any *sylvanesti,* let alone my sister. He understands and respects the gulf between us, he respects our culture as we should respect his. Do not let your prejudice blind you or make him into a monster who would despoil our *sylvanesti.* He is a Man, a wise Man, and would not dare dream of dragging one of us down to his level by visiting abominable acts upon her."

Aarundel's words sank arrowlike into my heart and pinned it painfully to my spine. I understood everything he said, and I knew how he meant it, but somehow I had never expected to hear such things from his lips. In the time we had traveled together—an eye blink for him, but my entire adult life—I had grown closer to him than any other living being, even my brother. We had shared good times and bad. We had fought side by side, staunched each other's wounds, and done insane things to save each other from situations that were beyond reasonable hope.

If I had a sister, I would have thought nothing of marrying Aarundel off to her. The person I knew him to be came first, his race came later. I did not think of him as an Elf, but as my friend, my confidant, my co-conspirator. I would have been proud to have him in my family, and for that reason, I was filled with pride when we set off on our journey to Cygestolia.

Because I thought of him as my equal, I assumed the reverse was true.

His curiously split attitude slammed me in the face. Here he was willing to put his reputation and his honor on the line in arguing before the Consilliarii that I should be allowed to be his *vindicator*. In doing that he openly proclaimed me his best friend, a person in whom he had no doubts. He trusted me and honored me with the selection, and that honor and trust I held dear.

Yet, at the same time, among his own people he set me apart. He held me at arm's length. He praised me and honored me above all of the Sylvan Nation by his choice, yet he still felt it was right and suitable to point out that I was still just a Man.

More's the pity, he likely did not know he had done anything to hurt me.

Worse yet, I was thinking, I held similarly conflicting views of other Men, including some in my command.

Calarianne stood. "The argument offered by Lomthelgar is correct and persuasive. We are not the Reithrese. We do not revel in morbidity. Executing the Man for a crime he has not committed and has no intention of committing would be an act of veneration for the Dark Goddess. We shall not be party to such action."

She looked over at Aarundel. "Your selection for *vindicator* stands. You will be well represented."

Lomthelgar popped up from his crouch and spryly stepped closer to the center of the chamber than where I stood. "Listen well, for this is the First Time: as another's voice, he speaks for himself."

That announcement, which I could not understand, started a new debate, and I found myself wanting to be away from all the noise and the voices. I worked my way to the right to where—as I had seen from above when entering the *legislatorium*—I could gain access to a stairway spiraling down the massive oak that held the seat of Sylvan government. I wanted very much to be alone, and, by chance or out of fear, I met no one as I traveled to the ground.

The stairs were long, and I managed to do a lot of thinking on the trip to the island below. The island itself was deserted, and sitting there between two small rootlets of the grand tree, I managed a lot more thinking. I didn't like all of it, but I've found that when you finally sit down to do the thinking that must be done, chances are there's not much of it that will make you smile.

"I have been told what my brother said. I am grieved."

I looked up at where she stood with one hand still on the bark banister of the stairway. "Why? He said what he saw as the truth."

"But you have been hurt by it."

I gathered my knees to my chest with my arms and smiled without looking into her eyes. "The hurt was in the hearing and because of what the words have made me think about. It is difficult to discover you have been deceiving yourself."

Larissa walked away from the trunk of the tree, then settled herself on the ground two body lengths away from me. She arranged her skirts delicately, and I drank in the beauty of her until I realized how dangerous it could be. As if sensing my thoughts, she deflected me with a question. "How is it that you consider yourself deceptive, when I have heard nothing from my brother or you to indicate this is so?"

I tightened the grip of my hands on the opposite forearms. "When I left the Roclaws two decades ago, I left with nothing but the horse between my legs, the clothes on my body, and the blade at my belt. I wanted it that way. I wanted nothing—not because I was spurning my homeland or because I hated my family. I wanted nothing so that all I did, all I became would be because of *me.* I wanted to be different, not burdened with possessions and titles and lands. I just wanted to be Neal Roclawzi, a warrior known across the face of Skirren for the things I had done."

"An admirable goal, and one you have accomplished."

"An admirable goal, but one I have not attained." I shook my head. "I own little more than my horse, my armor, my weapons—and I thought I had succeeded. Here, however, I have learned that I have acquired many things that I didn't realize I had gathered, and I realize that I have wanted many other things."

I tipped my head back and looked up toward the *legislatorium.* "Up there I learned that I had acquired an inflated view of myself. I learned that I wanted to be considered an equal by your brother and your people, and I realize that I was foolish or vain enough to think I was worthy of such consideration."

"You *are.*"

"Thank you for saying that, but yours is a minority opinion." I bit back pain. "The damnable thing is that your opinion is the only one that really matters to me right now."

I wanted to reach out to her, take her and hug her, to leech serenity and warmth from her, but I stopped myself. "Aside from wanting to be elevated to standing within an elder race, I find I also want you, but total success in that regard will be fatal."

Larissa smiled slightly and blushed, then plucked at a piece of clover growing amid the grasses. "You heap upon yourself too many burdens, Neal Roclawzi, and you do not take stock of your successes. You *are* the first Man ever to walk in Cygestolia. You *are* the first Man ever to be accorded the honor of being a *vindicator.* You *are* the first Man ever to argue within the *legislatorium* and the first to win a victory there."

"But all of those things are an offshoot of my being the first to visit."

"However, the fact of your visit did not bring with it

any of the others. Those are mantles you have won, and no one will ever take them away from you." She closed her right hand into a fist. "Ten of your generations from now there will still be Consilliarii in the *legislatorium* who will remember you and your words."

She rose onto her knees and leaned forward; her long-fingered white hands sank deep in the greensward to steady her. "To you, to the rest of the world, the Sylvan Nation appears to have one mind and one voice. It is defined for you in the verses of the *Eldsaga*. We are a cold, superior people who place no value on Humanity. This is how most Men see us, and it is not without good reason that they do so. Half a millennium ago our troops marched forth to destroy the fledgling empire your ancestors had created. My grandfather has told me tales of that time, horrible, brutal tales. Through them I know why Men fear us, and because of them I admire your courage in coming here and your bravery in befriending my brother.

"My family is not like all others here. The chamber in which you sleep was built nearly four centuries ago when Lomthelgar ordered it fashioned after the halls and castles he had seen and razed. While others crusading through the *Eldsaga* saw Men as half-witted beasts whose civilization was nothing but a crude imitation of our own, my grandfather felt the truth was otherwise. Others looked at the things that were similar between Elves and Men, then decried Men for being unable to match us—making us superior and consigning Men to inferiority. My grandfather looked at the *differences* and used them to mark Man's creativity. He fashioned your chamber in homage to what he had seen, and as physical proof of his vow to get all of us to see in Mankind what he did."

Passion and bitterness wove through her words as she explained things to me. "Though we were taught that Men were worthy of respect, that is not what made my brother respect you enough to bring you here and make you his *vindicator*. You *earned* that respect in his eyes. You have proved to him that Lomthelgar was right. In your argument in the *legislatorium*, you proved to many others that at least one Man is capable of thought and worthy of respect."

I nodded briefly. "But not worthy of his sister?"

Larissa clutched her hands together over her heart. "I cannot tell you that *I* would consider you worthy of any *sylvanesti* if I did not feel the love for you that I do in my heart. If my brother had come home with a woman he had won, I cannot say that I would welcome her. Inasmuch as my feelings for you conflict with how I would treat another Man and a *sylvanesti* being together, I know the attitudes that would condemn them are wrong. Because they are wrong, I know I must change them, but change does not come immediately.

"As much as I want to go over to you and embrace you, I will not and cannot." Frustration seaming her brow, she frowned heavily. "I know the laws that keep us apart are wrong, but to flaunt them also seems wrong and would serve no purpose but to have you terminated and me exiled. Others would point to us as an example not of an injustice, but of justice done because we proved ourselves unable to respect the laws of society."

Everything she said bored into my chest through the wound Aarundel's words had opened, but they did no more rending and tearing. They touched me deeply and awakened the part of me that I let loose only in battle. I began to reshape my perceptions along the lines of combat, spying out strengths and weaknesses along the enemy line. I ran through dozens and dozens of strategies in my mind, all the while my competitive and predatory hunger growing more and more ferocious.

I saw my situation paralleling that of the Red Tiger's war to overthrow Reithrese overlords. As I fought in his army, I did not fight for myself—I fought for others. I fought for generations of Men who would someday remember us only as characters in songs half-forgotten and best left unsung. I fought so they could live lives dictated *by* them, not *to* them.

So it was here in Cygestolia. I fought here so the whole of the Elven Nation would see in my example what Mankind truly was. Though I knew us deserving of respect, I also knew I had to earn it. That meant I had to do battle in their arena, by their rules, as much as it would hamper and hurt me.

It would be the true test of a hero, a challenge unlike any other.

A challenge before which I would not surrender.

I smiled as I stretched my arms and legs. "It is my understanding, my Lady Larissa, that as *vindicator* I am to be your partner in a dance—a dance in which we will not touch. Despite that handicap, I want my performance to be worthy of your people, your brother's wedding, and above all, my partner. Will you find me someone to instruct me?"

She smiled and rose to her feet. "My grandfather has already volunteered to be your teacher. You have a week in which to learn the steps to the *torris.*"

I stood and waved her toward the stairs ahead of me. "Then let us go find him and get started. This I vow: in a week's time your people will see a dance they will never, ever forget."

My prediction almost came true in a way I had not intended.

The *torris* is not a simple bow-and-wheel-your-partner dance with four steps that are repeated over and over. It's symbolic of a number of things, from life and nature to Sylvan history to bits and pieces of the lives of the dancers and the lives of those for whom they dance. I know of at least three different schools of swordsmanship that contain fewer independent moves than the *torris,* but I have to admit that I never worked so hard to learn them as I did this dance.

The different parts of the dance were individually very difficult for me because many of them relied upon a flexibility and fluidity of motion I could not easily reproduce. Lomthelgar, with wisdom born of eight or ten centuries of life, managed to draw parallels between some of the motions and things I might do in combat. Very quickly I found the dance built up of encounters in a series of shadow-fencing duels. Not only did this approach make the whole thing possible for me to master, but also allowed me to feed my defiance directly into my lessons.

Lomthelgar started me learning by using the Dreel as my partner. Shijef seemed as enamored of the pairing as I was, which provided me the perverse delight in commanding him to follow Lomthelgar's orders. There were one or two moves—the low sweeping ones—which the Dreel performed with more skill than I did. This made Shijef happy and, therefore, intolerable at certain points.

After only two days Lomthelgar pressed Shijef into other duties. Given two sticks, the Dreel was to beat out a consistent rhythm. This he did without fail, which allowed me to get down the timing for the steps. Lomthelgar also had me count to myself in sets of six, so I found myself hitting my steps correctly even when Shijef sped up or slowed down to confuse me.

By the final day Lomthelgar brought Larissa and me together to dance, but he did not allow us to see each other. First I performed blindfolded, and then she did. Lomthelgar hemmed and hawed, picking out little problems in our performances, but I knew from his criticisms that we had succeeded in learning apart how to dance together. And the next day we would each see the other dancing, and that, in and of itself, would make the dance more special than even I dared imagine.

My duties as *vindicator* were not limited to learning how to dance. Aside from being fitted for appropriate clothing and taking meals with various kin and allies of Aarundel's family, I had to assist him in the forging of the *insignii nuptialis* he would give Marta during the ceremony. Marta's brother would forge the wedding token for Aarundel, but both Marta and Larissa would help him, and both of them had a far better idea of what they were going to do than I did.

The process began at a forge set back in a rocky cavern on the eastern side of the Cygestolia valley. A smith smelted down silver-bearing ore and poured it into a baked-clay mold that made two silver bars, and two rings, with a long strand of threadlike silver twisting between them. We watched him fill the molds one day, then returned the next when he shattered the mold and severed the two sets of silver pieces.

Aarundel and I, because we were to work on the gift being given to Marta, obtained the smaller of the two sets and only a third of the silver thread. The piece we would create for her would be more delicate than the piece being given to Aarundel, which did not mean it would be any less work. Had the task of creating the item been left to me, I would not have known where to begin, but my friend did. As he noted, one nice thing about being so long-lived was that each elf-child had the chance to study different trades for years, obtaining a level of expertise a Man could only get over a lifetime, just to choose yet another career to make his life's work.

The first thing he set me to doing was making a short length of silver chain. Aarundel handed me an iron pipe roughly a quarter of an inch in diameter. Fixed to one end was a cross bar and running perpendicular to it was a groove cut through the top of the pipe. Viewing the pipe from the end made it appear to be a broken circle. The gap between the two sides of the circle ran straight down the cylinder and the edge appeared to be slightly worn.

As instructed, I coiled the silver thread around the pipe and wound it tightly. Satisfied with my work when I showed it to him, Aarundel handed me a device that looked akin to an arrow with only half a broadhead on it. I inserted the broken arrow into the pipe, fitting the triangular blade into the slot. With a hammer I gently tapped it down, and the blade cut each turn of the thread. Once through, I turned the whole assembly upside down, and two dozen links of silver poured into my left hand.

These I linked together, closing them with a very small set of tongs. By the time I had all that done, which shouldn't have taken so long except that it required more delicacy than my normal work, Aarundel had sized, filed, and set the ring with two small lapis ovals. He drilled a small hole between them and linked the chain in there at that point.

"Half-done," he announced proudly.

I had my doubts, because we had the armlet yet to finish. I assisted him in working it by holding the bar of silver in place while he hammered it into a sheet, and by positioning the crimp-molds correctly while he raised an edge around the whole armlet. He decorated the armlet with four oval gemstones: opal north and south, lapis east and west. The drill produced a hole near the cuff, into which we ran the chain's last link.

Aarundel smiled as he wiped sweat from his brow. "Drawn from the same metal, yet shaped by different hands and forces, they are just like Marta and me. We come from one people, yet we have been hammered into who we are by all manner of forces. In the wedding we shall be magically bound together, and our marriage will last as long as it takes for the metal to wear away to nothing on our flesh."

I tapped the bracelet at the end opposite the cuff, where the edge came to a gentle point. "Good thing the metal is thick, for a love like yours should take forever to die."

"Spoken truly as a *vindicator*"—he smiled—"and as a friend."

"My honor." I nodded and slapped him on the back. "Are we done?"

"One more thing." Aarundel turned the piece over and, using a small gouge, worked his mark into the metal. "There, I have signed it. Now you must."

I worked carefully and inscribed the six-line symbol for the Roclaws, then added my initial in the heart of the mountain. "Satisfactory?"

Aarundel looked at it and laughed. "When my grandfather was young, the mark of the Roclawzi was one that inspired terror and hatred. I am glad it now betokens a friend."

"A friend to the death, Aarundel. No one and no thing will stand between us."

"Agreed, unless," he smiled slyly, "you fail at the *torris*. In that case, I will have to kill you."

"Do not worry on that account." I quickly ran my right hand through one of the complex twitch-jerks that made the dance difficult. "If I fail, I will kill myself—if embarrassment does not kill me first."

Elven wedding traditions are different from those of Men in a number of ways that I found annoying. The bride and groom spend the week before the ceremony apart, except for when they meet to see the silver poured for their wedding tokens. Aarundel and I attended a number of functions with his in-laws, to the point of all but living with them. From what Aarundel told me, a great deal of the conversations involved politics and other things of concern to the Elves.

My job during these gatherings was to stand around and look the part of the *vindicator*. This meant I ate a lot because I could not understand what was being said. I also needed a lot of energy for my dancing lessons, and it would have been rude of me to refuse food. In fact, the various hosts and hostesses seemed to be relieved to be able to deal with me as easily as setting a bowl of something in front of me.

Sylvan cuisine is not bad, but it's not Man-food. Because they view fire as that which makes metal malleable, and because cookfires would use up an incredible amount of wood, Elves prepare food in an unusual way—though the results are quite remarkable and very edible. They combine all sorts of vegetables and herbs and spices together in huge cauldrons, pour over them juices and vinegars and let them marinate. Things added to this plant-mash right before serving are crispy, and meat soaked in it becomes tender and delicious without firing.

Breads and the like were also available, and quite good, but I understand less about their preparation. All I know about cooking bread involves mixing up a dough, scraping as much as possible off my fingers onto a flat rock, and trying to keep the fire around the rock going without getting too much charcoal in the bread. I think the Elves steam a lot of their bread, and I've heard talk of silver sun-ovens, but I was not overmuch concerned with pursuing more information about bread. Aarundel might have lived long enough to learn how to be a silversmith and a warrior, but I was too old to become a cook.

The night before the wedding, Aarundel and Marta were brought together in seclusion within a new chamber in Woodspire. As they contemplated their lives together, I was taken by Lomthelgar to the grassy, bowllike depression where the ceremony would take place the next day. Trees gave way above it, allowing me a clear view of the starry sky. Without realizing I had been uncomfortable, I found seeing the sky set me more at ease. Being trapped within so many trees is difficult for someone raised in the mountains, where trees are sparse and summer is the season when mud lakes cloak themselves with a grass thatch.

The elder Elf sank down on his haunches, and Shijef huddled behind him like a swollen shadow. "*Vindicators* guard this ground against violators."

I nodded. "Tomorrow, I know, I dance. What else?"

Lomthelgar gave me a lopsided grin. "Vindicate."

I frowned as the Elf and the Dreel shared a chuckle. "I should have known you two would become allies. You are united by a common enemy—me."

Both of them sobered. "Master you are, enemy you were."

Lomthelgar patted the Dreel on the shoulder. "And you are my *vindicator* as well."

"What?"

The Elf stood and shook his head. "You are to be left alone here. Good evening, Custos Sylvanii."

Lomthelgar led the Dreel from the circle, abandoning me at its heart. I dismissed their comments as mischief and nonsense and began to see to my duties as *vindicator*. I looked the area over by first walking the perimeter of the flat, then working my way up along the edge of the amphitheatre. It might have started as a natural formation, but the Elves had clearly worked on it and had shaped it. From a military standpoint it was a disaster to defend, but in the heart of Cygestolia the likelihood of an invasion approached the likelihood of my ever setting foot again in Cygestolia after the wedding.

Once I had satisfied myself with the military details of the situation, I sat at the upper edge of the amphitheatre, with my back to the woods, and other thoughts began to come to me. Because Larissa was for Marta what I was for Aarundel, we had been kept apart except for the pouring of the silver and the dancing. She had sent me flowers once by her grandfather, and I sent her back a garland I'd woven, using Shijef as my envoy, but that summed the total of our contact over that week.

I did not know where she would be stationed as part of her duties, but I dearly wished she could be here with me. It was not that I felt lonely without her, but that I felt so much more complete in her presence.

I began to wonder why Lomthelgar had brought us together to dance, yet kept one or the other of us blindfolded while we did so. I understood parts of it, of course. By seeing her I became used to the distraction of someone moving opposite me. Larissa's grace and elegance came as a marked contrast to the Dreel's shaggy, brutish movements, and in watching her I knew we would be very good at the ceremony.

In dancing opposite her while blindfolded, I learned two things. The first was that I had to concentrate on the timing and remain locked in thrall to the rhythms. The *torris,* for me, was more deadly a game than even the visit to Jammaq. One slip, one accident, one gust of wind blowing one strand of her hair against the back of my hand, and I would be slain outright. Never before had I placed myself in a situation where the most innocent of errors could kill me. Any wavering from the discipline that Lomthelgar had taught me would doom me and the *sylvanesti* I loved.

Blinded, I learned one other thing, and that realization made me wonder how much Lomthelgar knew about me and about his granddaughter. In challenging fate and death I was not alone, and in that most dangerous contest I had to trust absolutely and completely in my partner. Had I been asked if I *would* trust Larissa, if I *could* trust Larissa, I would have shouted my willingness to do so from Jammaq to the heart of the Haladin Outlands and back again. After the dance, though, I did not have to take her trustworthiness on faith; I *knew,* I had proof, that she would perform her part in our lethal dance perfectly.

I am not normally a daydreamer, walking about all moon-eyed. It's not said to be good for one born under the Triangle, for the moons will stare back at such, but the rest of the night passed in contemplation of things past and present. I found myself wandering through memories that I would have liked to have shared with Larissa, and in their remembering I wondered if I hadn't already told her of them. If the feeling of contentment I experienced thinking about her approached what Aarundel knew when thinking of Marta, then I envied my friend even more than I had imagined.

The night passed quickly and with the dawn's light Lomthelgar came and fetched me back to Woodspire. I ate a breakfast of pure water and plain bread, then slept a bit. After two or three hours of peace, the Dreel awakened me so I could wash. By the time I had cleansed myself and dried off, Lomthelgar finished laying out the clothes I would wear for the ceremony.

My tunic and hose had been cut from soft, shiny silk and dyed the iridescent color of emeralds. The fabric's light weight made me think it would be cold, but the silk warmed against my flesh quite quickly. My leather jerkin, gloves, and boots had all been dyed a light grey, lighter than dusk but darker than curing-smoke. The boots came to my knee and the tops flopped down; the gloves came to midforearm. The leather garments had been a bit large, but sized themselves instantly, as had Aarundel's glove during my fight with Tashayul.

Because I would be asked to dance, I removed Cleaveheart's scabbard from the belt I normally wore and affixed it to a longer belt that I looped diagonally over my torso. A second, more narrow belt threaded through the first at my left hip and buckled around my waist. The grand result of all this fussing was that Cleaveheart hung across my back, with the hilt jutting up above my right shoulder. Drawing it would be difficult, but I anticipated no trouble, so that did not concern me very much.

The other reason I was not concerned about my ability to draw Cleaveheart was that in my role as *vindicator* I was to bear Aarundel's favorite weapon. The Dwarven battle-ax rose to the height of my shoulder when I placed the butt end on the ground, and the broad curved blade all but eclipsed my chest. The wickedly hooked raven's-beak on the opposite side of the head actually looked more cruel than the ax blade itself, but I knew the blade's razor edge could chop through armor and warrior easily and efficiently. The spike at the top of the weapon might have been considered overkill, but it made the ax also function as a lance, which was important in a cavalry company.

Suitably attired, I followed Lomthelgar back to the amphitheatre and took my place at Aarundel's side. He wore black except at his throat, where an azure scarf had been knotted. He smiled when he saw me, then composed himself as gentle piping began from somewhere behind us.

The amphitheatre had changed in the short time I had been away from it. A small wooden altar had been raised at one edge. Looking like a tree stump, the altar had been shaped so that the feet resembled roots, and aside from the impossibility of it, I wondered if it had been grown in that spot in the hours since my vigil had ended. On its flat, polished surface rested a red velvet pillow which bore both *insignii nuptialis*.

Behind us, both on the flat and on the hillsides, many Elves had come to the celebration. All of them wore bright costumes, and I noticed, as I looked around, that the only green I saw in the whole place, aside from that which I wore, came in the few spots where the underlying grass peeked through the crowd. Paranoia over being the only person wearing green began to nibble at my mind, but I decided such thoughts were not part of my duty as *vindicator*, so I dismissed them.

The piping picked up in pace as the bride and her entourage entered the amphitheatre. They came up and over the berm at a point just barely on the far side of the altar. In the lead came an Elven priest I put at Thralan's age, though the white of his hair almost made me second-guess that estimate. Following him came Thralan and Ashenah, walking hand in hand. They wore black yet did not have blue to lighten the severity of their clothes. Still, the smiles on their faces left no doubt that they were very happy.

In their wake came Sidalric and Marta's mother, Grationa. They did not walk hand in hand as parents, but her hand rested inside the crook of her father's elbow. Vincelan, Marta's father, had chosen to go *excedere*, which meant he was unable to attend his daughter's marriage. I did not have a clear understanding as to what it meant to go beyond, but his departure had been spoken of in a mixture of reverence and sadness that made me think it was not the same as being dead, but close.

Aarundel's parents came over and stood behind us, and Marta's people stood opposite them. The piping stopped, then started again with a more sedate tune and I felt the attention of those gathered in the amphitheatre swell. Coming up over the crest of the hill, Larissa appeared in silhouette for a moment; then she started her descent. As did I, she wore emerald-green chased with black and looked utterly ravishing. I felt a jolt run through me as our gazes met, and relief as we both looked away—she gazing toward her brother while I glanced back up the hill to where Marta stood.

Aarundel's sharp intake of breath put into sound what I felt as I saw Marta descend the hill. Wearing an azure gown the same color as the scarf around Aarundel's neck, she strode forward with grace and a regal bearing. A black scarf trailed behind her as if a pennoncel proclaiming her link with Aarundel—though of that there was little doubt. She radiated happiness and love so brightly, and Aarundel reflected it so completely, that had I been standing between them, I felt certain I would have burst into flames. Everyone else seemed to sense the heat and the power of their *vitamor* as well, for the whole community was drawn together like a thirsty herd of antelope around a cool, clear lake.

The priest at the altar raised his hands and laboriously spoke in Mantongue. "As a community we come here to recognize and celebrate the union of this Aarundel and this Marta." Shifting to the Sylvan language, he spoke again, likely repeating much of what he had already said, but filling it in with ceremonial words that made the bride and groom smile.

The priest looked beyond them to Aarundel's parents. "Is this your son, free of obligations to another?" They nodded, and he turned his attention to Marta's mother and grandfather. He spoke to them in Elven—his foray into Mantongue only for my benefit. When he received a similar nod of assent, he spoke to Larissa, and she gave him short answers that prompted Aarundel and Marta to look at each other and blush.

The priest focused on me. "Neal of the Roclaws, *vindicator,* is this Aarundel known to you?"

"He is."

"Is he free of obligations and committed to this union?"

"He is."

"And has this place remained inviolate through the night?"

"It has."

My replies seemed to satisfy him, so he pushed on through the ceremony. At points he lapsed into Mantongue, and given the selection of things he allowed me to hear, he wanted me to understand both the sanctity of the situation and the incredibly long tradition of which I had been made a part. This consisted mostly of theological recountings, many of which I had heard before in slightly different forms, but with an emphasis on why Elves were greatly superior to Men.

"In the time before all time, Levicius and Alosia, the sky and the earth, became aware of each other. In this awareness came knowledge of their divinity, and in their wisdom they created the Dwarves to shape the world and the Elves to shape all that existed within the world. All that their creations brought forth were manifestations of their love for each other. Lest the world and their love become stale, they also brought forth another race, those who now claim the mantle Reithrese, to husband the elemental forces of Chaos, to inflict change upon their world so that it could change and grow and become more perfect.

"In time, through the pleasure of their creation, Levicius and Alosia chose to share their world with children born of them, not created by them. Kyori and Jistan came first, then Bok, Chavameht and Herin. Last came Reithra, who, in her jealousy against her mother over the love of her father, shaped her hatred into death. Thus began the first rebellion.

"Kyori and Jistan fought on behalf of their parents and won a truce with their siblings that forced Levicius and Alosia to go beyond. In the war of the gods, the Elves had defended the gods who had created them, and in that defense won the right to attend their creators in exile. The Dwarves, who remained neutral, were not touched by Death in the fullest first blush of its power, so now elude it still. The Reithrese embraced it and now it defines them."

Never before had I heard names put to the parents of the gods, and the antiquity of the Sylvan Nation made itself manifest in the Elves's knowledge of those who had birthed the gods that now ruled the world. The timing of the creation of the Reithrese also explained some of the animosity between them and the Elves. To the Elves they were created later, making them inferior. The Reithrese must have held that because they were created to change that over which Elves and Dwarves had been given dominion, they were the superior people. Their subordination in service to a lesser goddess meant nothing from their twisted point of view, I was certain.

Speaking in Mantongue again, and addressing only me, the priest continued. "Kyori and Jistan married and saw among their siblings the seeds of strife. In their wisdom they created Men and gave them to the others to use as soldiers so wars that *could* be fought on Skirren would *not* be fought in the heavens. Bok created the Dreel as his playthings, the Dwarves chose Herin as their patron, and Chavameht took pity upon the beasts, leaving only the Elves true to the first gods and above that which had been born in or through the Rebellion."

Feeling firmly fixed in the Elven cosmology down with snakes, slugs, and the occasional Dreel, I forced a smile on my face. It was not the first time I had seen a priest use a ceremony and his position to correct an evil in the world, though it was the first time I had been singled out as that evil. The smile at first felt wooden, but more life poured into it as I figured that if he didn't like my presence at the ceremony, he was absolutely going to hate the *torris*. After all, co-opt my friend's wedding day for your purposes, and you deserve all the pain you can get.

Having decided I was chastened or an idiot or both, the priest ignored me. For the rest of the ceremony he spoke only in Elven, but with his hand motions and the cadence of his words I could tell he was reciting prayers and formulas designed to bring Aarundel and Marta together. At appropriate moments each of them stepped closer to the altar and each other until they stood side by side in front of the priest.

Aarundel lifted his wedding token and slipped the ring over the middle finger on Marta's right hand. She did the same thing to him, then they clasped hands and let the bracelets clang against each other. Larissa came forward and grasped the armlet dangling from her brother's ring, and in imitation of her I started forward, but Lomthelgar held me back and took my place. I stiffened for a moment, then realized how closely I had come to destroying Aarundel's happiness on his wedding day.

In unison Lomthelgar and Larissa slipped the armlets in place, and a great cheer went up from among the Elves gathered there. Lomthelgar smiled knowingly at me as he retreated. "You spoke as my voice, I worked as your hands."

Aarundel gently enfolded his wife in a hug and kissed her deeply. I watched, not out of any voyeuristic fantasy, but because I could not bring myself to look past them at Larissa. I wanted to, but I knew I had to refuse. If I gave in, I knew I could lose myself in her, and that would shatter the composure I needed for the *torris*. Without it I might do to her what I almost did to Marta.

Around us the amphitheatre came alive. Some of the people filed away while others moved down to the flat and spread out blankets. They seated themselves on the ground while Aarundel's family retainers moved among them presenting pitchers of wine, bowls of vegetable stew, and small loaves of soft-crusted bread. All of the guests accepted the food with thanks, it appeared, but they did not partake of it immediately.

Before the altar, retainers lay down a huge black silk sheet. The bride and groom centered themselves on it; then four smaller sheets in azure were set to cover each corner of the black diamond. Larissa and I were pointed to the sheets on either side of the couple, while the four parents sat behind them. No one sat on the sheet in front of them, and I assumed that was to symbolize children, or perhaps in the case of a second or third marriage, the children from previous unions would occupy that place of honor.

The bride and groom were served last, and I wished they would take a drink of their wine, because my nervousness had me bone-mouthed. I waited patiently for them to act; then I felt Lomthelgar's hand on my shoulder. "Before they will begin the celebration, you must dance."

I nodded. "You'll be proud."

The elder Elf smiled. "The dance is everything. As it goes, so will go their life together."

I felt a shock as he said that; then I nodded and steeled myself to do the best I could. I already knew I was prepared for the dance. I had trained enough that I could perform it blindfolded. If my *torris* would predict the future of their marriage, I would make it perfect.

Leaving the ax in its place, but still wearing Cleaveheart over my shoulder, I stood and walked around the sheets until I stopped directly in front of the bride and groom. I bowed to them, then turned to the left and bowed toward my partner. Squaring around again, I smiled at Aarundel, then executed an about-face and paced away from him and his bride until I stood two steps beyond the center of the circle on the flat ringed with Elves. I did not look back, because I knew Larissa would be similarly bowing to her brother and his wife, then moving to take her place opposite me. Back to back, though separated by a Man-length, we were together to dance for my friends and her kin.

The pipers started the *torris* melody slowly, perfectly in keeping with the tempo Lomthelgar had used in instructing me. I moved to my right, curving to take up a quarter of a circle. Had I been an Elf, Larissa and I would have been touching shoulder blades. As our arms extended, we would have laid them out against each other and interlaced our fingers. Our hands would have risen toward the sky together, and our dance would have burned with the fire we both felt inside.

Apart, that could not happen.

A sharp, shrill note spun both of us about, like wild animals spinning to snarl at a pursuer. We froze for a second, barely a heartbeat, both because the dance demanded it and because, for the first time, we locked eyes in the dance. At that moment the resolve I had built up in myself to remain under control evaporated. I saw passion blossom in her eyes, and her lips pull back in a snarl to mirror the one on my face. There, turned inward, we knew the world consisted of us and those opposed to us. Wordlessly we agreed that if we filled the dance with the impossible love we had for each other, Aarundel and Marta would be that much more blessed: denying what we felt for each other, would deny them the perfect *torris,* and that we would not do.

Our hands came down from above our heads and around and up until our fists closed in our lines of sight. Whirling away from each other, we opened our hands as if to cast out to those gathered around us what had passed between us. Some may have comprehended at that moment, others never would, and I looked for hostility I could devour and use to fuel me.

The music picked up in pace, but the pipers began to follow us instead of the other way around. Spinning, leaping, and turning, we orbited each other in perfect unison. I held my hand out to guide Larissa through a pirouette, and though two feet separated us, she moved as if I had propelled her. As she whirled down into a crouch and I arced over her in a long leap, she snapped her head back and whipped her golden hair less than a foot from my hip and flank. Landing on my knees and sliding on my side, I spun around and came upright at the same moment as she did, each of us with our hands outstretched and moving as if we had risen together.

We both came forward until mere inches separated us. I turned to the right and she to the left, as a pair facing Aarundel and Marta. We ran at them, then stopped as one and reversed ourselves. Spinning outward, our hands passed within an inch of each other's stomach, her hand flashing past a second after mine.

I had stopped counting and had stopped listening to the music. I cared no longer for what the dance was or was supposed to be. I knew it was just us, *we* were the dance. Apart, yet touching each other on a level deeper and more potent than physical, we flowed through the rest of the *torris.* We laughed aloud and smiled at each other, our eyes blazing with the giddy excitement of love and the fear-tinged exhilaration of playing on the edge of oblivion. One false move, one miscalculation, and the thrilling sense of defiance would crash into defeat.

It didn't matter that I forgot steps and improvised others. I knew where Larissa would be, and I managed not to be there at the same time. I could see her and hear her, and I could *feel* her as if we were bound together with a million strings. Puppets and puppeteers both, we controlled and worked with the other, transforming the *torris* from a dance in celebration of love and union to a dance of love and union.

All too quickly and yet after much too great a time, the music ended and froze both of us in place at the heart of the circle. We stood so close that I could feel her breath upon my face, and I feared a single droplet of sweat might roll down my nose to connect us. If that happened, I knew I would die, but I did not care, because my heart felt full to bursting with such joy and contentment that death did not frighten me. I had milked everything possible from life—death would just crystallize the moment and allow me to exist within it forever.

I thought it was my heart beating madly when I felt the first tremor ripple through my body. I started to sway and realized that if I fell, I might fall into Larissa. Fighting a growing disequilibrium, I threw myself backward. Still working in synch with each other, I saw she had done the same thing, and we both laughed like children at the embarrassment of it all. Rolling from my back into a sitting position, I winked at her and wanted to say something, but what I saw between us made me silent.

The ground where we had stood had begun to blur the way a bowstring quivers after the arrow has been released. Individual blades of grass merged with others as the ground began to vibrate very quickly. The tremblings increased in power as their speed slowed, and I watched a six-foot circle of earth ripple back and forth as if it were water. As a circle of little wavelets closed on the center, a spike of dirt shot into the air. A small grass-studded ball pulled free of its crest and hung at head-height for a moment, then fell back to the earth. It merged with the dirt without a splash, though stalks of grass, roots and all, danced across the waves and settled outside the circle.

The earth within the circle began to boil. Lumps rose up like bubbles in broth, but when the muddy dirt over them retreated, they revealed stones from the size of my fist to one bigger than my skull. As they bounced out of the circle, I scrambled back on my hands and feet, then stood and looked over to see if Larissa was safe. She nimbly danced back out of the way of a stone, then smiled at me and returned the wink.

The dirt circle shifted from a deep, dark brown to a reddish color, then geysered upward. I raised my left hand to shield my eyes, but the dirt remained solidly locked in a column. It began to spin fast and faster, akin to the dustwhirls I'd seen in the Centisian plains, but did not move from the spot to which it appeared rooted. Then it all swirled down and resolved itself into a varicolored cloak fastened with an agate clasp at the throat of a Reithrese sorcerer.

"I bring you greetings from the Reithrese Nation." He hovered in the air and slowly turned a circle, studying the Elves as they came to their feet. His circuit complete, he faced forward again. His eyes narrowed as he saw me, then his lips spread apart to reveal a diamond smile. "You I find in the most unusual places, Manchild."

"Nor had I expected to see you here, Takrakor." I brought my right hand up to Cleaveheart's hilt, but did not draw the blade as Aarundel came up beside me. He placed himself in the way of any drawcut, so I assumed he wanted no violence, and his having left his ax behind confirmed that assumption. "It seems we only meet at ceremonies: here a wedding and at a funeral in Jammaq."

"Such circumstances will change in due course, Manchild."

"Pity, I *like* Reithrese funerals."

Aarundel held up a hand to silence me. "Neal, he is here as a guest."

I blinked. "You invited Takrakor to your wedding?"

My friend shook his head. "An invitation is always extended to a representative of the Reithrese people, for marriage is change and they are the masters of change."

"Marriage is also the death of solitary life." The Reithrese ran his tongue from crystal fang to crystal fang. "We are the masters of death."

I smiled. "Ah, there's a truly appropriate sentiment for a wedding."

Aarundel sighed and looked up at Takrakor. "It is seldom that the Reithrese accept the invitation."

Takrakor shrugged easily. "Could we ignore the wedding of one who has proven a fierce foe? Not only do we celebrate your nuptials, but we celebrate your coming life here, in Cygestolia. Your retirement from the battlefield will remove from us our concern for your safety among Men."

"The Haladina have hardly been a threat to Aarundel." I smiled at him. "Were I you, I'm thinking I'd be more concerned about the safety of Reithrese among Men."

The sorcerer's red eyes tightened down into bloody slivers. "I have not forgotten your antics, Neal. Not at all. You could but *hope* I would forget." He waved me away with an idle hand, and I felt a light breeze buffet me. "I will not let you spoil this joyous occasion among your Elders, youngling."

He clasped his hands together for a moment, then spread them wide apart and sprayed out a rainbow of gems that carried from Larissa's feet to mine. "These are for you, Aarundel, and your bride, Marta. Your skill as a jeweler is not unknown to us, and any gift you craft for her will be enhanced by her beauty."

Aarundel knelt and held up a blue diamond as long as my thumb and half that wide. "This would be reckoned a fortune even in Dwarven halls, Takrakor. Your earlier words could cause one to construe this as a bribe for me to remain here in Cygestolia."

The sorcerer's eyes flared wide for a moment, then returned to normal size as Takrakor smiled. "They are offered in friendship and fellowship, Aarundel, not as a bribe. We know you do not want to leave your bride for the war trail. And do not take it that I think you a coward easily swayed by wealth into staying here. I no more think that than you should imagine that the Reithrese fear an Elf consorting with Men."

"Then we share comprehension?"

"I believe we do."

"Good." Aarundel smiled carefully and raised his voice so all could hear him. "My wife and I, last night, came to an understanding. After a fortnight I will again travel from Cygestolia and continue my work as a warrior."

As the people murmured together in shock, Finndali came up from behind Larissa and rested his hands on her shoulders. "You were not granted permission to marry so you would leave again."

"And no condition was placed upon my return here to marry. You and the Consilliarii may have decided marriage would keep me here, but that was not *my* decision." Aarundel hesitated for a moment and glanced at his sister before continuing. "You have met Neal Custos Sylvanii. You all saw the *torris.* In his dance and in his conduct here you have seen why I have come to call this man *friend.* As Neal has come here to stand by me in my world, I will again travel from Cygestolia to stand by him in his. To do less would dishonor my *vindicator.*"

Takrakor's bass laughter cut through the buzz of Elven voices. "Very good, Aarundel, wonderful. I told them that you would not be gelded in Cygestolia. The Cold Goddess will eat your soul as eagerly as any other."

I eclipsed Aarundel's body with my own. "I'm thinking we can test that theory whenever your troops decide to come out and fight in front of their Man-mercenaries."

The sorcerer's cloak began to decay as his anger wore away his control. "When *I* choose to fight, youngling, you will once again long for the days of fighting the Haladina."

"That could well be true, Takrakor," I growled at him. "Until then I'll content myself with remembering how easily your brother died."

The Reithrese sorcerer snarled in anger and started to sink toward the ground. With a downward snapping of his wrists and windmilling action of his arms, he again raised the cloud of dust. Either because he had lost control, or because of deliberate contempt, the sandstorm lashed out and scourged me on the left side of my face. I went down on one knee and felt the blood starting to trickle from a gash on my forehead, but I drew Cleaveheart and had it poised for a thrust into the heart of the whirling cloud. The dust funnel collapsed in on itself, leaving only the dirt hole in the center of the clearing.

The Reithrese wizard had vanished, denying me a chance to make his clan yet more angry with me. His gift of gems remained scattered over the ground. I wished they had been his teeth and it had been my fist that had sown them there, but such evil thoughts were scarcely the proper things for a *vindicator* to be thinking at his best friend's wedding.

I pressed my left hand to my forehead to staunch the blood flow. Looking up, I saw Larissa move forward to aid me, but her husband held her back. Horror washed through her eyes—not at what she had almost done, but what custom would not allow her to do. I gave her a smile to let her know I was not seriously hurt, then nodded as her husband tried to turn her away from me.

Aarundel knelt beside me and took a look at my wound. "A little cut. Nothing really."

I laughed lightly. "And this was an event I was thinking I'd not need a scar for remembering."

"But if anyone was going to get hurt here, I would have assumed it would be you." He took the scarf from around his neck and wadded it into a bandage. "Here."

"Thanks." I could see he wanted to say something, but words or his voice failed him. "Had you told me I might be hurt, I might not have come."

He smiled politely, then took Marta's scarf from her to tie his around my head. As he leaned in close to knot the cloth, he kept his voice low. "Neal, in the *torris*, you and my sister . . ."

A shiver ran down my spine. "We did *not* touch. Not at all."

"No, no, I know that." Aarundel stared at me. "What passed between you, what drove you . . . it was obvious. Do you know what it means?"

I looked down and felt drained of energy. "Takrakor could have made a lot of Elven allies by having taken my head clean off?"

The Sylvan warrior shook his head. "It means that I am very happy for my sister and my friend."

"Thank you."

"And," he added grimly, "if you violate Elven law in this matter, when I kill you, I guarantee it will be without pain."

Chapter 15

To Mourn a Man's Passing

Early Spring
A.R. 499
The Present

"Where, man?" Count Berengar grabbed the servant by the front of his tunic and lifted him from the floor.

"Northwest of the Low Market, m'lord, in an alley behind the Haladin leatherworker's shop."

Berengar dropped him and raced from the chamber. In shock, filled with disbelief, Gena shivered, then scrambled to her feet and trailed after him. She wanted to shout to him to stop or slow down, but a growing hole inside her trapped the words. Her mind conjured all sorts of grotesque and hideous pictures to coincide with the servant's phrasing, "killed him dead." As she ran down the hallway, the images became stranger and stranger, layering eons of decay and abuse on a man who had been alive and with her only six hours previously.

It could be a mistake! Her training in wizardry overrode her emotions. The servant had seemed positive in his declaration of Durriken's condition, but what did he know of life and death, injuries and recovery? The servant might have assumed Rik dead when, in fact, he still lived. With her abilities and magic, she could strengthen Rik. She could keep death at bay. If the barest spark of life remained in him, she would nurse it into a bonfire that would bring him back to her.

She reached the courtyard in time to see Berengar's back as he rode out the gate. Gena turned on the nearest groom. "Saddle me a horse. Get two. You will take me to the place where Rik lies."

The youth looked flustered. "M'lady, I cannot . . ."

"Do *not* incite my fury." She grabbed a handful of his tunic and propelled him toward the stables. "Do it, do it *now!* My patience grows short." She curled her voice down into a sinister croak, hoping to invoke memories of *Eldsaga* atrocities to speed the groom.

Though he ran off to comply with her command, her anger did not remain under control. It exploded in her as she saw Rik telling her he was not worried about his trip into the Haladin section of Aurdon. *How could you have been so stupid? How could you have done this?* Her anger coiled with betrayal. *You should have known! I should not have let you go!*

Again her intellect attempted to intervene. She knew that she could not have stopped Rik even if she had wanted to. He always had been independent despite his devotion to her. And he had always been a risk taker, as the late fight with the Haladin Raiders had proven clearly. She knew that he had been smart enough to decide there was no threat, but bold enough to have gone ahead into danger if he felt the reward warranted the risk.

She realized in an instant that her anger came from the surprise of losing him so soon. Somewhere in the back of her mind she had seen staying with him as he grew old. That prospect held horror for other *sylvanesti,* but she had embraced the idea because the person Rik was would only get better with age, no matter what happened to his physical shell.

Unless he dies young.

The groom led two horses from the stable, and Gena vaulted up into the gray horse's saddle. She stared down at the groom as he mounted his horse, then let her impatience erode what little control she had left. "Lead the way!"

"I don't know where you want to go, m'lady."

Gena snarled, then concentrated. "Low Market, in the alley behind the Haladin leatherworker. Go, go, we will see a crowd, I am certain."

The groom touched his heels to the horse's ribs, and Gena whipped her reins across the horse's rump as it went past. She sent her mount after the first horse, cursing the groom's timidity and the roundabout travel the siege gates forced upon them. Everything and everyone conspired to slow her when she knew her magick might be all that could save Durriken from death.

The city flew past in a blur, then they reached the street off which the alley ran. The crush of the crowd made continuing on horseback impossible. Gena leaped from the saddle and waded into the crowd. Half a head taller than the largest of the people in the street, she forced herself through to where Aurdon Rangers held a perimeter around the alley-mouth. She did not care who she thrust aside or stepped upon. All she knew was that she would not be kept away from Rik and she would deal harshly with anyone who sought to stop her from reaching him.

She burst through the Ranger line. "Rik? Rik?"

Berengar whirled around from his station at the edge of the alley and stepped toward her. "Lady Genevera, no."

"I have to see him."

"No!" Berengar caught her wrist. "Don't go there."

She tried to pull free of his grasp, but could not. "Unhand me!"

"No!" Berengar pulled her to the side and trapped her against the adobe wall of the leatherworker's shop. "He's dead, Gena."

Despair swallowed her anger. "No, don't say that. I can help him."

"No one can help him."

"You don't know that." She pounded a fist against Berengar's chest. "He might not be dead."

Berengar secured her other wrist and pressed her back against the wall with his body. "Gena, he is dead. I have seen death. I know."

"I have magick."

"I know, but it can't do him any good."

She bit back an agonized wail. "Please, m'lord, please. I must see him."

"No, Gena, no." She saw him fight for control of his own emotions. "You don't want to see him like that."

"I need to see him, please."

"Gena, Durriken wouldn't want you to see him that way." He gathered her wrists together and held them against his chest in his right hand. He looped his left arm around her shoulders and hugged her close. "Allow him the dignity in your memory that the Haladina denied him in death."

The compassion in Berengar's voice broke through and eroded the urgency and resolve that had held pain at bay. She gripped Berengar's shirt and brought her head down to her hands as the tears started. "It's my fault. I should have been here with him."

"No, no, you cannot blame yourself. His death here is no more your fault than your death would have been accounted to him had we died yesterday." The count stroked her hair. "You would have done anything to save him, and he would have done the same for you, but not being there does not make you his murderer. Had you been here, I might be mourning the murder of two friends."

"Why did it happen?"

Gena initially resisted, then allowed Berengar to move her away from the alley. "I don't know why, but I do know we will find those who did this. My best people are dealing with it. They will bring the . . . they will bring Durriken to our home and he will be interred in the Fisher vault."

"I do want to see him, to say good-bye."

"I know. I shall see to it."

Gena lifted her head and kissed Berengar on the cheek. "Thank you." She shivered and nestled beneath his arm, availing herself of the refuge he offered until a cart came to carry them both home.

Genevera found herself surprised to think of Durriken as being so small in death. Except for a folded towel covering his loins, he lay naked on the gray granite-topped table. His body had been washed and his limbs straightened so that she could almost have imagined him to be sleeping. She stared at him, wishing and hoping his hairless chest would begin to rise and fall again, but from the chalky pallor of his flesh, she knew that would never happen.

Berengar stood with his back to the door. "The city's mortician thinks this odd, but I told him this was an Elven ritual."

"It is that, really." She slowly made one circuit of the table. "Unlike Men, we return our dead to the earth unencumbered by tokens and trophies of their mortal existence. Those who loved the deceased are asked to soothe their hurts; then we release the dead from any obligation they had to us."

She started to reach out toward Rik, but she hesitated. Death being so uncommon among her people, yet with so many dying back in the time of Neal, the ritual had become sacrosanct among Elves. She wanted to honor Rik for the person he had been inside, ignoring utterly his mortal shell, but she knew countless Elves who would take more offense at her honoring him in this manner than they would at her having slept with him.

Apostasy and heresy are no strangers to my family. She shook her head. *It is* right *to do this.*

She extended her left arm, lowering her hand, and allowed the tip of her middle finger to trace one of the purple cuts on Rik's chest. The first extended three inches from his breastbone up toward his throat and similar wounds scored the flesh beneath each breast. Identical diagonal cuts marked his chest near his shoulders and the lower edges of his ribs. The last laceration was the worst; a long, ragged crescent cut that had opened his belly.

The part of her inclined toward being clinical cataloged the likely damage done by each of the smaller cuts. The Haladina preferred the curved *jambyja* dagger for close work, and she knew each of the cuts ran down and in to meet in Rik's heart. He would have died quickly, almost without pain, but as she touched each hole, she could feel the outrage Rik had known as his life ebbed away.

Clinical detachment dissolved in an ocean of memories.

Gena forced away the few bad ones, releasing Rik from his part in any negative thoughts. She clung to those wonderful and wondrous visions of the time they had spent together. It seemed such a short time, yet she had never felt they would end. Cloaking her wounded soul in the happy times, she let go of the last bit of resentment—that of having been abandoned by Rik—and looked up as Berengar spoke in a gentle voice.

Berengar slowly shook his head. "The Haladina refer to that form of death as *tmeinja tal-karti.* It translates as 'Eight Cuts,' but each blow has significance to them. They reserve it for traitors."

Bile rose in her throat as she touched the start of the curved wound on Rik's stomach. Her fingers found cold, waxy flesh where so often she had felt only warmth before. Rik's stomach had been flat, but now gapped slightly open at the wound. Deep inside it she could see the blue-white rope of his bowels. Though Berengar had tried to shield her, she had heard the rumors about how the Haladina had looped Rik's intestines around his neck, draping them over him like an obscene bloody garland.

Clenching her teeth, Gena forced herself to trace every inch of the wound. She felt its cruelty and choked back her anguish and fury. She knew Rik would never have screamed in pain, but would have just glowered in anger at his assailants. She vowed she would not dishonor him by breaking down, even though her throat hurt with suppressed emotion.

You will be avenged, my love, by my action, because of my love.

That wound salved with her vow, Gena looked up at Berengar. "Why would they think Rik a traitor?"

Berengar would not meet her eyes. "Who can know the minds of the Haladina, my lady?"

"You need not spare me more pain, Berengar, for it cannot be worse than what I already feel." Gena touched the corners of Rik's mouth and gently brushed her fingers across his split lips. His right cheek and eye bore livid bruises, and a small cut had a curious right-angle twist to it, as if it had been made by a ring. She raised her hand to her lips, kissed her fingers, then again touched Rik's lips.

"He betrayed no one. They could have taken him as a spy for your family, I suppose."

"That might explain their killing him, but not in this manner." Berengar hesitated, then frowned. "I have heard a rumor . . ."

Her head came up. "What rumor?"

"A disturbing one. I had heard disturbing stories about Durriken and his vocation. I accepted him on the strength of his traveling with you, but . . . "

"You wonder if Durriken was playing some game on the Riveren side of things?" Gena shook her head adamantly and let fire play through her voice. "I may not have known Durriken long by Elven standards, but I knew him well. I knew everything about him because he opened up and shared himself with me." Her voice caught as she realized there had been many things she had not shared with Durriken, and she wondered if he knew she had held things back from him. "He would not have betrayed us, my Lord. Of this I am certain."

Berengar nodded once, curtly. "Then that is no longer a consideration. I do not know how their minds work, but the Haladina killed him and the Haladina will pay." His expression slackened for a moment, losing its fierceness. "That is, they will pay if you still feel able to undertake the trek for which I summoned you here. Without Rik, well, there is no onus upon you to do this thing. I can understand if you wish to mourn. I do not know enough about the Sylvan culture to know what you will do in that regard."

Gena nodded. "We mourn privately, at moments in which we feel a closeness to the deceased. Death is not as common among us as it is here, and seldom does it come prematurely, so there is not often that much regret." Looking down at Durriken, she brushed hair from his forehead. "I have so much to regret, and so little to remember."

Berengar extended his left hand toward her and opened it. "Perhaps this will allow you to remember him."

From his palm she drew Lord Orvir's ring and the silver chain to which it had been married. "My Lord, this was your brother's ring."

"No, it was Durriken's ring. I gave it to him and promised that I might give him the land grant that went with it if we succeeded. He gave his life in pursuit of our enterprise, so I deem it right that the title has passed to him, for however brief a time." The count shrugged uneasily. "The rest of Rik's effects, including his flashdrakes, are in your room here. I separated the ring only because I wanted you to realize that I meant for you to have it in his memory."

Gena slipped the chain over her head, past her ears, and let the ring rest between her breasts. "I thank you for your kindness." She closed her right hand around the ring and waited for it to warm at her touch. "I think there is no question that we must go forth with your plan. Neal Elfward fought against the Haladina throughout his life. No one who forged an alliance with the Haladina should be safe beneath his protection."

Berengar nodded in agreement and folded his arms over his chest. "Do you know where Cleaveheart is?"

"Not beyond question, but I think I remember its having been entrusted to my grandfather at the time of Neal's death. He and my grandaunt conveyed it to Jarudin."

Berengar smiled. "The imperial capital? Do you think it is still there?"

"I don't know, but that is the last place I know it has been." She glanced back at Rik, then nodded. "We bury our dead, then go to find Neal's weapons so we can avenge them."

Chapter 16

To Celebrate an Empire's Death

Early Autumn
Reign of the Red Tiger Year 3
Five Centuries Ago
My Thiry-seventh Year

Battles during the spring following Aarundel's wedding brought the final consolidation of Centisia under the Red Tiger's banner. Swinging up to the northeast, we nipped off a bit of Ispar, then retreated quickly as the Reithrese responded with a battalion of Reithrese Dragoons and a virtual horde of Haladina to hunt us down. The Reithrese did not follow us back into Centisia, though their allies did, and we sent the Haladina running back across the border after we'd left a quarter of their number bleeding on the north Centisian plains.

After that victory Sture renewed his call for an expedition to Irtysh. The Red Tiger said he would entertain the idea of that strategy and—in accord with a plan that Sture knew nothing about—I pulled the Steel Pack out of the Red Tiger's force in a fit of pique. We headed back toward Aurium, then slashed on into the mountains on the Kaudian/Esquihiri border to wait.

Word of the strike at Irtysh got out very quickly, and the Reithrese started shifting forces toward Ispar to harass our lines. Despite reports of new Reithrese activity to the north, Sture continued in his preparations for the expedition. When he was ready to go, he met with the Red Tiger for one last time and was given the news that he was going nowhere.

The Red Tiger wheeled his army around and drove hard into Kaudia. With the Exile Legion to guard his back, the Red Tiger pushed into the central reaches of Kaudia, and the Reithrese scrambled to oppose him. They brought Home Guards in from Reith and put up a spirited defense.

The Reithrese garrison and their Haladin allies held and fought well until the Steel Pack shot west and looped down south. We ended up well behind their lines and successfully raided a paymaster's caravan. As with all good mercenaries who have not been paid, the Haladina fighting in Kaudia began to look at returning to their homes. The Reithrese pulled back to defend key fortresses in the northwestern parts of the nation while the Steel Pack returned with our booty to the Red Tiger's freestate.

Both sides wintered in position; then with spring we brought the Exile Legion up and pushed sharply north. We skirted the line of Reithrese fortresses, but kept enough skirmishers out that the Reithrese didn't dare abandon them to attack us. As a result we stood poised for a hard march through Esquihir and Batangas to Reith itself. The Reithrese began to move troops from Ispar into Esquihir to press us from the north. Aarundel sent a message to Cygestolia demanding that passage through Elven Holdings be denied to them, so the Consilliarii immediately granted the Reithrese the right to come around the mountains and down. They swung wide a bit, venturing into the Batangas bulge to resupply after the long march. By the middle of summer they were prepared to send us back through the mountains into Centisia.

While battles are actually won or lost in the field, things done outside battle can almost guarantee the outcome before the first arrow flies or the first man falls. Aarundel and I both agreed that the Consilliarii would do anything they could to punish him and me for our audacity. He had defied them in rejoining the Red Tiger's army, and I dared love a *sylvanesti* without acting like an animal that they could destroy. While they hated the fact that Larissa and I were as heartbound as Aarundel and Marta, they also respected the fact that I fully observed their laws, so they had to find other means to destroy me.

The request to bar Reithrese passage through Elven lands came largely because the Red Tiger's plan would be ruined if the Reithrese moved into the Hiris mountains. Likewise, Aarundel's demand that our army be allowed the same sort of passage was denied, making it clear to the Reithrese that they had us trapped against the Hiris mountains. While I would not have seen that as a great threat, since our army could melt away into the mountains and another Human army could not stop them, the Reithrese and their wizards saw things entirely differently.

As the Reithrese armies pressed us north and east, their Haladin allies cut us off from a southern retreat to the freestate. We pushed back into the Hiris mountains, and, wary of being trapped the way Tashayul had been in the Roclaws, the Reithrese advanced carefully. Using small scouting parties and relying largely on wizards, they decided they had us precisely where they wanted us until spring. Employing their formidable elemental magicks, they brought winter early to the Hiris range, filling all the passes, leaving the Red Tiger and his rebellion trapped in a high mountain-valley forest.

Their magicks were potent indeed. Winds howled demonically and blew away any lingering summer warmth. Snow fell heavily during the days, then the night brought such bitter cold that the snow froze over into a crust. The day following such a freeze would bring rime-tinged winds that drove corn-kernel ice crystals across open meadows in the winter equivalent of desert sandstorms. Because of the time of the year, bringing winter to the mountains early was not terribly difficult, so the Reithrese wizards put a great deal of effort into bringing us the worst winter ever seen right there in the mountains.

The reason they were so willing to brutalize us with the weather was because they truly believed they had the entire Human rebellion trapped in the mountains. What they really had was a volunteer force of just over two thousand individuals, including two score of our sorcerers, who agreed to make it look to the Reithrese as if a much larger force were in that valley.

The soldiers in the force divided their time between setting up ambushes for Reithrese scouts and maintaining the appearances of a camp suitable for housing an army fifteen times the size of the mountain force. They did that by pitching tents and maintaining fires—both difficult tasks in the unnatural winter.

The sorcerers worked more subtly to annoy the Reithrese. Since Reithrese magickers are powerful, they tend to hold their Human counterparts in contempt. Our sorcerers used that arrogance against them by weaving concealment spells that functioned on multiple levels. The result was that any Reithrese sorcerer trying to use his powers for reconnaissance ended up with an incredible amount of spurious data and reports. Thus the Reithrese could not sort the truth from fictions concerning our army.

This heroic effort bought us the time we needed for the Red Tiger's plan to work.

The snow in the passes, which was so easy for the Reithrese to dump on us because of the seasonal proximity to winter, would, for the same reason, be impossible to melt away until spring approached. That meant that in trapping us, the only way the Reithrese could get to Jarudin would be to move back through the Elven holdings, or down and around through Kaudia and up through Centisia. In blocking the mountains, the Reithrese had cut themselves off from the most direct route back to Jarudin. However they ended up going back to the capital, it would take too long for them to counter our grand plan.

The army itself had pushed on hard through the Hiris mountains and had reached the Ispari side before the snows began to fall at all heavily. Aarundel and I remained in the mountains to organize the camp while the Red Tiger regrouped and rested the army in a valley two hundred miles south of Jarudin. There they brought in an early harvest, built siege machines, then slowly moved north toward the capital.

Once we were satisfied about the situation in the mountains, Aarundel and I used the Sylvan *circii translatio* to rejoin our forces. The trip that time proved even more tiring for me than before, but we had two days to recover before the army caught up with us. More remarkable was the Dreel's ability to accompany us on the trip despite his refusal to wear the silver chains that Aarundel and I needed to travel.

"Magick I am," he hissed, tapping his chest, "things I need not."

As much as I wouldn't have minded leaving him behind in the mountains, I was glad he came through. In fact, he seemed less tired than either one of us. While he did not steal a sheep during the journey, he did hunt down a stag when we arrived, and having to sup on venison did my recovery no harm.

Within a fortnight, at the culmination of two long, bloody years of fighting, the Human host reached Jarudin. An inelegant sprawl of local redstone, imported marble, and, for one tower, Reithrese basalt, the imperial city had been designed by Tashayul as a monument to the vitality he had once known. With his death the grand drive to finish the city had faltered, so Reithrese architecture gave way to Human as the walls surrounding the city were completed.

Tashayul's death hurt more than the desire to complete his capital. Without Tashayul's leadership, the Reithrese Nation broke into antagonistic political factions. While there was still a strong, imperially-minded contingent—led by Takrakor—the opposition groups appeared to wield enough power to prevent further expansion. The Red Tiger felt, and I agreed, that if we could take Jarudin away from the Reithrese, the imperialists would be terribly embarrassed and might be consumed by their isolationist foes in Reith.

Toward that end the Red Tiger's army stood arrayed around the imperial city. Sixteen thousand Centisian warriors made up the core of the army, with three thousand in light cavalry, two thousand archers, and the rest distributed among pikemen, swordsmen, axmen, and irregulars. Despite their name, the latter troops were the best, being huntsmen and errant warriors classed as bandits or heretics by the Reithrese Empire. Sture's Exile Legion added a thousand light cavalry and some well-drilled infantry. The rest of our infantry were farmers, who, despite two summers campaigning, had been more at home harvesting crops for the march north than waiting to lay waste to Jarudin.

The light cavalry formed the wings of our host, with the infantry and archers in the center. In front of them was the Steel Pack and the newly formed Steel Hunt. With my blessings and support, Drogo had split from the Pack and formed up his own heavy-cavalry company. Being from Centisia himself, he picked more of his countrymen to fill the ranks, and they all pledged their personal fealty to the Red Tiger. While they were not quite as fierce as the Pack, I took pride and pleasure at having the Hunt behind us.

The fact that we had arrayed ourselves in a classic battle formation must have astounded the Reithrese in the city. They had massive walls between us and them, and enough supplies in the city that they knew they could wait us out. Even if our catapults and ballistae, onagers, and trebuchets were able to cast stones or shoot missiles over the high walls, the damage done would be minimal, and magick could be employed to destroy the most offensive machines. Their troops, who seemed to enjoy standing on the walls and shouting taunts at us, were clearly not of a mind to sally forth and give us some sport.

Ours was, to their eyes, a halfhearted attempt at sieging an impregnable city. They could easily wait us out and send for troops to lift the siege if we became a nuisance. They grew contemptuous enough of us to let Human traders come out to sell us various wares and intelligence about the city itself. The only chance we had of taking the city would involve a miracle, and both sides knew it.

The Red Tiger sent a runner to bring Aarundel and me to his tent. The miracle was at hand.

A giant of a man, bigger than either Aarundel or myself, Beltran greeted us warmly and poured each of us a goblet of wine. "Tonight we dine at the emperor's table."

"I can hardly wait," I lied as I acknowledged Sture's stiff nod in my direction. I gathered, from the redness on the tips of his ears, he had been again at Beltran about some special mission for his Lightning Elite cavalry or using his coal-mining sappers to bring Jarudin's walls down. "How nice to see you again, my Lord."

"The pleasure is all mine, Neal." Sture, while not a small man, was shorter than any of the rest of us in the room and used a woolen cap to hide the fact that his black hair had thinned dramatically in the last three years. His brown eyes glittered with intelligence, but there were times I wondered if he was actually able to see beyond the tip of his long, slender nose. "I wish your Steel Pack the best of luck in the coming assault."

If I could have bottled the tone of his voice, I could have used a drop of it in Jarudin's wells to poison the entire population. Ignoring him, I smiled at the Red Tiger. "Plans have been finalized, then?"

"I believe everyone understands his part in this." Beltran gulped his wine and swiped the excess from his bushy red beard with the back of his left hand. "Will you be ready to ride in an hour?"

I nodded. "The Pack will. What is our target?"

The Red Tiger moved to the table sitting in the middle of his tent and used his goblet to pin down one corner of the map he unrolled. Sture held down the other side and studied the map as if he could change the writing on it by force of will alone. "The Steel Pack will go in at the Dragon's Tower. You will have the Veirtu riders coming after you." He shifted a finger along to point at a separate tower. "The Steel Hunt and I will hit the Griffin's Tower at the same time."

The plan made sense. The octagonal city, as I could see from the map, had been laid out like a wheel with the Imperial Tower at the hub. Each of eight main roads led out from it to the eight main towers on the walls. Entering the city at the Dragon and Griffin towers, we would pass through the quarter of the city given over to Men. We hoped that our fellow Men would not be as hostile to our attack as their Reithrese masters, which might let us get deep into the city before we met serious resistance.

I looked up at him. "You expect the Veirtu to draw their sorcerers to us?"

"I agree with Neal's skepticism on this point." Sture's head came up and he nodded condescendingly toward me.

"My Lightning Elite is a mounted force that has sorcerers more fully integrated into it. We would be a lightning rod —no pun intended—for any sorcerously inclined defenders."

Aarundel grabbed the back of my belt, preventing me from stepping forward to throttle Sture. "I believe, Duke Sture, you mistake Neal's question. He was not doubting the Pack's ability to work with the Veirtu, merely wondering what the Red Tiger's intent was in attaching them to our unit."

The Red Tiger, having ignored Sture's comment and Aarundel's reply to it, nodded grimly. "I know that will make it difficult for you, Neal, but the Veirtu should be able to offer some protection. If the sorcerers cannot raise the walls again, the rest of our host can get through and the battle is won. Both of our forces have to push on through and head straight for the Imperial Tower. The more effective we are in drawing the Reithrese to the heart of Jarudin, the more likely our success."

Aarundel studied the map, then nodded. "Speed, then, is our armor and spear point."

"And the Lightning Elite is the swiftest cavalry we have, my Lord."

Beltran sighed. "I agree, my Lord, which is why I have designated it to consolidate our gains once the Pack and Hunt are through the gaps. If your men fail, we will be trapped with no hope of victory."

"I understand, my Lord." Sture studied the map a little longer, then looked up wearily as if certain of a coming disaster.

"Speed is vital, Imperator, as it has been throughout our war." The Red Tiger lifted up his cup, and the map rolled up into a tube, slapping against Sture's fingers. "When next we meet, my friends, the Reithrese capital will be ours."

"Provided the towers come down," Sture muttered.

Beltran confidently plucked a small piece of marble from the table, tossed it in the air, then caught it in a fist. "They will fall, Sture, they will fall, and when they do, the empire goes with them."

• • •

The tactical application of magick in combat is very difficult for reasons that are relatively simple to understand. As with sword fighting, for every strike there is a parry. In magick each spell has a counterspell. The efficiency of a sorcerer, or the skill of the swordsman, determines success, but with magick it takes a lot of energy to accomplish a result, so having it countered could be quite debilitating. A wizard capable of throwing a spell only once is akin to an archer with only one arrow. If he misses, he becomes useless.

The best use of magick in our assault would have been to cause huge upheavals of land at the base of the walls to bring them down. Aside from the fact that none of the wizards on our side, including the whole lot of the Veirtu, had sufficient power to do such a thing, that plan had problems because the Reithrese had already laid counterwards against that kind of spell. In effect the walls were immune to magickal attack, which accounted in part for the incredible confidence of the defenders.

The Red Tiger had worked out a way around their wards. Magick considers part of a stone the rough equivalent to the whole stone itself. Mages call this the Law of Holomorphism. It says that a part is considered a model for the whole, and the larger the part, the stronger the link.

The little stone the Red Tiger had shown me in his tent had been brought out from the city by one of the traders and had come from either the Griffin or Dragon Tower. Had the Reithrese wards not rendered them proof against it, magick could have been used to crush the small stones, thereby crushing the larger ones. Because we had to use other methods, Beltran had dozens of such small stones married to far bigger stones with a little mortar. Those larger rocks were loaded into our trebuchets and made ready to shoot at the walls.

The spell created by the Red Tiger's wizards was cast upon the smaller piece of stone attached to each missile. To avoid a counterspell working against it as it approached the magically warded walls, the spell itself would function only until the stone had reached the apex of its arc. Until that point the magick would alter the flight of the missile to keep it flying on a course that would reunite it with the piece of the wall from which it had been taken. As it began to fall from the sky, natural forces would guide it into its target, so no magick could cancel the spell and spoil the rock's aim.

Though not as powerful as an earthquake, I was willing to gamble on its effectiveness. The spell had been tested while the siege machines were being built and, so I was told, had worked very well. Fursey Nine-finger and Gathelus had watched the tests on behalf of the Pack and agreed to the plans the Red Tiger had laid out at the start of the campaign, so I saw no reason to hold reservations about the magick.

Then again, I did make double and triply certain that Sture had not managed to secret a rock in my armor as I prepared myself for battle. Assaulting a fortified city is one thing, but tempting fate with magick is another altogether.

Aarundel came for me just as I finished dripping wax onto a folded parchment and pressed the butt cap of my dagger down to seal the missive. Flipping Wasp around, I returned it to its sheath in my right boot. "I want to entrust this to you. Send it to your sister if things go badly for me out there."

Aarundel held his hand out for it. "As I have in each battle before, I will hold the message for you and return it when the hostilities are terminated."

I shook my head. "I appreciate your confidence, but this is far nastier a battle than we have faced before. In the open field the Steel Pack is a force to be reckoned with. Breaching a wall is something else entirely."

"The nature of the task matters not, Neal." Aarundel slipped the message into a pouch on his swordbelt. "You wield *Divisator*. You are destined to win an empire. Until then I harbor no trepidation concerning your safety."

"The sword didn't do much to protect Tashayul."

"He deluded himself with an ambitious reading of a flawed translation."

"I hope your translation is better."

"I have the prophecy in the original."

I stood in a rustle of mail. Had we been riding into

combat against another line of heavy cavalry, I would have donned a full suit of plate armor. In a charge the sheer weight of heavy cavalryman in collision can shock, stun, or even kill an enemy, which is why few troops choose to become the target of the Steel Pack. In addition to the weight, the full plate helps turn Haladin arrows, which, at close range, have an annoying habit of sticking into ring mail.

If things went as planned, we would be fighting in the city, so I chose to armor myself with my Roclawzi ring mail and supplemented it with a limited amount of plate. The combination would not sacrifice mobility or speed if I had to travel on foot, and yet it would keep me safe. My hauberk covered me from midforearm to midthigh and included a hood that protected the back of my neck and my ears. To that I added bracers, gauntlets, greaves, cuisses, and knee-cops. I decided against armoring my feet because I wanted a good feel for the stirrups in case I had to kick free of the saddle, but I did add a toe spike to my boots in case fighting became far closer than I hoped.

Cleaveheart rode on my left hip, and I chose to carry a small target shield on my left arm. I planted a steel cap on my head because I had less confidence in the prophecy than Aarundel and because only an idiot would go into battle without a helmet. Even a glancing blow to the skull can put a man down, and being knocked senseless in this fight would mean death.

I followed Aarundel from the tent to where our horses waited. Once again the nature of the fight we would face had forced a choice when it came to armoring Blackstar. I decided to encase him as completely as practical in metal. The steel chamfron had two ram's horns curling out from just in front of the ear holes and ring-joined plate made up the crinet and cuello armoring his neck and throat respectively. The peytral had a spike in the center, and the wings came back to cover Blackstar's shoulders as far as the saddle. Flanchards hung from the edges of my saddle to protect his ribs, and they joined with the crupper covering his flanks, thighs, and rump. The armor added nearly a hundred and fifty pounds to our weight but guaranteed his safety in case the prophecy did not.

I pulled myself up into the saddle without assistance. Despite the fact that my armor weighed at least half what Blackstar's did, it was not deadweight and, therefore, did not tax my strength to move. The day men start wearing armor so heavy they cannot get into a saddle without aid is the day I go into battle naked except for a big stick with which to knock them from their mounts and a small dagger to finish them off. In the battle between strong and swift, swift wins every time—provided there is room to run.

Thrusting aside my misgivings about a city not providing much room to run, I accepted a lance from one of the grooms and reined Blackstar around. In riding over to where the Steel Pack awaited me, I rode past the Veirtu. They recognized me and set to howling and hooting in a way that I might have found mocking if I didn't know who they were. As it was, I just howled like a wolf back at them, and they took that gesture in great humor.

The Veirtu go into battle all but naked, though they use weapons more powerful than sticks and little daggers. They worship Chavameht and claim to be possessed by one or more of the many animalistic spirits that are that god's servants or avatars in the world. They gravitated to the rebellion against the Reithrese more because I'm known as the Dun Wolf and Beltran is called the Red Tiger than out of any real hatred of the Reithrese. Warrior-priests all, they wear the skins of their particular totem spirit, use bows, and in close combat wield knobby war clubs that are painted up with all sorts of strange and arcane symbols. They also employ strange battle magicks that do not have great range, but tend to leave their targets with gaping and horrible wounds akin to those one would find if the target had been mauled by wild animals.

Fursey Nine-finger rode up to me as I joined the Pack. "I see we have the screaming idiots following us. It's for real, then?"

"It is. We're the Dragon Tower. Form up in double file, on me."

Fursey turned and repeated my orders. Each of the five companies formed up in double ranks forty riders long. With Aarundel at my side and the Dreel loping along on the left, I started us out at a walk on a serpentine course that would parade us at the extreme edge of range for Jarudin's mangonels. We would ride parallel to the walls, as we had done at this time for the past four days, and if we were lucky, we would again attract a crowd of defenders watching and laughing at us.

Out ahead of us the Steel Hunt performed a similar parade maneuver. From behind, as we drew opposite the Dragon Tower—so named because of the dragon motif used for the gargoyles festooning it—a trumpet sounded from our lines. The sharp snap of axes chopping through cord, and catches being slipped, presaged the mighty groan of wooden catapult and trebuchet arms as they bent to their duty. In a whirring whoosh akin to a quick breeze rising, huge boulders flew skyward and arced up high above our heads.

Our siege engines, because they were larger than those mounted atop Jarudin's towers and battlements, had both a greater range and a greater capacity than those used by the defenders. The stones they hurled, some spherical and others rectangular quarry blocks, spun lazily, end over end. As the first passed the apex of its flight, another trumpet blast sounded, and the whole of the Steel Pack turned to face the walls. When that first stone hit, we began our advance.

The initial strike against the Dragon Tower hit low and hard. Though the missile shattered when it struck—pieces rebounding and tumbling back out toward our lines—portions of several foundation blocks crumbled right along with it. Two more boulders pounded into that same area, enlarging the wound. The thunderclap of their hammering shuddered through me. Though a growing cloud of dust obscured the base of the tower, screams and shouts from the people in it told me severe damage had been done.

The next three stones hit higher. One bounced off the top of the wall, reducing an onager to flinders and the men tending it to bloody memories, then fell down to wreak havoc in the city below. The other two did not hit so well or dramatically, but the tower wavered under their blows. More people screamed, and black cracks ran a geometric zigzag through mortar up the front of the tower.

The last four stones hurled came down on target. One

hit the tower near the top, breaking off finials and merlons as if they were teeth. The other three crashed down through the dust at the tower base. Splinters and fragments from them flew back out of the dust. The stones' impact sounded hollow, and I guessed that they'd actually punched through the tower's exterior. That had been the plan, and if it worked, the tower should come down.

Down it came.

The cracks running up the front of the tower spread out like plant roots. Dust shot from the windows and arrow slits as the tower's internal structures broke away. Support for them eroded from the ground up, creating stresses that ripped them apart. Through the dust I could see blocks and gargoyles beginning to fall away one by one, then that became a cascade and finally an avalanche of stone. As if the Dragon Tower had been built from glass, it collapsed in a rumbling roar that shook the ground. With a dust cloud billowing out like fog, the tower's stone flesh fluidly spilled out into the field as if it were a stony carpet being rolled out to greet us.

A great cheer rose from behind us, but the warriors in the Red Tiger's army knew the battle had not been won with the fall of one tower. As we spurred our horses into a trot, one whole unit of archers came running out behind us. Armed with longbows, they sent shaft after shaft over our heads and down into the gap. At that range none of us expected the arrows to have enough force to pierce armor, but soldiers on the other side would take cover sooner than test that idea with their lives. For similar reasons a number of our smaller siege machines had been loaded with stones ranging in size from thumbnails to fists. Our soldiers used them to sweep the walls and gap to force defenders down.

The stones that had been used to build the walls had varied in size, shrinking in accord with their distance from the ground. As the tower came down, the stones ground against each other as if they were pressed together in a giant mill. The leavings from the stones high up filled the spaces between the larger blocks, which did not move much, creating a crushed-gravel roadway. While it was not level, and oily smoke poured up from pockets where things burned below, it provided solid enough footing that Blackstar took to it without any hesitation and only a slight slackening of speed.

I cut Blackstar back and around a marble midden as Shijef dashed past. He leaped from the stone mound to the broken edge of the wall and clung there as if he were a titanic, rabid squirrel. Tail twitching, he dove down, and I lost sight of him just before I crested the hill. A blood-curdling scream of triumph rang from the walls, followed by frenzied shouts that ended in gurgles and moans.

Up and over I went, the first of the Steel Pack's riders into Jarudin. Blackstar slid down the far side of the wall's ruins, then sprang forward to flat ground. He shied to the left, moving away from where the Dreel yodeled in delight. Shijef shucked a Reithrese warrior from his steel carapace, carrying away more than just metal as he did so. Blackstar's movement brought me into range of another warrior perched on a rooftop. He screamed some oath at me and leaped, but I reined Blackstar around even closer to the house and caught the airborne warrior on the point of my lance. He curled up around it and clattered to the ground like a tin pot.

I released the lance and drew Cleaveheart. Giving Blackstar some spur, I drove forward down Dragon Street. Riding clear of the dust and smoke from the collapsed tower, I split one man's skull with an overhand blow. Aarundel rode another man down, then stabbed him with the spike on his ax before reining up beside me.

Dragon Street led a mile straight on to the Imperial Tower. Every quarter mile between the wall and the city hub, where the three ring roads cut across the street, it widened out into a square, at the center of which stood a fountain or monument. If we were to meet resistance, it would be at one of those points, so the faster we moved in, the less likely we were to be stopped. As nearly as I could see, no one had formed up to oppose us, but the Reithrese had barracks deep enough in the city that I had no doubt we would yet run into stiff resistance.

Aarundel pointed his bloody ax to the west. "Griffin Tower has fallen."

Fursey rode up behind us. "First Company is through."

I nodded. "Form up eight abreast." Looking up, I saw

Shijef running across rooftops, leaping street-wide gaps as if they were cracks between cobblestones. With so much death he had to be all but out of his mind with glee. I knew that if I saw him hanging from the eaves like a gargoyle in Jammaq, I'd be getting near trouble, and that little bit of information might be just enough to keep me alive.

Out of the corner of my eye I saw something further down the street. Instinctively I brought my shield up and felt something hit it hard. A cruciform broadhead pierced the steel, but did not pass entirely through the shield. As I lowered the shield, the Reithrese archer turned and started to run. Aarundel yelled at him in Reithrese, and the warrior started hollering back when the Elf's words reached his ears.

I tipped the shield toward me to get a good look at the shaft buried in it. "It was lucky I raised my shield."

"Prophecies are not easily frustrated."

I rolled my eyes. "Well, that Reithrese should have known enough not to waste the arrow, then."

"So I scolded him while he fled."

Fursey returned with his men right behind him. I let them file around us to take up a forward position. As the Second and Third companies came through—commanded by Senan and Ross—they positioned themselves behind the First Company. Four and Five slipped into the smaller streets east and west respectively. I put Gathelus to the west because he had worked with Drogo before, and let the new man, Benedict, have our eastern flank.

Riding up to the front of the Pack, I saw no change in the city during the five minutes it had taken for us to get inside. As the Veirtu started through the gap, I led the Steel Pack forward. For the first quarter mile we might as well have been parading through Polston, because we ran into no trouble and even had Humans in the windows cheering us on. I forbade the men any shouting or accepting of flowers or jugs of wine and picked up our pace.

Our advance into the second ring of the city was marked by a distinct change in architecture and inhabitants. Leaving ramshackle and widely disparate human dwellings behind, we rode into a sector of the city that housed the Reithrese lower classes and their Human allies.

The buildings had been constructed in a blocky style that had strength but no artistry. The houses had been gaily painted and gaudy drapes covered windows, but still seemed lifeless.

Not so the intersection with the second ring road. A Reithrese officer rallied a small patrol and two dozen Haladina to take up a position between us and the intersection. That made tactical sense, given that his position would allow any reinforcements to come from the ring road or from Dragon Street. Not knowing if he had troops following him, I had to admire his dedication to duty.

I also had to go through him.

Raising Cleaveheart, I waved my men forward and let the Steel Pack do what it does best: charge. Less than four hundred yards separated us from the defenders, so we cantered forward for roughly half that distance. I expected the defenders to break just at the sight of us, but stupidity or arrogance kept the Reithrese in their place, and Haladina admiration for the jewel-grinning warriors overrode their better sense.

Three hundred yards, then only two hundred fifty. As we approached, I could feel the blood start pounding in my temples. Blackstar impatiently tossed his head, and I found myself chuckling in a most sinister way. Aarundel raised his ax and screamed out an inhuman challenge. I squinted, trying to see if I could pick out individuals I could identify as sorcerers. I saw none and knew, as we passed the two-hundred-yard mark, it wouldn't have made any difference if I had.

Slashing down with Cleaveheart, I squeezed Blackstar with my knees and sent him into a gallop. The first rank of the Steel Pack surged forward, using Aarundel and me to fill in the gaps. Steel-shod hooves struck sparks from cobblestones. The rolling thunder of hoofbeats echoed down the Dragon Street canyon. Arrows loosed by the Haladin horse bows glanced ineffectively from armor. Clutching the reins in my left hand and pulling my shield in tight to my chest, I howled like a madman and plunged forward into the defenders.

I had no chance to strike a blow, because the initial impact blasted the Reithrese officer back. Blackstar had hit his mount in the shoulder, tipping the horse up and back over on its rump. It twisted to the side, rolling sufficiently to pulverize the officer's leg. Bucking and leaping, Blackstar pushed forward, eager to get at the Haladin ranks. His efforts carried us clear of the officer and on into the Haladina.

Riding lighter mounts, wearing boiled-leather or stripscale armor, the outlanders were no more suited to withstanding our charge than they were to enjoying a harsh winter. Horses screamed, nostrils flared, and eye whites poached brown eyes as Haladin horses scrabbled ineffectively to retain their footing. Some managed to turn after an initial shock, then another horse would hit them broadside. Shrieking curses, riders slashed at our horses while trying to control their own mounts. Cleaveheart fell silver and rose crimson as I cut a man from the saddle to win free of the roadblock.

I knew that I had to keep riding, because to stop or turn would have been as suicidal as the stand the defenders had made. The Steel Pack would roll over me as easily as it had them, and I had no intention of dying beneath the swords and flashing hooves of my own men. We had a mission to accomplish, and with each jarring hoof-fall I came one stride closer to completing it.

I raced into the middle intersection and saw, to the east, a troop of mixed Reithrese and Human pikemen running forward to set up another roadblock. I never even considered turning my riders to face them. A charge against set pikemen would be suicidal, and they could set up in the time it would take us to cross the two hundred yards to where they ran. But they were not between us and the tower, so their threat to us was minimal.

It became even smaller when Benedict and Five Company burst from the alleys and streets to catch them on the flank. Buildings swept that battle from my sight as I rode on. To my left, inside a hundred yards, a Reithrese longbowman stepped from a shadowed alley to shoot at me. Before he could loose his arrow, a furry shadow detached itself from a building across the way and in one bound carried the archer back into the blackness from which he had come. I heard no scream, but riding past, I saw blood anointing both sides of the alley.

The third ring of the city had buildings and homes that appeared more elegant and graceful, despite the rigidity of squared designs. Recessed doorways, open balconies, and hints of interior courtyards marked this as a more affluent section of the city, and I would have been willing to bet that we were the first free-Men to ride down the streets since its construction. It may well have had a beauty that I could have appreciated, but with the architecture being so inhuman, all I felt was the unsettling, unfocused threat of being an invader in an enemy stronghold.

At the last ring intersection I saw a knot of figures setting up, and their actions intensified that hostile sensation. Cloaked in black, with variously colored sashes, hems, and hoods, a dozen people stood where Dragon Street opened into the last courtyard. Several of them touched hands; then as they spread apart, a bluish line of lighting linked their hands and glowed out through their eyes. Others took up positions behind the sorcerous line, with two even climbing into the geysering fountain. The water began to form itself around them, encasing each in a shifting, spiky rainbow armor.

Even a hundred yards away I could hear the energy crackling and humming between them. I had no doubt their line would be lethal, but short of its instantly evaporating everyone who touched it, it could not stop us. I guided Blackstar directly at one of the sorcerers in the vain hope that he might be a weak link holding the chain together. I tightened my grip on Cleaveheart and for once hoped Aarundel was right about the prophecy's prophylactic properties.

Suddenly, from the eastern side of the square, a volley of arrows raked over the Reithrese. The centermost sorcerer in the line fell transfixed by a half-dozen Veirtu arrows. The energy linking him with the other sorcerers blinked, then died in a stink of ozone just before our whirlwind charge blew into the square.

The Veirtu, who had moved beyond Benedict's men as they fought with the pikemen, had flanked the sorcerers and had knocked the linchpin from the defense of the square. More arrows shot in at the water-warded sorcerers. The fluid armor caught and shunted aside arrows, but had no such luck against Veirtu magicks. I saw water rent as if by claws and one of the two sorcerers go down with most of her abdomen sliced open.

One or two of the Reithrese did cast spells at us. I felt the heat of a flamewall materializing behind me and heard the screams of riders at my back, but the fire winked out as Aarundel harvested the Reithressa's head with one long swipe of his ax. A bolt of lightning missed me, but struck another of the Steel Pack, and somewhere else an explosion cast a horse and rider high into the air on the left flank.

We rode on, a metal tide rising to the heart of the city. The lack of resistance over the last quarter mile had me wondering what we would face at the Imperial Tower. A number of scenarios ran through my mind, the most dire of which placed a sorcerous bodyguard for the emperor raising magical wards around the tower itself, but I doubted it. I suspected that even more troops than we had dared imagine had been summoned away from Jarudin to prevent the conquest of Reith. The sorcerers we had ridden over had not been that powerful, and I began to think that more trust had been placed in walls and defensive spells than was prudent for the emperor.

As we rode, the Imperial Tower loomed taller and taller. It reminded me of Jammaq in that on its faces had been carved countless little scenes. These depicted everyday life, laws in action, history and folktales, in an illiterate's monument to the empire and people that put it together. And while it did not have the profane displays and elements found in Jammaq, to me it felt no less malevolent. The life carved into its flesh was not life as it naturally occurred, but life as the Reithrese intended it to be. The fact that Humans appeared at the bottom of the tower and Reithrese occupied only the upper precincts sent a not-so-subtle message to the conquered people of Ispar.

It was a message I wanted to expose as a lie.

We came into the central promenade surrounding the tower and saw the Steel Hunt arriving at the same time. Our troops began to rein up, and I saw the Red Tiger himself leap from his saddle to run up the stairs at the two sentries stationed there. Taller than either one of them, with his red mane flowing back from his head, the man who would be emperor ran at the Reithrese soldiers with a broadsword in each hand and roaring laughter falling from his throat.

Behind the soldiers the tower's huge iron doors slowly began to close in an effort to keep us out.

Without a second thought I jammed heels into flanchards hard enough for Blackstar to feel it. The horse took the stairs as if they were level ground. One of the guards turned toward me and I flung my shield at him. It sailed through the air and bounced up off the steps at him. He parried it, but dealing with it delayed him enough that he could not stop me. In a clatter of hooves on basalt, Blackstar crested the steps and plunged on through the narrowing doorway.

I kicked free of the saddle and twisted down to the ground. I let myself go to one knee and continued my spin, with Cleaveheart whipping out from left to right two feet above the floor. A Reithrese warrior's slash passed over my head while my cut took his left leg off at the knee. He went down screaming and I came up quickly. I parried a thrust back to my right, then smashed my gauntleted left fist into another soldier's face.

He reeled back, spitting out a fortune in broken teeth, and bumped into the two Man-slaves working the windlass to close the door. One of them turned around and jumped on his back, while the other cowered in place. "Throw it wide open," I shouted at him, then spitted the Reithrese. "You're free men now. Where's the emperor?"

The slave who had jumped the Reithrese pointed to a sharply arched doorway. "He's in there, waiting."

I ran toward the archway as Aarundel rode into the entryway and the Dreel edged in around the door. "The emperor is in here."

A shiver ran down my spine as I entered the long, narrow room beyond the archway. Aside from flames dancing in the pit-fire at the far end and in the circular firepots built high up on the walls, nothing in the room moved. Squares of prayer carpet had been piled along the wall split by the doorway and were the only furnishing in the room. They helped me identify the chamber as a Reithrese chapel.

Six black pillars shaped like giant femurs held the ceiling aloft. As I looked up into the vaults, I noticed they had been curiously shaped. With reddish highlights slithering across the relief like snakes, it took a moment or two to put the shape above me together. Overhead, as if I stood within a giant sarcophagus, the ceiling had been carved as a mold for an effigy. Though rendered in reverse, I recognized Tashayul's form—the metal skeleton surrounding him providing a big clue for me.

Silhouetted against the firepit located beneath Tashayul's eyes, the emperor leaned on a sword, waiting. Even encased in blackened mail, he appeared taller and a bit more slender than the average Reithrese warrior. The set of his shoulders marked resignation, but I did not know if that concerned having to fight, or having to die. As his head came up, I saw gold glints from the crown he wore.

"So, it is you, Neal." He slowly shook his head. "You have indeed earned your nickname: *Sikkatura*."

I smiled. "Sikkatura?"

Aarundel slipped through the door and stood at my right. "It means 'annoyance.' "

The emperor laughed. "The Elf gives you the polite translation." He straightened up and waved me forward. "Come to me, Neal, let us fight. If you win, the empire is yours. And when I kill you, I shall have *Khlephnaft* and shall build the empire anew."

I shook my head and walked down the aisle between columns toward him. "If you win the sword, I trust you will ward your capital more appropriately?"

"There will be no need, once we have sent every last Man to the goddess." He turned his back to me and dropped to one knee before the firepit. Bending his head forward reverently, he slid the tip of his blade into the lapping flames and intoned a prayer aloud. *"Bierek dmir Tieghi, Alla falz mara minn Hajja ta'dejjem."*

Rising and turning to face me, he brought his sword up in a salute. What had been a black blade before, now only served as the core of a sword edged with indigo flames. I saw lettering on the blade begin to glow. I recognized the letters as being Reithrese in origin, but their meaning and importance I could not begin to fathom. As the emperor brought his sword down into a guard, the flames brightened, and dull red tongues played off the tallest spikes.

I closed my left fist around the latter half of Cleaveheart's hilt and kept the blade between me and the Reithrese emperor. Until I knew what the sword could do aside from burn, I could not take the offensive. Likewise I needed to gain a feel for the emperor's skill. Had I approached him the way the Red Tiger went after the sentries, I'd have been spitted and roasted with one lunge.

The emperor obliged my taste for caution and came in faster than I expected of him, but not so fast that I could not counter his attack. He feinted a head-high slash, then whipped the blade down and around my parry. Twisting my wrists around, I managed to invert my blade and stop his attack, but not before the edge of his blade sliced a piece out of my right greave. I felt the heat against my shin and heard the metal clink on the floor, but I'd jumped back out of range before another little cut could do to bones what that blade had done to my armor.

Cleaveheart had weathered the parry without so much as a nick, so whatever the magick was that allowed the sword to chop up my armor, it had no effect on my sword. That was good because with my armor being useless, we would be reduced to a battle of skill. The emperor had skill, there was no doubt about it—as Aarundel had noted in Cygestolia, having a long life allows one to learn a lot about a subject.

The emperor came at me again, lunging low, then flicking the blade up and around in a cut meant to carve a furrow through my chest. Pivoting on my right foot, I drew myself out of line with the attack. Two hands on my hilt, I chopped Cleaveheart down, momentarily trapping his blade against the floor. He pulled back, and I whipped my sword up in a quick cut at his throat.

He twisted around and went down, eluding Cleaveheart's sharp kiss by an inch. The flat of his blade slapped across my flank, and half-melted armor rings tinkled as they bounced off the floor. I jumped back from that hellish sword as the burning sting started in my side. My retreat gave him time to roll to his feet and step away from the smoking impression his sword had made in the floor.

"As always, Manchild, time is on my side."

"Neal, give him to me." The Red Tiger stood in the archway, bloodied blades at the ready.

"No, the emperor is mine." I raised myself up to my full height and struck a single-handed guard with the tip of my blade pointing down toward the emperor's knee. I opened my mouth as if to speak, then advanced a step, extended, and lunged. The emperor batted my blade aside, then snapped his blade down and around in riposte aimed at my heart. I brought my left hand down and slapped the white-hot blade away with my gauntlet. I felt the searing kiss of hot metal against the back of my hand, so I flicked my hand forward like a cat ridding its paw of water and threw the gauntlet at the Emperor.

He slashed his fiery blade back through the space between us, cutting the gauntlet in half. The cuff flew in a fluid blob to splash steel-gray against one of the pillars. The candescent hand, leather straps burning merrily, struck him in the middle of the chest and dripped down the front of his ring mail. The quilted gambeson beneath it began to smolder. The emperor retreated quickly to escape the smoke rising in his face, but his swift movement only made the fabric burn faster.

A quickstep to my left and he came into range again. I brought Cleaveheart down in a heavy cut that caught him on the left shoulder. Rings snapped apart, and he screamed as I chopped down through muscle and bone. He tried a halfhearted cut at my midsection, but I slid Cleaveheart free and parried him strongly. Shifting my sword to my left hand, I brought my right fist up and caught him in the mouth, smearing crimson across his white face and chin.

He staggered back, then collapsed. He sat down hard enough to jar the crown from his head, but he retained his sword. Tears filling his eyes, he tried to roll up to his feet, but the punch still had him too unstable to be able to manage it. He slipped again and tried to regain his balance by burying his sword in the floor. It sank into the stone as if cutting through nothing more substantial than water, so it did not help steady him.

Unbalanced, he released the blade. That quenched its flames and froze it in place, but he had fallen too far from it to use it to lever himself to his feet. He crashed back to his buttocks, then rolled over onto his ruined left shoulder. He screamed, arching his back, then went limp. The smoking cloth sent a gray column toward the ceiling, where it gathered into a cloud and filled the face of Tashayul.

I leaned forward and scooped the crown up with Cleaveheart's tip. I slowly turned and was surprised to see the Red Tiger had advanced from the doorway. He looked at the crown and then me and back at the crown again. Straightening up, with both swords at the ready, he looked me in the eye, saying nothing, yet saying everything by raising one eyebrow.

Back by the door Aarundel held his ax at the ready, and the Dreel tensed in the shadow of a pillar. Between them stood Sture, the captains of my Steel Pack, and the Steel Hunt's Drogo. I saw them study the both of us and I knew their thoughts. Though I had fought beneath the Red Tiger's banner, the Dun Wolf was his equal in song and legend. I wielded Cleaveheart, and as everyone knew, the man who possessed that sword was destined to win an empire. I had killed this emperor, and I had been responsible for Tashayul's death. While the Red Tiger might have inspired the uprising against the Reithrese, no man, not even Beltran, had a more legitimate claim to the crown than did I.

All I had to do was slip it from my sword and place it on my head. Beltran might fight me for it, or might pledge his fealty to me. Through that simple action I would become the most powerful Man on the face of Skirren. I would become the hero of heroes. I would be the liberator of Mankind, and everyone, including the Elves, would have to respect me. They would have to deal with me as an equal. They would have to please me, placate me, and that could mean they might even give me Larissa.

The stink of blood and burning wool cut through the idyllic fantasy my mind began to weave around her image.

I looked over at the Red Tiger. "There is a prophecy that says he who wields Cleaveheart will win an empire."

He nodded stiffly if solemnly.

"And so I have." I flipped him the crown. "I have chosen to win it for you."

Chapter 17

Memories of Childhood

Spring
A.R. 499
The Present

Durriken's death affected Gena in ways it took her a long time on the road to sort out. She recognized almost immediately the utter irrationality of her becoming angry with Rik for having died on her. His death spoiled the dreams she had not even realized she harbored until he was killed, and she felt betrayed by that. Knowing that such resentment was not logical did not help abate it, but did let her feel it coming on and shunt it aside before it could prompt behavior.

She also felt pain at Rik's loss and found herself quick to take offense at even the slightest hint of disdain for him. Within hours of his death the Fisher family suffered another loss: Waldo was found dead, the victim of ingesting poorly prepared mussels. His body had swollen up, and his tongue turned purple as it filled his throat and cut off his air. He literally strangled to death in the night on his own tongue, and she found that death fittingly ignominious for a man she detested.

The tears cried for Waldo annoyed her because she felt there should have been much more of a display for Rik. She found herself unable to cry in public and knew that her upbringing made public displays of grief and emotion as alien to her as the custom of burying valuables and favorite items with the dead. Among Elves those things were shared out as keepsakes. She almost laughed when one Fisher proclaimed the family vault proof against grave robbers, because Gena believed if Men refrained from interring jewelry and other such things with the dead, no thief would bother even to try to break in.

Looking up ahead of her on the road, she saw Berengar gently shift his weight with each step his horse took. She owed him a debt of gratitude because he had insisted that Rik be buried before Waldo and in a place considered more honorable within the tomb. That had brought arguments, but Berengar would not be denied. She smiled as she recalled him telling a reluctant relative, "Gainsay me, you scheming snake, and instead of Neal Elfward, *I'll* be haunting your nightmares."

Gena gave Spirit a touch of her heels and brought her horse around the string of spare mounts and pack horses to Berengar's side. "My Lord, I owe you an apology."

Berengar feigned polite surprise easily. "An apology?"

Gena nodded. "We have been on the road for a week now, and I have been singularly poor company. I have returned silence and apathy for your care and concern for me."

He shrugged his broad shoulders eloquently. "You have had good reason to be quiet. You have suffered a loss."

"As have you."

"Waldo? Yes, he was a loss, but I was not as close to him as you were to Rik." Berengar hesitated for a second, then frowned. "Not wishing to speak poorly of the dead, but Waldo was pusillanimous and prickly. He traded more on our family name than he did on his own deeds, and he judged people not by their own worth, but the worth of their position in the world. I think I actually liked Rik more than Waldo, and if offered a choice to summon one of them from the grave to join us here, I would choose your friend."

"You are most kind in excusing my behavior."

"Actually, Gena, your silence has allowed me to think about our mission and all that attends it, well away from the pressures and politics of Aurdon." Berengar looked back over his shoulder to the south, where Aurdon lay seven days back down the road. "Away from the city, traveling into the heart of this decaying empire, I am becoming aware of how petty and trivial our struggles are."

"How so?"

"Here, were I traveling in the company of Aurdon Rangers, our journey would be taken as an invasion from over the border. There, in Aurdon, my name and my family can get things accomplished in an instant. Here, in Ispar, my crest would mean nothing if a Red Tiger were not standing on top of it." His blue eyes flashed with amusement. "Realizing that something which you value is worthless outside a very small, confined place is humbling. And, of course, this whole discussion must seem very silly to you because of the chronological view your longevity affords you."

Gena started to deny his claim, but the wary way in which his eyes began to narrow stopped her. "There once was a time when what you have said would have been accepted by Elves as akin to a natural law. The struggles of Men were seen as battles between herds of animals. They were interesting and even diverting, but they were not seen as causing much in the way of permanent change in the world."

"Until Neal."

"Neal *did* influence our way of looking at things, yes." Gena wiped some sweat from her brow with the back of her left hand. "Some Elves, my great-great-grandfather among them, thought Men had been dismissed too lightly. Neal proved a boon to those wishing to advance that view. Men, and their actions before and since the time of Neal, have proved that view to be correct."

"Even so, the snarling battles between Men cannot be seen as being nearly as important to Elves as they are to those of us involved in them."

"That is a valid point, but one that cannot stand without analysis. Take, for example, the situation that we are riding now to correct. There are those among my people who might argue that the Fishers and the Riverens fought five hundred years ago and they are fighting now, so that Neal's effort to keep the peace failed utterly. To suggest, however, that the failure means his attempt should never have been made is wrong and even dangerous."

Berengar nodded slowly. "So your perspective over time suggests that anything which waxes will wane, like the tides rising and falling."

Gena smiled. "That is an excellent example. The fact that the tide will reach the same low point in the night that it saw in the morning does not mean the beach will not be wet at noon."

"I see that holding for natural forces, but Human enterprises?" The count looked around at the rolling green meadows covering the hillside up which they rode. "If that idea is valid, then it might be imagined that the Red Tiger's empire will rise again."

Gena frowned. "I suppose that is true, but things do not necessarily run in circles, though they may be cyclical. For example, we know there will never be another Reithrese Empire to conquer. If the empire is to become powerful again, it might be as a federation of strong provinces."

"Or a strong leader may rise up and reunite it under his leadership." Berengar shook his head. "The one thing that I have not liked about having been placed in the imperial line is the amount of politics into which I have been thrust. My family branch broke off from the main line four generations back: my great-grandfather was the emperor, though my great-grandmother was scullery maid or somesuch. My mother's uncle managed to convince Hardelwick, the current emperor, to legitimize our line. All that did was get my two cousins killed, it seems. I am hoping that I am far enough removed from things that I won't be a target."

"I hope you're not a target as well. This uncle who got your line legitimized, he is the Atholwin we are going to visit?"

"Yes. He is my mother's uncle. We used to come up here, my brother Nilus and I, in the summers to get away from Aurdon during the humid season. Just over the rise we can see the town of Blackoak with the castle at the other end of the valley." He hesitated for a second. "In fact, if I remember correctly, on the down side of this hill is a grand old oak in which my brother and I built a tree house. We hung a rope from one of the branches and used to swing on it while pretending we were soldiers preparing to storm the castle."

Gena flicked a horsefly off Spirit's neck. "You speak of that time as if you treasure it."

"I do." He turned to look at her with curiosity in his eyes. "It is easy for me to remember my childhood, because it was not that long ago. I remember things like running and laughing, my first taste of a raspberry tart, and the first time I ever fell in love. It occurs to me that while I envy you your long life, I think I should feel the loss if I were to be so far removed from times of simple pleasures."

"Such memories do not fade, no matter the years." Gena took time to look around as she considered how much she wanted to tell him. Still stung by the fact that Berengar knew things about her that she had not shared with Durriken, she chose to husband facts for the moment. "Among the Elves, children are a rare and blessed event, with the gulf between parent and child often being measured in centuries. Even so, because we have such a long life, as adults we are not so pressed to accomplish things that parents cannot take time to nurture and enjoy children. A child is, in essence, property of the family into which he is born. When my brother and his wife conceived and bore a son, all of us raised him, from great-grandfather on down."

She smiled at the count to soften the blow of not telling him everything. "My great-aunt, before she went beyond, spent a great deal of time with me, despite having duties to her husband's family. From her I learned what I know of magick as well as much about Neal Elfward. From her and my grandfather I learned of him directly, whereas all you have are stories that have been told and retold until they no longer resemble the truth."

"I know that, yes. Still, the stories have some validity. For example, I know of Neal's love for Elvenkind from the stories. I even heard of a story sung in Najinda that tells of

Neal's true love for an Elven maid. Is that true or an example of exaggeration?"

Gena shrugged the question off, avoiding a direct answer. "In those days, for Neal to touch a *sylvanesti* would have resulted in his death and her disgrace."

"Not so today, I take it."

Gena blushed. "No, not so."

"I'm sorry. Please, I didn't mean to embarrass you." Berengar hunted for the proper words. "Your affection for Durriken was obvious yet circumspect. I didn't know . . . not that I cared . . . well I cared, but I did not wonder . . . " He blushed in turn. "Forgive me. This is none of my business."

"You are forgiven if you wish, but I did not count it a fault against you." Desirous of moving away from a discussion of her personal life, she smiled at Berengar. "How long is it since you last visited your uncle?"

"I was a child when last I spent any real amount of time with him, but most recently I was here when I traveled to Jarudin for our family's investiture." Berengar shook his head slightly. "The years have not been kind to Atholwin. His health was declining then, and I do not imagine his sons' deaths have improved things very much. It will be interesting to see him again."

Gena looked up as they came over the hilltop. Hoping to burn the melancholy note from Berengar's voice, she pointed to a huge budding oak halfway down the hillside. "There, is that the tree you remember?"

"Yes, yes it is." Berengar's face brightened. He touched his heels to his mount's ribs and started to trot toward it. "There, on the eastern side you can see a couple of boards still in the branches. Likely not our fortress, but another. Uncle Atholwin must have great-grandchildren who still play in those boughs."

Gena laughed and rode after him, then reined back when Berengar raised his left hand. "What is it?"

"Something we never had in that tree."

Closer in, swinging from a limb jutting north, Gena saw a stretch-necked corpse. She rode forward and worked around to the east to keep the wind coming from her back so she'd not smell the body. By the look of the flesh and the clothes, it had been hanging there for the better part of four days, for the weather had been dry and hot and the corpse showed every sign of being desiccated by the wind and sun.

Drying had tightened the lips to reveal a meagre collection of yellowed and rotting teeth in the dead man's mouth. His eyes were gone and a raven perched on the branch above him. It had a bit of something in its beak, but flew off to the north when she came in too close for the bird's comfort. "There is a sign on his chest."

Berengar rode up beside her and studied the corpse as it slowly twisted around and back again. "The Truth is life. In life he lied, now he is denied the Truth."

Gena shivered. "That's not the sort of acorn I would hope my oaks would produce."

Berengar focused his eyes further down the valley. "This is not the same place I remember from last year. . . . I mean to say, we have come to Atholwin's holding, Blackoak, but the village looks smaller, and the roof is gone from one of the castle's towers."

"Yes, but there are still people down there, and fresh pennants flying from the other towers."

"True enough." Berengar took a deep breath, then exhaled slowly. "Let us ride to the castle and see how things stand there. If Atholwin lives, there will be an explanation for this."

"And if he does not?"

"That, Lady Genevera, could also explain this."

They rode around the village instead of through it, keeping to a huntsman's trail that had partially returned to the wild. The bridge over the dry moat had a few rotted timbers in it, but the patches proved strong enough that their horses did not punch a hoof through. In drawing nearer the gray stone structure, Gena did see that the smallest of three towers had fallen into disrepair, though the walls looked strong and were manned by soldiers in livery that Berengar identified as belonging to his mother's uncle.

Two young grooms accepted their reins in the small courtyard, and an elderly servant answered the sergeant-at-arms' call for someone to attend them. The old man, stooped with age beneath a pate festooned with thin threads of gray hair, smiled when he saw Berengar. "Come, come, Count Fisher. My master is expecting you."

Berengar and Gena exchanged surprised looks, but followed the man nonetheless into the musty, dark building constructed around the base of the main tower. Torches burned in every fourth sconce, providing just enough illumination for Gena to pick her way around haphazard barricades and caches of weapons stored in shadowed niches. She could see no rhyme nor reason to any of it except to wonder if the master of the castle feared a coming need to defend his home even into the hallways.

The servant led them into a small room with moldering tapestries covering all the walls. Across from them, behind a thick oaken table set with a pair of burning candles, a wizened old man sat huddled in a huge chair. His pale flesh had faded past the white of his hair and long beard to the point where it appeared blue in some places and ivory in others depending if it covered meat or bone. Most of it covered bone, leaving Gena with the impression that she stood before a skeleton encased in glass.

One hand rose as if a puppet's limb being manipulated by an arthritic puppeteer, and the long-nailed finger that came out to point at them quivered. In a voice not much more stable than the finger, the old man croaked, "So you are Berengar Fisher. My spies told me you were coming."

As if on cue, a raven descended from the blackness overhead and landed on the table. Its talons scrabbled against the wood as it walked forward, its head bobbing. It twisted its head to peer down into the heavy goblet on the table; then the bird swung around to face them. It cawed loudly, and the old man started as if he had drifted off to sleep after speaking.

Berengar took one step forward. "I am Berengar Fisher, pleased again to be in the company of Earl Blackoak."

"Is that so?" The man's cloudy blue eyes barely seemed to move, and Gena wondered if he could even see her in the gloomy light. "Then you will indulge me, nephew."

"As you wish, uncle."

Gena heard noise in the hallway and glanced back to

see a number of the castle's soldiers gathering at the threshold.

"If you are Berengar Fisher, then you are an assassin. Tell me how you will slay me." The old man's eyes sparked with energy. "And tell me truly, for I will know if you lie, and you will not like the consequences of trying to deceive me."

Chapter 18

Anticipation of Children

Autumn
Reign of the Red Tiger Year 3 /
Imperium Year 1
Five Centuries Ago
My Thirty-seventh Year

A shiver ran down my spine as I again stepped into the Reithrese chapel at the base of the Imperial Tower in Jarudin. Though the month since I had fought here had wrought many changes in the city and the world, the burn scar on the back of my left hand reminded me how close I had come to dying. While I was not so certain that the average member of the Elder races was that much tougher than the average Man, I knew the elite among the Elder races had great power, and I wondered how long I would be able to defy such people without paying for my audacity.

Xerstan, the balding, bulbous architect whom the Red Tiger—better known now as Emperor Beltran Primus—had assigned to designing new constructions and renovations, bowed his head to me as he entered the room. The yellowed light given off by the tallow candles illuminating the room made him look jaundiced, but I preferred that to the bloody pallor that the now-dead fires had spread across the room when I first saw it. "Forgive my being late, Lord Neal, but my apprentice was tardy in making the wax impressions of your dagger."

He held Wasp out to me, and I returned it to the sheath at my right hip. "I trust, then, that the emperor has agreed to the plan we discussed?"

The small man nodded confidently. "He is still of a mind to fill this room and seal it for all time, but your idea has piqued his sense of irony. Preparations will take a year, though if things go the way the first month of conquest has gone, we may be ready by spring." He walked past me and squatted awkwardly beside the hilt of the emperor's sword. "I do not know if I am comfortable with this being here, or if I would feel less so if we removed it. It was rather nasty as I understand it."

I scratched at the twisted flesh on the back of my hand. "I think leaving it here is appropriate." I glanced up at the effigy of Tashayul. "Strikes me as appropriate that it should have burned out in roughly the same spot as Tashayul's heart. I think it requires a prayer to Reithra to activate, and I'm thinking I've no desire to hear such a thing uttered in earnest here."

"May the gods grant everyone your wisdom in that matter. Fortunately I don't think there is a Reithrese left in the city, so this will not be a problem."

He was correct. The Red Tiger had declared martial law immediately and dealt harshly with looters and vandals. Because Jarudin was a northern city, the Reithrese population tended to migrate back to Reith for the winters, and a great number of them had taken time to travel with the army that had moved through the Elven Holdings to trap us in the mountains. As a result, the Reithrese population remaining in the city was relatively small. The empress gave Beltran her parole and led the remaining Reithrese back toward their homeland with no more than they could fit on wagons. Haladina rode as their guards and departed in good order.

I had not expected things to go as well as they had. Sulane, the imperial widow, accepted Beltran's terms quickly, as if she had anticipated something harsher. Aarundel said she'd heard stories about my intent to make her my wife, prompting her to leave as quickly as possible. While that rumor might have been a contributing factor, I assumed she agreed because Beltran asked only one thing for ransom for her and her people: time. In return for five years of peace, he let her go.

The Human population in the city moved from their hovels into the grander homes of their Reithrese masters, but that migration likewise worked on a system Beltran had devised. That the transition went smoothly made me thankful once again that I had avoided temptation and had given him the crown. Not only was he a leader, but he was thoughtful. He considered laws and policies, their implications and problems, before imposing a solution.

The trade of time to the Reithrese was a brilliant example of his forethought. He knew that time meant nothing to them. Five years would pass before they noticed, but it would be seen among Humanity as a veritable eternity. It would allow him to consolidate his grip on Ispar and to promote revolts in Barkol and Esquihir, while Sture headed off to Irtysh to liberate it. Thousands of Human children would become world-aware with a Human empire dominating the world's geography. They would take pride in it, and when the time came, they would rise to defend it.

Likewise, his system for parceling out homes worked to bring people together and make them mindful of the sacrifices endured in winning the empire. The grandest houses were given over to his allies and commanders in repayment of their service to him. A whole section of the Inner Ring was set aside for the Mountain Men, and everyone was looking forward to the spring and their liberation from their icy prison. Aarundel and I were given homes in that area, but I declared mine the Roclawzi embassy and sent word to my brother that he should send an ambassador or two.

The rest of the homes were given out based on the number of years individuals and families had been in thrall to the Reithrese. An effort was made to redress the losses of those who had seen their homes destroyed, their families slain, and their wealth stolen by Tashayul's host. Disputes arose and there was some fraud, but Beltran and his judges cut through all, meting out justice swiftly and sharply to those who deserved it, rewarding honesty and redressing tragedy wherever they found them.

In many ways I think the two most difficult cases for the Red Tiger to deal with were Aarundel and myself. Sture had been easy to appease. Newly freed Irtyshites who had been brought to the capital by their Reithrese masters swelled the Exile Legion's ranks to nearly double. With Beltran's blessing, Sture left amid fanfare to liberate his frozen homeland.

Aarundel studiously sought to downplay his role in the affair, but did accept a home and a title. Beltran sought to reward him with more, but Aarundel continually refused. Finally the emperor offered to write and send to Aarundel's kin an accounting of his exploits, and the Elf relented with the proviso that the Red Tiger would no more press him on the matter of reward.

The Red Tiger could understand, with Aarundel being an Elf and all, why he might refuse Man-offered honors. I confused him more when I turned down his request to become his warlord. He wanted to bring the Steel Pack into imperial service as one of his two bodyguard companies—an idea to which I agreed after polling my Men and discovering they wanted that as well. I granted him that pleasure and nominated Fursey Nine-finger to replace me. Other than that, as I told him, hot food, a warm bed, and cold ale would be more than enough reward for me.

That was not sufficient for him, however; he advanced a number of reasons for his opinion, and I had a hard time disagreeing with any of them. If I did not accept some sort of position, it would be assumed that I had repudiated our alliance and it could be taken that I had no confidence in him. Moreover, I had become a symbol of the revolt, as had he, and order had to be imposed over things while it still could be, or the rebellion against the Reithrese might fall apart without any preparation for the battles that would still come.

He pointed out, for example, that a number of very idealistic young men had taken to burning the backs of their left hands with brands and glowing irons to ape the scar I had from killing the emperor. The Red Tiger and I agreed this was nonsense—and regretted the clumsy ones who managed to burn their hands off—so we established that the soldiers in Emperor's Own Steel Pack were to wear a branded leather glove on their left hands in honor of Lord Neal, Knight-Defender of the Empire, and that they would not take kindly to anyone lampooning this tradition outside their ranks. As the brand they used the six-lined rune for the Roclaws, which didn't look anything like my scar, but reminded people of me anyway and got their point across.

Being so honored both gratified and terrified me. I must admit pleasure at how readily the men of the Steel Pack agreed to wearing the gloves. What the Red Tiger and I had created as the solution to a problem, they embraced proudly as a newborn tradition. A greater troop of warriors I could not imagine commanding, and I admit to feeling a thrill when I heard ballads sung in our honor.

I had agreed to the title only because the Red Tiger trapped me into it. If I had no title, then the honor the Steel Pack showed me would be thought a fraud, and I would dishonor them by refusing a title. I bargained hard, so the purview of the Knight-Defender of the Empire was to go where I wanted, do what I wanted, all the while answering only to the emperor himself—that latter coming only if I wanted to answer to him, too. The position included a stipend, which I didn't want, but it proved useful for keeping Shijef in sheep so he'd stop eating dogs and cats.

A messenger skidded slightly as he rounded a corner and burst into the chapel with youthful exuberance. He sucked in a great breath as he regained his balance and tugged his tunic into shape. "My Lord Knight-Defender . . ."

"Neal will do, there." I squinted at him. "Clarmund, is it?"

He looked surprised. "Yes, sir, my Lord. Ah, my Lord, I have been sent by the emperor to request your presence in the imperial audience hall. An embassy has arrived, and he deems it important for you to be present."

I smiled. As much as I eschewed anything that had the vaguest hint of officialdom about it, I had been looking forward to seeing whomever my brother might have sent to represent the Roclaws in the imperial court. Not having spent much time in the Roclaws since Tashayul's death, it occurred to me that I might not have any clue as to who the ambassador might be, or where that person stood amid the various Roclawzi factions, but seeing a fellow countryman would be a joy nonetheless after all this time.

I followed Clarmund out from the chapel and around to the staircase that spiraled up and around the tower. It had a twin on the far side with which it danced around but never intersected. That stairway had been cut more broadly and had been decorated with carvings that must have excited the Reithrese. Mercifully the Red Tiger had their artwork covered with tapestries, and not a few rugs hung to the same end. While that stairway served well for formal parties going to the second level of the tower, I preferred the plain servants' stair, because ostentation makes me itch and you can't beat a servants' passage as a place to pick up great gossip.

The imperial audience hall had been designed and decorated by a Reithrese who appeared not to have been as lugubrious as the chapel's architect. The whole room had a woodland feel, with columns carved to look like trees, their branches spreading out and up to form the ceiling vaults. The ceiling rose high enough to break up through the next level, and little viewing galleries had been carved within the branches so anyone in the chamber above could look down upon the proceedings. The walls had been painted with pastoral and woodland art, though the creatures represented ran long toward predators, and more than once Men were pictured as the object of a hunt.

Though I should not have thought it odd of a people who have gems for teeth, the throne was a remarkable piece of work. Fashioned from a smoky quartz, the throne's back appeared to be a giant incisor. The seat and arms were shaped from molars, and two long, upturned fangs arced up and out to curve above the emperor. The fittings that joined all of these teeth together were gold and set with gemstones which, I knew from previous examination, were Reithrese teeth and were rumored to have been taken from Tashayul's rivals for power.

What I did not know, and really did not *want* to know, was if the giant teeth were carved by artisans or had graced the mouth of something far too big to make me comfortable.

The chamberlain was about to announce me, but I waved him to silence and wandered down through the stone garden to where a small delegation of four stood speaking with the emperor. I recognized Aarundel but didn't question his presence initially, because he had met my kin in the mountains. His presence made sense. It was not until I saw him gesture with his right hand that I realized in it he held the hand of the woman standing next to him. I mentally revised that to *sylvanesti* next to him and felt my heart begin to beat faster.

Beltran looked up and eased the crown back on his head. "Ah, my Knight-Defender hath arrived. You know him, of course, Ambassador."

The Elf standing opposite Aarundel on the left side of the throne turned and nodded in my direction. "He served as *vindicator* for Aarundel when he and my granddaughter Marta were wed." His voice remained neutral, but I felt a bit of respect when he inclined his head toward me. "I am pleased to see the Reithrese have not yet harvested you."

"And I am pleased to see you again, Sidalric Consilliari." I stopped and bowed formally to him. As I straightened up, I smiled at Marta. "And you, Lady Marta." Turning back toward Sidalric, I racked my brain to remember Marta's mother's name, for I felt certain she had to be the veiled *sylvanesti* attending the ambassador. *Grationa, that's it.*

As I started to speak, the *sylvanesti* stepped away from the ambassador and, with hands sheathed in fawn leather, raised the white veil she had worn. Words died in my throat, though my mouth did remain open. I blinked, twice and again, then forced myself to resume breathing. "Doma Larissa, I am honored."

"It is my honor to be in the presence of the Knight-Defender of the Empire." She gave me a smile that set my heart to burning more fiercely than the old emperor's sword ever had, and I hoped it was a fire that would never go out. "Tales of your bravery and ferocity have reached even unto Cygestolia."

I coughed into my hand, then shook my head. "My Lady, you are far too wise to believe even a portion of them, for you know they are nine parts lies to one part rumor."

Larissa just smiled serenely. "But even if those rumors were nine parts exaggeration, the one part truth in them would make you more than worthy of the praises sung in your name."

"You are most kind, my Lady."

Beltran clapped his hands. "You are indeed special, Lady Larissa. I have fought for a month to get Neal to acknowledge his part in our victory, and he evades it as if praise were a whipping. You tame him with a glance and a turn of phrase."

I gave him a stare of pure poison. "She's had years of dealing with stupid animals, Majesty."

"Centuries, actually."

I clutched my chest with my left hand. "And in all that time, never so deftly did you wound one so deeply."

"I'd vouchsafe never had she dealt with one so contrary as my Knight-Defender."

"I believe you will recover, my Lord." She smiled at me teasingly.

"Your words are balm to my wound, my Lady."

"Wit and charm from Neal?" The Red Tiger scratched at his beard. "My Lady Larissa, you are a miracle worker. Though I regret being parted from your company, I might suggest you minister to my Knight-Defender in the stone ocean on this level. And you, Aarundel, if you would care to show your lovely wife yet another part of this tower, the ambassador and I can begin some discussion of issues common to his realm and mine."

I bowed deeply toward the throne. "Then, my Liege, I beg of you leave to escort Lady Larissa to the ocean."

Beltran frowned. "I believe I prefer reluctance to satire."

"Your wish is my command."

"Get out of here, Neal!" he shouted in mock command. "My Lady, go with him, cure him if you can, and give me back the Neal of old. If you cannot, this one you may keep with my compliments."

Though built by the Reithrese, I found the stone ocean interesting. The room in which it had been placed had been constructed to appear to have been rough-hewn out of black basalt. The floor had been covered to a depth of nearly a foot with knucklebone-sized marble stones of the purest white. Big jagged hunks of azurite and turquoise decorating the floor erupted through the white stone ocean like fangs tearing through flesh. I knew they were meant to be islands, but because of the throne, the tooth image stuck in my mind and would not go away.

A mahogany shoreline hemmed the ocean in and provided enough of a walkway for observers to circle the ocean and study it from all angles. Caretakers—once slaves, now respected freemen and part of the imperial household—raked the marble stones into patterns that corresponded to constellations or anything else that struck the caretakers' fancy, I imagine. The patterns were not openly representative, but held shapes the way clouds do when you take the time to look at them on a lazy afternoon. Depending upon the angle and your mood, the still waves of the stone ocean could form anything.

I had taken to spending a lot of time there. I appreciated the quiet, yet liked being nearby in case a question arose upon which the emperor might like or tolerate my opinion. I also know the stone teeth and the white stones reminded me a lot of the Mountain Men trapped to the south and also reminded me of my home. I found I did a lot of thinking in that room, which is not a bad thing in and of itself, but having spent my life preferring action to contemplation, it marked a new and slightly scary change.

Larissa's face brightened as she passed through the threshold. "Oh, this is magnificent."

I blinked away surprise. "You like it?"

"It is beautiful. Of course I like it."

"But it's so devoid of life, I thought . . ."

She stopped and looked at me. "You spend a lot of time here, do you not, my *vitamora*?"

I nodded.

She smiled and stretched out her arms. "I can feel your presence. This may once have been a Reithrese place, but you have made it your own. And as you love this place, so do I."

We sat down in silence, studying the flow of stones. Though no signal passed between us, I knew we were letting our eyes track across the same frozen waves and swirls in the pattern. As we traced our way through the ocean's currents and eddies, the two years since we had seen each other evaporated.

"It has been so long, yet it feels as if we danced together yesterday." I wanted to reach out to her, and started to, then withdrew my hands. "It is very good to see you again."

Her chin came up and her eyes sparked with mischievous fire. "We have seen each other since then, my love. There have been dreams."

I blushed. "The dreams, I remember many. I often feared for my life if I mumbled in my sleep, since your brother and I often shared a tent or a room during the campaign. Never did I dare tell him about the dreams."

"Nor did I speak to my husband of them."

I frowned. "You speak as if we had the same dreams."

"We *did*, Neal." Larissa knelt on the floor and delicately shifted a stone from the crest of one wave to the next. "This is but an aspect of being *vitamorii*. My brother would never have noticed your midnight whispers because likely he was sharing dreams with Marta. At least, she says it was so."

I smiled, but felt cheated. Had I known those dreams were more than just my imaginings, I would have clung to them more tightly and fought to remember them. "I had no idea."

She pressed a gloved finger to her lips. "Nor do any of the others. If they imagined we shared dreams, there is no telling what the reaction would be. This is our secret."

"Agreed." I leaned back against the wall. "How is it that you have come here?"

"When Beltran's missive arrived in Cygestolia, the Consilliarii decided to send an ambassador to open relations with this new Human empire."

I did not conceal my surprise. "That is a change from the last time they dealt with a Human empire."

"And that change is largely your fault, my *vitamora*." Larissa plucked at a fold of her skirt and smoothed the cloth against her thigh. "Your example helped blunt the forces that wanted a second crusade."

"Of that, then, I am thankful. Still, that explains why Sidalric is here. Why have you come?"

"I had no choice." She adjusted the folds in her brown dress's skirts. "As *vindicatrix*, I had to be present at the time when Marta presented her Petition of Fecundity to the Consilliarii."

"Her what?"

Larissa nodded, her eyes narrowing for a moment; then she smiled. "When Levicius and Alosia created us, they gave little thought to reproduction. For them it was sufficient that there was a mechanism by which we could increase our number. They chose, therefore, to make Elven women fertile for the period of a month or so after ingesting the fruit of the apple tree."

"Apples?"

"Not the red and green fruit you know, but a special apple with golden skin that grows in a single grove in Cygestolia. Because we have long lives, we determined that access to that fruit should be limited and only those who have done something remarkable should be allowed to bring offspring into the world. This is why Elven children are rare and treated as a great gift to the parents and to both of their families."

Part of me thought that tyranny; then I remembered seeing hordes of children running through the streets with no one to tend them or care about them, and I wondered if the Sylvan system might not have advantages. "Marta has petitioned the council to be allowed to have a child?"

"She has, and the Consilliarii have granted the petition." Larissa shrugged. "As much as they might like to deny it, Aarundel's exploits here in the Manworld have been remarkable, and having a child will mean he will not venture from Cygestolia for the next half century."

Half century? She said it so matter-of-factly, yet I knew I would be dead and gone before that time had passed. "So you accompanied Marta here so she could tell her husband about the petition grant?"

"Yes, and for another reason."

My spirit buoyed up. "And that was?"

"I am the *vindicatrix* and you are the *vindicator*. As we stood with them at their wedding, it is our duty to stand with them when they are given the golden fruit."

I folded my arms over my chest. "But we don't have to be there for the conception part, right?"

Light Elven laughter filled the room, forever banishing the last bit of gloom from it. "No, we do not, though remembering those dreams, were my brother to require instruction, you would be an excellent tutor."

I fought to keep a blush from my face. "I tend to dream larger than life."

"What harm fantasy if it gives pleasure?"

"None." I laughed to myself, then rubbed a hand over my face. "So is the ambassador speaking to the emperor about where the ceremony will be held?"

"I do not know, but of what concern it would be to the emperor I don't know."

"Larissa, the emperor owns this city. Everything is his concern."

"Ah," she smiled, "I see your confusion. No, he is not speaking to the emperor about that aspect of the ceremony."

"Then what are they discussing?"

"Among other things, the ambassador is conveying to the emperor a request from the Consilliarii." She innocently tucked a lock of golden hair behind her left ear. "The presence of his Knight-Defender is required in Cygestolia for a ceremony, and Sidalric is requesting permission for you to travel there with us immediately."

Chapter 19

The Hospitality of a Strange House

Spring
A.R. 499
The Present

Gena watched in stunned silence as Berengar shifted his shoulders to loosen them. "Being an assassin come to slay you, uncle, I will cause to be brought here a company of nubile girls who will sorely test your virility. I will give you a week, no two weeks, for you to exhaust yourself."

The old man's jaw gaped open ever so slightly. "Two weeks of wenching would not slay me."

Berengar shook his head. "I know that, uncle, but after the two weeks, when you lay in your bed, I would sneak up and tell you that your wife was again alive."

Atholwin's eyes widened, and Gena thought for a moment that his heart had ceased beating; then he began to laugh aloud. His laughter reminded her of the raven's call, and the black bird joined its master in cold mirth. "Hildegarde! The sight of her alive nearly slew me, so after forty years in a vault she would be my death. You win."

Berengar bowed his head. "I win only because my brother is not here."

"There are many who are not here." The old man's voice drained of pleasure, and he seemed to refocus his eyes on Berengar in a way that made Gena uneasy. "Who is this you have brought with you? Have you a wife now, Berengar?"

"No, uncle, I have no wife, though were I to marry, I could think of worse matches." The count turned and gently guided Gena forward with slight pressure on the back of her elbow. "May I present Lady Genevera of Cygestolia."

"An Elfess?"

Berengar frowned slightly at the use of the clumsy term. "Yes, uncle, she is Sylvan, and a companion in an important quest. We are bound for Jarudin."

The old man nodded for a moment, then his head froze in position and his eyes focused distantly. Gena felt uncomfortable because his eyes looked beyond her, as if into a world she could not sense and could not influence. "Elves have not been about in the land for a long time. Last one I saw was with Neal Elfward."

She started, and Berengar gave her elbow a gentle squeeze. Gena looked up at him and he shook his head slightly. His eyes promised an explanation, so she controlled further reactions to the old man's words.

"Uncle, we have ridden a long way. If you would grant us the hospitality of your home."

"Yes, yes." The old man clapped his hands inaudibly, but the servant who had shown them in appeared as if summoned by magick. "Tobert, take them to rooms. Give my nephew Osberic's room and this Elfess, give her Mildred's room. They will join me for supper, so we will have the best of the house."

"As my lord wishes." The servant bowed toward them. "If my lord and lady would follow me."

"Until this evening, uncle."

The old man nodded, then slipped into another fugue that left him staring at the goblet on the table. The raven cawed defiantly and hopped to the man's shoulder. Gena shivered and gladly left the room.

The upper floor of the main building had not been cluttered with debris and weapons' caches, but it seemed only slightly less forbidding than the hall below. In her room Gena found a layer of dust thicker than that which the road had deposited on her boots. Dust kittens followed in her wake, snatching playfully at her heels before they rolled beneath the bed. The bed itself, with musty sheets and sour straw mattress, creaked horribly when she sat upon it. She imagined the whole thing collapsing, bringing all four posts and the canopy they upheld down on her as if they formed a snare.

Berengar gently knocked on her half-open door. "May I?"

Gena nodded. "Please, and you might want to close the door."

"Agreed." He started to sit in a chair, then tipped it forward and banged it against the floor to knock free most of the dust. "I had heard stories about Atholwin, some of which I related to you, but I did not think things had gotten this much out of hand. His sons' deaths have clearly hurt him, but he's harmless, I'm fairly certain."

She arched an eyebrow at him. "Forgive me if the Man hanging in your oak does not reassure me of that. When he asked you to tell him how you would kill him, I started looking for a way out."

"Yes, I can imagine how odd that appeared." Berengar seated himself and slowly stroked his beard. "Uncle Atholwin has forever been obsessed with inheritance, death, and ancestors. I don't know why, he just has been. He used to tease my brother and me with his 'secret knowledge' of our plans to do away with him so we would inherit his holdings. I know he did this with his own sons and grandsons as well, so it was not isolated behavior."

"Nonetheless, it is ghoulish."

"True, though I guess I always just saw it as an eccentricity." He sat forward and rested his elbows on his knees. "His obsession led to his petitioning the emperor to legitimize our line. I don't think he did that to give him or his descendants a reason to try to overthrow the emperor as much as he wanted it to be part of his legacy. I think he felt our gratitude to him would mean that he would live forever in the annals of his family."

That made an odd sort of sense to Gena. "But you said

before, that his sons had been killed because of throne politics."

"Well, that is the rumor, I don't know that for certain. Still, there are a number of families with imperial holdings that take claims to the throne seriously. The legitimization of our line has effectively distanced older families from the throne, since we descend from one of the more recent emperors."

Gena frowned. "Your uncle seems to think he met Neal and Aarundel."

"Atholwin was a scholar of folktales and legends in his younger days. I learned all that I know of Neal from him during the summers I spent here. Atholwin thought it his duty to keep Neal immortal. Like the emperor, he has sought and cataloged a great deal of information about the history of the empire and its establishment. Since uncle always willingly shared his information, and corresponded voluminously with the current emperor, the emperor looked kindly upon the suit to legitimize our line." Berengar shrugged. "At least, this is my belief."

"So you are suggesting your uncle's mind is failing him?"

"I think he so loved stories of the past that he is now retreating into them. It is a pity, really, because he was quite witty and charming. His wit, for example, spawned the assassination game, which you witnessed. The object was to come up with the most entertaining method for killing him." Berengar chuckled lightly. "My brother Nilus was given to elaborate devices and grand plots. I usually appealed to Atholwin's vanity and had greater success."

Gena walked over to him and gave his shoulder a squeeze. "I am sorry the Man you remember is being lost to you. For us, when an Elf reaches an age where he tires of this world, he travels beyond and begins a new life there. We are spared watching our relatives age so severely."

Berengar patted the back of her hand. "What is this *beyond*? I have heard it mentioned at various times concerning Elves, but I do not understand it."

Gena folded her arms and began to pace as she considered how much she could tell him. "In the time of the gods, when the children opposed their parents and drove them out, the Elves stood by the parents. As a reward we are allowed to pass from this world into the place where the gods have taken up their exile. It is a parting from our kin, but it is not as sorrow filled as death because we all know we will meet again there, when we go beyond ourselves."

"If you are not slain in this world."

"Correct."

Berengar glanced up at her. "Men are barred from this place?"

"That is also correct. I do not know if children of mixed parentage would be allowed to go or forced to stay because none have survived to the point of asking to go beyond."

The count sat back and smiled slightly. "So those Elves who believe Neal's influence has destroyed Sylvankind do have a place where they can retreat from Men after all."

"True, but I do not think Neal would gainsay them that sanctuary." Gena smiled as she remembered something her grandaunt used to say when speaking of Neal. "Neal Elfward was a hero for this world. Not a hero for Men, but for the world itself. He would be happy nowhere else and would begrudge no one what they had, if they would permit him and his world to remain at peace."

"It sounds as if the world now has not changed much since his time." Berengar stood and headed toward the door. "Let us hope we can change it for the better before his dream dies forever."

Gena used the two hours between Berengar's departure and the call to dinner to rest. Dreams came to her in broken pieces that included a gang of men wearing masks and white robes dancing around the oak tree while a man twitched at the end of a rope. That scene brought her awake in a cold sweat. She tried to sort through the symbolism in the images, for she did not believe the dream prophetic or clairvoyant. She decided she had imagined the scene at the tree in the worst possible way, and clad the men in ghostly white robes because they had to have been vassals of Atholwin, and she already saw him as a living spectre of a man.

She washed up in a basin and changed her clothes, using her old blouse to wipe the dirt from her boots, then went down the stairs. Tobert met her at the bottom floor and conducted her to a dining hall, which, though many times larger than the audience chamber she had first entered, had been illuminated by only four more candles.

He seated her in the middle of a table over two Manlengths long and a quarter that in width. Berengar sat at the end of the table on her right hand, with Atholwin and his bird taking up the other end. Tobert brought the food in seven courses, though, sum and total, what he served each of them would have filled only two normal plates. Gena thought, at first, that she might have been slighted because of a mistaken belief that she did not eat meat, but she noticed Berengar's rations were as small as hers, and both of them were given food in generous proportion to that which was placed before the master of the house.

While possessed of a healthy appetite normally, Gena did not regret the meager amount of food offered. The soup, a largely vegetable dish, came thin and neither hot nor cold. She understood that its being springtime meant fresh vegetables were rare, but the grit of sand beneath her spoon as she ate made her wonder why the food had not been washed before preparation.

She picked at what was served and largely contented her stomach by consuming some potatoes that were small and odd looking and only slightly mealy. The bread likewise proved edible if bland, but the slatherlard was rancid, so she avoided it. She was offered a tiny cut of a greasy meat that Tobert called "rock rabbit," but she gently refused it, having no desire to learn what rat or squirrel tasted like.

Atholwin hardly ate at all. He spent most of his time talking, and chances were, when he remembered to eat something, the raven had already consumed most of what had been served in that course. The old man showed no affection for the bird, nor gave any sign he even noticed it, yet Gena sensed a bond between them. The old man would stop all speech and movement until the bird shrieked, bringing him back to the present with them.

His nattering proved easy to ignore, primarily because Earl Blackoak's cellars contained superior vintages. A different wine came with each course, and the better ones actually made up for the paucity of food and the state of the cuisine. Gena took care in drinking because she did not want to be drunk when it came time to sleep in this strange place. Berengar and his uncle consumed their wine with much more enthusiasm, and the more intoxicated Atholwin became, the more sensible and coherent was his conversation.

With uncharacteristic strength he hammered his fist against the table, then thrust a finger toward Berengar. "You *are* here to kill me. You want it all yourself, don't you, boy?"

Berengar smiled at first, then became wary when the angry tone in Atholwin's voice cut through the wine. "No, uncle, I do not want you dead. I came here to see you because I am traveling north."

"Spying for Hardelwick are you? He doesn't trust me, though I have pledged my fealty to him. I'll see you swing for this betrayal, Berengar."

The vehemence and energy in the old man shocked Gena. "My lord, Berengar speaks truly. He is not here to kill you."

The old man turned on her, his eyes frighteningly clear. "Lies! I have my sources. I know his mind and yours. Betrayers both, now and forever."

"Uncle!" Berengar threw his napkin on the table and came around to Gena's side. "You have had too much to drink."

"I am not powerless, Berengar." The man's eyes widened, and spittle gathered at the corners of his mouth. "You will see. You and the *sylvanesti* witch. You plot against us and you will pay!"

Tobert stepped from the shadows and helped Atholwin from his chair, then passed him into the keeping of two soldiers. The raven took one last morsel from his plate, then flew off into the shadows in the room's vaults. Tobert shivered and slid his master's chair into place.

"I must apologize for him, my lord and lady."

Berengar straightened up and folded his arms. "Is he normally like this?"

"It has been getting worse, my lord. This outburst, it is not unique. This time he directed it at you, but often he rebukes the shades of his sons Osberic and Analdric for their plots against him. Please, wait here a moment."

Gena looked up at Berengar as the servant disappeared. "What now?"

"I don't know, but I do not like the idea of my weapons' being in my room."

Tobert returned with an old bottle and two tiny glasses. "Your uncle is considerate when not in one of his moods. He specifically told me to make sure this brandy was served tonight. It is very good and will help steady your nerves." He looked off in the direction the soldiers had taken the old man. "I will get some into him later and make arrangements for you to leave by first light so this encounter is not repeated."

Gena accepted the brandy and forced herself to sip it. It did taste very good and warmed her throat and stomach. She watched Berengar quaff his drink, so she followed suit with the remainder of hers. Tobert then led them from the dining hall back to their rooms.

"Please, do not think harshly of Earl Blackoak. He remembers many enemies without remembering they are dead."

"We understand, Tobert. Lady Gena and I will be ready to ride at dawn."

Gena bowed toward Berengar and bid him a good night before retreating to her own room. Once she had closed the door, the musty, dusty room made her think of a tomb. She got herself ready for bed and lay down, but her mind remained active enough to hold sleep at bay. Every creak and windsigh sent shivers down her spine. Her reactions disgusted her because she knew she was far too old to be cowering in bed like a scared child.

She got up again and remembered how Rik's presence had made her feel secure no matter how unsettling or difficult a circumstance had been. *Things could be worse, he'd say, unless we take steps to make them better*. She smiled at the memory and decided to take his advice to heart. After some preparation, which included sliding the chair beneath the doorknob, she returned to bed and surrendered to sleep.

• • •

"Arise, Sylvan witch, and look upon the instrument of your death!"

Gena's eyes came open, and her breath caught in her throat. A half-dozen men in white robes stood around her bed. Three of them, two at either side of the head and a third far back at the foot, remained motionless and bore thick black candles with odd sigils worked into them. The flames wavered and capered in perfect synchronization with each other. With each flicker she felt the ebb and flow of energies that blocked her ability to concentrate enough to work magick, and she knew that as long as those three men remained magickally linked, she would be powerless.

Within the triangle, two men with silver swords flanked Atholwin. The old man, whose limbs showed none of the signs of the weakness or palsy she had seen earlier, held a wavy-edged dagger out for her inspection. The raven on his shoulder made no sound, but its eyes glowed with an unholy red light that splashed bloody highlights over the blade's razor edge.

"We saw betrayal in you, witch, and that will not do." The old man cackled, and his lips quivered as he raised the blade and leaned forward. "Betrayal is lying, and now you must be severed from the Truth."

Chapter 20

The Hostility of a Familiar Wood

Autumn
Reign of the Red Tiger Year 3 /
Imperium Year 1
Five Centuries Ago
My Thirty-seventh Year

Despite the desire by the Elves to leave immediately, Emperor Beltran Primus talked Aarundel into being feted before we departed. While the formality of the feast, and the lies called testimonials, made me twitch, I genuinely enjoyed myself. And when the Steel Pack lined the road leading out to the east so our party had to pass beneath their crossed lances, my heart swelled with so much pride, I thought it would burst.

And even the emperor wore a branded glove on his left hand when he saw us off.

The ambassador remained in Jarudin along with his servants and a dozen Lansorii. Another dozen Lansorii accompanied us on the road and, to an Elf, they seemed less than pleased to have me along. The Dreel filled out our party and we traveled light because, using the magical Elven pathways, our journey would take only four days to reach the edge of the Elven Holdings and another week to reach Cygestolia itself.

We departed from Jarudin early in the morning and rode east despite Cygestolia being almost due west of the capital. The nearest grove in the Elven network lay to the east not more than twenty-five miles, so we took our time reaching it. Our party actually spread out on the road, with a half-dozen warriors as point and flank guards and six as the rear guard. The fact that Shijef ranged far and wide through the woods surrounding the road did not appear to attract their notice, nor did Larissa's and my riding slowly and trailing the whole company.

The two of us did not talk much on the ride, but not out of fear of being overheard, for the Lansorii stayed as far away from us as they could. We didn't need to speak as we rode through sun-spotted forests and beside gurgling streams. It seemed enough that we were sharing the experience of the ride together. I drank in every detail I could of the landscape and would have gladly used it to replace my recollections of all the battles I had fought during my life. My martial past seemed but an illusion when Larissa and I were together.

When we reached the grove, I set up a campsite removed from that shared by the Elves. While Aarundel, Marta, and Larissa—especially Larissa—were solicitous toward me, the other Elves clearly wanted as little as possible to do with me. Aarundel was so happy to be with Marta again, I don't think he noticed their attitude toward me. Though I could not blame him for their feelings or for his ignorance of them, I did feel a bit abandoned. Seated alone, poking deadwood sticks into a fire, melancholy began to smother me like clouds descending on a mountaintop.

The Dreel sat himself down on his haunches across from the fire and watched me with scintillating red eyes. "Alone you are now. Alone am I, by your doing."

My head came up. "You are alone because you entered a contest and lost."

"And lost you have here, Dreelmaster Neal."

I raised an eyebrow. "Lost, have I?"

Shijef nodded solemnly. "In war you live. Wither in peace, you will. Aarundel leaves and you die."

"Ah, you have become a soothsayer, have you?"

A growl rumbled deep in his throat, and I saw the flash of bright claws, but the Dreel remained where he sat watching me. "Defeated I was, and abided by our bargain I have. I will. You my master are."

"But you could now defeat me."

"Could. Will not. Lost once I did." Shijef shook his massive head. "Not again. My master I will survive."

I said nothing because I knew he was correct. At best I had another decade or two in my life. I could already begin to feel myself slowing down. I went to sleep with one series of aches and woke up with another. When Aarundel and I had begun to run together, we were both long, lean, and strong, and he had remained that way, but I had become scarred and old and slow. I was dying by degrees, and Aarundel had been too polite to call this fact to my attention.

The Dreel felt under no obligation to spare me the truth, but I marveled at the fact that he did not exploit my weakness. He could have slain me at any time and run off, but he abided by his bargain. In fact, I found I had more confidence in his service to me than I did of the Reithrese's abiding by the deal made between Beltran and Sulane. I felt confident Shijef would stay with me until my death freed him, and the majority of my traveling companions felt that would come sooner rather than later.

Larissa appeared not to share that opinion. She came to me in dreams that night, and we once again danced as we had at the wedding. Wearing the same riding clothes we had worn during the day, we spun and whirled and danced along the trail leading away from Jarudin. Despite the both of us wearing gloves, we never touched. We just moved about each other, slicing across each other's paths in an intricate weave of flirtation and teasing seduction in which I felt not slow nor old nor as if I were dying.

In the morning she and I shared secret smiles and readied ourselves for the journey through the *circus translatio*. We said nothing to each other, but our chuckles appeared as irritating to the Lansorii as they were pleasurable to us.

Our nonverbal communication continued, even on the ride from Ispar to the fringes of the Elven Holdings, and though not a word had passed between us, when we arrived at the grove on the far side of our ride, we led our horses away from it and on for a short distance before stopping.

Exhausted, I dropped to my knees beside a small woodland stream and splashed cold water in my face. She knelt beside me and pulled her hair back with her left hand as she lowered her face to the water. Larissa drank deeply, then licked away the crystalline droplet hanging from the center of her lower lip.

Sitting back, I watched her, then laughed. "Thank you."

She wiped water from her chin with her right hand. "To what do I owe these thanks?"

"For being you." I slowly levered myself to my feet, and my knees popped audibly. "Yesterday I heard my joints groan and snap and I felt old, but that was when I was apart from you. In your presence I am rejuvenated. I know it is only temporary, but it is enough for me."

I snagged Blackstar's reins and patted the beast on the neck. "I think I will make camp up over there, in those rocks. It seems a likely place."

"No, Neal, let us work our way down this brook. Where it curves around that hill there is a small pool and a clearing. There is grazing for the horses, and the copse beyond it will yield enough deadwood that you can kindle a small fire."

I turned and looked at her, then on up to where the others made their camp in the grove. "I had hoped not to be so far removed from you."

"The clearing is large enough for two." The dusk's growing shadows hooded her hazel eyes. "If you would permit me to join you."

My heart began to beat faster as an icy viper coiled in my stomach. "But what would they think?"

"They will think what we already know." She gathered up her horse's reins and started to lead the gelding down the path along the stream. "My brother trusts us both implicitly. He knows us better than we know ourselves. He knows that though we might wish it to be otherwise, we will not violate the laws that divide us."

Aarundel's words to the Elven Council rose from my memory to sting me as I followed her. "Your brother told the council that I knew my place and that I would never dream of dragging a *sylvanesti* down to my level by visiting abominations upon her. He said I knew I was not worthy of you." As I repeated his words, I felt the hurt they caused me throbbing anew. I tried to keep the pain out of my voice, but I knew I had not succeeded when I saw it reflected in her face as she turned back to look at me.

"My brother regrets those words." She looked up at the sky through a hole in the forest canopy. "He has given them a great deal of thought, and he knows that what he said was wrong. He knows that on an intellectual level and believes it fervently. You know he would give his life for you."

I nodded. "And nearly has on occasions too numerous to count." I sighed. "That is precisely why it is so difficult for me to reconcile his actions with his words."

"Please understand that our family is noted and even reviled for my grandfather's belief in the equality of Humanity. He filled our father with his belief, which is why Aarundel was never recalled by my father and enjoined from continuing his adventures with you. My father is even more opposed to anti-Man prejudice than Lomthelgar, and he did his best to instill his beliefs in us, his children."

I bent down and plucked a yellow daisy, then Larissa took it from my hand and tucked it behind her left ear before continuing. "What my father did not realize was that we had a whole culture that had retrenched itself behind anti-Man revetments. Before Lomthelgar, everyone had been anti-Man, so no laws to petrify that attitude were necessary. As Lomthelgar began to make Elves think about their prejudice, legislation slipped into place to prevent the denaturing of our Elven heritage. My father, in his early years, was considered all but heretical. As Aarundel and I grew up, we were merely seen as peculiar for our attitudes. The placement of laws meant we were not a threat; therefore, we were not pressed as hard to defend our beliefs as

Thralan had been, which means we did not consider them as deeply as he did."

I began to understand where she was going with her explanation. "You're saying your brother accepted me as an equal without realizing exactly what that meant?"

"Yes, my love. He never considered what it would mean if you were to fall in love with a *sylvanesti.* He might have risen to your defense, but your being in love with his sister came utterly unexpected to him."

"Both because you are married and are his sister."

"Yes. As his sister I am sexless, and in being married any sexual needs are assumed satisfied." She shrugged. "Everything struck too close to home for him, and he reacted without thinking along the lines our culture had defined for him."

The stream curved around a hillock and widened into a placid pool. We led our horses across the stream itself and onto a grassy plateau that, in the spring, would be flooded by the stream. The long grasses had gone to seed and rustled underfoot. A couple of logs had been deposited on the flat by previous floods and gave us a good start on a campsite.

I used grass by the handful to rub Blackstar down; then I hobbled him where he could graze and drink as much as he wanted. Larissa did the same for her horse, Valiant, then helped me gather up stones for creating a firepit and the branches with which to fill it. As we worked, our conversation detoured from the serious course, but both of us knew it would return when we had no more tasks to deflect us from the thought it demanded.

Shijef showed up just as I got the fire started. He casually tossed a dead quail at my feet, then slunk off into the growing shadows to gnaw at a second, larger bird. I checked the quail to make sure it was a fresh kill and not carrion, then dressed it out, plucked it, and arranged a spit on which I hung it to roast.

Sitting there on a water-worn log, I looked from the fire over at Larissa. "It strikes me, Lady Larissa, that come spring there will be no sign we were ever here. One simple flood, and the snows in the mountains will guarantee that easily, and all this will be swept away. Time will do that with me, as well."

She smiled. "You will never be taken from my memory, Neal. I could not forget you, my *vitamora,* the warrior who refuses healing and does not acknowledge defeat." She laughed lightly. "You have not made yourself easy to forget among my people. The council was surprised when you gave the crown to Beltran. Many had predicted you would keep it yourself and be coming to Cygestolia to destroy us."

I shook my head. "That was never a consideration."

Her eyes flashed in the firelight as juices from the quail dripped down and sizzled on a stone. "Why did you refuse it? You are a leader of men and could have been emperor."

"I may be a leader, but I am not an emperor." Even though I knew I would tell her anything and everything she asked, I hesitated for fear my admonition would make her think less of me. "In the Roclaws my brother, Jarlath, rules. He is two years my senior, yet only half my size physically. By the time I had seen my sixth summer, I towered over him and could best him in any sport and give him a good match in games of strategy and thought. By the time I was ten years old, I could defeat grown men in combat, and using a spear and Wasp here, I slew a snow-wolf that winter. As I grew older, there were many soothsayers who predicted I would become a great leader and hero."

"And they were correct."

I nodded. "That they were. Roclawzi nobles saw me as the leader who could rebuild the Roclawzi Empire your people destroyed in the *Eldsaga.* I was groomed for that task. I was raised to believe I was fated to do great things in the name of Humanity. I would be the instrument through which Men recaptured that which had been stolen from us. Of course, my brother remained an impediment to this plan, but I was young and did not realize it." I shook my head. "I wanted to believe all that was said of me, and I almost did. . . ."

Larissa's dark eyes looked through me. "But you love your brother."

I smiled. "You inhabit my dreams and know my mind."

"I know your heart, my love, and I do not think you could bear your brother any enmity."

"But you don't know my brother."

"Yes, but I see how you have become Aarundel's friend. He would not accept you if you were false or fickle, and your loyalty to him and to Emperor Beltran tells me enough about you to conclude what I have."

"My brother is a thinker. Whereas others looked at the Roclawzi past and sought ways to recreate it, he saw that our empire had been destroyed by forces from the outside. He looked for ways to make certain the people of the Roclaws could prosper without inviting another invasion by your people or the Reithrese. He determined that trading with the Dwarves and with other nations would accomplish this goal, which many of our nobles saw as an abandonment of our warrior heritage."

I looked deep into the fire, down to where the flames had no color and the coals below glowed bright red beneath onionskin flesh of white ash. "He came to me, when I was sixteen, and outlined his plans for our people to me. He asked my opinion and told me that he would abdicate any claim to the throne in my favor if I thought he was wrong. He didn't care about power or ambition, he just wanted to do what was best for our people. He put his future and their future in my hands, and I saw I could not handle them."

I glanced up and my eyes slowly recovered, bringing Larissa into focus and form. "I told him I was bound off to be a hero, one who would make the Roclaws proud. It was his job, I told him, to make certain the Roclawzi still existed to sing my praises. We agreed to that division of responsibilities. I fled the land where politics almost turned me against my brother." I shrugged my shoulders. "Many of the Roclawzi lords who wanted me to supplant my brother were very angry with me, which made me more than glad to have tangled them in their own web of schemes. With that as my nearest entry into politics, I had no desire to be the emperor."

Larissa smiled at me. "I would not have guessed that was the explanation. Even with all my brother has told me . . ."

"Even your brother does not know about that. Aside from my brother and me, you are the only one who knows."

Shijef took that moment to audibly crunch a bone between his teeth.

I smiled. "So there it is. Neal Roclawzi left the mountains to become a hero. He left not to win an empire for himself, but to avoid having to lead the Roclawzi to ruin."

"Then he has satisfied that ambition." Larissa broke a stick in half and tossed both pieces into the fire. "Has he other ambitions?"

I watched the sparks from the fire spiral upward until they died. "I had none until I met you, but I fear Sylvan law will prevent me from satisfying them." I shook my head. "For the longest time I assumed I would meet someone with whom I would have a brood of children and live out the twilight years of my life. Now that I have met the person with whom I would like to do those things, I cannot. I suppose I will have to return to the mountains and teach my nephews all the things I had intended to teach my own sons."

Larissa's faintly bemused expression slackened slightly. "You have no children?"

"Despite all you have heard about the proclivities of Men, I have none I know about." I shrugged. "Given that plotters almost turned me against my brother, I was reluctant to provide them bastards of mine that they could use against him or his heirs. I always supposed I would father children someday, but the war against the Reithrese preoccupied me; then I met you, and since then no woman has kindled more than a flicker of interest for me."

"I thought, I did not know . . ." She seemed at a loss for words and still filled with distress.

"What's wrong?"

Worry-furrows creased her forehead. "I realized just now that because of me you will have no children to carry on your tradition."

I shook my head. "Fortunes of war."

"No, do not say that." Worry melted into stern resolution. "Among the *sylvanii,* children are a privilege granted the few by the many in acknowledgment of their contributions to the world. My brother and Marta are being so honored because of what he has done fighting side by side with you. The thought of your line ending with you . . . for me to deny Humanity your progeny . . . this is unthinkable."

"But I have no interest in getting children on any woman. Were you and I able to create a child, that would be an honor and a child blessed in so many ways that even the gods would smile upon him. And I understand the importance you see in children, but if our lines cannot be united, I will not overmuch regret dying without heirs of my blood."

"But, Neal, while you and I may never be able to be together, your son and my daughter might be able to be together."

My heart felt twisted around inside my chest. The idea of a child of mine and a child of hers being able to share what we could not filled me with happiness. Yet the happiness came with a bittersweet tinge as I realized it meant she would have a child with Finndali and I would have to couple with someone other than her. The only time before I had felt a similar conflict in my heart came when I first rode away from my home, abandoning it so I could preserve it for the future.

I swallowed away the lump that had risen in my throat. "I understand what you have said, and I acknowledge the wisdom of your thoughts." I opened my hands helplessly. "I just don't have any interest in selecting a woman to play broodmare for me. I . . . I don't know."

She gave me a little smile that melted away the anxiety and confusion nestled in my breast. "I will find someone for you. I will find you a mate who loves you as much as I do. When you are with her, it will be as if you are with me."

"You can't do that."

"I can, and I will because I love you too much to let you go out of the world. Perhaps I am being selfish, but I do not have to acquiesce to what others say is inevitable."

"Such as my aging and withering away in front of you?"

Larissa nodded once, her golden hair sliding down to

veil her face. "I knew that could happen when I first saw you, but by then it was too late. I accept the pain that will bring me because it will be nothing in the face of the joy knowing and loving you has brought me. What we have together is too special to allow it to be hampered by laws and customs, superstitions and fears. Our love will transcend it all, even if it takes generations to do so."

The passion in her voice filled me, and had Shijef not splashed his way out into the pool to remind me of his presence, I might have crawled across the clearing to her and courted death. Because of his intervention, I remained in place and poked the roasted quail with a finger. "It seems done. Are you hungry?"

She nodded. "Yes. I will eat and then, I think, sleep."

I smiled. "Yes, sleep, and perhaps a dream."

"*One* dream?" Larissa feigned a pout. "Dreams, my love, very sweet dreams."

I woke with a start as the Dreel shook me to consciousness. "What?"

"Lifeblack floods." He pressed Cleaveheart's hilt into my hand. "The grove."

I threw back my blankets and stood. "Keep her safe."

Shijef growled as I started to run off. "That's a command, Shijef!" I shouted back over my shoulder as I sprinted into the night. Wearing only my breeches, I splashed through the stream. Its cold bite turned my bare feet into blocks of ice. The chill night wind puckered my flesh and burned my throat as I gulped down air. My ears strained for the sound of steel on steel and screams as I ran, but I heard nothing, and that fact worried me.

Running in the dark along a path that meanders through a forest is not the fastest or wisest way to get from one point to another. Thick roots clutched at my feet and ankles, bringing me down again and again. Each time I fell, I bounced back up and continued on, my speed only slightly abated. When I saw large branches in my way, I ducked beneath them, but countless of their smaller, skeletal kin scourged me over the length of my journey.

I crested a hill, then took a rolling tumble down the

other side into a small valley barely twenty yards from the *circus translatio* grove. I concentrated on keeping Cleaveheart in my hand as I somersaulted down through brush and bracken and somehow missed solid collisions with moss-covered stones and the few thick trees on the downslope. At the bottom I regained control of my body and huddled in a crouch, waiting for a reaction to my noisy appearance.

Again I heard nothing, and goose pimples rose on my skin, though they were not caused by the cold breeze caressing me. Slowly, moving in fits and starts and going as quietly as I could manage in the midnight blackness, I moved to the grove. While my ears and eyes failed me, my nose did not, and even before I broke through the circle of trees, I knew what I would find. As I entered the grove, the moon's wan light carved a nightmare from the darkness.

Elves lay twisted and strewn around the clearing in various boneless poses of death. Ambushed while they slept, most of them were naked, and those dressed wore no more than I did, save one. He had managed to pull on one boot before two arrows crossed in his skinny chest. The four or five—no, it was four, but one was in two pieces—showed signs of having been cut down by swordsmen. The copious hoofprints in the soft sward had so chewed the land that I could not clearly identify how many horsemen had attacked them, but I would not have been surprised to know two dozen or more had been in on the assault.

I squatted next to one of the arrow-slain bodies. The shaft and fletching were familiar to me from countless battles with the Haladina. I rolled the body up and over onto its side, the flesh still warm to my touch. One of the broadheads protruded from the Elf's back, and the appearance of the barbed tip confirmed its Haladin manufacture. I eased the body back to the ground, then stalked through the clearing, counting.

When I reached a dozen, I ran out of bodies. I went back through the camp and reconfirmed my count. The Lansorii were dead, all of them, slaughtered while they slumbered after their hard ride through the *circus translatio*. On the edge of the Elven Holdings they had not bothered to set out pickets, and Aarundel would have been too preoccupied with his wife to have noticed.

"Neal!" Larissa appeared at the edge of the clearing with the Dreel rising behind her like a shadow. "By the gods!"

Her hands rose to cover her mouth as she drifted forward, and I opened my arms to offer her a safe haven. In that moment I needed her as badly as she needed me. I saw her tears glisten in the moonlight, and I wanted to brush them from her cheeks. I reached out to do that, but the Dreel swept her out of my grasp.

"Shijef?"

" 'Keep her safe' your command was."

"Then you should not have brought her here."

"In my care, safe she is."

Anger erupted in me. "Then keep her on the edge of the grove. That is my new command, *slave!*" A third time I searched the camp, picking and poking through the collapsed tents and discarded blankets. I listened for any sound of life and looked for any clue beyond the obvious concerning the identity of those who had laid the ambush. And I looked for my friend and his wife.

I don't know how long I searched, but by the time I returned to where Larissa sat, the Dreel had found her a blanket. She rested with her back against the bole of a tree, her knees drawn up and hugged tightly to her chest. Her cheeks remained wet, and a few strands of her golden hair were pasted to her face with tears.

I tossed Aarundel's ax at her feet. "Your brother and Marta are not among the dead. I saw no blood among their belongings, though there were quite a few arrows in their tent."

"Did they run off?"

I knelt and patted the ax. "If they had run, this would not have been left behind. Aarundel never would have run from Haladina without a weapon in hand. He also would have run toward us, to warn us. There are tracks leading away from here that I will follow in the morning. The attackers, it appears, started an area search, but abandoned it quickly. I'm thinking, though, I'll not find your brother or Marta out there."

"Why not?" Her question came wrapped in hope.

"A lot of things, some I probably won't recognize for days, but I know a couple of things that aren't right. Some of the wounds are bloodless, which means they were inflicted after death. The Haladina have never been neat and orderly when fighting, but they don't beat up on corpses as a rule. More important, though, there's not a single Haladina lying out there, and I'm not going to believe your Lansorii couldn't account for at least one of them, even in an ambush."

"But who would do this? Would the Haladina risk adding to the *Eldsaga* by raiding here in our lands?"

I shook my head, then balled my fists against my desire to stroke her hair and kiss away her tears. "This was an act of cruelty—as cruel as the laws that keep us apart right now—and an act of revenge. The Lansorii died because your brother dared fight beside me to overthrow Tashayul's empire. He and Marta were taken as hostages so they can be traded for something of incalculable value." I raised Cleaveheart and watched the moonlight skitter down its unblemished edge. "With this sword comes a means to win an empire, and those who staged this raid mean to have it in exchange for the lives of your brother and his bride."

Chapter 21

The Cleansing Effect of Fire

Spring
A.R. 499
The Present

The raven on Atholwin's shoulder hopped into the air, and as it spread its wings, it began to change. Feathers melted back into black flesh that stretched taut between the bony fingers of the demon's batwings. Its head expanded and fattened while flattening. Its two eyes swam up into the center of the forehead and merged, then split apart into three eyes that formed a triangle pointing down at the serrated beak. The bird's feet remained the same, but the body and legs changed to become more anthropomorphic. Little infant arms sprouted from its sternum, vestigial limbs that could only clap and grasp and, at points, looked as if they were part of a baby trying to fight its way to freedom from inside the demon.

Gena recognized it from descriptions given of the foul creatures that had served Reithra. It was a *ferghun,* a demon from some obscure pit of her inferno that seduced men through their fear of death, promising them much and denying them everything in the end. Such creatures, as nearly as she could determine, had not been seen on Skirren since the fall of the Reithrese, and the presence of this one meant Atholwin had dabbled in dark practices best left forgotten.

Fear sent a jolt through her that burned away the magical fog generated by the syncopated candle flames. With a deliberate speed that seemed ever so slow to her, she brought her hands out from beneath the thick bedding, flicked the primer covers off, and thumbed back the talons on Durriken's flashdrakes. Stabbing the first handcannon forward, she pulled the trigger and braced as the talon sparked into the primer pan. After a heartbeat or perhaps two as hers raced, earsplitting thunder followed a bright flash and gout of smoke.

The first ball took Atholwin clean in the chest. It made a neat round hole over his heart amid the peppering of unburned powder that flecked his robe. The old man sighed explosively, then seemed to collapse in around the wound, while his dagger twisted and bobbled up out of his grasp. His body flew back into one of the two swordsmen behind him, but before they could collide with the candlebearer, Gena fired the second flashdrake.

The shot blew straight through the *ferghun* and the muzzle-flash burned a ragged hole through the center of the beast. It screamed in the voice of the raven, wrapped in anguish and threaded with madness, then began to dissolve from wound outward. Behind it the candlebearer snapped forward in an abrupt bow as the ball took him in the stomach. His candle dropped, the flame dying seconds before he did, and Gena felt her ability to work magick return.

Dropping the flashdrakes in her lap, she grasped the heavy coverlet and threw it forward to entangle the lone standing swordsman at the foot of the bed. Without moving from her place, she swung her hands wide and gestured at the two remaining candlebearers. Even as their eyes cleared and focused on her, the black candles they bore immediately and completely combusted. Each man reeled away in a flash of light, with singed hair stinking and white robe burning.

The first swordsman regained his feet as Gena rolled from the bed, but never got a chance to close with her. The door to her room disintegrated beneath a powerful kick. Berengar, his eyes blazing, swept into the room, turned the swordsman's thrust with a casual parry, then riposted with a slash that carried clean through the left side of the man's chest. A recovery and a lunge sent the entangled swordsman stumbling back into a human torch, and the both of them crashed against the wall. The tapestry hanging there immediately caught fire, and flames leaped from it to the canopy over Gena's bed.

"Come on, this place is a firetrap!"

Gena scooped the flashdrakes and her old clothes into her satchel, then picked up her boots and ran out behind the count. As big as a bear and growling in a suitable manner, he stalked through the house awaiting attack. She followed behind him with a spell or two in mind to use if any more demons opposed them, but they reached the courtyard unmolested.

"Wait here." Berengar turned to head back into the manor, but black smoke had already begun to pour out of the doorway. He ducked his head and disappeared into it, then came running back out coughing loudly and swiping tears from his eyes. "Too much fire."

"It was a tinderbox. Lots of debris and old wood."

Berengar smeared soot across his face. "When I heard the flashdrakes go off, I came running. Now my boots and clothes are burning up there." He scowled for a moment, then looked from the building to Gena and back. "You said the first spell every magicker learns snuffs fires. Can you?"

Gena shook her head. "Magick I can work, but miracles, no." She reached out and pulled him back away from the building as burning wooden shingles crashed down amid a shower of sparks. "Let it burn, all of it, then scatter the stones and salt the earth."

Berengar looked strangely at her. "What happened in there?"

"I'll tell you as we get our horses and get away from here. Maybe in the stable we can find you more than just breeches to wear."

The count nodded, and they did find an old polish-stained shirt amid the tack in the stable. They pulled Spirit and Teague from the stable and got their packhorses out as well before the fire spilled over to engulf that structure. While they worked, Gena told Berengar of what she had seen in her room and shared with him the conclusions she had drawn from her experience.

"If I had not chosen to load the flashdrakes and keep them with me because I felt frightened, I would be dead right now, because they knew how to neutralize my magick. I think the *ferghun* would have supplied them with that information—it is rumored that those demons know a great many things, including facts hidden in the past or lurking in the near future."

Berengar shook his head slowly. "A *ferghun*? I cannot believe . . ."

"Believe it, Berengar, I saw it. Its presence there with your uncle suggests he let his studies of folklore and legend carry him too far." Gena found her anger growing hotter than the fire consuming the castle. "It is known that some of the Haladina worship the Cold Goddess, but I had thought civilized Men would have found her a detestable mistress."

"It was not his fault, Gena."

"How can you say that? He would have murdered both of us."

"He was a frightened old man, haunted by ghosts. It is not surprising that he sought assurances from the Goddess of Death concerning his fate and that of his sons."

"The Cold Goddess is a curious mistress to court if you want sanctuary against death. She and her people are abominable!"

"But *you* remember that, *we* do not." Berengar raked hair from his face. "Time wears away the cruel edges of history. Your grandfather fought against the Reithrese, so you have the tales directly from him. You know how horrible the Reithrese were. We do not. Men hear only the seductive tales of power that will make us the equal of the Elder races. For an old man, one who has seen his dreams of immortality evaporate, that is very seductive. I'm certain he felt he could master her."

"Another myth disproved."

"Yes, yes, you are right, Gena, but he was sick and not thinking correctly. Had he been the Atholwin I had known in my youth, he never would have dabbled in Reithrese magicks." Berengar shook his head as he led the horses through the gate and away from the burning castle. "It is odd, of course, that in his ravings he was correct: we did kill him."

"But we did not go there to kill him." Leaving Spirit with Berengar, Gena slipped away behind a tree to change from her nightdress into traveling clothes. "We did not betray him, merely stopped him from murdering us, so accusing us of being betrayers was wrong."

"Point well-taken." Berengar took a deep breath and seemed to slow down. "Please, forgive me, I am overwrought."

Gena smiled at him as she returned from changing. "It was a difficult ordeal for us both."

"Let us hope we face no more in the future." He swiped a hand over his face, then yawned. "Castle there, burning hot / roasting and toasting all the clothes I've got . . ."

Gena laughed at his rhyme, and that brought a smile to the count's face. "So, Berengar, do we press on to Jarudin, or do we go back to Aurdon and resupply ourselves?"

He frowned and thought for a moment, then nodded. "We go on, if that appeals to you. We are almost halfway to our goal, and a return to Aurdon might mean that my Elders change their minds about our mission. I would rather fail in Jarudin and return than fail here and return."

"I understand. I have a little gold, and if we forage while on the road, I think we should be able to make it to Jarudin. If we need more, we will put you to work spinning rhymes in taverns for food and lodging."

Berengar groaned and hauled himself into the saddle. "I would sooner flaunt the Emperor's justice as a highwayman than sing for my supper."

Gena mounted Spirit and brought the horse alongside Berengar and his horse. "That may be well and true, but when we get to Jarudin, explaining away bad rhymes and worse songs might be easier than dodging reports of criminal activity, especially when it comes to getting us an audience with Hardelwick."

"As always, Lady Genevera, your beauty is exceeded only by your wisdom." Berengar laughed lightly and gave his horse a touch of his heels. "Let's find a place where they will trade food for song and pray we get the better of the bargain."

Chapter 22

The Fiery Effect of Truth

Autumn
Reign of the Red Tiger Year 3 /
Imperium Year 1
Five Centuries Ago
My Thirty-seventh Year

Though I had slept for nearly a day and a half since my arrival in Cygestolia, I felt very tired as I stood before the Elven Council. Every seat in the council amphitheatre itself was filled, and Elves of every description clung to the branches and boughs above and around it. The story of the massacre and our unescorted journey back to the Elven capital had spread firefast through the city, and everyone wanted to be present when the council summoned me.

I suppose that it should not have surprised me that I had been brought to the council with a charge of misconduct against me or the death penalty hanging over me. I should have been used to it. In fact, as much as I abhorred politics, I had to admire the way the charge had been laid so there would be an excuse to destroy me if I proved to be as much a threat to Elvendom as some feared I was.

I breathed in slowly, pleased with the calmness I felt

dwelling inside me. "My answer to the charge that I engaged in physical contact with Lady Larissa is that the charge is false." I glanced to my right where she stood with Lomthelgar and Shijef. "I charged the Dreel with the duty of keeping her safe."

I let an edge slip into my voice. "Even at the moment when she saw the slaughter, in a moment of horror when any two living creatures would search out a companion for comfort and reassurance in life, he kept us apart. We abided by your law even in a situation where that law stripped us of all that makes us living, breathing, feeling creatures. Your law robbed us of the most basic consideration and compassion. As unjust as the law was in that situation, we respected it. On this you have my word, as well as that of Lady Larissa and the Dreel."

Most of the Consilliarii met my defiance and anger with defiance of their own, but when Larissa nodded toward me and gave all of them a stern stare, some shrank back from it. Whispers from the gallery buzzed and hummed above me. Though the words escaped me, tones of shock and outrage did not. I could not tell if they were directed at the law or my audacity, but I took heart in my ability to provoke a reaction among a people who saw me as little more than an animal.

Thralan stood at his place in the council. "Calarianne, so there is no stigma upon my daughter, I demand these charges be dismissed by acclamation."

Lomthelgar capered forward. "Second!"

The *sylvanesti* overseeing the proceeding nodded. "If there are no objections . . . seeing none, I have it that the charges are dismissed without opposition."

She raised her staff to bring it down and adjourn the session, but I raised my hand. "Wait! I must speak to the council on another matter."

Calarianne hesitated and another of the Consilliarii rose to move that I be allowed to speak. Thralan seconded the motion and it passed on a voice vote. "The council will listen to you, Neal Roclawzi."

I bowed my head respectfully to her, then looked up at the Elves facing me. "I understand that it is believed Haladin raiders slew the Lansorii and carried Aarundel and

Marta away. I must inform you, lest the reputations and abilities of those Lansorii and my friend be slandered, that the Haladina did not kill them. The Reithrese *did.*"

"What proof have you of this?" A black-haired Elf stood in the front row. "By all accounts you arrived too late to see the raiders."

"I've been thinking on the problem all the while we traveled here." I held my left hand up with the palm facing me and my fingers all splayed out. I curled the smallest under saying, "First off, there were no Haladin bodies present, and there is no way at least one of them would not have died. And, without a doubt, the Haladina could have carried off their dead, but they're not much of a mind to do that when there is so much loot."

The Elf nodded carefully. "But the bodies were not looted."

My ring finger curled down. "Another atypical fact about the fight. I'm thinking I've never seen a battlefield where the Haladina didn't make off with as much in the way of booty as they could pile on their horses. Elven armor and arms were left behind, as well as the personal effects of the slain Lansorii. The Haladina would have treasured those things, for they would have been seen as powerful both among the Haladina and as symbols of their skills to their Reithrese masters."

The Elf let a sly grin steal across his face. "Perhaps you scared them off, Neal Roclawzi."

I shook my head and tucked my middle finger down. "Any Haladin raider who had just succeeded in slaughtering an Elven patrol wouldn't be frightened by a half-naked man with a sword. They had bows and could have feathered me while I stumbled about in the dark."

My index finger came down. "This all contributes to why I know the Reithrese staged the raid. I heard nothing of the fight, which meant it was over before the Dreel awakened me. The Dreel remained unaware of the fight until all the killing had been done, which tells me that some powerful magicks had been worked to keep the attack quiet and secret. Those same magicks point out how your Lansorii could have been taken so quickly. Also I found evidence of a limited search of the area. That meant they were looking for Larissa and me. The attackers obviously knew who we were, and had they been willing to spend more time in your forests, I'd likely not be here."

My thumb came in, leaving me a fist. "What happened that night is this: two dozen Reithrese warriors approached under cover of powerful magicks. Because they can see as well in the dark as you can, there was no need for torches, which meant there was one less clue as to their approach—and the Haladina would have had to come with enough torches to set the whole forest ablaze. They slew most of the Lansorii with arrows, then herded the rest together. When they determined I was not there and no one would tell them where I was, the Reithrese cut down all the survivors save Aarundel and Marta and carried them off."

"Your arrogance knows no bounds, Neal, if you suppose the Reithrese hate you so much to slaughter Elves to get at you."

"You're a fool if you think I believe it's me they want." My fist pounded down on Cleaveheart's hilt. "They want this sword because they think it can be used to restore Tashayul's empire. Had I been there, all of us would have died, you would have launched a new campaign to destroy the Haladina, and the Reithrese would have offered to help you destroy Mankind."

Another of the Consilliarii stood. "Your tale is fanciful, Neal, but untrue. The Reithrese have already sent us a message of condolence for the deaths and have promised to turn over the Haladina who did this once they determine who they were. They are being most cooperative."

"Of that I have not a doubt, Consilliari, because those leaders with whom you correspond likely do not know who did this. More correctly, they suspect but are without proof. Without proof, or without pressure from you, they will not act just on the off chance that the person who planned this deed succeeds in having me trade the sword for his two hostages."

"Impossible! The Reithrese would never condone aggression against us."

"Why not? What would stop them?" I folded my arms across my chest. "They play the long game, the same way you do. Five hundred years ago, at the time of the *Eldsaga*,

Lomthelgar's ideas about Men were blasphemy, yet little by slowly, I'm thinking, enough Elves softened in their views that you enacted laws to codify and punish what would have been unthinkable before he began to share his insights. In the same way, the vast majority of Reithrese might shudder at the thought of conflict with the Sylvan Nation, but if this act of aggression is not punished, they will begin to assume they risk nothing attacking you. The barrier between you and their lust for power and greed will be worn down."

"As you say, Neal, we play the long game. *If* your fantasy were true, we would have much time to deal with it."

I thrust a finger at the speaker. "It is true *you* would have a long time to deal with it, but *my* friend and his wife would not. Every second they spend in Reithrese captivity is an eternity. That's the problem with you long-lived beings, and the advantage of being a mayfly. You have perspective, but *I* have *urgency*! I am impatient. I will not tolerate my friend, my *brother*, remaining in captivity for a moment more than I must. In fact, I ride tonight to free him."

The Elf folded his arms across his chest and scoffed at me. "You speak as if you know where Aarundel is being held and the identity of his captor."

"I do." I pointed off south by southwest. "Aarundel and Marta are being held in Jammaq. They are Takrakor's prisoners, and he wants this sword in exchange for their lives. That's why there have not been ransom demands from this mythical band of Haladina. Takrakor knows I know what he wants, and I'll see to it that he gets it, though not in the manner he expects."

Lomthelgar cackled aloud. "Mark him, this is the Second Time—he speaks in his voice for himself!"

The leader of the Consilliarii struck her staff to the wooden floor once, quieting the hubbub Lomthelgar's remark had provoked. "What you have said is disturbing, Neal Roclawzi, but you are mistaken if you believe we will give you permission to act against the Reithrese in this matter."

"With all due and sincere respect, Calarianne Consilliari Primus, *you* are mistaken if you think I came here to ask permission. I'm telling you what I'm going to do because I'm going to use the *circii translatio* network to get me to Jammaq and back again. My explanation here is a *courtesy*, not a petition."

"No one will teach you how to activate the magick."

I shook my head. "I have already learned, from Lady Larissa, to facilitate our return here. She did not know I might have other uses for what she taught me."

The first Consilliari to question me again rose to his feet. "We *can* stop you."

"How? Execute me? On what charges?"

He smiled. "I move we reconsider the misconduct charge against Neal Roclawzi."

Thralan shot to his feet. "Impossible, it was dismissed by acclamation and cannot be brought up for reconsideration because of that fact."

I smiled over at Lomthelgar, who had come up with that bit of strategy in our discussions earlier in the day. "You cannot stop me, which is good, because Takrakor is not known for his patience."

The declaration sparked a heated debate and not a few shouts from the gallery. I watched it rage, but because I did not understand the words, I gained more from visual cues than I did from the angry voices. In the heart of the council older Elves exchanged grim glances. They looked at me, then quickly away, and finally one of them nodded solemnly.

This older member of the Consilliarii stood. Though his white hair and slightly thick middle would have had me dismiss him as a threat in combat, he moved with the energy of a snake coiling. "I am Disantale, and I applaud your instruction in our laws, Neal. I applaud your respect for them. I value your bringing to our attention the need for urgency in action, as well as your taking us to task for the unjust nature of our laws concerning Men."

As Disantale spoke, I felt a cold dread start to crystallize in my stomach. The council had grown quiet as he spoke, and apprehension seemed to condense in the air. I wanted to run because I knew, as much as he was praising me, so would he damn me, and I wanted nothing to do with a condemnation delivered so coolly as this.

"Neal, your presence here has impressed me, as have my son's reports of your exploits. If you are exemplary of Men, perhaps we have misjudged them and you. I offer you a bargain in return for your cooperation in this matter."

I felt pressure close on me tighter than Shijef's jaws. "I cannot be swayed from my course, Disantale Consilliari."

"I am known for being persuasive. Hear me out." He pointed down at a group of Elven soldiers, and I recognized Finndali among them. "If you abandon this quest, my son will divorce his wife and we will repeal the law that keeps you apart from Lady Larissa."

His words hit me harder than any punch I had ever taken, and were far more effective in driving my breath from me. My stomach imploded and I felt my heart begin to ache. I began to fold up around my middle, and I did sink to one knee, but I used my left hand to stop myself from collapsing. Despair and joy warred in my brain as dreams came to life and sought to erase what I could remember of Aarundel.

Finndali stepped forward stiffly. "I willingly pledge obedience to the decision of the Consilliarii in this matter."

I hammered my fist into the floor. "You bastards. You sanctimonious, superior, scheming monsters." The emotional turmoil in my head and gut converted instantly into anger, and I let that anger fill the void in my body. "I already know you hold me in contempt, but to think me *so* simple and *so* easily manipulable . . . How could you? Is it arrogance or just cruelty that makes you think I would jump at this offer?"

I rose from the floor slowly and straightened up to my full height. "I'm not a dog to be thrown a bone. You greatly dishonor Doma Larissa to cast her as that bone. I am well used to being an object of scorn to you, but to show her such disrespect is unworthy of even your kind. Had I not a pressing engagement, I'd use Cleaveheart here and now to slay the lot of you."

I shook my head, still fighting to clear Disantale's words from my ears. "With one hand you offer to make me worthy of Lady Larissa under your law, but to receive that boon I must refuse to save her brother. Were I to agree, I would no longer be worthy of her. And you, those of you who think of Men as oxen with thumbs, you would be victorious. I would have shown that I was willing to trade friendship for the embrace of *sylvanesti* thighs. And you would have denied us the chance to have children, so this tasteless compact would have died when I did."

I laughed and wiped away tears. "You know, if I accepted this bargain, I *would* be worthy of your revulsion. The thing of it is that none of you would hate me as much as I would hate myself.

"I am *not* an animal. I cherish all those things that you believe ennoble you as a people. I cling more tightly to personal friendship and loyalty than you do. It is not a peculiarity of Man or a man, because I know had I been taken, Aarundel would be speaking these same words to you. He would even risk your denying him and Marta the child you used to lure him into this trap."

I opened my hands and arms to take them all in. "So there you have it. I, Neal Roclawzi, Elfward, Knight-Defender of the Empire of Man, refuse your offer. I am bound for a cold, dangerous place to free my friend and his wife. You may take that as a sign of madness. Many of you will. But I'd rather be mad and away from here, than sane and living among a people that could offer such a shameful bargain to block the rescue of one of their own."

Larissa met me in the chamber I had been given in Woodspire. I was busy stuffing a blanket into saddlebags, so I did not see her at first. When I looked up, I saw her lower lip tremble, then white teeth bit at it to still its quivering.

I could not meet her gaze. "I want you to know, Larissa, that your brother almost lost out today. I almost chose you over him. Please, do not think my choice, my deciding to leave, means I love you any less." Frustration balled my fists.

"You had no choice, Neal." Her words came calm and certain, and she did a good job of covering her pain. "I very much wanted you to choose me, and I hated myself for that. I love you for the fact that you were strong enough to keep from capitulating to them."

I shook my head. "Unchecked arrogance cannot be rewarded." I looked at her again and found I could have lost myself in the dark pools of her eyes. "I don't ever want to be apart from you, but I will not sacrifice your brother for our happiness. I'll be back soon, with them in tow."

"I was thinking that I might accompany you on your quest. They might need a healer. . . ."

"You may be correct, but so was the Consilliarii. If I were to lead Elves, even one, into Jammaq, whatever happens down there could kindle a war that your council wants to prevent." I grinned wryly and sat down on my cot. "Having just come through a war, I cannot blame them for their caution. By going alone, with no sanction from them, my actions can be denied. Succeed or fail, stay or go, the Consilliarii wins as long as conflict with the Reithrese is not heightened. The Reithrese cannot assign to the Consilliarii blame for anything I do. Best case for the Council is my death in a successful rescue."

"But that would leave *Divisator* in the hands of the Reithrese, and they will destroy the empire."

I shrugged. "True, not the best case for Men, which is why the council and I have our differences."

Larissa shivered. "I cannot stand the thought of you alone in Jammaq."

I grinned. "There will be plenty of Reithrese to keep me company."

"That is not what I meant."

"Alone he will not be." The Dreel squeezed past Larissa in the doorway, then sat in the middle of the floor. "Together we travel."

"I travel alone, Shijef. This is *my* fight."

The Dreel thumped his chest. "Slave I am, master you are. Lifeblack pools."

I narrowed my eyes. "Listen to me, Shijef, for master I am. *Your* master. I'll not be having the Reithrese hunting down the Dreel for sport because you joined me in a mission that fails."

Shijef flicked both of his paws forward to ward that suggestion off. "With Shijef, fail it will not."

I snarled. "With Shijef I am *not*. I expressly forbid you to follow me. *That* is your master's command!"

His agate eyes all but shut. "Keep Larissa safe?"

"Keep her safe. Do that, Shijef, please. That, too, is an order."

The Dreel bellowed angrily, then growled at me as he stalked out of the room. Larissa looked at me and raised an eyebrow. "He is not happy."

"That's because he wanted to go along and kill things, not because he wanted to protect me." The second I said it, I knew it was not true. "He will see to your safety."

"I would rather he saw to yours."

"You need not worry about me, *vitamoresti.*" I slapped the scabbard on the bed and smiled. "I've got your father sending a message to the Red Tiger requesting the use of the Steel Pack by the Knight-Defender, and I imagine that any Reithrese agents left in Jarudin will mark their departure at my request and relay that information to Jammaq. Takrakor will assume I'll come with an army because only an idiot would travel to Jammaq alone, and that means I'll have the element of surprise on my side."

"Will you be careful?"

"As careful as I can." I shrugged and smiled to reassure her. "Don't worry, I will return."

She shivered. "How can you say that?"

I winked at her. "Remember, the gods are perverse when playing with us lesser races. What will hurt more, my dying in Jammaq, or my seeing you again knowing that the Consilliarii will never consent to let us be together?"

"You trust in the gods more than I do, I think."

"No, in your love I trust, and in this blade," I smiled as I stood and shouldered my saddlebags. "Of the gods I just hope that *if* they notice me, they find me diverting and let me live just a little longer so I can endure that much more torture."

Chapter 23

The Empire of Dreams

Spring
A.R. 499
The Present

In retrospect, Gena thought, having lost most of their possessions to the fire at Castle Blackoak had been a blessing of sorts. At various times, as she had grown up, her grandfather and grand-aunt had both mentioned that the gods were perverse and would do all they could to make life miserable for mere mortals. This had clearly been a case of their meddling, and though Gena did not find traveling inexpensively that much of a burden, it clearly wore on Berengar.

On the road before the fire Berengar had not been soft or particularly prickly, but there were little rituals of civilization that he liked to observe. Each evening, for example, he had brewed tea and always made an effort to select aromatic woods to burn while his water came to a boil. He was not experimenting to find a new source of pleasure, but clinging to an old pattern of behavior because it helped define who he was.

Gena knew, from stories and observation, that Men

fought hard to carve out strong identities. Elves, with their long lives, were content merely to live, while Men seemed determined to build around themselves some sort of legend that would live on beyond them. Berengar had been no exception to that rule, and while he had his baggage and the trappings of an Aurdon noble, he acted much as she imagined he would have.

She looked up ahead at where the count rode in front as they neared a small forest. He still sat up in the saddle, but the steel shaft that had straightened his back had softened. He had tied his hair back with a strip torn from the hem of his shirt, and the ends of the cloth flapped in the light breeze like pennants over his right ear. Bare leg showed between the hem of his breeches and the low-cut leather shoes he had won in a game of knucklebones. He moved stiffly, still bruised from their village visit three days before because the local tavernmaster would not pay for song, but did offer them lodging and food if Berengar could best the local champion in a bare-knuckled fight.

As if he knew she was watching him, he turned slowly in the saddle and looked at her sideways with his still-blacked left eye. The swelling had gone down, and the edges of the bruise had turned a jaundiced yellow, but his eye remained bloodshot and rimmed with purple. "I have been thinking, Gena, that you are a bad influence on me."

"Me?" Gena feigned surprise and urged Spirit forward with her knees. "How, pray tell, did you reach this conclusion?"

Berengar half shrugged but stopped as a grimace seized his face. "All this talk and thinking about Neal is what prompted me to fight with that monster back in Elmglen. I think I wanted to impress you with my heroic ability."

"And you did, my lord." She glanced down at his scabbed knuckles. "I never expected you to get up after he knocked you down the second time, and no one in the village thought you would send him down with a single punch."

The count grinned and brought his right fist curling up into a short uppercut. "It was a good punch, but only one of many . . . on both sides. I've not been so stiff since I fell down two flights of stairs as a child."

Gena shrugged. "I offered to fix you."

"You did, and I refused." He laughed, then cut it off abruptly and hugged his left arm to his ribs. "I thought that I could show how tough I was by letting my body heal naturally, without magick."

"My lord, even Neal was not that foolish." She smiled at him. "If you wish, when we stop for the night, I could help you with the pain."

The count paused to consider her offer, then shook his head. "No, I think the worst of it is over, and I think it is good that I let it linger. Traveling hurt and living hand to mouth gives me a perspective I have not had before. Take, for example, the caravan that you and Durriken rescued from the Haladina. When I heard of them and when they arrived in Aurdon, I pitied them. Now, after this, I think I begin to understand them."

"It is not without good reason, my Lord, that people are often enjoined to consider other perspectives when making a judgment." Gena looked around at the rolling meadows and woodlands. "In Cygestolia there is nothing even close to this sort of open territory. It is difficult for most of my people to imagine anyone wanting to live outside a forest. In fact, I cannot think of but a few Elves who would have accepted the lodgings we did last night."

"Yes, spending a night sleeping in a sod house was interesting. I think, before arriving at my current state, I would have looked down upon those people. While they were a bit crude in their manners, their hearts were generous, their wisdom sound, and their concern for two travelers rather inspiring." He shook his head. "They even had dreams for the future, of expanding their farm and providing enough for their children and children's children."

"I think that admirable."

"As do I."

"Then why the shake of your head and the beetling of your brow?"

The count's expression lightened immediately. "Oh, I was not thinking ill of them or their plans. What had me confused was Neal again. When he and the Red Tiger entered Jarudin, the tales say that Neal killed the Reithrese emperor and took the crown."

"Yes, but he gave it to the Red Tiger."

"Why?"

"Why?"

"He could have had an empire. He could have shaped it in ways that would have made it last for all time. He could have made himself into a hero for Humanity, one that would not have been so easy for us to forget." Puzzlement again knotted Berengar's brow. "I don't understand his choice."

"Is that because it was a bad choice, or just the choice you would not have made in his place?"

Berengar chuckled carefully. "I had not separated those questions, and I guess I assumed since his choice was not my choice, it was by definition a bad choice. Had he chosen to keep the empire, I might have been able to trace my lineage back to him, not the Red Tiger. He had his chance at eternal fame and passed it by."

Gena nodded sympathetically at first, then hesitated. "I do not know Neal's mind, but I wonder if he did not think the Red Tiger would make a better ruler than he would."

"Perhaps, but to pass up a chance at being able to make your dreams for the future live—and I know he must have had them, every man does—I guess the ability to let that chance go by is what makes him a hero."

"It may well be that indeed." Gena ducked her head beneath an oak branch as they rode into the forest. "Since you would not have made Neal's choice, what would you have done had you won the crown?"

"A good question, that."

"You yourself said every Man has dreams for the future. What are yours?"

Berengar looked straight ahead and focused distantly. "Had I been in Neal's place, I would have moved swiftly to consolidate the empire and bring it under a strong central rule. The Red Tiger did bring it together, but only because he was the only power in a vacuum. He contented himself making arrangements with local strongmen instead of imposing his view of the empire from the top down. As a result, it was only ever really a confederation of states, and as you have seen, it has broken apart into the commonwealth within the last century."

He waved his hands at the surrounding countryside. "Even here in Ispar the instability is palpable—my late, unlamented uncle being just one example of how badly things have gone awry. You are right to condemn his dabbling in forbidden knowledge, but you must understand that when things become so out of control, Men search for ways to gain control. My uncle chose incorrectly, but the need for stability and control cannot be disputed.

"Stability and control would have been my keys." He turned toward her, and she saw his eyes alight with an inner fire. "In a year I would have brought Barkol, Ludhyna, and Ysk into my empire, and that would have provided me with enough forces to take Kaudia. I would have pushed on through the Haladin Outlands and Quom to destroy Reith."

"My kin might have objected to so strong a Human presence."

"But your people are not stupid. Our war would have been with the Reithrese and, more important, my empire would have rebuilt and structured Human settlements. Your people rode out on the *Eldsaga* crusade because Men were encroaching on Elven homelands. Under my rule the old borders and remnants of Reithrese political structures would have been swept away. Isn't it ridiculous that we now, after five centuries, still call the imperial capital by the name *they* gave it? The Red Tiger, while he did free us from the Reithrese, left us culturally enslaved to them forever."

Gena laughed. "There *are* Elven cartographers who believe you have stayed with the old names as a courtesy to them."

"That's an interesting perspective." Berengar shook his head. "Perhaps it comes from being raised in a merchant's house, but I would have organized the empire in a manner that built economic ties between regions and promoted both economic and cultural growth. I would have permitted ethnic and social identities to remain distinct while sublimating nationalism within pride for the empire. Strict laws and swift, sure punishment for violations would guarantee a lawful society that would, in turn, promote harmony and increased economic strength."

"But once one part of your empire determined that its economic best interest lay in another province or, worse yet, the Elven Holdings, you would have a serious conflict."

"Not at all. We have ridden for half a day, and aside from the croft we left this morning, we have seen no sign of Human habitation."

"Aside from this road."

"True, and were I emperor, there would be many more of them. They would be wide and well built because commerce demands swift and certain transport. Each province would have market centers. With land grants and tax amnesties I could promote immigration to new areas of the empire to create growth. I would have an army that would keep the Haladina in their deserts and put down any internal conflicts. And had I been Neal, your people and I would have had only one conflict."

Gena raised an eyebrow. "Yes?"

Berengar grinned despite a split lip. "The *sylvanesti* he loved would have been my empress."

A thrill shot through her as she read more into his statement than his words contained. She had always seen him as attractive and flirtatious, but Durriken's presence, and then his memory, had seemed to keep them apart. Their current conditions and the attention they demanded had pushed larger issues away and had created a bond between them that could have easily slipped into more than mere friendship.

Gena immediately began to poke and probe her own feelings toward Berengar, subjecting them to intellectual scrutiny in hopes of killing them. Merely considering her attraction to Berengar seemed to be a betrayal of Durriken, both on her part and by Berengar. She resented that intrusion on her, yet she knew that mourning a dead man forever would only destroy her. She had seen that before and resolved she would not fall into the trap.

Her attraction to Berengar did not wither away under examination, but neither did it blossom into the all-consuming passion of *vitamor*. It remained a seed, not yet sprouted, content in dormancy. Gena realized that their current situation was too odd and strange to provide a solid foundation for a relationship, and she dared not risk her friendship with Berengar by surrendering to his charms in such an atypical setting.

She recovered herself and smiled carefully. "That would have created quite a conflict with my people, my Lord. You must recall that five centuries have passed since Neal and the *sylvanesti* were in love. While my culture now permits what it denied them, it does not encourage it and barely tolerates it."

Berengar nodded. "This I understand, though I can dream of your Elders finding my arguments persuasive."

"Indeed, they might well have." She laughed and winked at him. "But if you have dreams of being persuasive, I would focus them away from Elves at this point."

He frowned for a second, then let himself laugh. "And upon what would you focus them?"

"Hardelwick, the emperor." Gena narrowed her eyes. "After all, he must be convinced that you actually are who you say you are, and to entrust Cleaveheart to you. They way we look now, you will have to be more persuasive than even Neal could ever have dreamt of being."

Chapter 24

The Emperor of Nightmares

Autumn
Reign of the Red Tiger Year 3 /
Imperium Year 1
Five Centuries Ago
My Thirty-seventh Year

I never felt so alone as when I rode from Cygestolia to the first *circus translatio*. I had said all my good-byes at Woodspire and at the base of the tree had been given five horses in addition to Blackstar. Three were laden with supplies, and all had been outfitted with the same sort of silver chains I wore. I was told by the groom who gave the horses to me that they were meant as a gift to the Man-emperor in Jarudin, but I knew that was a fiction that would make it easy for Aarundel's family to deny ever having given me any aid in my quest.

No one accompanied me to the grove. No soldiers along the way showed themselves. Shijef, whom I expected to wheedle and whine until I consented to his going with me, stayed away. Riding out from the city inhabited by virtually immortal beings, one of whom I loved with my whole heart and soul, I felt incredibly small and insignificant. That was how they saw me, and how the Reithrese saw me, and part of me knew they were right.

But it is the small pebble deep down in a boot that can hobble even the greatest of warriors. I smiled as my brother's old defense to criticism about his size came to mind. My success, if I was to have any, would come from the fact that I would be in Jammaq before even the Reithrese thought it possible, and even more so if they accepted the bait concerning my recall of the Steel Pack. If I had any luck at all, as a small pebble I would pass into their nation unseen and remain unsuspected until far too late for them to do anything about it.

The now-familiar wave of dizziness passed over me as I entered the grove. I led the horses around so they strung out one behind another; then I drew Cleaveheart. As I had learned in traveling with Larissa, a torch was not needed to activate the magick, just a touch and the repetition of an Elven phrase: *translatio mysterioso arcanum nunc.* I started before the tree that would send me south, then circled the grove, touching all the other trees, save that one, with my sword.

The torch used the first time I had traveled this way had given off sparks, which had cycloned around inside the grove to provide a wall through which I passed. Cleaveheart did not produce sparks per se, but rang loudly and clearly. The notes manifested themselves physically as spheres of differing colors, multiplying with each blow. The low notes, thick and blue, drifted toward the ground while the sharper, high notes darted about as if they were yellow and red hornets. All of them shivered the chains, binding me and the horses to the magick.

As I rode around, the sound built as if ten, then a hundred and a thousand swords, pealed in discord and unison. On my third circuit I reined Blackstar around, then drove him straight at the tree I had neglected. As I dashed forward, the sound grew louder and louder until I could feel the notes tremble through me. The spheres melded together into a rainbow wall through which I burst at the point of near deafness, and on into the network I rode with the sound receding behind me.

The network dragged on me, and I wondered if my plan

was doomed to fail. I knew Takrakor was not a fool. Despite the Steel Pack's recall, he would realize that it was possible for me or a troop of Elves to head down to Jammaq on a rescue mission. While other Reithrese would be negotiating with the leadership in Cygestolia, giving him a gauge on how much of my suspicions the Elves believed, he had to assume I might try something. He could discount much Elven participation since the only Elf likely to instigate trouble in conjunction with me was his prisoner, but as the raid had already proved, Takrakor was nothing if not calculating.

The network had three groves between Cygestolia and Reith. At three days of rest to one day of travel, that put any rescue attempt at a minimum of a week and a half. A longer time would be logical to expect, because the nearest grove lay nearly 120 miles from Jammaq. If he assumed we would take two weeks to get to Jammaq, he would not be considered overconservative in his thinking.

This was the reason I had decided to push as hard as I could. What I intended to do had been described as possible by Lomthelgar, suicidal by Thralan, and necessary by all three of us. When I reached the next grove, I would get off Blackstar, tie him to the end of the string, and mount the next horse. I would repeat that process a second time at the grove after that, and wind up in Reith in less than a day. From there, if I could do it, I would ride into Jammaq, free Aarundel and Marta, and ride off with them. Our supply horses would double as mounts, which meant, if we abused the network and ourselves, we could reach the edge of the Elven Holdings before Takrakor would expect a rescue attempt being made.

At least that was how I hoped it would go. The distance between Jammaq and the nearest grove did concern me, but before I worried about escape, I wanted to have the rescue completed. While I knew Takrakor was a cunning and ruthless adversary, I also knew he was not omnipotent, and I counted on that fact to guarantee our ability to flee.

Riding alone into enemy territory, even along a magickal highway, is not generally considered a way to earn a retirement pension. In thinking about what I wanted to do, I realized that Takrakor was not as powerful as I first thought, and that Tashayul had been limited as well. Before he had obtained Cleaveheart, Tashayul had controlled an army, but not one large enough to let him secure his empire. Until he had the sword in hand, resources had been denied him. Once he had it, and had the prophecy reading in his favor, support in Reith had been more forthcoming, which was why he had been able to fulfill his destiny.

Internal politics in Reith, as with Elven politics in Cygestolia, doubtlessly placed limits on what Takrakor could do. In taking Aarundel and Marta, the Reithrese sorcerer had made a bold bid for power that could just as easily doom him if it came to naught. If it won him Cleaveheart, he could find as much support for his imperial ambitions as had his brother. If his bid failed, the political powers in Reith could disown him and kill him or turn him over to the Elves for justice.

I was betting my life on the idea that Takrakor had acted without sanction or knowledge of most or all politicians in Reith. I knew he had at least two dozen individuals with him when he staged the raid that took his captives, and I could not imagine him handling many more than twice that number if he wanted to keep the operation a secret. As Jammaq remained abandoned for most of the year, it made a logical hiding place for the captives, and I already knew Takrakor felt quite at home there. I also felt certain he would be there because he would want to force me to return the sword to the place from which I had obtained it.

What everything boiled down to was this: I would face fifty or so Reithrese, including at least one powerful sorcerer, in the city of the dead in my attempt to free my friend and his wife. If I succeeded or failed, the most likely result was that the Elves and Reithrese alike would insist my mission had never existed and that things I said about it, if I survived, were the ravings of a lunatic.

Such are the privileges of being a member of an Elder race.

The first transfer worked well. I had dismounted before the last packhorse came through. Though my limbs felt leaden, I untied Blackstar and attached him to the end of the string, then hauled myself into the saddle of the second horse. Not having carried more than a saddle on its first run, it had not worked incredibly hard, though it looked back walleyed at me when I gave it some spur. I applied sword to tree again, and within two minutes we were into the network.

The second leg dragged on more slowly than an old drunken veteran's war stories. My sense of urgency concerning the rescue had made it possible for me to switch mounts, but having to sit still for what felt like eons eroded my strength. My head kept bobbing down to my chest as I dropped off to sleep. The shock of my chin hitting my chest would bring me awake again, and I shook my head to clear it, but I continued to get more mush-minded with each passing second.

Seeing the third clearing all dark and swirling in the white-for-black world through which I rode alarmed me and burned away the fatigue enfolding me. Peering into the depths of the inkstorm, I saw no one and nothing, but I prepared for trouble nonetheless. Something was definitely not right.

As we came through a tree on the north side of the clearing and normal vision returned, I saw immediately what had happened. A whirling cyclone of reds, browns, blacks, and greys rioted about. For some reason I could not fathom in my tired state, the grove was active, and as nearly as I could determine, the outgoing tree was the one I had intended to use.

I reined back immediately and brought my horse in beside the next horse in the string. Without touching the ground, I switched mounts, then drove my new horse forward into the correct tree. In an eye blink we were off again as the warm, musty wall of earth-tone colors gave us passage.

As I used my belt to tie myself to my saddle, I wondered how the Elves had managed to hide a *circus translatio* terminal grove in Reith. I did not remember seeing very many trees on my first journey there. Most of those had been single, wind-scoured, and twisted trees defiantly clinging to rocks no self-respecting lichen would have called home. I tried to let my concern over this point alarm me enough to make me alert, but my body could not muster enough energy to allow me to panic.

Before we got there, I fell asleep.

As much as charging into enemy territory alone is stupid, arriving exhausted is even more so. Apparently, when I arrived at the appropriate point, I functioned well enough to unsaddle my horses, water them, and tear open a bag of grain for them before I wandered off to collapse. I say "apparently" because I have no conscious memory of doing that, but when I awoke, I saw that it had been done.

Upon waking I also saw how and why the Elves had been able to maintain a *circus translatio* terminal within Reith itself. I awoke in a subterranean cavern of considerable size with a huge gash cut in the ceiling. Bright, cold sunlight poured down through it and the raindrops dripping from the edges misted enough for a rainbow to fill part of the air above me. Below the gash, placed carefully to take full advantage of the sunlight, was a grove of miniature trees. I recognized all of them and for the barest of seconds wondered if I had not been transformed into a giant through my misadventure.

I realized quickly enough, of course, that the miniature trees were the product of woodwifery. They had been grown specially and probably maintained carefully to provide the link needed to give Elves access to the interior of Reith. The cavern itself, with a pool collecting downhill from the grove, provided water and the cover needed to conceal at least a hundred warriors and their mounts.

I checked the horses and found all of them in good health. Though I had no way of accurately judging the time, I estimated that I'd slept for at least twelve hours, maybe more, and decided I would wait until the sun went down before moving on toward Jammaq. In the meantime I put more food out for the horses and scouted out the tunnel that led to the outside. Confident I could lead horses through it in the dark, I returned to the cave and slept some more.

The nicest thing I can say about the countryside in

Reith is that it is as equally beautiful at night as it is in the day. More so, actually, because at night there is enough heat radiating from the broken, black rocks to fend off the nightchill, whereas in the day it would have baked me. Mile after depressing mile of pulverized landscape would grind down anyone's resolve to continue, but nighttime seriously limited my circle of vision, so I was spared the brutal tableau.

Reith did have a lot of caves. I had no trouble locating sufficient housing for myself and my mounts. In one I found bones and in another I found feathers, but aside from those things, I saw nothing even approximating a sign of life. Given my status in the country I thought that a good thing.

Reith is a nation made of mountains and more mountains, yet it is not like my homeland. The Roclaws are old mountains; while Reith is a land still in the grip of volcanic upheavals. At night I could see fire glowing in numerous mountain-tops. The hiss of steam or the bubbling plop of mud-flats filled the night with unsettling sounds. Sulphurous fog choked me and made my eyes water from time to time. It was such a foul place I had no difficulty seeing why the Reithrese would want to win an empire that would allow them to live elsewhere.

It took me three days to reach the outskirts of Jammaq. I left my supplies and three horses in a cave outside the city, then led Blackstar and two other horses with me into the city itself. I fastened a set of silver chains to each saddle so we could slip them on whenever we had a chance during our ride away, even though I expected us to have at least three days on the road before we reached the cavern—if we reached it. I stabled the horses in one of the sidestreet mansions and headed out on foot for the last part of my journey.

I armed myself with Cleaveheart and Wasp, the latter homed in the top of my right boot. I slung Aarundel's ax across my back, with the head at my left hip. I had chosen to wear studded leather armor for two reasons and did not regret the choice. After the grueling ride I relished the relative lightness of that armor. More important though, ring mail's incessant rustle, and the metallic ringing in my ears caused by a coif, would have made my stealthy advance through the city of the dead impossible.

Autumn brought to Jammaq even more of a chill than it had known on my last visit, but I did not mind. Back then, in my youthful bravado and stupidity, I had come to beard the Reithrese in their own den. I felt confident that all the prophecies about me—both those others told and the ones I wove myself into—would protect me. I could not have failed to carry Cleaveheart away, so confident was I in my immortality.

Now, well into the autumn of my life, I felt a kinship with the city of the dead and comfortable in its sepulchral chill. In each leering gargoyle I saw an enemy I'd ridden down or slain with the sword I now bore. Having killed so many people did not necessarily make me a citizen of Jammaq, but it did confer on me visitor's privileges, and I meant to abuse those very privileges before the sun came up. A few more Reithrese would come to rest in Jammaq, and the living would depart.

A cold breeze cut at my face right then, and I realized I found a subtle strain within a great truth. As I had explained to Larissa, the gods were perverse. What I realized as I stalked toward Takrakor was that Reithra was the most perverse of all. She knew I was in the city and easily could have warned those who waited for me, but by betraying them and allowing me to send them to her, she let me feed her. That amounted to an act of worship toward her, and the last thing I wanted to do was to be counted among her acolytes.

Having placed my trust in the perversity of a perverse goddess, I should not have been surprised to see what awaited me at the mausoleum from which I had liberated Cleaveheart. In the dozen and a half years since I last saw it, a portico had been added to the building. Broad, circular steps led up to a landing that allowed access to the rest of the building. Four pillars carved in the shape of intertwined Human and Elven zombies upheld a roof. The figures making up the pillars were paired Man and Elf, male and female and like-gendered, mocking Elven laws and decorum with their crudity.

The merlons on the roof itself made the edge appear to be a huge jawbone, and it had been set with massive diamond teeth, the value of which was incalculable. Standing tall over the incisors in that jaw, Takrakor gestured, and all around me torches flared to life on the surrounding buildings. "Welcome to Jammaq, Neal Elfward," he shouted as light poured into the small courtyard before the mausoleum. "You have arrived far sooner than I expected. My allies, whom I invited to witness your submission to me, will be disappointed."

"I'd beg your pardon, Takrakor, but had I known you had a ceremony planned in my honor, I would have been more considerate."

"Considerate, yes, I believe that is how I often characterize you." The Reithrese sorcerer bared his diamond teeth in a soundless snarl. He regained control of himself and shook his head. "You possess something I mean to have."

I raised Cleaveheart into a guard. "Come here, I'll give it to you."

"Droll, Neal, and pathetic." Takrakor reached down out of my sight and dragged Marta to her feet by her hair. She did not cry out, nor did she move to defend herself. In the wavering light that poured through the teeth I could not see her clearly, but the gauzy garment she wore revealed a lot of flesh that appeared almost as pale and mushroom-hued as that of the sorcerer who held her. "You recognize Marta, of course."

I said nothing.

The sorcerer shifted his grip to the back of her neck, then brought her face down to his. He kissed her savagely. Her jaw shifted down as he forced his tongue into her mouth, yet she did not push him away or struggle. I wondered at why she did not fight him or do something, and then, when a pitiful, animalistic wail filled the courtyard, I thought finally she had returned to her senses.

Then I realized the sound came not from her but from the black door in the mausoleum. A tall, slender figure marched and stumbled through it and across the portico to the head of the stairs. He stood tall and quivering, while twenty feet above him Takrakor abused his wife. I saw Aarundel tense and try to move from where his feet had been rooted to the stone, but his efforts went unrewarded.

"Run, Neal. It is lost."

Aarundel's harsh plea barely made it past his clenched teeth, but it brought a sharp laugh from the Reithrese sorcerer. He released Marta, and she remained standing behind him, his spittle running down her chin. Takrakor licked his lips, then smiled diamonds at me. "He wants you to run because I have given him a choice. To save his wife, he must slay you and give me your sword. To save Marta, you must slay him and leave me *Khlephnaft.*"

I shook my head. "No bargain. I want both of them, alive, and away from here."

The Reithrese laughed loudly, but I could tell he forced it. "Do you think that if you rescue them, the Elves will be kindly disposed toward you?" He reached back and caressed Marta's breasts. "Do you think they will consent to let you touch a *sylvanesti* the way I have? Is this what you hope?"

"What I hope is that you've cleared up your affairs, because it looks as though I'll be killing you to take my friends back home."

"You jump ahead of yourself, Neal. If you do not kill Aarundel, or he does not kill you, *I* will slay Lady Marta here." He extended his left hand, and a dagger slid from his sleeve into his grasp. "It will be quicker than she deserves, but it will happen."

"Is this what you hope?" I mocked him.

"It is what I know and what I will cause to happen, even if I die." His face darkened and his voice took on a cutting edge. "I have already sent a message to certain of my brethren in Reith telling them I have *Khlephnaft.* They are coming here, now. Even if you were to kill me, there is no way you would be able to get your friends out of Reith. It is over, Neal Roclawzi."

"Strikes me those were the words I used in talking about your brother dying in the Roclaws."

Takrakor snarled and flicked his right hand in my direction. As if a puppet on invisible strings, Aarundel leaped from the portico and charged at me. He wore Reithrese ring mail, though his head remained bare. The barbed Reithrese scimitar in his right hand whistled as he swung it back and forth through the air. Hatred burned in Aarundel's eyes, but his brows slanted back toward the sides of his face as if he sought forgiveness for what the sorcerer was forcing him to do.

I noticed something wrong with Aarundel, but his first onrushing attack gave me no time to figure it out or to exploit it. He brought the sword down in an overhand blow. I parried high and normally would have swung around wide to the right to get my body out of line with his cut, but Takrakor's control took the edge off Aarundel's speed. I pivoted quick and tight to the right in a move that caught Aarundel's hip on mine and sent him up and over in a midair flip.

He crashed hard to the ground on his back. He hesitated there for a second, giving me a chance to split his skull from nose to crown, but I did not press my attack. I let him roll over to his stomach and scramble to his feet because that first pass had told me a number of things. If I could sort them out, I might be able to avoid killing Aarundel.

Aarundel was never a great swordsman—his weapon of choice was the ax that I wore on my back. I was better than he was at swordplay, and I had a magickal sword as well. Cleaveheart had already notched his sword when I parried him. I could easily do to him what Tashayul had done to me in our fight, which would leave Aarundel unarmed and vulnerable.

The Elf came at me again, but I parried his attack aside and forswore a riposte. Whipping my blade up and around in a grandiose slash, I rained three quick blows down at Aarundel's head and shoulders. He managed to parry each one easily enough, but each cut carved another piece from his sword. Like a woodsman notching a tree before felling it, I worked on Aarundel's sword with two other attacks, then I moved in close, bound his blade, and pushed him away.

What I knew about magicks could have filled a thimble

and left room for an ocean, but I did remember that the small stones taken from the towers in Jarudin had a link between them and the towers from which they had been removed—a link that made magick possible. Takrakor's control over Aarundel meant he had to be linked to the Elf in some way. If they had both worn a similar crown or something else that bound their brains together in some way, the source of the connection would have been obvious. As it was I could not see Takrakor well enough to notice anything odd about him, but I spotted the difference on Aarundel as we stood face-to-face before I pushed him back.

Between his eyebrows, up against his forehead, I saw a scab barely an inch long and a lump beneath Aarundel's flesh at that point. I knew that had to be the focus of Takrakor's link with my friend, and as the Elf came back in toward me, I dropped my guard to invite a lunge.

The point of his blade shot in at my heart, but I twisted to my left and raised my sword arm up and over his lunge. As Aarundel overextended, my left fist arced out in a punch to the right side of his head. That staggered him and he began to fall sideways. I brought Cleaveheart down and sheared through his blade, then hooked his heels with my left foot, dumping him to the ground.

I pounced on him instantly and sat on his chest. I trapped his arms with my knees, then pressed Cleaveheart's pommel straight down on his forehead. The lump did not shatter, but the flesh split anew, and a thin sliver of a diamond tooth sat like an island in a welling pool of blood. Smearing crimson across Aarundel's forehead, I brushed the tooth fragment away and stood.

Takrakor stared down at me, furious. I shifted Cleaveheart to my left hand and filled my right with Wasp as the sorcerer started his turn toward Marta. I whipped my arm forward, sending Wasp up and up toward him, but Takrakor took no notice of my action. Intent on Marta, he brought his dagger up, aiming it for her soft belly.

Wasp skipped off a toothy merlon and tugged at the shoulder of Takrakor's cloak before bouncing off into the tower's shadows behind him. The sorcerer looked back at me with disdain, his knife frozen for a heartbeat. "Know that what happens now is what you have wrought."

"Neal, save her!"

"I can't!"

Looking up as I was, I saw it descending before Takrakor had even the slightest inkling of his peril. Leaping down from a perch higher up on the mausoleum tower, Shijef flew through the night and landed short of the gap between Takrakor and Marta. The Dreel's left arm stabbed forward and swept back. It caught Takrakor in the face and battered the sorcerer back into the shadows. With his right arm Shijef gathered Marta up, then the beast vaulted the toothy balustrade and landed in the courtyard with the grace and stealth of a cat.

I shrugged the ax off and tossed it to Aarundel as the Dreel ran over to join us. "Set her down, Shijef."

The Dreel did as I instructed. "One claw, Shijef, carefully." I pointed to the scab line on Marta's forehead, above and between her staring eyes. "Cut the lump out. Easy, very easy."

The Dreel produced one razor claw and carefully reopened the wound. As with Aarundel, the skin split cleanly and revealed a piece of one of Takrakor's teeth. I was about to order the Dreel to flick it away, but Marta blinked and raised a hand up to pluck it from her brow. "Leave this to me."

Had I been of a mind to argue with her about collecting souvenirs, I would have demanded she discard it, but the arrival of a half-dozen Reithrese warriors from within the mausoleum demanded my attention. Clad in mail similar to that which Aarundel wore, they bore swords and bucklers. They looked tough, but were coming at us from a direction in which we did not want to go.

"Shijef, I have an order for you. Will you obey it?"

"Obey always I do."

"You disobeyed me by following me here."

"Followed not, *preceded.*" The Dreel smiled most horribly. "Obeyed I did."

The third grove being active with the colors of his fur suddenly made sense, as well as did his absence at my departure. It also explained how I managed to dismount and care for my horses upon my arrival in Jammaq without remembering any of it. "Do you smell the horses?"

"I do."

"Get Marta to them, and Aarundel." I glanced at my Elven companion. "Get going, I'll hold these clowns back."

Droplets of blood etched dark lines around the corners of Aarundel's mouth. "The Reithrese are more than just your enemy. Shijef, get Marta away from here."

"Go, Shijef, now."

The Reithrese approached us almost casually, as if already confident of their victory. I brandished Cleaveheart. "This is the sword that stole your empire. Are you brave enough to take it away from me?"

Before any of them could answer, I darted forward. Wrapping both hands around the hilt, I brought it across in a waist-high slash at the nearest of them. My foe dropped his buckler down to parry me, then screamed as Cleaveheart sliced through the small, round shield and took the lower half of his arm with it. His right arm had already started to come up in a thrust at my chest, so I spun inside his arm, brushed his attack aside with my right shoulder, and shifted the grip on my blade. With my back to his chest, I reversed Cleaveheart and thrust it back past my right hip and through his abdomen.

Letting gravity and his fall pull the dead man off my blade, I freed my right hand from Cleaveheart's hilt and appropriated my victim's own blade. Continuing my spin, albeit late and slow, I came around and, with the borrowed sword, swept aside a lunge at my midsection. I kicked forward with my right foot, catching the swordsman in the stomach. Breath exploded from him as he fell back. I split his skull with an overhand blow from Cleaveheart.

His brains had barely spattered the cobblestones when the third warrior came in quickly. He wanted to use his speed to defeat me and feinted at me with the dagger in his off hand. As I had with Aarundel's sword, I slashed Cleaveheart through it, then down into the warrior's left leg. He screamed as he went down, but caught himself on his hands. That presented his neck for me perfectly, and I did to him what I would have loved to have done to Takrakor.

My work done, I looked over at Aarundel. Two of his foes lay in a pile, and most of the third in another, with scattered bits between them. "Good work."

"And you."

I pointed to the dead Reithrese. "I assumed Takrakor had two dozen when he killed the Lansorii. Where are the rest of them?"

"I have no idea. I think some were sent as messengers, but the rest should be patrolling the city to keep Takrakor's enemies away."

I brought my sword up into a guard as I heard the clatter of hooves on cobblestones. "Mounted. This will be difficult."

"Anything to let Marta get away."

But Marta had not gotten away. With her bangs brushed back from her bloody face, she rode the lead horse into the courtyard, bringing Blackstar and the third horse behind her. Shijef jumped down from a rooftop, squatted on the cobblestones, and flicked dust and pebbles at the dead Reithrese. Aarundel ran over to his wife and hugged her around the waist, then mounted his horse.

I hauled myself up into Blackstar's saddle and patted the beast on the neck. "I have horses off to the north."

Shijef sniffed the air in the direction. "Lifeblack pools."

"We may have to chance it. North is where we can reach the *circus translatio*."

The Dreel shook his head. "Lifeblack deeply pools." He pointed toward the east and on around the compass. "And there. And there and there and there."

Aarundel frowned. "Surrounded. Takrakor's allies must have taken his announcement seriously."

I raised Cleaveheart in my right fist. "This sword is mine, and a lot of lifeblack will pool before it's pried from my hands."

Marta held her fist out. "Whoever is coming is very anxious. I can feel through this bit of tooth that more than one person is trying to magickally communicate with Takrakor."

I looked over at the Dreel. "Did you kill him?"

Shijef looked crestfallen. "Broken, not dead."

"Dammit." I looked around the city. "There has to be a way out of here."

The Dreel's face brightened, which normally is not a good omen. "The Elven Way. Roadfast."

"We need the grove for that." I turned to Aarundel as we all snapped ourselves into the chains we would need to use the *circus translatio*. "There's not a grove here in Jammaq?"

"In this necropolis? No."

"Use Roadfast, not grove."

I frowned at Shijef. "We can't use Roadfast without a grove, and the nearest one is three days' hard ride from here."

"We need to do something." Aarundel pointed to the north. "I hear riders out that way."

The Dreel rose up to his full height. "Use Roadfast."

"We can't."

"Can."

"How?" I looked at Dreel as if by willpower alone I could make him understand. "We need the magick of the trees."

"Magick the trees have." Shijef pounded both paws against his chest. "Magick I *am*."

The Dreel started off at a dead run around us. He circled us once, and the colors in his fur began to blur. On the second circuit he moved so fast that I had difficulty following his movements, and on the third only the intensification of the colors in the circle when he passed allowed me to see him.

When he got back to the point where he started, he stopped again instantly. His arms looped out to circle us all, then pull us in toward him. Blackstar fought against his touch, but I looked up and saw Reithrese riders pounding down toward us from the north. I spurred Blackstar forward, and he plunged on into the Dreel. The color wall parted, and once more I found myself in the odd place the Dreel named Roadfast.

As the familiar weariness began to pull at me again, I looked back and saw Aarundel and Marta riding behind me. Back beyond them I saw Shijef's shadowy form. Any attempt at figuring out how he could possibly be moving with us on a pathway for which he was the entry point threatened to overwhelm my senses. Facing forward again, I contented myself with feeling safe for the moment and smiled as I imagined Larissa's expression when we all arrived, once again safe, in Cygestolia.

Chapter 25

Finding Your Place In History

Spring
A.R. 499
The Present

Despite the grey haze hanging over it and the ragged sprawl of mud, wooden, and stone buildings surrounding the walls, Genevera could see beauty in the Imperial capital. The bits and pieces of Reithrese architecture yet visible added an exotic touch to what clearly was a thoroughly Man-wrought city. She knew there had been extensive reconstruction after the fire that took place around the time of her birth, but natural weathering had taken the edges off new buildings and gave them the same grimy patina that marked even older constructions.

Berengar and Gena entered the city through the southern gate and immediately headed toward the second circle and the immense bazaar. There they managed to bargain their way into far fancier clothing than any they had obtained on the road—though none of it seemed to Gena quite good enough for visiting the emperor. Closer to the palace itself they took rooms at The Branded Hand and used the inn's bathing facilities to wash away the road dust.

She would have preferred waiting until the next morning for making their attempt to see the emperor, but Berengar's impatience warred with his solicitousness toward her, making him edgier and less predictable than a wounded bear. Dressed and perfumed, they hired an open carriage to take them to the palace. The choice of action over patience calmed Berengar, and he grew silent as the palace loomed closer.

The central tower itself had not been damaged in the fire, but reconstruction had allowed the emperor at the time—Rudolf, the grandfather of the emperor from whom Berengar's family claimed descent—to expand the Palace. He added a series of rectangular buildings that surrounded the original tower, though to what purpose Gena could not imagine, because the Reithrese tower easily had more habitable space in it than Woodspire or the Fisher mansion in Aurdon. More curious, given the fact of the tower's size, was the continuing construction on the buildings surrounding it.

The coachman let them off at the gate, then moved off a short distance to wait. Gena took this as an ill omen, but Berengar seemed barely to notice. As she adjusted her green cloak and woolen head scarf, the count strode boldly to the nearest of the soldiers standing at the gate. "I am Count Berengar Fisher of Aurdon in the province-state of Centisia. This is Lady Genevera of Cygestolia. We are come on an important mission to speak with His Sovereign Majesty, the emperor."

The soldier looked from Berengar to Gena and back. He appeared unimpressed, but turned to walk back through the gate. Berengar started to follow, but the man held his left hand up to stop him, while dropping his right hand to the hilt of his sword. The count stopped, his smile dimming, while the man disappeared. He returned quickly enough, leading an older man who stood not quite as tall as Berengar, but was decidedly more stout than Gena's companion.

The new arrival, a sergeant according to the armband he wore, ignored Berengar and walked over to Gena. The scent of garlic reached her before he did, and with the swipe of his gloved left hand, the sergeant removed the last trace of his dinner from around his mouth. "Drop the scarf, missy, let me see your ears."

"This is an outrage!" Berengar's shout came with enough anger that in a bar it would have spawned a fight in an instant.

The sergeant shook his head. "Best be having your boy be quiet or we'll steel-leech him."

Berengar's eyes blazed, but Gena raised a hand. She removed the head scarf, then raked her hair back from her left ear. "Is this sufficient, Sergeant, or do you wish to touch it?" She twisted the ear sufficiently to have torn the pointed top off had it been prosthetic. "I am one of the *sylvanesti.*"

"So your patience and help here confirm, my Lady." The sergeant cocked his head toward Berengar. "And you will vouch for the likes of him?"

"I will and do."

He turned toward Berengar. "Claimant or pretender?"

Berengar blinked. "I beg your pardon?"

The sergeant sighed. "Do you wear the tiger over your crest or not?"

"I do."

"There we go." The sergeant waved both of them after him. Once inside the gate the man led them past a small guardhouse and pointed them to a doorway. "Go in there. Find yourself and you will find the emperor."

Gena could see the tension rising to an explosion in Berengar, but she bled some off as she touched him on the arm. "Come, my Lord, let us see if we have a clue to the puzzle we have been presented."

Berengar exhaled audibly but said nothing as he nodded and followed her through the doorway. Beyond it they found a small, relatively featureless room. They entered through a door in the south wall. Doorways to the east and west led back out of it. In the center, on a stone dais, stood a scale model of the castle surrounding the tower. Twenty-seven small golden circles marked different points on it, and each circle had a number engraved on it.

Gena could not figure out what the numbers meant,

though she did notice that they grew larger the further they were located from the room in which they stood. She also saw that only half of the new construction had been marked with them. "This is quite curious."

"Hmmm," Berengar grunted. He had barely glanced at the map and instead peered up along the walls near the ceiling. "Look, the name of every emperor has been carved into the wall, along with a number to designate his position in our history. See, it begins with Beltran Primus and ends with Hardelwick."

Gena looked up and saw the number twenty-seven carved beneath Hardelwick's name. "I think I have an idea. What was the name of the emperor from whom you claim descent?"

"Aufrey. He is number twenty-four."

Gena looked down at the model of the castle. "Twenty-four, here it is. We go east." Without explaining she grabbed Berengar's hand and led him off through the eastern doorway. She felt him resist at first, then he moved with her willingly. As they passed through numbered chambers with doors to the north and south, they increased their speed, but held back from running.

They stopped in the chamber with "24" carved in the center of the floor. To the north, carved on the wall, they saw the names of Aufrey's legitimate children, save that of his eldest and heir, Caselmund. That name had been inscribed over the lintel leading into the next chamber. A doorway stood open beneath each of the other three children. The centermost opened into a chamber, while the other two led to stairs.

To the south they saw four doors, and above the second Berengar pointed toward a name. "Loreena, that is the woman from whom my line descends."

The door beneath her name stood open. Gena also noticed that of the four doors on that side of the room, only one other had the name actually engraved in the wall. The other two names had only been painted on the wall. Gena suspected their impermanence had something to do with the strength of the claim to the royal house, and could easily mark the difference between descendants being able to wear the tiger or not.

" 'Find yourself,' the guard told us." Gena waved Berengar on toward the door.

Berengar preceded her, then led her around a sharp corner and up some stairs to a second floor. The both of them had to stoop, since the ceiling rose to a height of only five and a half feet. Along the walls she saw more names carved above even lower doorways, and Berengar led her on through one. Up more stairs, through another two rooms, up one more flight, and Gena began to fathom how the twists and turns had been laid out. Primary heirs remained on a level with their forebears, lesser kin and bastards went up a level. In a couple of places she saw doorways that had been bricked up, with names scraped from the rock.

A tight spiral staircase took them up into the smallest of the chambers in which they had yet found themselves. A lantern set on the floor illuminated Berengar's name and, beside it, that of his dead brother. Squatting back away from the lantern, a man in a cloak like puddled shadow clapped bony, long-fingered hands. "Quicker than most." He laughed, slightly sarcastically. "But not as fast as the most hungry."

The man moved like a spider as he crouch-walked over to where Berengar and Gena hunched with their spines pressed to the ceiling. "You are Berengar Fisher and you are Genevera of Woodspire, of Aarundel by Marta and through Niall."

Gena made no attempt to hide her surprise. "You are well informed, Majesty." She dropped to one knee and bowed to the gangling man.

Berengar aped her. "This is an honor, Highness."

"I am certain I believe it is as well, Berengar." Hardelwick dismissed Berengar without a second glance. He settled back on his haunches and, resting his knobby elbows on his knees, clasped his hands together. "I am so glad you are here. There are many things I must ask you and discuss with you. In the fire we lost records, which is part of the reason we have this monument to our posterity as an ongoing project. You should be able to bridge some chasms in our knowledge." The long-faced man smiled quickly, his dark eyes flashing with reflected lantern light. "With your help, I believe I can salvage much of the empire's early history, and especially details about Neal Roclawzi."

"I would be happy to be of any service to you, Highness."

Berengar cleared his throat. "Imperial Majesty, we have come to you on a mission that is most urgent and of the utmost importance to Centisia and the empire itself."

"Yes, yes, I am certain of that, Berengar. Interesting that you come to me *with* a mission as opposed to come *begging* one. Quite a nuisance, that is, thinking up quests for those who wish to etch in stone what we have only in paint here." Hardelwick combed the few remaining strands of his hair across his balding pate. "With Elves it is so hard to tell, but I would not put you a day over two hundred years. Is that right?"

Gena nodded, impressed with the man's guess. "I am a little older than that, but I have spent a century studying magicks, which has left me relatively isolated concerning news of the world. I do know my history, though, and I have a particular interest in Neal Roclawzi."

"Inspired by your grandfather?"

"Grandaunt, really. My grandfather often spoke of his friend, but there were some memories he chose not to share."

"This grandaunt, she would have been Larissa, Aarundel's sister?"

Gena nodded. "She was."

The emperor reached out and took Gena's hand. "You will have to see one of the things that survived the fire. It is a small painting made from the time when Beltran, the Red Tiger, feted Neal, here in Jarudin, and your grandfather and grandmother and grand-aunt were here. I am certain the artwork does not do her justice—none of them in fact: the emperor looks as if he has a potato for a nose when he should look like Berengar here—but I know you will appreciate it."

"I would like that very much, sire."

"My Liege, if you please." Berengar frowned and eased himself down onto his other knee as well. "Our mission is very urgent. Once we complete it, we can discuss history or anything else you wish."

The emperor casually brushed Berengar's statement aside. "You of Aufrey's brood have always been impatient, and it never does you any good. Impatience killed Atholwin's sons and has him dabbling in the ways of Reithra."

Berengar's jaw dropped. "You know of my uncle's foul practices?"

"Know? Certainly. He tried to hide it, but not that hard, because he wanted to brag about having information I did not. He did have some useful things, of course, but nothing I could not have found out without enslaving myself to a *ferghun*."

"You knew of *that* and did nothing?"

"Why should I do anything? Your uncle still had historical information to give me. Still does."

Gena shook her head. "Not anymore."

The emperor's eyebrow came up. "Dead?"

She nodded. "Fire. It started when he tried to murder me."

"Oh, dear, oh, dear." The emperor shivered. "Nothing salvaged, was there?"

"No, dammit, we almost died." Berengar's eyes hardened. "How could you have let a threat to the safety of the empire like my uncle exist? Reithra worship has been proscribed since the birth of the empire! How could you ignore your duty to the empire like that?"

The emperor sighed heavily. "Impatience, impatience. When Beltran won the empire, and while his heirs sustained it against threats internal and external, they required direct control of everything. Since that time a bureaucracy has built up and sustains itself. All that I am really required to do is to sign taxation decrees and deny leave to warring nobles to attack their neighbors. This I do, and do willingly. My passion, however, is recovering the history we have lost, for it is my duty to maintain our proud traditions as completely and accurately as possible."

Berengar rubbed his hands over his face. "But you should know how corrupt and broken down things have gotten out there. We have Haladina raiding in Centisia."

"And you have the Aurdon Rangers to fight them."

"But we, the Fishers, pay for them when the Rangers are maintaining *imperial* security."

The emperor shrugged. "Their budget is but a tenth of the money your elders and the Riverens withhold from my tax collectors. Oh, don't look so surprised, Berengar. You knew they were underreporting trade and production, and if you didn't, you're more stupid than even I would have imagined."

He released Gena's hand and scuttled around to face Berengar more fully. "I know wearing the tiger above your crest has filled you with all sorts of ideas about the empire and imperial traditions, but it is the fabric of fantasy. If I were to force your Elders to correctly report what they have earned and send me my due, they would chafe beneath my rule. As it is, I have set tax rates at double and triple what I need to sustain my army and other imperial functions, because I know half to two-thirds of the money collected in my name will never reach me. In turn, because local nobles do not want imperial scrutiny, they handle all but the most major of problems. I do not mean to disillusion you, but the first emperor was, really and truly, the last heroic emperor. Since his time we have been little more than accountants because the Empire has not required more from us than that."

Berengar sat silently for a moment and Gena thought him completely depressed. She recalled the enthusiasm with which Berengar had outlined how he would have put the empire together had he been Beltran, and she knew that Hardelwick's apathy toward the empire's maintenance had to be a shock.

The count shivered, then looked up at the emperor. "I understand what you have said, at least on the surface, and I am certain I will come to understand more as I think on it. Which I shall do. However, that has no bearing upon our mission. Consider my request as that of a minor noble who does not wish to impose on His Imperial Majesty, but has no other choice."

Hardelwick nodded wearily. "What is it you ask of me?"

"I, we, have come here to request that you make available to us the sword and dagger Neal Roclawzi used five centuries ago." Berengar opened his hands. "Certainly you know where they are, and we need them most seriously."

"A mission to find Cleaveheart and Wasp?" The emperor sounded almost surprised and definitely amused. "Perhaps it is fated that you come here with that request, for I have recently learned of the sword's resting place. Due to Atholwin, actually."

"Yes? Yes? Can we have it?"

Hardelwick chuckled lightly as he shuffled toward the stairway. "You're welcome at having a go at getting it, but I'm not certain there is a Man or Elf alive who can actually lay hand to it."

"I can."

"So we will see, Berengar." The emperor patted Gena's leg. "Come, my dear, follow me. You will enjoy this."

"Is there a specific reason for that, Highness?"

"Oh, I believe so." The man nodded as he perched on the edge of the circular opening and extended his legs down into it. "After all, magickal wards that have lasted for five centuries are not common, and these were well woven. You can take pride in Larissa's handiwork, and we shall both be there to applaud if Count Berengar can defeat the spells she laid down."

Chapter 26

Carving a Niche in History

Autumn
Reign of the Red Tiger Year 3 /
Imperium Year 1
Five Centuries Ago
My Thirty-seventh Year

The Dreel's magick somehow superseded the nature of the *circus translatio* network and brought us directly to the grove outside Cygestolia. Upon arrival I did not feel nearly as weary as I had in my outbound trip, but I was not, by any measure, well rested and full of energy. We all managed to dismount and lead our horses from the grove, but before we left it, Aarundel used the blanket tied to his saddle to cover his wife's near nakedness.

As she huddled beneath it, my friend turned to face me. "We shall not speak of what Takrakor did to her, or the state in which you saw her. There are those among my people who would view that as an offense equal to your having touched her, and they would erase your gallantry in a foolish act meant to salvage the honor of the person you almost died to save."

I nodded. "I saw nothing, and I defeated you through a subterfuge."

"You need not go that far, my friend." Aarundel's eyes grew distant. "When I first met you, back when you fought Tashayul, I thought you brash and arrogant in the things you said. You bragged about becoming a hero, and like a hero, you did not back down when faced with Reithrese and Elven scorn. I knew then that I had no desire to fight you, ever, for you would defeat me. And I also knew you would become the hero you prophesied yourself to be."

"Not without you at my side."

Shijef lifted Marta into his arms, and I took charge of her horse in addition to Blackstar. Elven warriors slipped from the surrounding woods as we approached the city, but their challenges to us died as they realized who we were. With Aarundel and Marta both having bloody streaks on their faces, and me with a week's worth of grime and a splattering of Reithrese blood on me, we looked a suitable sight to have come back from the Reithrese city of the dead.

Word spread quickly that we had returned to Cygestolia. I fully expected the surprise I saw on many faces, but I read fear on so many more of them. It did not appear to be focused upon me—the fear, though the surprise came fully in my direction—leaving me to wonder why the Elves would find terror in the return of two people presumed dead by the Consilliarii.

Lest I leave the impression that our homecoming was met with sour looks and silence, I must note that it was not at all. Everyone cheered once they were over their initial shock. Aarundel quickly found himself unable to translate all the questions and comments directed at us. Laughter, catcalls, and applause followed us as we made our way from the grove to Woodspire. There loyal family retainers relieved us of our horses, and we were taken up to our chambers.

Once there I washed quickly, then collapsed in my bed. I had hoped to see Larissa before dropping off to sleep, but I thought it best that I had not. Given the growing state of euphoria in which I found myself—spawned because snatching my friends from Takrakor's lair was quite a feat

—I might well have swept her up in my arms and have given her a proper welcome.

As I found in my dreams, she'd feared throwing herself at me, so she had stayed away as well. And forced herself to lie down to sleep so that we could be together in the heart of a city that wished to keep us apart.

I saw little of Thralan and Lomthelgar because the Consilliarii met in almost constant session from the time of our return. I could only guess at the type of discussions that kept them going so long, but after my last encounter with them, I was not of a mind to go there and see if my conclusions were correct. More important, I knew that their ideas and their wishes would really not make a difference in what I saw as the course for the rest of my life.

I spent a great deal of time away from most of the Elves during the first week after our return. Aarundel had been obsessed with the fact that Takrakor had taken both his and Marta's wedding tokens, and set about making new ones. I accompanied him to the smithy and worked on a project of my own under his able tutelage. Neither of us spoke much, but that didn't bother me. He was thinking of his wife and their ordeal, and I was thinking of my future and the likely events to unfold in it.

I knew the Reithrese and the Elves might be able to come to an accommodation concerning the kidnapping, but I also knew that I would never be able to escape retribution for my part in the desecration of Jammaq. The Reithrese could easily brand Takrakor a renegade and deliver his head on a stake to satisfy Elven sensibilities. My problem lay in the fact that enough Elves viewed me with the same disdain as the Reithrese. While I might be considered inviolate while in Cygestolia, I would be fair game outside the Elven Holdings.

I could not spend the rest of my life in Cygestolia. I was not one to cower in safety when faced with a threat. Moreover, the Reithrese merely had to press the Red Tiger, and I would come out to oppose them. They knew that, I knew that, and I felt certain most of the Elves knew that. Without much trouble at all the Reithrese would be able to dislodge me and destroy me with impunity.

Oddly enough, I did not find the idea of once again fighting the Reithrese all that disquieting. Even if the Elves didn't see it, I knew the Reithrese would never be at peace. Men had taken their empire away from them. We had defeated an Elder race. We laughed at their retreating troops, and they had to rely on our good graces to escape. We had shamed them in a way that they could never allow to stand. Just as a man would never abide a dog that tricked him and stole food from his table, so the Reithrese would have to punish their rebellious inferiors.

I had no doubt that the next ten or twenty years would spell the end to Humanity or to the Reithrese. One way or the other we would be wiped out, or they would all die off. We could not live together. Perhaps the long Elven perspective could have allowed us to see a way to peaceful coexistence, but Men did not have it, and the Reithrese did not use it. The rebellion and overthrow of the empire had been an overture to genocide.

Just as I had felt a duty to go free Aarundel, so did I feel a duty to be with my fellow Men to oppose the Reithrese. I harbored no illusions about a long life sinking into glorious old age. I had chosen to tread the Hero's Path, and my journey was not yet at an end. Had I the freedom to marry the woman I loved, perhaps I would have wished my journey had ended, but facing the consequences of my choice would still not have been removed from me.

Of course, there always was the possibility that the Consilliarii had been locked in battles over whether or not they would grant me dispensation to marry Larissa, but I doubted that sincerely. If they were to do that, they would more tightly bind me to them, which would increase the chances that they could be brought into the Man-Reithrese conflict. More than likely, it occurred to me, they were devoting themselves to figuring out how to punish me for leaving three horses meant for the emperor in Jammaq. Surely that was a crime for which someone could claim my head.

After a week my work at the forge was finished, and at the same time the Consilliarii summoned me to appear before them. I agreed to go to them, but instead of dressing in my finest clothes, I wore the leather armor that I had used in Jammaq. I belted Cleaveheart on and left Wasp's empty sheath tucked inside my right boot. Regardless of what they were going to say to me, I intended to let them know my thoughts and plans, and the reasons behind them.

Calarianne, the *sylvanesti* overseeing the Consilliarii, did not hide her surprise when I came to the council armed and in armor. "Welcome, Neal Roclawzi Elfward. I trust you do not think you will be required to defend yourself here."

"I do not, Doma Calarianne. I felt it fitting that I come dressed for war because I know I will be leaving soon to conduct a war." I bowed my head to her. "However, I suspect you did not summon me to discuss my sartorial preferences."

"You are quite correct in your supposition, Elfward." She looked away from me toward one of the Consilliarii standing before her. I recognized him as the first Elf to oppose me when I said I was leaving on my rescue mission. "We have brought you here, Elfward, to reward your bravery."

The Consilliari bowed first to Calarianne and then more formally to me. "You are aware, Neal Roclawzi Elfward, that the title Custos Sylvanii is one that we bestow upon other races and peoples in whom we trust and whom we admire. Aarundel of Woodspire, as was his right as an Imperator, bestowed that title upon you and, at the same time, petitioned this body to ratify his decision. His petition has been granted, making you the first Man ever to earn that title. Henceforth you will be known among us as Elfward, and any that would bear you malice because of your Humanity or your birth in the Roclaws are enjoined to set their animosity aside, or be forced to reside apart from us."

Despite his obvious reservations, the Consilliari spoke the words sincerely. I felt a lump rise in my throat, and that surprised me. I had spent so much time expecting and living with hostility from the Elves that having even this begrudged acknowledgment of my worth unbalanced me. A smile came to my lips unbidden and I tried to kill it, but I failed because I found it mirrored on more Elven faces than I ever would have dreamt possible.

Calarianne nodded her head. "Thank you, Vorrin Consilliari. Neal, it has come to our attention that in your recent adventure you lost a dagger that had seen much service with you. While we know we cannot replace it per se, we offer you this inferior substitute, lest it be said we do not know how to show gratitude."

Marta stepped forward and walked across the flat of the chamber toward me. On a satiny blue pillow she bore a dagger that looked as closely as I remember to be Wasp's size, shape, and design. Of course, Wasp had been rusty steel with fittings of brass, while this had a blade of silver-washed steel, a crossguard of gold, and a gold pommel with a diamond set at the very end of it. As I reached for the blade, I felt a slight tingle, and Marta nodded to me almost imperceptibly.

Her voice came in a whisper. "The diamond is the one you saw taken from my brow. I have worked a spell onto the blade. I know there is nothing that will keep you and Takrakor apart, so this magick will help bring you together."

"To my advantage I am certain." I hefted the blade and relished its improved balance over that of Wasp. "The better for throwing."

Marta smiled. "The better for not missing."

"Thank you." I reversed the blade and tucked it into my boot sheath. I bowed to Marta, then acknowledged all the Consilliarii. "Now I no longer feel naked."

"This pleases us greatly, Elfward." Calarianne smiled warmly at me. "As a Custos Sylvanii, Cygestolia is open to you. Thralan Consilliari has said that your chambers in Woodspire will be available to you whenever you need them and for however long you require them. We would like you to consider Cygestolia your home."

"That is a most gracious offer, but I cannot accept it." I reached into a pouch on my swordbelt and pulled from it the silver bracelet I had labored to create over the week. "Cygestolia is the home of the Elves. I am not an Elf. I cannot remain here.

"This bracelet is what I am." I ran my thumb across the

runes I had scored into its surface: Man, Mountain, Sword, Luck, and Friend. "Crudely made, just like me, and nothing in comparison with Elven majesty. It defines me completely and even has errors made in its manufacture, which lets you know I have a grasp on my worth and importance in the world."

I let the bracelet dangle from the fingers of my scarred hand. "Rather pitiful, I know, especially from your point of view, but it serves its purpose well. And that purpose is for it to remain here, so I will not be forgotten. When I leave Cygestolia this time, I don't count on returning."

I took a deep breath, then continued. "The Reithrese are out there. They will be looking to do to Men things so horrid that the *Eldsaga* will pale by comparison. I don't say that to inspire you to destroy Humanity before they do. I want you to know that savagery in the name of racial superiority is not your talent alone. I have seen the Reithrese at practice, I have heard stories, and I saw what Takrakor did to a party of your Lansorii. What comes will be lifeblack delivered in oceans."

I looked around the room, trying to meet as many pairs of eyes as I could. "You and the Dwarves and the Reithrese are all Elder races, but I do not hate you because of it. Hatred is too strong an emotion to be wasted on harmless differences such as race.

"Malevolence, however, deserves hatred. The Reithrese are malevolent. So it is that I hate them. I know, even as I stand here, they are preparing to destroy Humanity—if not this year, then next, or ten years from now or a century from now. They can and will destroy us because they choose to hate us over simple things. Perhaps that is a good definition of malevolence: hatred based on arbitrary and benign differences."

I held my arms open. "You have seen Mankind in me. Men have hopes and dreams, just as you do. We have the petty and cruel, as you do, but we also have the noble, the kind, and the wise. We are not Elves, nor shall we ever be, but that does not mean we should be butchered by the Reithrese.

"My urgency, the urgency that sent me out to Jammaq, tells me that there is no room or time for compromise with the Reithrese. After they subdue Men, their suspicions will fall on you and the Dwarves. The Reithrese place themselves in service to death. There is no living in harmony with them. There can only be fearing when they will strike."

I let my hands sink back down by my side. "I am going to war. I am going to fight the Reithrese. When you judge my actions, do not look at me as a madman, but remember I am Custos Sylvanii. Do not ask why I choose to oppose the Reithrese, but remember I act as a Man *and* as a friend of the Sylvan Nation."

Lomthelgar stood out from the line of Elves near the front of the room. "This is the Final Time! In his voice he speaks for all others."

I did not understand the significance of the elder Elf's comment, but its effect on the Consilliarii was what I would have expected had he up and tossed a hornet's nest into the center of the room. Angry shouts in Elven echoed back and forth. Calarianne hammered her staff against the chamber floor a half-dozen times, but that only cut the volume of the discussion, not its virulence. Finally things calmed down, and two Elves were chosen to speak on whatever subject was at hand. The first went on at great length and with incredible eloquence, though I didn't understand a word of it, whereas the second man pointed at me, made a quick statement, and sat down again to a round of applause from the gallery and most of the other Consilliarii.

Calarianne polled the body and the side with the long-winded speaker lost decisively. She made a pronouncement, then looked over at me. "You are a curious man, Neal Elfward. We offer you hard choices, and you accept their burden without complaint. You offer us hard choices, and we are forced to fight before we accept the burden. It is maddening to many of us that centuries of discussion dissolve beneath your urgency and passion."

I wasn't certain how I should reply to that remark, so I said nothing.

"It is the decision of the Consilliarii that the Legionnairii Sylvanii will assemble and march on Reith for the purpose of destroying the Death-lovers. As you have protected and rescued us from them, we deem it our repayment to you to end the scourge of the Reithrese for all time."

I stood stunned for a moment; then I smiled and bowed to the Elves. "I am honored at your choice. When do we leave?"

Vorrin stood forward. "This is our battle now, Elfward. Your part in this is finished. You will not go."

Lomthelgar opposed him. "Vorrin Consilliari, Neal is the Man who has spoken with Three Voices."

"Superstition. It does not apply."

Thralan shook his head. "If it did not apply, Vorrin, why did it make you change your position from your earlier votes on this subject?" He ignored the Elf's stammered defense. "You understand the significance of this—all of you do. This is the reason, the last sign. Because of him we embark on the Second Great Crusade. You deny this because it marks a time of chrysalis and you do not wish to face all that entails."

"He is a *Man*. This is a War of Elders."

"He is Custos Sylvanii and, therefore, not to be dismissed for his Humanity." Thralan pointed toward me. "Neal wields *Divisator*. By his hand the snake will lose its head."

Vorrin hesitated for a moment, then shook his head. "We cannot chance *Divisator* falling into Reithrese possession. He could lose it."

"I'll tie a lanyard from my hilt to my wrist."

Lomthelgar clapped at my suggestion and a few other Elves laughed. Vorrin became furious. "And if one of them takes your arm? What then?"

I stared right back at him. "Then I place my trust for the world and the future in the hands of the Elven Legions. If each warrior fights only a tenth as well as Aarundel Imperator, a thousand swords like Cleaveheart could not delay the destruction of the Reithrese. Mark me, Vorrin Consilliari, auguries and prophecies, signs and fears be damned. I will be there to destroy the Reithrese. The question for you is this: will you wait here to be told later how the day was won, or will you fight at my side and guarantee victory?"

Chapter 27

False Goal, New Beginning

Autumn
A.R. 499
The Present

Gena followed the emperor back through the generations of Berengar's family to the main imperial line and then on deeper to his own chambers. When they reached the corridor with vaulted ceilings, Gena straightened up, as did Berengar, but Hardelwick still hunched a bit. While older than Berengar by a good bit, Gena did not think the Man so old that his skeleton had begun to deteriorate. She decided, instead, that his hunch came from long years spent poring over manuscripts or haunting the corridors of the stone genealogy.

The emperor's own chambers confirmed her guess concerning his stoop-shouldered posture. If not for the profusion of two items she would have thought the room belonged to a soldier who could only be comfortable in the spare, spartan surroundings of a campaign tent. The bed, wardrobe, desk, and most chairs were little more than pieces of wood hastily cobbled together. Functionality superseded form, and the desk itself looked solid enough to support the weight of the whole palace.

The two things that dominated the high-ceilinged room were books and mirrors. Shelves had been built into every wall, and bookcases started to form a labyrinth in two corners. Every available surface, save but one chair and the center of the desk, had books stacked on it, around it, or above it. The sour scent of the straw in the mattress mingled with the more powerful, musky scent of a Man, making Gena wonder if—absent the necessities of entertaining visitors—the emperor ever left the room.

The mirrors hung all over the room, suspended from the ceiling by slender cords. Other cords secured them one to another, and anchored them to the shelves. None of them were low enough to provide the emperor with a good image of himself, though she suspected the man hardly cared how he looked when or if he dressed for a special occasion.

She also felt a spell woven into the room. The sensation of the spell was maddeningly familiar, but it took a quick, surreptitious casting of a diagnostic spell to tell her what it was. When she got the answer to the mystery, she smiled and blushed. "Of course, a fire-dampening spell. You do not want to chance losing these books."

The emperor nodded distractedly. "Exactly. No fire in this room."

"And the mirrors, they collect the light from the windows and direct it to your desk."

"Yes, Genevera. I work from dawn to dusk, while there is light." The emperor pulled himself up to his full height. "These tomes contain all I have been able to reconstruct of the empire's history. That shelf there, those half-dozen books, those are all I have been able to collect about Neal. I have some questions for you, if you don't mind. . . ."

"Highness, you were going to show us something?" An edge crept into Berengar's voice. "Cleaveheart."

"Yes, yes, that's it." The emperor, hunched over once again, waved them on through a door that led out into the courtyard and the Reithrese tower. "I'd not have found it again if your uncle's vague hints about Reithra worship had not made me compare some accounts from the time of the empire's founding. Of course, the story of Neal having destroyed the Emperor's Legion of Immortal Bodyguards in battle right here is well-known, after which he killed the emperor himself and crowned Beltran on these steps, but I have always been suspect of it. An architect at the time, Xerstan was his name, kept a diary concerning his projects, especially the ones involving changes to the tower here. He had copies made for his family and prospective clients, which is how I happen to have his account, since the original was likely lost well before the fire."

The emperor led them up the steps to the doors of the tower, but required Berengar's help in opening one sufficiently wide to permit them entry. The darkness inside threatened to stop them in the entryway, but Gena conjured a floating witchlight sphere that gave off a cold blue light as it preceded them through the quiet halls. The place felt quite dead to her, but grit grinding beneath her feet and a profusion of shovels, picks, and axes leaning against the walls made her think the tower saw a certain amount of activity from time to time.

"Xerstan mentions meeting Neal and undertaking for him, with the emperor's blessings, a special job. He refuses to give any details about that job, citing confidentiality and honor. He notes, in another place, having helped Lady Larissa of Woodspire complete a monument to Neal, but I found no record of such a thing being created, or any sort of public event being held to memorialize Neal—at least none at which Lady Larissa was present. Xerstan, who was something of a moralist, also devoted a number of pages to the foul business of Reithra worship, and he took great delight in pointing out the tricks and oddities built into the Reithra chapels, one of which every good Reithrese maintains in his home for her worship."

The animation on the emperor's face as he spoke made him seem more alive than ever before, even despite the washed-out, bone-white pallor the witchlight poured into his face. Berengar's impatience narrowed his eyes, and Gena felt convinced he would have swatted the emperor had the man not been leading them further into the dark tower. Gena smiled at the emperor and found she was not forcing it at all, because she actually did find the man's information fascinating.

"Xerstan said each chapel had a firehole. He notes this was a circular pit anywhere from three to six feet in diameter. Plain ones extended down for twice their diameter and were kept burning by the family tossing wood, coal, rubbish, bones, and anything else that would burn down into it. Some of the more sophisticated ones tapped into natural gas vents to keep them burning, and more than one pit actually led down into subterranean tunnels that could be used for a variety of purposes."

Berengar could contain himself no longer. "How does this pertain to Cleaveheart?"

"Always the impatient ones." The emperor stopped and lifted his head to be eye to eye with Berengar. "It occurred to me, Berengar, that Xerstan said every Reithrese dwelling had such a chapel and such a firepit, but I had never seen such in this tower. Xerstan reported that he had learned all he knew about Reithrese chapels by destroying them, which led me to believe that if there had been one in here, he had destroyed it. I began poring over architectural drawings of this tower and remeasuring everything, and I found where the chapel used to be. Therein, I believe, I have found Cleaveheart's resting place."

"You could have said that in the first place."

"Those who only want answers will never learn how to find answers." The emperor yawned, covering his mouth with the back of his left hand. "I have had men excavating the chapel. Wizards I brought in said they felt two foci for magick, so we dug to them first. I think you will find both fascinating. Come."

The emperor held aside a huge tapestry, and Gena saw an opening where bricks had been knocked out of the wall in a haphazard pattern. She sent the witchlight in first, and it revealed a low, narrow tunnel shored up with stout timbers. Gaps on the sides showed her that the architect had used almost anything as fill for the chapel, including broken masonry, bones, dirt, and metal that had been reduced to rusty streaks. Dust clung to everything, and Gena regretted ever having changed out of her road clothes.

At the far end the tunnel opened out into an area that

had been entirely cleared of debris and cleaned up substantially. She could see details on the walls, and as she sent the witchlight upward, she got a shock when it revealed a face looking back down at her. She kept the witchlight up there until the emperor emerged from the tunnel. Berengar followed him, rubbing at his forehead.

The emperor looked up. "That, I believe, is the face of Tashayul. He is carved up there, akin to a pâté mold." The man laughed lightly. "I believe this is the room in which Neal killed the emperor, and I am certain the irony of having Tashayul watch it all was not lost upon him."

Berengar folded his arms. "Why do you think the fight was held here?"

Hardelwick shrugged and aped Berengar by folding his arms. "As Lady Genevera has likely already noticed, there are two sources of magick here. One is this sword, which is the blade the last Reithrese emperor used to defend his empire." The emperor toed the hilt and blade protruding from the floor. "He failed to do so."

Berengar dropped to his haunches. "Nice blade."

Gena brought the witchlight down and smiled. As the light circled the blade, the sword's shadow retreated before it, as if the sword were a sundial in a world gone mad. Berengar reached out toward the blade, but refrained from touching it before either Gena or the emperor could warn him away.

"Very nice blade. Depending upon the story, according to my uncle, this sword became a dragon or screamed out a death song or blazed with fire." The count dug his thumbnail into the stone near the blade, and it flaked up rather easily. "I would guess fire?"

The emperor nodded his head. "Very good. I think it was fire as well—that story predominates the tales, though the dragon story is a better one, I think."

Gena summoned the witchlight over to the object, from which she distinctly sensed powerful Elven magick. Six feet in diameter, the circular piece of white marble had been set flush into the basalt. Elven, Reithrese, and Human runes spiraled out from the center to the edge. She reached down to touch the words and feel them slide beneath her fingers, but before she could do so, the stone shimmered, as if a reflection in a pond that had been disturbed by a rock being dropped into the center of it.

"What was that?"

Gena looked up at Berengar. "It is a simple ward, but I suspect it is meant to keep casual and inexperienced sorcerers from attempting to disturb the stone. The image we see here, the one that rippled when I touched it, is a glamour, an illusion. What we see is nothing like the surface of the stone beneath it. Glamours are often woven into Elven spells that are meant to last for a long time. It presents an image that does not age and does not change, which is suitable for a memorial."

The emperor knelt down and carefully moved his index finger around above the spiraled runes. "I cannot read Elven or Reithrese, of course, though I do recognize them. The Man runes are an archaic form. I believe they come from the Roclaws. The Roclawzi ambassador does not have a linguist with him, but he has sent a request back to the mountains to send one to me. I can make out some of the message, but the fragments do not make much sense."

"The Elven is older, but I can still read it." Gena concentrated, canting her head this way and that to follow the line of script. "Glory does not lie within, Merely a sword that did win / An empire washed in blood, In the name of the common good. Let he who puts hand to hilt, From sacred duty never wilt. An empire won will yet fall / If not governed for the good of all."

"I had less than a third of that."

"Not great poetry."

Gena looked over at Berengar. "Less the fault of the poet than my retranslation of something likely written in Mantongue and translated over into Elven. I would say it is rather common in terms of a burial warning."

"Yes, but how many burial sites are warded by Elven magick?" The emperor smiled as he dipped his finger down and the image rippled. "Quite potent, this magick."

Gena nodded. "I agree, which means it is keyed."

"Keyed?" Berengar frowned. "Is that different from using some sort of fuel to power the spell, as you explained to me after the ambush?"

"Ambush?"

"Haladina, Excellency, and the reason for our mission."

"Ah."

"To answer your question, Berengar, yes and no. If you will recall, I described to you a spell that worked on arrows to increase their speed and power."

"The one you used on the sand."

"On sand?" The emperor leaned in toward Gena. "Fascinating."

"Yes. That spell was keyed to arrows after a fashion, but it worked with the sand and could be made to work on rocks or spears or any other sort of projectile weapon." Gena pointed to the stone circle. "This spell, because it is protective, is keyed magickally. It is, in essence, a lock that requires a specific key or set of keys to unlock it."

"I need Cleaveheart. Can you unlock it?"

Gena thought for a moment, then nodded her head. "I know I can, but doing it without the key will be all but impossible. If Larissa cast this spell, and I feel enough of her in it to make me think His Majesty was right in saying she was the author of it, I should be able to learn what the key is. With that I can break the spells and we will recover the sword."

She shrugged. "Getting that information, however, is not going to be easy."

Berengar stood. "No expense is too great, Lady Genevera. You know that."

"It is not expense that worries me." She sighed as heartache and anxiety washed over her. "It will be difficult, and those who have the information may not want to give it to me."

"I will convince them."

Gena almost laughed. "You are persuasive, my Lord, but even the emperor could not guarantee our getting the help we need."

"I don't understand." Berengar frowned. "Why will this be so difficult?"

"To get the key we have to travel, my Lord." Gena looked down and shivered. "To Cygestolia, where we will have to convince those who knew Neal and his wishes to betray his secrets to us."

Chapter 28

True Goal and the End of Everything

Early Winter
Reign of the Red Tiger Year 3 /
Imperium Year 1
Five Centuries Ago
My Thirty-seventh Year

The Elves began assembling their host immediately. Word went out by means mundane and magickal telling the warriors, archers, lancers, Imperators, and sorcerers to assemble for the Reithrese campaign. Sparks constantly shot from the forges of Cygestolia, making that section of the city glow as if the Reithrese were forcing a volcano up through it.

I was informed that the assembly would take place near the borders with Batangas and Kutchtan. It made sense from the strategic point of view because that would put us closest to Reith while allowing us to remain in Elven lands. We would march through Batangas, its vast plains making for swift travel and allowing our horses to feed on grasses, which meant we did not have to carry with us as much in the way of supplies. In addition, the Human population of

Batangas was largely nomadic and would be able to move out of our way.

Use of the *circus translatio* to move troops had been ruled out. There was no need for speed or stealth—the Elves wanted to give the Reithrese every opportunity possible to gather together in defense of their nation, because they wanted them all in one place. Besides, a genocidal war is not something to be undertaken in haste. I did not doubt we would prosecute the war, but I think all of us wanted a long march in which to embrace the responsibility.

The host would proceed in three columns. The main column, the one to which I would be attached, would go directly in at Alatun and lay siege to the city. The other two columns would guard our flanks and then sweep down to seal the country and destroy all the Reithrese trying to flee. None of the Reithrese would be allowed to live, a concept that made my nights sleepless as I considered mothers and babies falling under the sword.

While uncomfortable with that idea, I came to terms with it on the journey. My brother's plans for the Roclaws looked at moving us away from a warrior tradition and toward a more constructive and productive trading base, but his choice to make the people of the Roclaws peaceful and prosperous would not stop the Reithrese from destroying them. Any Reithrese left alive after this would have such a hatred for Elves and Men that retribution, as justifiable as it would seem, would become the core of their lives. And while the survivors, were any permitted to survive, might be small in number, there was no way to underestimate the regenerative or reproductive powers of the Reithrese.

My sleeplessness over this point isolated me from Larissa. As Finndali's wife, she spent her waking hours making preparations for him to go off to war. I did not begrudge him her service, I envied it. For my part, I had Shijef and Lomthelgar attending me, but neither of them could offer me the comfort she could, though both did prove distracting.

Finally, in the wee hours before we were scheduled to ride from Cygestolia to the rendezvous point, my restless peregrinations took me to the empty Consilliarii amphitheatre and there I found her. The moonlight that snuck through branches glowed from her face. She wore a gown of silver, trimmed with lace at bodice and wrists, that left her shoulders bare where her long golden hair did not hide them.

Even when we danced, even in our dreams, I had never seen her look so beautiful. She saw me, and the dour expression on her face lightened. It never reached full joy, but her being able to change a grim frown into one of mild concern made me smile, and that brought another degree of relief to her face. Had I died right then, I do not think I could have died happier.

I bowed to her. "I cannot tell you how happy it makes me to see you this night." I looked out at the city in the trees. "Everyone is consumed with family concerns tonight, which is expected. Your family has been very kind to me, but this is their night to be with Aarundel and Marta. I would have thought you would be with your husband tonight."

She glanced down. "I was."

I nodded, covering the pain that simple reply stabbed into my heart.

"I'm sorry, Neal, if that hurt you. I would spare you hurt, but I want no secrets between us, no distrust."

I walked toward her. "I trust you completely, in that which you tell me and that which you do not. Not *needing* secrets between us does not mean they will not exist, by intent or omission. I love you, so nothing you could do would hurt me." I laughed aloud and looked around at the empty seats. "Can you imagine what would have happened to me if the Consilliarii were here when I said that?"

"Could *anything* they chose to do be worse than the choice they gave you three weeks ago?"

I shook my head. "It could not."

Larissa slowly began to circle me, and I turned to keep facing her, but she held her hand up. "Stay still. I want to remember you here, tall and strong, ready for battle."

"Should I be smiling, or do you wish the face I will give the Reithrese?"

"You will always be smiling in my memory, Neal of the Roclaws."

I fumbled with the pouch on my belt and removed the bracelet I had created. "I made this for you, for it truly is all that I am. It is not much—the same goes for me—but the bracelet and I are all yours." I held it out to her.

She completed her circle and delicately took it from my fingers. Two inches, one, separated us, yet remained a gulf as wide as all the oceans. My heart pounded, and inside I wanted to reach out to pull her into my arms. I wanted to hold her so closely that I would never forget the press of her body against mine. I wanted to smell the night air through her hair and taste her lips on mine. As my gaze met hers, I saw she wanted the same thing in that same instant, yet both of us held back, restrained by laws created in the very place where we stood alone and unwatched.

I released the bracelet and looked down. "I'm going to die out there. You know that, don't you?"

"Don't say that. You could survive."

"Lies should not be our fantasies, Larissa. We both know I will not be coming back here."

In silence she slipped the bracelet onto her right wrist, then raised it to her bosom and held it there with her left hand. "That is . . . it is the nightmare with which I have lived since the decision was made to go to war."

I swallowed hard. "I don't fear death, really. I resent it, because it will take me away from you, but I know there is no way I will survive this campaign. If no one else dies, I will, because the Reithrese cannot let me live. And I am willing to trade my life in order to make sure they are destroyed."

"I resent it as well, Neal." She smiled sheepishly. "I have fantasized about stealing away in the supply train that will care for the army. I would be there to heal you when you fall."

I looked down at my burned left hand. "And deny me another scar to explain to your husband in twenty-nine years? This is a collection of which I am not proud, and had I felt your healing touch at the start of my career, a collection I might never have allowed myself to assemble. Now? I think the time for stubborn old fighters like me is passing."

"And employing my art to save you would doom you."

She nodded solemnly to me. "I would gladly accept exile, but I will not be the instrument of your death."

"And I would not rest easy if I knew I had caused you to be sent away from your people." I looked down. "Though leaving you will tear my heart out, I cherish the time we have had together, the dreams we have shared and the joy we have known."

She smiled. "I love you, Neal, and will forever."

"And I love you, Larissa, and will love you forever."

Wordlessly, but by mutual consent, we lay down there on the floor of the council chamber, slept, and dreamed together of forever.

The forest was alive with Elves as we gathered in the morning to ride out. The Cygestolian contingent was to be twenty percent of our force and Aarundel conservatively numbered it at twenty-five thousand individuals. Five Legions, each breaking down into fifty companies with one hundred individuals in it, the Cygestolian force combined two Lansorii legions, one each of light and heavy infantry and the last a mix of archers, engineers, and sorcerers. Each company had its own bright banner, and the Elves gathered in hollows and on hills, in glens and in meadows, to say good-bye to their loved ones.

I sat ready to ride with Aarundel's company, in a legion commanded by Finndali, so I was honored to have Calarianne, Thralan, Lomthelgar, and other important Elven officials present to see us off. Most of the conversations took place in Elven, but the tears and brave words carried their meaning to me easily. I had been part of this sort of scene all my life, and this time I was reminded of the occasions I had ridden from the Roclaws in search of adventure.

"If I might intrude here for a moment," I announced cautiously. I looked over at where Shijef squatted in deep conversation with Lomthelgar. "I have something I would like to say, and I can think of no other group of witnesses I would rather have present."

Everyone quieted and looked at me. "Shijef, I have not been a perfect master, nor have you been a perfect slave. You have disobeyed me as often as I have given orders that should not have been obeyed. While desiring my death, which would mean your freedom, you have ever kept me safe. And in my most recent misadventure, you saved Marta when I could not."

The Dreel stared up at me, his garnet eyes unblinking.

"Shijef, we embark on a war to forestall forever the domination of one race over another. Into such a war, for such a cause, I will not take a slave. I free you now of any and all obligation you have to me. Go, you're free."

Shijef dug at the earth with a claw, but said nothing.

I smiled at him. "Go, go on, get out of here. Go home."

The Dreel frowned. "No more my master are you?"

"I am not your master. Go home."

"If no more my master, why orders give me?"

Mild laughter rippled through our assembly. Aarundel, frightening in his dark, sharp-cornered armor, pointed off east toward the hills of Irtysh where I first met the Dreel. "You may go away now. You are free."

"Free I am, free I have been." The monster pawed his own chest. "Stupid I am not, you I understand. Understand you me. I not the Reithrese love. What they would do to Men, they do to Dreel will. Slave I have been, and slave no more, ever. If Elves will have a Man in their army, a Dreel they will have."

The Elves, along with me, were speechless.

Shijef tapped his chest, then walked over and pounded my breastplate over my heart. "Have the same heart, we do, you and I. Pledge, do I, to you what compelled was before. My line and your line, friend and allies are, for all time."

I reached up and held his paw to my chest. "We have the same heart, you and I. I accept your service in return for mine and that of my line."

The Dreel laughed, which made Blackstar shy; then Shijef pulled away and sat down again with Lomthelgar. I saw Aarundel's parents and Marta gathered near him, and other families saying their farewells to their warriors. I felt utterly alone and isolated for a second; then I heard her voice and reined Blackstar around.

"Neal." Larissa smiled up at me. "I have something for you. A gift for a gift."

I noticed, as she extended her hands toward me, she wore the bracelet I had given her. She held a braided circlet of golden hair up to me. I pulled my gauntlet from my right hand and leaned down. She slipped the circlet around my wrist and, using the blue ribbon that had been woven into the braid, knotted it in place.

I raised my hand and caught the scent of her from the hair and the ribbon. "I thank you, my Lady. Its medicinal properties are working already."

She raised an eyebrow at me. "Medicinal properties?"

"Clearly you have woven some of your healing Arts into it, for it eases my heartache straight away." Reluctantly I again shut my hand away in its prison of leather and steel. "Just remember, we have had forever together."

Larissa nodded carefully. "If you come back to me, we will have it again and again."

"It wouldn't be enough."

"No, but it would be superior to any alternative." She took a step back and looked over at Finndali. "I should bid him farewell."

I nodded and watched her go to him. As she walked over to him, she began to move stiffly, and they seemed to treat each other very formally. Yet, at the end of their conversation, he bent over—to kiss her, I suppose. I don't know because I turned away and started to concentrate on the horrible realities of the coming war.

A thousand miles separated Cygestolia from Alatun, and we crossed it at what could almost be described as a leisurely pace. Elven foot soldiers, by virtue of their longer legs, make better speed than their Human counterparts, but even so we planned on taking two months to make the journey. With every step closer to Reith we knew the Reithrese were preparing for us, but that was as we intended it to be.

Our ranks swelled when we reached the rendezvous in the southwestern bulge in the Elven Holdings. There our fighting force grew to over twenty-five legions, making it more than triple the Man-force that had rebelled against the Reithrese. For every three individual soldiers, two other

Elves came along with us as support. They handled everything from the preparation of food and tending the sick, to sharpening our weapons and shoeing our horses.

After five weeks we had penetrated halfway into Batangas. In that time I had learned a great deal of Elven and Dreel—one of necessity, and the other so Shijef and I could both stave off boredom when the Elves ignored us. About that time Elven scouts came back and reported a mounted Human force approaching from the northeast. They said the warriors rode beneath a banner with a left-handed glove and mountain rune on it. Finndali granted Aarundel and me leave to ride out to the Human force, and we welcomed the Emperor's Own Steel Pack to our number.

Their arrival actually solved a problem I had caused for Finndali and other Elven leaders. While they were bound to have me with them, they had severe reservations about having me in combat. Even the creation of a lanyard to keep Cleaveheart with me did not seem to address their concerns. When the Steel Pack arrived, they installed me at its head and then designated my unit as reserve.

There was grumbling about that in the Pack, but it died down as we drew closer to Reith. The weather turned cold, but very little snow fell on the plains. Ahead of us, dead to the south, we saw the mountains of Reith, but not well because of the heavy clouds cloaking them. During the day not being able to see our destination helped lower tension by keeping it distant. At night, even a hundred miles away, Reith became very close and very threatening.

In the dead of night bright, brilliant flashes of light would transform the clouds into luminiferous beasts with wispy tentacles just waiting to pluck us from our saddles. Lightning, red and green and other colors unnatural and unusual, shot through the sky. Distant thunder echoed and rumbled toward us, turning Reith into a land where the very stones seemed to be preparing to grind us down.

Aarundel reported that the light and noise, according to Elven sorcerers, were meant to make it difficult to read the truly powerful spells being woven by the Reithrese. When I likened the show to the magical equivalent of gilded parade armor, my men took to watching it as if it were a drama being unfolded on a distant stage. Each night they wove a different folktale around what they saw and by the time we had gotten near enough that thunder sounded close by when lightning flashed, even the Elves seemed to have some respect for the bravery my Men exhibited.

We entered Reith through a mountain defile that the Reithrese should have defended. They stationed scouts in and among the mist-haunted rocks and canyons, but they never struck at us. I do not know if they felt we were not vulnerable, or if some twisted sense of Reithrese honor demanded they allow us to assemble on the battlefield before Alatun, but they missed an opportunity to slow us down and hurt us. It was not until the final battle was joined that I saw why they did not meet us there and, perhaps, why they did not feel they needed to.

Though only fifty miles separated us from Alatun, the clouds prevented us from seeing it. We posted small forces out in front of our host to warn us of any Reithrese attack. Those troops knew that if the Reithrese did press us, they would die well before any help could reach them. The Elves given those missions appeared to accept them without question, and I gathered it was something of an honor by the way Finndali rejected my offer to take a turn as we moved forward through Reith.

For two days we advanced cautiously. Fog shrouded us every inch of the way. Tinged with yellow and smelling of rotten eggs, I decided it was not wholly natural, and the testy nature of some Elven sorcerers told me I was not wrong. The last night we camped not ten miles from Alatun, but aside from thunder and a lurid red glow pulsing through the night, we had no way of telling where the city was.

I looked up as Aarundel entered my tent. I held out two letters for him. "I wouldn't want this battle to go any differently from any other. You will see these are sent?"

"As always, though I trust you will take them back from me and see to it yourself." Aarundel pulled up a camp stool and seated himself. "I want you to know I have argued with Finndali to let your unit go with mine in the first wave. I did all I could, but I could not convince him."

I shrugged. "He could open a chicken and read in its guts that my leading will make all the Reithrese fall down and die of laughter, and he'd not let me go first. He has his reasons."

"I know. I just did not want you to believe *I* had reasons why I did not want you along with me." He clasped his hands together and looked down at them. "There have been times, my friend, when words I have spoken have betrayed what I feel in my heart for you. It is not easy to shed centuries of thoughts and ideas. I know I have hurt you in this, and I wish to apologize."

"No apology necessary, because there are times when your words have told me exactly what was in your heart. In Jammaq, when you told me to run and again when you asked me to save Marta. In those two things I heard what you truly believe." I reached out and grabbed him by the back of his neck, then brought my forehead to rest against his. "We are brothers beneath our skin. We're not perfect, but brothers nonetheless, which means, I'm thinking, we understand."

Aarundel smiled, then sat back, and my hand slipped from his neck. "Then you will understand when I tell you that upon our return, I will do all that is possible to see to it that you and my sister can finally be together."

I couldn't speak around the lump in my throat, so I just nodded to him and smiled, all the while fingering the braid circling my right wrist.

Morning came cold enough to make fog when I breathed, and I thanked whichever god made wool that I had clothes to place between me and my armor. Over the quilted jacket and breeches I wore full plate. It had been made for me in Cygestolia, so bore the spikes and spurs the Elves favor. In addition, the face mask I wore had been fitted to me perfectly on the inside, but on the outside I appeared to be a snarling wolf. I had smiled when I first saw it, and even now it prompted a grin, because in this brass-washed, steel suit I truly became the Dun Wolf.

The Elven host assembled along a front over a mile wide. The battlefield sloped gently up toward Alatun over harsh ground. The earth, which had been baked by the summer sun, developed a thin film of slippery red clay because of the heavy fog. The plants that grew there were all needles and spikes, though some sprouted yellow or white blossoms. Big boulders dotted the battlefield. While insufficient to form a breastwork, around them the battles would swirl and eddy, and in their shadow, bodies would pile up.

Elven pikemen held the center, with cavalry wings and archers to back them up. Our supply train retreated, but not too far. Had there been sun, it would have glinted from a hundred thousand helmeted heads. As it was, the fog ebbed and flowed, revealing and stealing away whole portions of our line.

From the other side, out in the sea of fog, I heard a trumpet blare. As if a theatre curtain, the white fog began to lift, though in its wake rose up a bloody mist that hugged the ground. As the fog began to dissipate, I saw shadowy forms move through it. Without reference points I could not determine their true size, but that mattered less than trying to account for their odd shapes and strange gaits.

Then quickly enough there arose from our side a buzzing, as those who could see the Reithrese army communicated with those to the rear. As far back as I was, I could make out nothing of substance, and by the time I translated what was being said, I could see it for myself.

What the Reithrese lacked in numbers they made up for in incredible power. Creatures of every imaginable size lurked among their ranks. I saw giant figures carved from stone marching into place in the line among normal Reithrese soldiers. A whole company of scimitar-wielding cavalry skeletons brought their cadaverous mounts into place behind a unit of Reithrese Dragoons. Hordes of small, Man-like things nailed together from scrap wood and animated by magick held spears at the ready.

These were the least of the forces arrayed against us. As the fog burned away, I saw huge creatures with eight and ten legs, built of bones, hundreds and thousands of bits of ivory, bound together through magic. Hundreds of Reithrese archers, not all of them living by the looks of them, rode the spines of those behemoths. Similar but smaller things made of scrap armor and weapons walked upright like men, but were shaped like hedgehogs with swords and scythe blades forming their quills and claws. Just one of those animated, metallic creatures wading into an infantry formation would decimate it, at best costing the Reithrese the life of the sorcerer riding in the thing's chest, magickally commanding it.

Try as I might, I could not see Takrakor among the forces arrayed against us. I knew he had to be there, and I knew I would kill him, but locating him among fifty thousand of his countrymen would be no easy task. I would have thought he would command one of the bone-monsters, or a steel hedgehog, but discerning the identities of the sorcerers manipulating them would have to wait until the things had been destroyed.

Trumpets sounded loud and brassy amid the Elven forces, and the infantry began a slow advance. All along the line they moved as one. Green and gold pennants flew, emblazoned with Elven slogans and runes. The pikemen in the front lowered their pikes to accept any Reithrese charges, but the other side's cavalry appeared disinclined to engage the foot soldiers. Behind the infantry and flanking it, the Elven cavalry moved up.

The Steel Pack remained in place, and Shijef stationed himself twenty-five yards in front of us as if to fend off any Reithrese assault that got through the Elven host. Despite the nature of our opposition, I did not fear their winning through to where we waited. What I did experience came down more to a fear that treachery awaited the Elves and a general feeling that I would not be able to save them.

A hundred yards separated the Elven infantry from the wooden puppet men. Reithrese cavalry shifted restlessly, bright banners twitching listlessly in the nearly breezeless morning. The Elven pikemen pressed on, but their formation shifted subtly, with part of their central ranks holding back in a tighter knot. The Reithrese guessed at what was about to happen, and blaring trumpets sent horsemen forward. Their skeletal allies galloped into the fray as well, and the matchstick men lunged forward into the infantry formation.

The wooden men did little damage, but managed to weigh down the pikes used to keep live foes—especially cavalry—at bay. From the left the Reithrese cavalry charged in at the infantry. Hoofbeats thundered across the plains as red mud splashed like blood on the legs and bellies of the horses. In counterpoint the voices of Elven Lansorii raised in war cries dwarfed the Reithrese cacophony as they countercharged.

The Reithrese horsemen hit the infantry on the left flank. Their lead elements crushed the opposition and penetrated a quarter of the way in toward the heart of the formation. Horses screamed and reared up, blood flowing from their mouths and nostrils as if they were figures in a grisly fountain. Some pikes took them and their riders at the same time, but most failed to strike anyone. Reithrese riders pushed forward, urging their horses on as if stemming a rising tide. Had the impetus and momentum carried on, they might have gotten to the group of people they sought and done serious damage.

They did not because the Elven countercharge hit the cavalry wave on the flank and sheared it off. Elven Lansorii, transformed into metallic demons in their inhuman armor, sank into the Reithrese unit like a tent stake into soft earth. The force of their charge deflected the Reithrese effort, directing both Elves and Reithrese into the army of kindling warriors. The bloodmist swirled, and in the thick of it I saw Aarundel's ax clearing an arc in front of him.

The skeletal horde bore down on the Elven infantry. The wind whistled eerily through their empty rib cages, and their jaws bounced up and down as if they were shouting as loudly as the Elves, but no lungs meant no war cries. Instead the clitter-clack of their bones, barely heard as more than an annoying buzz, announced them.

The knot of Elves at the core of the infantry started to glow. A golden nimbus surrounded them and brightened, then shot out a nova-flare. The fiery lance burned a swath through the skeletons eight men wide and a hundred yards deep, leaving two rows on each edge and two ranks in the back untouched as the rest of the horde went from bone to smoke in the blink of an eye. A second jet of magickal energy—this one blue and unfolding into a blanket—washed over what was left of the undead cavalry. As if water, it eroded whatever held the skeletons together. Momentum tore them apart and scattered the bones over the battlefield.

As hedgehogs moved forward, and more sorcerers advanced with their bodyguards, dread began to rise in me. I looked up at the battlefield and beyond it to Alatun itself. Something told me the key to winning the battle lay therein. I knew instantly that I could ride in there and win the day. No more Elves would have to die. No Elven women would mourn lost kin and lovers. And the gratitude the Elves would bestow upon me, it would be without end and without restrictions.

All this came to me subtly, and I accepted it the way I accepted as fact that the sun would rise the next day. I drew Cleaveheart casually, as if I meant to inspect the blade for nicks and cuts I knew I would not find on its edge. I knew I could easily slip away from the Steel Pack and ride around the Reithrese army to Alatun. Nothing could keep me from getting there and fulfilling my destiny. *With Cleaveheart and the dagger Marta has given me,* I thought as I reached down for it, *I will not be denied.*

I felt a sting at the base of my skull when I touched the dagger and wondered for a moment if she had not somehow tricked me into carrying a weapon that would harm me. Quickly enough, though, I sorted out the flash of betrayal I had sensed and realized that she had given me a gift more precious than she had imagined. The dagger set with Takrakor's tooth had just saved my life and that of the army.

The spell she had placed on the dagger provided me with an instant and intuitive knowledge of Takrakor's location. It was not overly specific, but I knew he lurked in Alatun, and I could feel him waiting there for me. I realized that the thoughts I'd had about how I could win the battle had come from his mind. Like a spider in a web, he had used his magicks to lure me in. Had I not known, had the tooth and the magick that bound it not told me where Takrakor awaited me, I would have ridden into his trap and handed Cleaveheart over to him without much of a fight indeed.

But I *did* know, and that meant I could thwart him.

I raised my hand and nodded at my trumpeteer. He

blew a call that brought my Men to life and directed their attention to me. I pointed to the city, then gave Blackstar a touch of my heels. "To Alatun and victory!"

"To Alatun and victory!" they shouted as they rode after me. Shijef sprinted on ahead of us, harsh hissed laughter serenading us on our mad ride toward the Reithrese city.

As we swung out around the Elven lines, I knew what Finndali and others must have been thinking. At first they would curse me, for I was committing part of their reserves in a mad romp of dubious value and questionable efficacy. Our goal, as an army, was to destroy the Reithrese, not take territory from them, so capturing the city meant nothing. Its loss might blunt their morale, but how much can the fighting ability of magickal automatons and stone warriors depend upon emotion?

Down on the battlefield the armies closed. Golden lightning met black shields as magicians vied with each other to destroy and protect troops. Steel hedgehogs scratched and clawed their way into Elven infantry units. Sleetstorms of Elven arrows washed over the huge bone constructs, thinning the ranks of the archers riding on their backs. Giants of stone and ivory stumbled, charges faltered, and units collapsed, yet always the forces pressed forward, throwing reserve units in to replace those who had fallen.

"When we get to the city," I shouted at Fursey, "close the gates and hold them against the Reithrese. Cut off their retreat."

He nodded to me and we raced on. With each stride I could feel myself getting closer and closer to Takrakor. Each vibration pounding up through the saddle and into me marked off the time before I would destroy him. His magick grew stronger as I approached, coaxing me onward, and Marta's magick centered me on him as if I were an arrow that had been launched at a target. I would not miss, I knew that, and I could not wait until my target and I became one.

Before us the city's gates lay open as if she were a caravanserai whore eager for our business. I turned in the saddle, and through the mist roiling behind the Pack I saw one of the behemoths begin to disintegrate beneath a withering

Elven assault of verdant and blue magickal spears. Its skull exploded as the sorcerous energy engulfed it, and I saw what looked to be the burning body of a Reithrese magus ejected from the conflagration.

The explosion echoed from the black walls of Alatun, chased by a confusion of horns bleating out commands to soldiers on both sides. Skittering across the low grey sky like an aurora, a purple energy shroud originating from the Elven side of the field played through the air between the city and the Reithrese lines. It illuminated and caused to glow numerous lines of power streaming out of the tower central to Alatun itself. I saw those lines shift and the glow vanish as the top of the gate eclipsed the tower and Blackstar pounded up to the city's entrance.

Off to my right the Dreel leaped from the ground and scrambled nimbly up and over the soaring battlements while my horse and I charged straight down the cobbled expanse of the main street. Behind me a trumpet sounded, reining the Steel Pack in so they could command the gate while I raced on. I felt Takrakor's derision for their effort drown beneath a wave of avaricious joy as he caught sight of me speeding toward the tower. Emotions twisted through his brain too quickly for me to identify consciously, but they made the hackles on the back of my neck rise as I rode up to the base of the black tower at the city's hub.

Cleaveheart in my right hand and the dagger in my left, I vaulted from Blackstar's back and ran as fast as I could up the steps to the open doorway. The tower itself, though weathered and decorated in an archaic and chaotic style, reminded me of the Imperial Tower in Jarudin. I knew immediately the newer tower had been modeled on this one. Likewise would Takrakor model his fight against me on the emperor's defense of his title. Not that the sorcerer would fight me with a sword, but he would turn the site of my greatest victory into the place that would host my greatest defeat.

I sprinted directly toward where the chapel was in the Imperial Tower, and I saw the flash of a rainbow cloak lapping at the doorjamb as Takrakor headed in there before me. I reached the threshold unopposed and at first glance was struck by the nearly identical structure of the chapel here and the one in Jarudin. From femur columns to firepit and braziers, the rooms looked to be twins of each other. Then I looked up and saw the only difference between them.

Takrakor, silhouetted against the flames of the firepit, beckoned me forward. His diamond grin glinted in the bloody red light from the braziers. "Come in. I have remodeled this place in honor of you."

Where his brother's intaglio had graced the ceiling of the chapel in Jarudin, I saw my own likeness in this place. It showed me torn and bleeding in a number of places. Broken bones poked through naked flesh, and a huge portion of my skull was missing. It looked as if I had been drawn and quartered, then hacked and trampled. I had also been emasculated.

My voice echoed from within the mask. "I'm thinking that if that's an honor, then I'd just as soon be killing you without any ceremony." I took a step toward him. "You want Cleaveheart, now you'll have it."

The sorcerer brought his hands back against his chest. Suspended from a harness, Wasp lay in a sheath pressed against the sorcerer's breastbone. Aside from a black kilt edged with gold, leather sandals, and his rainbow cloak, the Reithrese was naked and seemed almost powerless. His slender arms and skinny chest proved him to be no physical threat to me, yet the moment he touched my old dagger, I felt powers gathering around me.

"Oh, I will have it, but only after reality mirrors my art." He raised his left hand and extended it forward, his fingers splayed. His body shook as if in the midst of a convulsion, then his fist closed and I felt a titanic hand grip me. It lifted me bodily into the air and held me as if I were as weak as a new-whelped pup. My armor groaned and my chest grew tight. Breathing deeply sent daggers through my chest. Every muscle in my body spasmed, and my limbs drew themselves in toward my torso.

Takrakor glanced upward, then shook his head. "Not at all a match." He brought his left hand down and touched it to Wasp, then used his right hand to pry his little finger out straight. As he did that, my left leg came down and almost touched the floor. Straightening his thumb brought my other leg down, two fingers brought my arms out at my sides, and his middle finger brought my head up.

He gently cuffed the edge of his right hand over the tip of his left middle finger, and my head snapped back as if I had been punched. My helmet flew off and my mask fell away, but I heard no clatter of their landing against the floor. I tried to turn my head to see if they hovered behind me, but I could not move at all. I hung there, crucified, my ears still ringing from the magickal blow.

Takrakor held both hands out in front of him at arm's length with palms facing each other. He kept them spread apart as if they lay on either side of my chest, and when he curled his fingers in as if making a fist, I felt his nails dig into my back. I coughed in spite of myself, and he laughed, then slowly pulled his hands further apart.

My Elf-made breastplate tore down the center and spine as if cheap cloth. He continued to move his hands sideways until a gap three fingers in width formed. My pauldrons stopped progress at my shoulders, so the sorcerer yanked down with his hands once, twice, three times until the leather straps snapped crisply and the armor fell away.

Each tug ground my shoulders around in their sockets. My body gave with the pulling, but his magick held my arms in place. I felt things shift and heard things pop, then pop again as my left shoulder noisily returned to its place in the socket. I wanted to scream, but the pain in my chest stopped me from drawing in enough of a breath to allow me even a weak whimper.

He must have seen my jaw working, because the pressure that kept me breathless eased. "Scream if you wish, Neal. I *will* hear your screams. I will delight in them, and I see no reason to delay my gratification."

I coughed again. "Not a scream."

"You will."

I wanted to say something foolishly brave or tough, as did all the heroes of song and legend when in such dire straits, but I could think of nothing. I could not even muster a stoic air, which I am certain would have inflamed him more than insolence. I had grossly underestimated his power and was paying heavily for my stupidity. Even so, I had no intention of giving him satisfaction by admitting that fact.

I could feel his puzzlement through the dagger in my left hand, and I let it fortify me. Every minute he spent changing me into the image hovering above me was one more minute in which his powers were denied to the Reithrese army.

Takrakor hooked his fingers over into claws, then raked both his hands down. Finger-width rents appeared in the armor on my legs, and it fell away in a curled, twisted tangle. On the bracers and rerebraces he took more time. In them he cut a spiral that left them hanging like a ribbon on my arms. He carefully tugged that ribbon off, letting the metal uncoil across my flesh. Blood dripped from countless cuts on my arms, and sweat burned into them.

With the wink of an eye he made my gauntlets disappear, yet my weapons remained in my hands. Except for my tattered boots, scraps of the gambeson and breeches I had worn, and the circlet of Larissa's hair on my wrist, I hung naked and gore-spattered before him. My stomach pushed out toward him with each labored breath I took.

I looked up at him. "Why don't you take the blade and be done with it?" I'd like to think I asked the question in hopes of luring him in close where I could strike at him, but I cannot say it was so. Held there and stripped so completely while I remained impotent to stop him, I felt worn and tired. I had told Larissa that I would not be coming back, that I would die in this campaign. So this was it, and I was willing to give up. I had been beaten by this Reithrese sorcerer, and I knew my time was at hand.

"Take it?" He shook his head slowly. "No, no, no, Neal Elfward, Neal of the Mountains, keeper of Cleaveheart, Scourge of the Reithrese, Murderer of Tashayul and Butcher of Jarudin, no. I will not take it. You will give it to me. You will *want* to give it to me."

His thumb and little finger came in on his left hand, and my knees immediately bent so I hovered in a kneeling position. He nodded his head slightly, and magick slammed me down against the floor. I felt my left ankle snap as it curled beneath me. The pain shot up along my leg, and I reached back with my left hand to touch the ankle; then a numbness entered me at the base of my spine. In the same instant I realized that he had freed me from the grip of one magick, then had used another to render my legs lifeless.

"There, now you know what my brother felt for the last bit of his life." Low laughter rolled from his throat, but the snap and whispered roar of the fire in the pit behind him swallowed it quickly enough. "I would have preferred to hold you as before, but a greater magick requires me to resort to a lesser one. And do be assured, though your legs are numb and useless now, I will let them share in your body's agony."

He stared down at me as he raised his hands. He folded thumbs and fingers into fists, then brought his index fingers out. He crossed them, middle knuckle against middle knuckle, right over left. "You will find this very painful, and the only way to end it is to offer me Cleaveheart." He raised his hands toward his face and placed his crossed fingers against his skull, where he had inserted the bit of tooth on Marta and Aarundel. Then, facing me, he whipped his fingers apart.

Pressure like a mule kick hammered me right below my breastbone. It drove the air from my lungs, then the pain started. I felt the panic of being unable to breathe, but the blow forced me back enough that my chest stretched and I involuntarily pulled some air in. As I leaned back consciously, to breathe more deeply, lightninglike agony stabbed through my chest and brought me forward again.

I looked down and saw a cruciform bruise forming between and below my breasts. The two lines barely an inch in each direction, where they met marked the focus of the pain. I hugged my hands to my chest, pulling my face back so the blades would not slice me up, but touching the bruise only increased the pain.

"It will hurt more if you rub it." Takrakor stared at me, his voice strained with exertion. "Over the next twelve hours, unless I stop it, that spell will slice you into four parts." He rolled his eyes up to look toward the ceiling. "I will ease the pain for you if you give me the sword."

Anger and fear and frustration came through the dagger to me as he spoke. Despite the pain and my weariness, I found his conflicting emotions fascinating. How was it that I was able to trouble him when he had me in so disadvantaged a situation? I could understand his wanting me to endure the mental torture of surrendering the blade to him —his treatment of Marta had displayed his cruel streak— but he seemed to *need* me to submit to him.

His confusion and need sparked in me the one thing he did not want. I thought I had detected a weakness in him, and that gave me hope. That hope and my pain twisted through bitterness into defiance. If I was going to be tormented, so would he be, and I could do that by refusing him over and over again until I died.

"I will never . . . surrender . . . this sword . . . to you." I forced myself to control my breathing.

"Bold words." He brought his right fist down like a mace, and an invisible fist smashed me to the ground. Stars exploded when my forehead hit the floor, and blood started flowing from my nose. "You will take a long time to die, Neal."

I snorted, spraying blood down my chest. "And you will never . . . ever . . . get my sword."

Outrage spiked through the dagger, and Takrakor flailed at me from across the room. I could no more keep track of the blows than I could move to avoid them, but few hit solidly. After his flurry petered out, I felt as if I'd been tossed around in the hold of a ship in the midst of a storm, but other than a twinge in a rib that got hit twice, I wasn't that much worse off than I had been before.

Takrakor stood back and folded his arms to his chest to consider me. In doing so he touched Wasp again, and I saw him smile most cruelly. My physical pain grew, and a new, sinister influence started to creep into my mind. Whereas he had been subtle before, teasing out thoughts that I wanted to believe, now he moved in to disrupt my thoughts and weaken my resistance to him.

He keyed on my frustration and despair, and I felt a smug superiority trickle in through the dagger I held. He had briefly lost control, but when he regained it, he knew I was a thing beneath him. He could compel me to give him the sword, and that would not do for him. If he peeled my mind like an onion, soon there would be nothing left to defy him, and the second this course of action suggested itself, he pounced on it. My frustration at being unable to strike back at him became twisted, and he used it to slice away options and plans as they came up, isolating me from anything but submission to his will.

Takrakor stepped closer to me. Our proximity both increased the power of the link we had and heightened my frustration. Having my arms free and not being able to hit him when he was across the room was one thing. Remaining impotent to strike as he crept closer and closer was entirely another. With each step he ground my spirit away beneath his feet, and I could do nothing but watch my life leak away from the wounds he opened in my mind.

He used my frustration against me and slowly warped every memory of past victories to which I clung. I used them as armor for my sense of hope, and he peeled it away layer by layer. My defeating his brother in our first fight became nothing more than a fluke, something that would never be repeated in a million years. The emperor had died less by my effort than by his own foolishness because he remained behind when the wisest of Reithrese had abandoned Jarudin.

Takrakor used his own special knowledge of events to show me how hollow my life had been. I saw myself through his eyes at Aarundel's wedding and felt his derision at my pitiful arrogance that day. With each step nearer multiplying the strength of our link, he managed to deconstruct my life, making each victory the calm before a Reithrese storm that would destroy Mankind. Each thought he changed, every remembrance he destroyed, cut away at my ability to resist his will. While he did come closer to torture me, I knew he would not close within Cleaveheart's striking range.

Agony racked me as he hit my last line of defense. He burrowed into all my memories of Larissa. He clutched at them, pawed them, and soiled them. He showed me images conjured from dreams where he substituted a rutting goat for me, then let me live through each and every tableau from Larissa's point of view. He turned everything all around until he got to the point where he started to make me believe she saw me as her perversion.

I pressed my hands to my temples, and enough anger flowed through me that my fists should have crushed the hilts of my weapons. Takrakor, sensing victory, pushed harder and harder. He rearranged things so I would think that Larissa, seeing herself soiled and degraded, would kill herself—already *had* killed herself in shame when I gave her the bracelet over which I had labored.

That did it. Standing barely five feet from me, he pushed one last time and broke through. He touched my hope and I acted.

I smashed the hilt of the dagger into the floor, shattering the fragment of his tooth. Takrakor screamed in mortal pain. Both hands shot to his jaw as he reeled away in agony. He stumbled back and half fell, screaming anew as I pushed off the floor and ground the little pieces of tooth into dust.

Pins and needles shot through my legs and new pain slammed up through my left ankle as I lurched forward. I staggered as a man drunk and dying. Clenched against the pain, my teeth ground against each other. With the diamond broken I no longer could feel his emotions, but the expression on his face as he scrambled to his feet needed no magic for translation. In his eyes I saw fear.

And the reflection of Cleaveheart.

I whipped the blade across his chest with all the speed and strength my desperation could muster. I hit him solidly and would have split him in half, but my blade caught on Wasp. Takrakor spun away from me, more from the impact than by his will. A scarlet froth and big bubbles marked where I had cloven ribs and torn a lung. Blood dripped from his mouth and nostrils and sprayed out in a spiral as he pirouetted around.

I stumbled to my knees and barely caught myself with my hands. I saw his blood splattered across the floor and heard the swish of his cloak as he fell back. I heard a muffled *thwump,* then the scraping of metal on stone. As I looked up again, I saw the last of his legs and the soles of his sandals as his body slid down through the hole to the firepit. For a second the room went dark, then sparks rose up. I watched them float toward my battered face on the ceiling, twisting around and flopping onto my back as I did so.

The stone felt cold, but the blood on my blade and chest burned. I raised my head enough to see that the bruise on my chest had grown a half inch in all directions; then I lay down. Looking up at the image Takrakor had fashioned of me, I reveled in the fact that though I knew I was dying, I was not dying defeated. As black oblivion swept over me, despite the pain, I managed a laugh that I intended to ring in my ears through eternity.

Chapter 29

To Come Home Again

Late Autumn
A.R. 499
The Present

With each mile closer to Cygestolia, Gena felt a sense of urgency building in her. When she first felt it, barely a week into the month-long journey, she dismissed it as spillover from Berengar's nervousness. At his insistence they had borrowed four horses from the emperor and money enough to see them through the trip to Cygestolia and back. Seeing Cleaveheart's resting place had focused Berengar tightly on his goal of obtaining the blade, and she knew his anxiety came from not knowing what was happening back in Aurdon.

As the sensation grew in her, she managed to name it. *Homesickness.* She had been gone from Cygestolia, wandering the face of Skirren, for a dozen years. For an Elf that amount of time passed in an eye blink, yet she felt a growing hunger inside her again to see the groves and vales of her homeland. Whereas before she returned, she would have dismissed Cygestolia's importance to her, as she drew closer, she wondered seriously why she had left in the first place.

Now, well inside the domain claimed by the Elves, she wished she had the implements necessary to use the *circus translatio*. She had not taken such things with her when she rode away because she was uncertain she would ever want to return. She slowly began to realize that her time among Men had worn on her because she had constantly been treated as a threat or a prize to be won. Never had she been given time just to be herself, and Cygestolia became a sanctuary where she could do just that.

No, not never. *With Durriken I found sanctuary.* She nodded to herself as she remembered hours and hours spent languorously entwined with her Human lover. When they were together, he treated her with deference, but she knew he would have acted so with any female, *sylvanesti* or Human. Rik had a way of looking into people's hearts. He pushed past what they appeared to be, or what they were supposed to be, and saw what they were. In his arms Gena had been able to be herself, and, she realized, as long as they had been together, she had not been looking for sanctuary anywhere else.

Berengar still remained solicitous and polite to her. Small kindnesses such as complimenting her on meals when it was her turn to cook or taking on more than his share of the heavy lifting and carrying marked his concern for her. Their conversations, after all the time they had spent on the road together, had grown deeper and more philosophical, yet somehow divorced of emotion. They even spoke of what it would be like if they were to become lovers or to actually marry, but that conversation seemed concerned more with cultural customs and mores than the attraction they felt to each other.

And there *was* an attraction. Gena blushed when she thought about it, less from prudishness than from her feeling that she was betraying Durriken in some way. She gave Berengar chances to approach her, and clues that she would be receptive to his advances, yet he did not act upon them. She was interested in the way he watched her sometimes at night—Men generally being forgetful at how good Elven sight is in the dark—but he held himself apart. She gathered it was from a sense of duty to his family—his willingness to marry for an alliance as much as for love—and she chose to respect that.

She also acknowledged that his focus upon their mission put her off at times. Durriken had been positively Elven in his attitude about time: his sense of urgency had not been driven by the passage of hours. Rik desired the correction of past wrongs—as with the return of Marta and Aarundel's wedding tokens to them—and was willing to take the time needed to make sure his missions would succeed.

In his single-mindedness concerning Cleaveheart, Berengar exhibited what Elves found least desirable about Men. Even so, she had no doubt he would be able to control himself when he reached Cygestolia. She smiled. *Berengar will charm everyone he meets.* Still, some Elves might balk at turning Cleaveheart over to a Man, and that was a possibility that made it hard to predict how Berengar would react in the long run.

Cygestolia had not much changed since she had been away. The groves appeared to her eyes to be more stately and grand than any Man-home she had seen. She felt a sense of anxiety slip away as once again she saw the island with the council tree on it. She smiled and pointed toward that island.

"Do you see that stone structure there, at the base of the tree?"

Berengar nodded. "Surely all the Elves in Cygestolia do not live in that one small house."

"No," she laughed. "We live in the trees. You will stay in my family's home, Woodspire. You will have the chamber Neal used when he stayed here."

"Thank you. So what is that building?"

"That is Neal's tomb."

He sat up taller in his saddle and shaded his eyes with his hands. "Yes? Could Cleaveheart be in there?"

Gena shook her head. "No. I have seen inside, and I saw no weapons of any kind. We came here because my grandfather and grandaunt made a journey from Cygestolia after Neal's death. I believe that trip was made to secret Cleaveheart away."

"You said your grandaunt had gone 'beyond.' " Berengar frowned. "You cannot do that and return with the information, can you?"

"No, but my grandfather still lives, and he might know what the key to Larissa's spell is."

Gena led Berengar through the city to the Seven Pines district and on to Woodspire. Elves took their horses and their baggage from them at the base of the tree; then they entered the tubes and rose through the heart of Woodspire. Wordlessly she guided Berengar through the tree and smiled when she reached the chamber that had once been home to Neal Elfward.

"Grandfather!" Gena ran across the room to where Aarundel slowly rose from sitting on the edge of what had been Neal's bed. It occurred to her that he had not been moving so slowly when she went away, but by then she was in his arms and reveling in his hug. "It has been far too long."

"It has, Genevera." The old Elf stroked her hair. "You are a tonic for an aged, one-eyed Elf."

She felt a tremor run through him. "What is it?"

"You have brought a guest."

She slowly released Aarundel, then turned and nodded toward Berengar. "Grandfather, this is Count Berengar Fisher of Aurdon in Centisia."

Aarundel nodded slowly. "You look the image of the Red Tiger. Seeing you there, I half expect to see Neal himself come around the corner."

Berengar bowed respectfully, then smiled openly. "It is an honor to meet you, Aarundel Consilliari. I have long thrilled to the stories of your adventures with Neal. Your granddaughter believes that you can help us with a problem that has brought us over two thousand miles."

Gena suppressed a frown because she would have preferred to ease into the discussion rather than deal with it so quickly. She tried to hide from her grandfather her displeasure with Berengar, but he gave her hand a squeeze.

"Remember, my dear, I rode with Neal. I understand." Aarundel waved Berengar to a chair and again eased himself down on the foot of the bed. "What is this problem?"

Gena, still holding her grandfather's hand, knelt at his

feet. "Do you remember Aurium and the first night you and Neal arrived there?"

The wizened, white-haired Elf slowly smiled. "Neal forced a peace on two families there. Riveravens were one and the Fishers the other. Did that peace not last, my lord?"

Berengar shook his head. "Not truly, Consilliari. Over the years the oath Neal made has kept our two families from destroying each other, but it is constantly tested. The intervention of his ghost, so it is said, enforces what he began five centuries ago. The Riverens—what you knew as the Riveravens—have recently entered into an alliance with the Haladina, and this threatens my family. We would strike back, but Neal enjoins us from doing so."

Gena looked up at Aarundel. "Neal said the two families would be joined until Cleaveheart and Wasp severed the knot he fashioned from the sleeves of two people. It is time for the knot to be severed, so we are out to recover the blades."

Aarundel shook his head. "Your effort is doomed to failure. The blades cannot be recovered."

"But we saw where Cleaveheart is hidden." Berengar frowned heavily. "Lady Genevera says she can undo the magick if you will give her the key. It is vital you do so."

"My lord, were she to ask and I were able to accede to her request, I would do so, but I cannot." Aarundel drew in a deep breath and sighed wearily. "Before Neal left Jarudin for the last time, he had made arrangements to hide Cleaveheart away. He wanted the architect—Xer-something it was . . ."

"Xerstan," Berengar offered.

"Xerstan to create a vault that could only be keyed by Wasp. A cast of Wasp was made for this purpose, and Wasp was used to key the spell that Larissa created to ward the vault." The Elf shook his head. "The cast was destroyed after use."

"And what of Wasp?"

"It was lost to the Reithrese in Jammaq, though Neal said Takrakor had it at Alatun."

Berengar shook his head. "Jammaq? Alatun?"

"Places destroyed centuries ago. You reckon the passing

of the years from the date of their destruction. This is the four hundred and ninety-ninth year since the annihilation of the Reithrese. Wasp has not been seen since then, which means there is no way to recover Cleaveheart."

"There *must* be another way." Berengar hammered his right fist into his left palm. "If there is not, everything is lost."

Aarundel shrugged. "Larissa, who cast the spell, is no longer here. Breaking that spell is possible, but it would take Gena here a century of specific and concentrated study to be able to do so. I gather you have not the time to wait for that."

"No, no I do not." Berengar growled and scowled. "I can't believe Neal would have been so stupid to have keyed Cleaveheart's hiding place with a simple, ordinary dagger that could have been broken in a fight or during a meal."

"Perhaps it was not stupidity, my lord Count, but caution."

Gena stroked her grandfather's hand. "And perhaps he had another way to get at the sword."

"That could be, Genevera, but I would not know. Only Neal would."

Gena slowly stood. "This I realize, which means I have little choice if I am to help Berengar save his family."

"I see no choices at all for my family's salvation."

Gena shook her head in Berengar's direction. "But there is one, Berengar, and the one we shall use because there is no other." She looked down into her grandfather's eye. "Tomorrow I intend to open Neal's tomb and bring him back from the dead."

Chapter 30

To Die Far from Home

Autumn
Reign of the Red Tiger Year 3 /
Imperium Year 1
Five Centuries Ago
My Last Year

The jolt from the wagon's wheel hitting a rut stabbed a fork of pain through my chest and brought me to consciousness. I coughed, spreading the pain evenly through me. I opened my eyes and wondered if I had gone blind; then my eyes focused, and I saw stars and moons in the heavens above. Either I was alive or the paradise promised by Jistani prophets fell decidedly shy of ideal to my way of thinking.

"Neal, are you awake?"

I turned my head to the right and saw Aarundel sitting hunched over with his back pressed against one side of the open wagon. The edge of the blanket covering me also covered his feet. He had raised his head above his knees, and I saw a thick bandage wrapped around his head. Blood had soaked through it, especially where it covered his right eye.

"Awake, my friend." My tongue felt thick in my mouth. "Water? Did we carry the day?"

"Healer, here, water." Aarundel snapped his fingers and pointed at me.

An Elf turned from another wounded Elf and knelt between Aarundel and me. He supported my head with one hand and pressed the nipple of a wineskin between my lips. I drank a little at first, bracing for the pain when I swallowed; then I took more. Finally I nodded and the Elf took it away.

Aarundel smiled wearily at me. "We were victorious. After you closed the gates, their magickal support from the city stopped. We crushed their army when their magick allies fell apart. We found you in the chapel and a cabal of dead Reithrese wizards higher up in the tower. I was told they were torn up."

I coughed out a laugh despite the pain. "Shijef . . ."

"I've not seen him, but it was probably the Dreel."

I nodded. "He knew I could kill Takrakor."

"Did you?"

"Returned the favor he did me." I tried to pull the blanket down so I could look at my chest, but my hands didn't seem to work too well. "He used a spell that will draw and quarter me."

Aarundel rested a hand on the healer's shoulder. "Cletine, can you counter it?"

The redheaded elf shrugged. "I know how to heal wounds. Dispelling other magicks is not my forté. I could try, but it might take me years of study before I would even have a chance at succeeding."

"Fret not, friend Cletine." Another cough racked me. "I'll not be having magick heal me up."

"This is different from before, Neal."

"It's not, Aarundel. The Reithrese are dead, so am I. If I were to use magick now, well, it would be cheating, wouldn't it?" I managed a smile for him. "Never before. Not now."

"Even if it would allow you to see my sister one more time?"

"Perhaps that would be worth it." I thought for a moment, then shook my head. "But I'm thinking I'm not dressed for courting. Besides, Cletine's healing art would be better spent making you prettier for Marta."

Aarundel raised his right hand to cover his missing eye. "No, this once I think I'll follow your example, my friend."

"You need not be stupid, Aarundel."

He gave me a brave smile. "Not stupid, Neal. *That* eye was my stupid eye, my blind eye. Without it I see many things, many injustices that I have condoned by not opposing them. Next to my wife, I love you and my sister more than anyone, and I kept you apart. Let's make a pact, Neal, you and I. This time I forgo magick for healing and you use it."

"I'd accept if I could, my friend, but I'm thinking I've not got much longer." I coughed and convulsed, but kept my scream trapped in my chest. "You have those letters?"

He patted his hand against his gambeson. "I can give them back to you."

"Not this time." I looked up at the healer. "Cletine, could I be troubling you for something to ease the pain? Not magick, a draught or something?"

Cletine nodded and drew a leaf from a pouch on his belt. He crushed it, and a faint scent like mint chased death from my nostrils. He opened my mouth and laid the leaf down in front of my lower teeth and let my lip hold it in place. "Suck on that. It will help. You may sleep."

"Thank you." I turned my head toward Aarundel. "You have Cleaveheart?"

He nodded.

"Good. I entrust it to you. Take it to Jarudin. Talk to Xerstan. He knows what to do."

"Xerstan." Aarundel nodded at me. "You know you've done more than destroy the Reithrese, don't you?"

"More?" I found it easier to smile as the pain in my chest dulled. "I think ending the Reithrese threat is enough for a Man, don't you?"

"A task worthy of a hero, Custos Sylvanii, and a task acquitted by a hero."

"By many heroes, Aarundel, most all of them Elven." My eyes began to want to close. "Thank you for being my friend."

"The honor has been mine."

"It is an honor we share." I shut my eyes and summoned an image of Larissa. "Tell her I died with her in my mind and my heart."

"Rest peacefully, my friend."

I felt him grip my shoulder and I tried to smile. I don't know if I succeeded, because along with the pain all other sensations faded. I hoped I had, because I'd rather have him remember my smile than my death. He was a true friend, and I owed him at least that much.

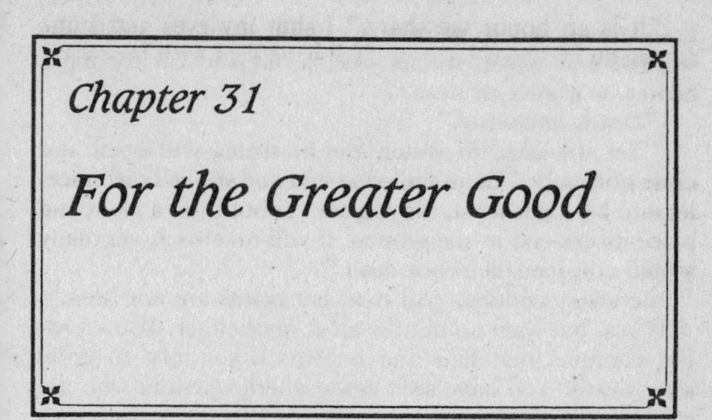

Late Autumn
A.R. 499
The Present

With a swift rub of the polishing cloth, Genevera removed the last bit of tarnish from the silver bracelet. She remembered her grandaunt taking it from her own right wrist and putting it onto Gena's wrist. "I make to you a gift of this because you can bear the responsibilities that come with it." She had not understood at the time, when Larissa had gone *excedere*, but now she wondered at her grandaunt's prescience.

Gena turned toward Berengar. "What was that you said?"

"I cannot believe you can do this—defeat death." His spirit had been dampened by her proposed actions, and his face remained a bit pale. "Neal has been dead for five centuries."

She shook her head. "Neal has lain in a tomb for five centuries. Death is a process that has some leeway in it."

"I don't understand."

"I'm not certain I do either, fully, but Larissa, my

grandaunt, used to provide me with examples while she worked and taught me. If you go out and cut for me a flower, is it alive or dead?"

"Dead, obviously."

"Yet if placed in water, the blossoms will open and close normally." Gena smiled at him and slipped the bracelet into her right wrist. "If you cut a shoot from a plant and place its cut end in the ground, it will take root, yet many would consider the shoot dead."

Berengar nodded. "All true, but plants are not Men."

"Yes, but Men do not die all at once either. You know, for example, that hair and fingernails continue to grow after death. You have seen cases where warriors who are struck in the head still breathe for a time even though they are dead."

"True, but none of them last five hundred years in that state."

"None of them had Elven magick to help them survive." She pointed Berengar to the doorway leading out onto the walkway that would take them to the council tree and the island with Neal's tomb on it. "The healers with the army, at least those being sent back with the wounded, could not counteract the Reithrese magicks used to kill Neal. Do you recall when I explained that magick dealt with the manipulation of chance and time?"

"Yes."

"The healer attending to Neal wove a spell that slowed the passage of time for Neal. He hoped that when Neal arrived in Cygestolia, someone would be able to reverse the magick worked on him."

Berengar raked fingers back through wind-tousled red hair. "So you are saying he is not really dead, just frozen in time before he died."

Gena shook her head. "No, he actually *is* dead. He is trapped in the midst of that process, anyway, and has not been revived. No one could be certain that their spells could counteract the Reithrese magick. Many sorcerers labored for centuries to find a way to dispell the Reithrese enchantments. They succeeded and turned the results of their research over to my grandaunt. I am certain she would have brought Neal back, but because there was a chance of failure, she did not want to take the risk of losing him forever."

"She told you this?"

Gena frowned sharply. "No. She did not like talking about Neal's death, but I was able to coax things out of her, and that is the impression she gave me. She would speak of him and his deeds, but never about the feelings they shared. Even so, I know she loved him deeply." She looked down at the stone tomb so far below. "Once a month she would enter the tomb and she would look at him. I think she wanted to take the chance to bring him back, but she dared not be selfish."

Shrugging, she continued. "I *am* willing to take the chance, because if I do not, your family will die and Rik's death will go unavenged."

They crossed the branch bridge in silence; then Gena stopped when she saw her grandfather standing alone in the middle of the Consilliarii chamber. On his right arm he wore his *insigne nuptialis*—the one Rik had recovered—and she knew he put it on only at times of importance and ceremony. "Grandfather? Are you going to try to stop me?"

The one-eyed Elf looked from her to Berengar and back again. "If I did, you would ignore me."

"I would listen."

"I know you would, Genevera." He watched her closely. "Are you prepared for this? It will not be easy."

"I know. I have studied Larissa's notes and I have rested. I can and will succeed, grandfather."

"I am certain you will. Please, indulge me in one thing: remember that for all the stories and legends, Neal is just a Man. And he was once my friend." Aarundel folded his arms, and Gena thought he meant his speech for Berengar and not for her. "If he cannot solve your problem, it is not his fault, but if he can, do not be amazed. I have learned there was not much he considered impossible."

Berengar narrowed his eyes. "You approve of what we are doing?"

"I will not gainsay you." Aarundel stepped aside, then followed them as they passed through the chamber and onto the staircase spiraling around the trunk of the tree.

Walking down to the tomb, Gena remembered all the previous pilgrimages to that site she had made with Larissa —only realizing this time that she actually *did* consider them pilgrimages. Her grandaunt had not spoken much during the visits, yet afterward they would sit in the shadow of the tomb, and she would entertain Gena's questions about Neal and his life.

It occurred to her that she had not visited the tomb since the last time she and Larissa had done so together. After that last trip Larissa had given her the bracelet and told her that she was going beyond. *When I asked why she was going away, she just told me her work was done.* Gena felt a shiver run down her spine. *She went beyond and I left Cygestolia.*

Each step down took her back in time to the previous visits. She wore the same sort of white cotton gown Larissa had demanded she wear on their visits, and she had gathered her hair back into a thick braid as her grandaunt had done. She imagined herself now taking her grandaunt's place, and that idea both chilled and pleased her. Larissa had always seemed more responsible than Gena had, so accepting that responsibility made her happy, yet it also inspired fear in her.

She rubbed at the bracelet and felt the Man-runes slide beneath her fingers. She knew they defined Neal and that it had been created by him, but its association with her grandaunt made it so much more to her. The bracelet was a piece of history, frozen in time, just as was the man who had pounded it out of shapeless metal.

The small stone building loomed larger as she walked across the grassy sward toward it. The grass felt cold on her bare feet, and the earth vaguely moist. Everything smelled very much alive around the stone monument to death. The sunlight poured down upon her, yet its warmth failed to reach her. A chill of doubt came to her as she reached the stone-blocked doorway.

Will Neal want this? That question had not occurred to her before, and it made her hesitate. Just as quickly as it had come, an answer followed, and she smiled. Larissa's tales had all stressed Neal's devotion to Mankind and to protecting it. If he had been able to foresee the trouble his actions long ago would have wrought, he would have refrained from taking them. And if he was forced to act to repair the damage, he would. Of this she had no doubt, and she took the Aurdonian ghost stories as confirmation of Neal's desires.

She turned from the rough-hewn, blocky granite building and faced the two males behind her. "Only I may enter the tomb. Larissa cast spells in there that protect Neal, and without this bracelet you could be hurt. You may watch from the doorway—I always did—but be quiet. I am not certain what I am going to find, and I will need to concentrate."

Aarundel nodded and stepped back a couple of paces. "Count Berengar and I will wait here."

Berengar's expression told her that he did not like that idea, but he withdrew to Aarundel's side. "Good luck."

She nodded and faced the tomb once again. The arched doorway had been filled with a single slab of stone polished until the surface reflected her face back at her. She forced a smile, but butterflies flitted through her stomach. She felt sweat rising on her upper lip, so she let her body shudder once to burn off nervous energy; then she set herself for the task at hand.

Gena looked up at the golden script carved into the stone above the arch. "Neal Roclawzi/Custos Sylvanii. A great hero and greater friend." As she spoke the words, she felt the thrill of hearing stories from Larissa and her grandfather race through her again. *With what I am going to do, I will add to the legend and become part of it.*

She raised her right arm and pressed the bracelet against the keystone of the arched doorway. The stone blocking the door went from grey with flecks of black to a milky white. It then faded through translucency to transparency before evaporating altogether. She caught a musty, dry scent from the tomb as warm air drifted out from the stone enclosure.

She lingered a moment in the doorway, seeing Neal again as she had seen him so many times before. Lying there on a stone slab, his feet toward her and his head on a stone pillow at the far end, he appeared to be sleeping, not dead. She knew the clothes he wore had been enchanted so the yellow silk tunic and green silk breeches would not age and decay, and she guessed that Larissa herself had sewn them together.

Gena stepped across the threshold with the reverence appropriate for entering into the presence of someone sacred. As she walked around his feet to his left side—exactly where Larissa had always stood—Neal's physical size impressed her. Not only had he been tall, but very robust as well. Scars crisscrossed the hands folded on his chest, with the burn scar on the back of his left hand being predominant among them. His sharp cheekbones, straight nose, and strong jaw gave him a look so vital, it mocked death.

She realized, as she looked down at him, that his chin and his cheekbones reminded her of Rik. His hands, though larger than Rik's were, had the same proportions. His hair, though a shade lighter than Durriken's had been, featured the same sort of ragtag utilitarian cut and length favored by Men who were more worried about being able to see than about being seen. Because of the resemblance she found herself liking the Man lying there in front of her even before life had returned to him.

Then she caught herself. *Do I see Rik in him, or did I see him in Rik?* That question shook her to her core. Gena wondered if, when Larissa went beyond, she had decided her grandaunt had abandoned Neal. Had that prompted her to go out into the world of Men to find her own Neal, and had she done that in Rik? She recalled measuring Berengar by her image of Neal, and she feared she had used the same yardstick to measure Durriken.

She shivered. *Enough time for that later. I need to figure out the spells here.* With her entry into the room, she knew she faced multiple sets of spells. The first came from the clothes on Neal and, she suspected, a glamour that kept the roses in his cheeks and the color in his hair. Larissa had warned her about protective spells, and she could pick some of them out from the background, but she could not identify all of them clearly. She felt she would have had more success trying to pick out individual instruments in an orchestral recital in Jarudin than she would isolating and identifying each spell.

That difficulty did not worry her because she knew the

bracelet she wore functioned as a key to all those spells. Larissa had woven her magick strong to protect Neal, but in giving Gena the bracelet she had transferred mastery of those spells over to her. Gena knew she would be operating in a safe environment. She had reread all of her grand-aunt's notes on what she had hoped would be a way to save Neal from his death, and she felt certain she could command all the spells she needed to do the job. Care and caution would allow her to take things one step at a time so she could do it right.

Gena rubbed her hands together and rolled her head around to loosen her neck. She ignored the sweat dribbling down from her temples and started to control her breathing. "Right. First thing is to remove this glamour. Once I see what I'm working with, I'll know which spell goes when."

Magery had any number of ways to counteract spells. Other spells could crush, dissolve, or slice through magicks, but each of them required an expenditure of energy greater than that used to cast the original spell. Gena chose to unweave the spell, and toward that end she used a small diagnostic spell that helped define the nature of the glamour. Once she had done that, she had an idea how the spell had been begun and completed, so she focused her attention on the end point. By simply manipulating time and chance, she unmade the end point; then the whole spell began to unravel.

As the glamour began to evaporate, Gena saw the true Neal Roclawzi, and she recoiled from him. Blood covered his pale, grey face—old, dried blood that had broken into tiny chips like a sun-dried mudflat. The silk clothes turned into soiled rags stiff with blood and dirt that covered his loins and little else. Open, ulcerated wounds formed a cross on his chest running from throat to navel, flank to flank. Multiple bruises covered him in purple, swollen bumps, and she saw an odd lump where at least one rib appeared to have been broken. His left ankle had swollen up to the size of a small melon, and his left foot canted in at an unnatural angle.

Her mind began to reel as she saw Neal's battered and abused body. She felt as if she could not breathe, and she knew she was beginning to panic. She fought to regain control of herself, but something in the tomb prevented her from doing that. Struggle as she might against it, she could not focus, yet through the fog in her mind she realized she had triggered a massive magickal trap and she had no way of counteracting it!

The spells that had lurked in the background swelled as they drew energy from her panic. They used the bracelet as their conduit. A red haze expanded from the corner of the tomb and washed over the body like a dust-cloud. Where it penetrated Neal's flesh, it liquefied the blood on him and sucked it back down through his pores. Flesh that had appeared bruised drained of color, and a pinkish flush colored his skin.

Silvery daggers of microlightning descended from a black cloud that coalesced from the tomb's shadows. Flicking down and back like the feathery kisses of a serpent's tongue, the lightning played over Neal's body. It lingered over open wounds and centered itself on his chest. The little forks all retreated into the cloud; then with a thunderous humming a single solid argent spear stabbed down into the cruciform wound at his navel. With the patience of a caterpillar inching along a branch, the incandescent lightbar worked its way up toward Neal's head. Flesh sizzled in its wake, the greasy vapor rising up into the cloud, but the flesh appeared seamless and unmarked as the smoke rose from it.

The beam lingered over the cross's center point, filling the room with a gout of sickly sweet smoke that made Gena want to vomit. She coughed and the beam flickered for a moment, then continued as she straightened up. It split into three pieces, two running across the wound and the last one up toward Neal's throat. The two flank beams vanished as the third jumped from his throat up to his nostrils. When it plunged in there, she saw light play beneath Neal's closed eyelids and shine out dimly through his ear; then the cloud imploded and the light vanished, leaving her momentarily blinded.

A wave of exhaustion rode over her, and a moment of mental clarity followed in the trough. She knew she was not as tired as she had been when she hastily cast the spell in the Haladin camp, but the two spells that had used her had drained her significantly. Moreover, they drew sustenance from her panic and fear in violation of the Elven dictum to keep emotion out of spells. The emotions made the spells incredibly powerful, but also unpredictable, and that frightened Gena horribly.

She tried to stop a third spell from vampirizing her, but that took more of an effort than she could muster. Gena did tenaciously cling to a small portion of vitality, bolstered in her efforts by knowing that if she lost it, the magicks could wring her free of life and discard her like a dry husk.

A blue-gray light bled up through the stone bier upon which Neal lay and became so bright that all she could see was his skeleton in silhouette. The light pulsed once, then dimmed, and it appeared as if Neal's flesh had become steel. The spot over his broken ribs suddenly glowed red, and sparks shot from it as a metallic hammering echoed in the tomb and shuddered through her. Likewise his left ankle glowed and sparked; then the light flared again and Neal returned to normal, save his ankle and rib no longer showed signs of injury.

Dizziness swept over Gena as the fourth spell started to draw on her for power. Somehow she knew this was the final spell, the one that would complete the task she had come to perform. She had wanted to be the master of the spell, directing it and using it, but she found herself just a component in it. Larissa had betrayed her, and the last spell sucked up her outrage like a sponge.

Heat flashed over her body and she thought she might faint. She fought the weakness, and the spell skimmed her defiance off to feed itself. Gena knew she was being manipulated, but every emotional response was anticipated and harvested.

Suddenly she felt short of breath. She could not breathe, her lungs lay useless and frozen in her chest. She felt her body begin to burn in its need for air, then that sensation vanished as well. She tried to puzzle together what was happening to her because Larissa's notes had said nothing about this effect—had said nothing about any of this—and she began to wonder if all she had been taught by her grandaunt had been nothing but bait for this trap.

Then she noticed Neal's chest had begun to rise and fall on its own.

Gena hunched forward as her heart began to beat wildly, then stopped altogether. When it started again, after only a second or two, her stomach convulsed. She felt her guts shiver and internal organs quiver. Her hands twitched, her toes curled inward. Every muscle in her body jerked and cramped and released. She thought at first that the spell was stealing seconds of life from her to transfer life into Neal's body, but she rejected that idea because the differences in their species and genders would make the transfer flawed and useless.

No, she decided, *I am just being used as a road map so the magick can show Neal's body what exists and how to make it work.*

Her head jerked back, exposing her throat, as she felt the spell plunge up her spine and into her brain. It prowled around in there, as Durriken might have prowled the curio vaults of rich Kaudian antiquities collectors, examining her memories. She saw everything flick across her mind's eye, yet the spell only lingered over the stories and thoughts, impressions and dreams she had experienced concerning Neal. As if it were picking up all the fragments of a shattered vase, it took every bit of him it could find and sent it flowing into his brain.

Gena knew it was not to rebuild his mind, but to remind him who he had been. If he were to live again, his soul would have to be plucked from Reithra's grasp and put back in his body. The stories, the memories, merely made it easy for him to return. It made his body receptive again.

The spell pushed against the last little reserve of energy Gena held. She resisted, but it pressed her. Without words it conveyed to her its need, not for something of Neal she yet possessed, but for a reason for him to return. It had to be potent and powerful, emotional and eternal. It could not come without sacrifice. *And it has to come from me.*

Gena opened up and fed directly into it the love for Neal she had seen in Larissa's eyes. Though her grandaunt had never spoken of her feelings for Neal, she never had to. Genevera had seen it from the beginning, and had never seen it dim. She wondered for a moment how Larissa could have prepared all this so lovingly, and then have walked away from it without using it. No logical answer came to her, so she funneled that mystery into the flow and felt herself begin to faint.

Her head came down, and she stumbled back against the wall of the tomb as the spell released her. She saw Neal's body convulse, and she cried out reflexively as his head hit the stone pillow on the bier. A second later she found herself slumping down in the corner, too tired to stand, too exhausted even to try to fight gravity. As she went down, she saw Neal's eyelids flutter, and even though she feared she was dying, she knew he lived again. In that realization she knew everything would be fine, and she surrendered to the blackness stealing over her.

Chapter 32

The Minority Does Suffer

Late Autumn
A.R. 499
The Present
My 536th Year

Sharp pain ripped through my chest; then came a blackness that I decided was death. Time did not flow, it grew stagnant. Shadow flashes of life, either dreams or visions, occasionally settled on my consciousness the way a leaf floats on a dead pond before slowly sinking to the bottom. They settled down there to molder with the rest of me.

Brilliant searing lights and heat and tingling shook me. The back of my head smacked something solid, but I felt more surprise than I did pain. The aching that had chased me through the darkness had eased. For the first time in eternity I summoned up the strength to open my eyes, and I found them responding to my command. As they opened, I saw a figure in white falling away to the ground off to my left.

I sat up enough to get my left elbow under me and took a good look at her. The sunlight pouring through the arched doorway showed me golden hair I could never forget and glinted off a bracelet I recognized. That she sat slumped in the corner with her chin touching her breast alarmed me, but I saw no blood and knew that were I to touch her, I could do more harm than good to the both of us.

A huge man eclipsed the sun as he ducked his head through the arched doorway. I recognized him more by his size and shape than by the hint of copper in his hair, but I couldn't imagine what he would be doing in Cygestolia. He looked at where Larissa had fallen and shouted *"Jenna!"* which was an oath I'd never heard the Red Tiger utter before. I wondered if I was dreaming somehow; then I saw him reach toward her, and I knew, dream or not, I had to act.

Sitting up and spinning around on my rump, I got my feet beneath me and launched myself at Beltran. "Don't touch her. You can't touch her."

Beltran looked utterly surprised at the sound of my voice. He folded around my shoulder. I heard a satisfying *ooofff* as my tackle carried him back out of the small building and crashed the both of us to the greensward. I bounced up off him and rolled through a somersault, but as I spun to face him, dizziness washed over me. The world swam before my eyes, and before I could focus them, a heavy left hand clouted me over my right ear.

The ground hit me harder than the fist had, but not by much. I rolled unsteadily to my feet and felt a hand grabbing my right shoulder. "Neal, hold. Berengar, stop."

I twisted around, pulling my shoulder from beneath the old Elf's hand. "He almost touched her, doomed her."

"Neal, friend, he will not hurt her."

I frowned. "Do I know you? The only Elves I call friend are Larissa and her brother, Aarundel. She is in there, and her brother will kill Beltran if he touches her."

"In the old days I would have indeed done that."

I blinked my eyes and took a good long look at the Elf standing before me. Long white hair draped over his shoulders. He wore a black eye patch and stood as tall as my best friend had, but his muscles had atrophied. His skin had an almost transparent quality to it, as if he were more spirit than flesh. "Aarundel? What did the Reithrese do to you?"

Aarundel shook his head. "They took my eye, Custos Sylvanii, but no more."

I frowned despite the pain growing at the base of my skull. "But you look so old. Your grandfather, Lomthelgar, he does not look so old. What happened?"

He shrugged. "I aged. Five centuries have passed since you last saw me."

That cut my legs out from under me, and I sat down hard. "Five hundred years? But . . ." I glanced back at the small stone blockhouse. "Your sister, she has not aged."

"She is my granddaughter, Neal, by my son Niall." Aarundel crouched, then sat on the ground beside me. "Many things have changed, my friend."

The man with whom I fought emerged from the blockhouse with a *sylvanesti* in his arms. I waited for a volley of Elven arrows to cut him down, but none came. I looked up and knew I sat beneath the Consilliarii tree and watched this most grotesque violation of Elven law being perpetrated right here. Aarundel barely glanced at the Man dooming his granddaughter to exile, and the Man seemed more concerned for her than for his own fate.

"How can he be carrying her?"

"I can because I am strong and considerate, old man." He lay her down in the shade and rubbed one of her wrists. Ignoring me, he looked at Aarundel. "She is breathing and has a pulse. She fainted from whatever went on in there."

I reached out and grabbed Aarundel's left arm. "What has happened? Why is Beltran here? Wait—can he be Beltran? Five centuries?" I closed my mouth as my mind became a chaotic jumble of ideas and fears warring for control of me.

Aarundel patted my hand with his right hand. "There are many things I will explain to you, my friend, gladly. I know this is abrupt and confusing." He pointed to the man kneeling beside his granddaughter. "This is Count Berengar Fisher of Aurdon in Centisia."

I frowned. "Aurdon? I remember the Fishers of Aurium. Are they related?"

Berengar looked up while his hands continued their

massage of the *sylvanesti*'s wrist. "They are the same, Neal. What you knew as Aurium is now known as Aurdon. It has grown and changed since you last saw it."

Five centuries! I stared down at the ground and picked at the grass growing there. It felt the same to me as it had when last I touched it. I plucked a piece and put it in my mouth. It tasted and smelled the same. That was something, something normal, and I clung to it. If this was all a dream, I would laugh in the morning and if not, I now knew a new definition for nightmare.

Aarundel's arm bones felt as light and frail as a bird's wing in my grasp. "Larissa?"

My friend shook his head. "She has gone beyond, Neal. With Lomthelgar and my parents."

"Marta?"

"She waits here, with me."

The *sylvanesti* responded to Berengar's efforts to revive her with a groan. She tried to sit up but would have failed had Berengar not shifted around and placed his hands beneath her shoulders. As her head came up, and I saw her face for the first time, I felt a fist crush my heart. It was not what I had experienced when I first saw Larissa, but an imperfect echo of it. She looked enough like her grandaunt that I was reminded of the person I had now lost.

The smile on Aarundel's face was all that kept my spirit from dying right then and there. "This, Neal Elfward, is my granddaughter, Genevera. Gena, this is Neal Roclawzi."

She bowed her head toward me, letting her thick braid slither over Berengar's hand and her shoulder. "This is a dream come true for me, meeting you."

I nodded, unable to think of anything to say. My mind yet reeled at my existence. My hands came up and touched my chest. I saw no bruise, no indication that my battle with Takrakor had ever taken place, yet the absence of Aarundel's eye told me it had. "My wounds." I grabbed Aarundel's shoulder. "I was dying. What happened?"

Aarundel glanced down. "You died."

Genevera smiled at me. "I saved you. I repaired you and brought you back to life."

My jaw dropped. "I was dead?"

"Yes, but I fixed you." She frowned at the disbelief in my voice. "The magick, the spells woven into the tomb . . ."

"Tomb?"

She looked back toward the stone structure, but my attention was drawn more to the fact that she moved so like Larissa, than to the building. "That was your tomb. I triggered the spells in there and brought you back. I healed you."

"You brought me back to a world I do not know. You have healed me."

Gena nodded emphatically. "Yes, that is what I did."

I stared at her wide-eyed. "But I never wanted to be healed."

"What?"

"I never wanted to come back. And you bring me back after Larissa has gone beyond?" I turned to Aarundel. "How did this happen? How did you let it happen?"

Aarundel steeled himself to reply. "There are many things that I must explain to you. . . ."

I wanted none of it and let my confusion slip over into irrational anger. "Why couldn't you just let me stay dead? I may not have been of an Elder race, but that should not make me your plaything. How could you think so little of me?"

Aarundel stood abruptly and, grabbing my arm, brought me up with him. He shoved me against the Consilliarii tree, and I saw the old fire smoldering in his eye. "Damn you, Neal, you know it was not that! You and I, we were brothers. You said so yourself."

"I would have let you die, brother."

"And I *watched* you die, *brother*, inch by inch as Takrakor's magick gnawed its way through you." He jerked his thumb back into his chest. "I was with you when you took Cleaveheart from Jammaq, and I have rejoiced every day that you were brave enough to come to Jammaq to steal Marta and me away from the Reithrese. Can you deny *me* wanting to rescue you from the last of their perfidy? Can you fault me for wanting to let you see my sister one more time? Can you fault me for hoping, one day, that you and I might walk again together through the vales of Cygestolia?"

He straightened up and watched me closely. "If you can, then know, *brother,* that the same fault is harbored in your breast, for I have done nothing here for you that you would not have done for me. Go ahead, tell me I am wrong. Do so and I will apologize, but I will not regret what I have done."

Chapter 33

The Puppet's Strings Justified

Late Autumn
A.R. 499
The Present

The man Gena had brought back from the dead covered his face with both hands. Leaning back against the Consiliarii tree, he hung there halfway between upright and prostrate. Part of her expected him to sob, but her mental image of Neal the hero killed that idea instantly. That was the sort of weak emotion of which she did not believe he was capable.

She shivered because much confused her. She had not considered what his reaction to being resurrected might be. Well, she had, but she had assumed he would respond with gratitude. All Men she had known carried with them a fear of death. In Rik it had been small and in others all but crippling. She had thought that any Man offered a chance to defeat death would readily accept it and be overjoyed at being returned to life.

Neal seemed to resent what she did for him, and resent it greatly. More surprising than that was her grandfather's apparent anticipation of that resentment. He had known what to expect from Neal, but he had chosen not to warn her. That was a side of her grandfather she had never known before, and it scared her.

"Grandfather, what is happening here?"

Neal lowered his hands. "Explain, Aarundel, if you can."

Aarundel lifted his head and appeared defiant in the face of their questions. "On the road, after you had been given that sleeping draught, it became obvious you would die. You had clearly stated your preferences about magick, and Cletine was unable to reverse the spell that had been cast upon you, so our disagreement on that point was moot. Cletine was able to use a spell to isolate you within time. It managed to slow the damage being done to you by Takrakor's magick. My intention, in having him cast that spell upon you, was to allow you to see Larissa one more time. That was, I felt, the least I could do for you."

The man nodded briefly. "For *that* I thank you."

"*That* decision led directly to this consequence." Aarundel opened his arms and took in Cygestolia with his hands. "In the wake of the annihilation of the Reithrese there was much mourning and rejoicing here among the *sylvanii*. And much thinking. You lay in state in the Consiliarii chamber for a month, with my sister there always. Your role in the Reithrese extermination and her love for you provoked much thought. And catalyzed much in the way of change."

He looked over at Gena, and she became fully aware of the pressure of Berengar's hands on her shoulders. "The law that separated you from Larissa was swept away in a vote that was nearly unanimous."

Neal looked up. "Finndali?"

"He died at Alatun. Those who voted against you were Vorrin and other reactionaries. The humiliation that came from their votes prompted them to go beyond shortly thereafter." Aarundel's eye focused distantly, and his face slackened slightly into an expression Gena recognized from when he used to tell her stories of the days he traveled with Neal. "There also arose among the mages a contest to counter Takrakor's magick. While your wishes were well-known on the matter, the mages said the spell cast upon you was the last trace of the Reithrese in the world and, therefore, should be expunged. They made it a matter of safety as well as pride."

Gena frowned. "What do you mean when you talk about Neal's wishes on the matter?"

Neal wearily raised his left hand and showed her the back of it. "I always refused magickal healing. That is why I am so scarred. Your grandfather asked me to reconsider as I lay dying. I refused."

Gena felt her guts twist into a knot. "I did not know."

"It is true, Neal, she did not." Aarundel looked straight at his friend. "We told her everything about you, but we hid your feelings concerning curative magick from her."

"What?" Gena struggled to her feet. "Why?"

"Because it was necessary." Aarundel cut her off by slashing his hand through the air. "The mages worked for over two centuries to figure out what they would have to do to counteract Takrakor's magick, and they created a regimen of spells that would successfully do the job. These they made a present to my sister. They—in reality *all* of the *sylvanii*—felt it was her decision to make, whether or not to use them. They raised this tomb and placed you inside it, giving her, through the bracelet you made, the only access to it."

Gena watched muscles bunch at the corners of Neal's jaw. "So Larissa accepted this gift even though she knew I did not want it? How could she?"

Fire sparked in Aarundel's eye. "*You* knew what you wanted. *I* knew what you wanted. *She* knew what *you* wanted. You didn't think to ask what *she* wanted. That is the burden of *vitamor*, Neal. It is not your wants or her wants, but what you want together that matters!"

The white-haired Elf stared up at the sky as the anger drained from his voice. "You will never know how much your death hurt Larissa, Neal. She always held herself in control, but there were times when I could see it. A tear. The way her voice would crack. The fact that her laugh was never unrestrained after your death. She loved you so fiercely that she would have done anything to bring you back—anything but violate your wishes."

Neal wrapped his right arm across his chest and covered his face with his left hand. "What I did to you, my love . . ." Gena could see his jaw moving, but no more words escaped his mouth. Suddenly he hammered his right fist against the bark of the Consilliarii tree. "How could I have been so cruel?"

His question hung in the air, leaving him open for recrimination, but Aarundel answered him gently. "We both wanted you back with us, but we respected your wishes. No matter how much it hurt, she would not violate them. Her love for you prevented action for the first century or so, then fear took over."

"Fear? Of me?" Neal's hand came away from his face. "I never would have knowingly hurt her."

"She knew that, my friend." Aarundel stepped forward and laid his hands on Neal's shoulders. "She was afraid of your reaction if she brought you back. You would have been three centuries out of your time. She was afraid you would hate her for being so selfish as to bring you back when the world you had known had vanished. I tried to tell her she was wrong, but she would not listen."

"And here I react as she predicted I would, justifying her fears."

"Your anger is understandable."

Neal shook his head. "That's not entirely true, but she should not have thought any anger would turn into hatred. We would have been together. A thousand years could have passed, and I would have been very happy to return to her."

Aarundel folded his arms. "I think she knew that, but it led into her other, far greater fear. What she dreaded—the thing that truly stopped her from using the magicks herself—was that she would not survive losing you again. That pain . . ." Aarundel raised his hands and let them fall again as he shrugged wordlessly.

Neal balled his fists in frustration. "I know her pain. I am here and she is forever beyond my reach."

"Remember she loved you very well and truly, for she did things in your name neither of us ever would have contemplated otherwise." Aarundel looked over at Gena and then away again. "We hatched a plot, my sister and I. My son, Niall, showed no aptitude for magick, so we had to wait. His daughter, Genevera, did have a talent for magick. Larissa taught her a great deal about magick and about you. I taught her mostly about Men and you. We created for her a very strong portrait of you, yet one that was incomplete. We wanted, we expected, that some day she would want to complete it. She would use the spells that Larissa would not to bring you back, and when my sister deemed her sufficiently powerful, she went beyond, hoping you would understand."

Gena's jaw dropped. "You used me to bring him back against his wishes?"

Aarundel faced her squarely. "You were not overly concerned about his wishes when you chose to act."

"I acted because doing that seemed a viable solution to the current problem! Had I known he never used magick to heal himself, I never would have done this."

Neal stared up at his friend. "I'm thinking, Aarundel, I cannot believe you would have done this. You warped your own granddaughter into bringing me back?"

"What is so hard to believe, Neal? Have you forgotten how the Consilliarii offered you my sister to prevent the war with the Reithrese? Am I not of the same blood and the same culture that offered you that devil's choice?"

"I thought you were different."

"I *am* different!" Aarundel's anger flooded through his voice. "Larissa would not bring you back. I *could not* bring you back, yet I knew that your death was the fault of me and my people. We knew and had known for ages that one day we would be forced to go to war with the Reithrese, yet we were willing to do anything we could to forestall that eventuality. We were willing to let them slaughter Men to build their empire because we thought it would deflect them away from us. *You* forced us to remember they had aligned themselves with Death, and because they had done so, there was no way to avoid a conflict.

"You also put a face on Humanity for us. You showed us that all the noble and virtuous thoughts and traditions we ascribed to ourselves also applied to Men. When you refused my sister to save me and my wife, you shamed a nation. You made us realize that for us to sacrifice Humanity to preserve ourselves was incredibly arrogant and the height of hubris. You died in a war we should have waged centuries ago, you died wrongfully, and I chose to do whatever I had to do to redress that wrong."

Her grandfather faced her and Gena saw pain in his single eye. "Had I a choice, Genevera, I would have done what you did and have earned the ire for it that you have earned. You were a tool in my hands, so all blame should fall to me. I do not expect you to forgive me, but I hope you will understand me."

Gena wanted to scream at him and almost did, but a voice inside her stopped her. Yes, she had been used. Her grandfather and grandaunt had deceived her. They had tricked her into doing something they could not bring themselves to do. For that they deserved all of her anger.

However, they had not *forced* her to raise Neal from the dead. She had jumped at the chance, for reasons she could only barely begin to fathom. She knew, in part, that her willingness to participate came from the fact that if she were successful, she would have done something her grandaunt, her mentor, had been unwilling and unable to attempt. Bringing Neal back had been her opportunity to prove how much she had learned and how skilled she had become. Her discovery of the deception turned that pride into a knife that sliced through her ego and stabbed deep into her self-esteem, but as an Elf she knew herself heir to a big piece of the hubris her grandfather had just described.

"I understand you, grandfather." Rik's image flashed through her mind. "I understand your wanting your friend back, and even your desire to see the wrongs committed against him redressed. And I can forgive you because my part in this was prompted by similar motivations."

She slipped the bracelet from her wrist and walked over to Neal. "You made this for my grandaunt, and she treasured it for the five centuries she agonized over you and your fate. She loved you more than you will ever know, and it was her love reflected through me that finished the process that brought you back to life. If not for her love, you would not live now."

The corners of Neal's mouth tucked back in a quick smile. "I lived for her love, fitting now that I live because of it."

Gena held the bracelet out toward him and saw him draw back from her. "I am not worthy to wear this. Take it, wear it in her memory. You made it so she could remember you; now it is your turn to remember her through it."

Neal took it from her and slipped it tight around his own right wrist. He smiled up at her, then looked back down at the silver bracelet. "Thank you." He frowned, then shook his head. "Forgive me for my reaction. I'm thinking that being dead does not do much for one's manners."

Gena smiled back at him. "No offense taken. This has to be a shock."

"That it is. So much has changed."

"Not as much as you might think, Neal."

Neal looked over at Berengar. "How is that . . . Berengar, was it?"

"Berengar Fisher. Five centuries ago you were chasing Haladin raiders through Centisia. Like locusts they are back."

Neal straightened up and stood free of the tree. "If you're half the warrior as was the man whose form you wear, those raiders would not be much of a threat."

Berengar nodded at Gena. "As Lady Genevera can attest, we give better than we get, but we cannot root them out of Centisia fully because some are there under the protection of the Riveren, er, Riveraven family. Because of this alliance, the Riverens threaten to overwhelm my family. The prohibition on violence between our families that you laid down prevents us from being able to fight back."

Gena nodded. "We have been searching for Cleaveheart and Wasp so we can undo what you did in Aurdon. We believe we have found Cleaveheart's resting place, in Jarudin, but the obvious way to recover the sword is keyed to the dagger Wasp. Wasp was lost in Jammaq and never recovered. We need to know if there is another way to get the sword, and to answer that question, we had to bring you back to life."

"A fair question that is, and I'm thinking you expect me to answer in the affirmative, else you'd not have gone to all this trouble." Neal's green eyes narrowed in a frown. "I'm afraid, though, that I was not smart enough to think of a second way to open the vault. I had sort of intended to have Cleaveheart locked away forever, which, I'm thinking, I would likely have pegged as five centuries or so, given how I was thinking at the time."

"Damn and damn." Berengar's hands bunched into fists. "Without that blade, my family is lost."

Neal cocked an eyebrow at him. "Well, we can't have that."

"But we can't fix it either, because only Wasp can open the vault, and Wasp is gone."

"Not at all." Neal pointed off to the northeast. "It's off that way."

Aarundel looked shocked. "What? How do you know that?"

Neal looked at his pointing finger as if it were an alien part of himself. "I don't know how I know, my friend, but it's out there. I know it the same way I knew where Takrakor was when we waited outside Alatun."

The two of them looked at each other. "Neal, you don't think . . . ?'

"Think, not likely. Fear, on the other hand . . ." Neal clapped his hands on her grandfather's shoulders, and she saw Aarundel smile proudly. "Tell you what, my friend, I'd be thankful for the loan of weapons and supplies. If we're right, I'm thinking I've got some work to finish, and five centuries is far too long a time to have left it undone."

Chapter 34

The Ties Even Death Cannot Sever

Late Autumn
A.R. 499
The Present
My 536th Year

Despite Berengar's statement to the contrary, I found very little to be as I remembered it from before Alatun. Aarundel's aging and the presence of a stone building on the Consilliarii island were but two of the changes time had wrought in Cygestolia. It was not grossly different—I still remembered my way around—but all the trees appeared to be a bit lighter in their shades of green, and a few of the smaller ones were sporting leaves of red and gold. Even though I had seen seasonal changes in Cygestolia and the Elven Holdings before the Reithrese campaign, I thought these new changes more chronic than seasonal.

Woodspire, by contrast, had grown larger and fuller. I saw more in the way of things that a Man might find familiar, and reorienting myself to its internal geography proved not that difficult. Even so, when I went to turn down a corner to the chamber that had been mine, Aarundel steered me on and up some stairs to a grander suite of rooms.

"These we created for you, in the event of your return." He smiled at me. "Larissa guided the project."

I could not help myself but to smile. The huge chamber had as its centerpiece a stone garden akin to the one in the tower at Jarudin. One whole wall had a map made from blocks of different woods, all textured to represent mountains, valleys, rivers, deltas, lakes, and cities. I recognized the general layout of the terrain, though some of the political borders surprised me. The room had been furnished with chairs and chest that I would have chosen, and I felt a pang in my heart when I realized the depth of care Larissa had put into creating this room for me.

"I am honored."

"Then we are very happy." A silver-haired *sylvanesti* slipped into the room behind Berengar and nestled in beneath Aarundel's right arm. "I have waited a long time to see you again, Neal Elfward."

"Marta?" I bowed to her.

As I straightened up, she surprised me and stepped forward to hug me. I tried to hold her back, fearful of what would happen when we touched, but neither she nor Aarundel appeared to be the least bit concerned of the consequences of her action. She wrapped her arms around my chest and squeezed. "I have long wanted to do this to thank you for saving our lives in Jammaq."

When Aarundel smiled and nodded at me, I let my hands slip from her shoulders and around her back to enfold her in a hug. The scent of lilacs rose from her hair, and the long silver locks tickled against my chest. She felt so frail and light in my arms, yet I sensed a strength flowing through her. Afraid I might crush her, I held her as tightly as I dared, then I eased myself free of her arms.

She looked hurt for a moment, then her alabaster flesh flushed pink. "Forgive me, Neal, I know this must all be strange for you."

I nodded. "It is, a bit. I can recall times when I wanted to take Larissa into my arms and could not, even though I sought only to comfort her, not seduce her. And now, the idea that I can hold you without Aarundel fearing your loss or my death—and I'm thinking the former is more his fear than the latter—it is something I will have to become used to."

"Because of you, it is possible." Marta retreated into Aarundel's arms, but smiled at me nonetheless. "The law that prohibited our touching was foolish, and I hope it remains in its grave ten times as long as you did."

I smiled and looked down at my hands, still feeling her in my arms and pressed against my chest. "Though it is five hundred years late, I must thank you, Marta, for saving *my* life in Alatun."

"But I was not there."

I laughed aloud. "Not in form, but in spirit, to Takrakor's regret. The spell you put on the tooth fragment in the dagger you gave me told me that he waited for me in Alatun. There he managed to do some things to me that, well, put me in quite a state. He kept getting closer to strengthen his link to me, and it strengthened the one you created. Then I smashed the fragment of his tooth against the stone floor."

Marta's hand rose to her own jaw. "Oh, my."

"That, I'm thinking, is likely the tamest of language he had running through his brain." I shrugged, then worked my shoulders around to loosen them. "He was distracted and I cut him with Cleaveheart. I thought I had killed him, but the link with Wasp seems to be working still, which means Takrakor might yet be alive."

My right index finger again wanted to point off to the northeast, but I held it in check. "We need Wasp if we are to get Cleaveheart back and solve Berengar's problems."

Aarundel nodded. "Recovering the dagger and getting back to Aurium/Aurdon will take some planning. The sooner we are started, the sooner we will finish."

It was interesting to watch the changes that time had wrought in Aarundel. He had always been a capable leader and a meticulous planner, but he served as an adviser to me by his own choice when we fought together in the Steel Pack. In the years since Alatun he had grown into the sort of leader that his father and grandfather had been. From the start I knew he would not be accompanying me on the quest to get Cleaveheart back, but he would do everything he could to guarantee us success.

The first thing he did was order tailors, armorers, and swordsmiths to come and begin preparing me proper clothes and tools for our journey. I learned quickly that styles had changed in everything from boots and tunics to armor and swords. What I preferred, of course, was considered archaic, but I conceded to conventional wisdom in the area of fashion, though I did insist on a blade rather stouter than this rapier-thing Berengar seemed to favor. Aarundel had a sword made to my specifications, but also commissioned a rapier for me.

Once I had clothes enough for a short journey, Aarundel arranged for me to travel with him via the *circus translatio* to a spot roughly three hundred miles north of Cygestolia. Before we left, with me sitting on the back of Scurra, a multiply-great grandson of Blackstar, Aarundel and some astronomers had me point off toward where Wasp was located. They planted stakes in the ground parallel with my arm and on a map drew a line up and off the edge of the map that corresponded to the direction in which I pointed.

After we arrived at the *circus* grove to the north, Aarundel had me again point toward Wasp. I noted myself that I pointed more easterly than northeasterly this time, and that appeared to please Aarundel. He looked at the stars and made some notes, then we settled down, just the two of us, to rest up for three days before we headed back to Cygestolia.

In the darkness, with the two of us swaddled in blankets to keep the cold out, it felt as if we had never been apart. We remembered bits and pieces of battles as if they had happened only yesterday. A light snow started to fall, and it seemed to me as if we were back in the Hiris mountains, tricking the Reithrese into believing the Red Tiger's whole army had been trapped there.

He told me about how the whole battle at Alatun had run. My heart swelled with pride as he described the Steel Pack holding the gate to the city despite attackers inside and out. When the magickal components of the Reithrese army fell apart, the Elven host had overwhelmed them. Those that could retreat tried to do so in good order, then were crushed against the walls of the city they had sought to defend.

"Those of us who were wounded were taken away, but the rest of the army scoured the countryside and killed everyone and anyone they saw of Reithrese descent. We prepared mass graves and buried the lot of them. We destroyed their cities and sterilized their land with fire; then we salted the earth and erased any trace of their having existed—at least any trace within Reith itself. As a people the Reithrese are forgotten except among degenerates and the Haladina, who drill their teeth and set them with gems in remembrance of their former masters."

I nodded. "It sounds as if you did a thorough job."

Aarundel stared into the little fire we had blazing near our feet. "I would have been happier had a complete record been kept of the Reithrese, along with a list of the dead, but there were thousands and thousands of them. I don't know if cataloging them would have been possible. For example, I would have preferred to have found Takrakor's body. If he yet lives . . ."

I shrugged. "He was the serpent's head. When it was struck off, the body died. Now we will have to make doubly certain the head remains dead. Do you think, with him alive, if there were a corps of Reithrese survivors they would not have tried to avenge themselves upon Elves and Men before this?"

"That point has merit, and I am foolish enough to take comfort in it." He leaned back against an old log and began to tell me of his life since my demise. He proved a proud father and prouder grandfather, citing some of the adventures Niall, Gena, and her brother, Finnwick, had enjoyed. He told me of Gena's lover, Durriken, and his having recovered the *insignii nuptialis* from the vault of some collector.

"You have prospered in my absence, and of that I am proud, my friend."

"But it was your sacrifice that made it all possible." Aarundel's hand came up, forestalling any reply on my part; then he pointed off toward the east.

Excepting the crackle of the fire and my own heartbeat, I heard nothing for a moment or two. Then I caught the faint sounds of something approaching our campsite. I reached over to where the hilt of my sword lay, but refrained from drawing it as, in one huge leap, a hulking shadowed form landed at the edge of the firelight circle.

It poked its muzzle into the air and took a healthy sniff. "Neal Roclawzi, you are."

In size and shape it looked a lot like Shijef, but its coloration differed radically. Half its face, starting from the muzzle and taking in the left ear, was black. The other side started white at the muzzle, but became grey-blue around the eye and across the cheek and ear. The body fur tended toward black except for a grey V-blaze at its throat and white on its paws. There was no doubt it was a Dreel, but its presence so far from its normal range surprised me.

"I am Neal Roclawzi."

"Defeated Shijef in single combat you did?" It hunched down on its haunches and cocked its head at me. "Show me."

I opened my blanket cocoon and lifted my warm woolen tunic. The Dreel peered in closely at the bite scars Shijef had left on me. "I was much younger then, so if you seek the same sort of contest, I will decline."

It shook its head, then raised its muzzle to the sky and let out a howl that chilled me more than the night air. "Stulklirn am I. Shijef-sired through Bactha, Sorrla, Skactin, Borna, and Byorii. Of the seventh generation am I, and the first to be honored by your presence." The beast lowered his head until his chin touched the ground. "The bargain is and fulfillment am I. The same heart have we."

Stulklirn's words echoed those of his great, great, great, great grandfather, bringing remembrance to my brain and a smile to my face. "We have the same heart."

The Dreel's head came up and he howled happily. His bushy tail stirred up leaves behind him, it beat so against the ground. "What service would you have of me?"

"Sit, for the moment." I pointed to a spot a bit closer yet still slightly downwind of us. "Does Shijef still live?"

"Lives in his children he does. Many kin, many lives." Stulklirn extended a paw toward the fire, then pulled it back and sniffed at it. "Waited, did we, for you. When you came, I was chosen."

"How did you know?"

The Dreel shrugged. "Knew, did I." His agate eyes sparkled with excitement. "Chosen was I because to you fast I could get. That Bactha's gift is."

I glanced over at Aarundel. "Dreelbands were small and not widely spread when I was alive. Are there more of them now?"

"I confess I do not know. With the spread of Mankind, I suspect many of their ranges have grown smaller, but I have heard little or nothing of the Dreel since the fall of the Reithrese."

"Hidden we have been, waiting. Shijef and Man-Neal allies. In service to the Dun Wolf are we. Protect denmen." The Dreel looked to me for some confirmation that what he was saying was true, so I nodded and smiled at him. "In Dreel-land, Shijef emperor. All Dreel him praise."

Aarundel shrugged. "When we return to Cygestolia, ask Genevera about the Dreel. She has a very good understanding of folklore—especially the legends that still are sung about you. I am certain she knows of the Dreel."

Stulklirn's ears pricked up. "To Cygestolia you go? Take you there I will."

He started to get up, but I restrained him with a hand. "We have the grove as soon as we are rested."

The Dreel shook his head. "Trees slow are. Stulklirn much faster with Bactha's gift is."

I glanced at Aarundel and decided from his raised eyebrow that we both had missed what Stulklirn believed he was making obvious. "Bactha's gift, it allows you to go between places?"

The Dreel thumped his chest with a paw. "Mastery of Roadfast, have I. Longstepper am I."

"Well then, Stulklirn Longstepper, tomorrow or the day after we will let you take us to Cygestolia."

"Until then?"

I shrugged. "Until then, we sleep and talk and wait."

"Waiting I have done." The Dreel opened his mouth in a canine leer. "Waiting with allies better is."

• • •

Over the next two days Aarundel had me point toward where I felt Wasp was, and the measurements he took always appeared to be roughly the same. He explained to me that he would draw the line indicated by my pointing on the same map as he had drawn the line for the first point. Where those two lines crossed would be the area in which we could find Wasp.

The Dreel took great interest in what Aarundel was doing, and from time to time I found them locked in conversations as deep as those that Lomthelgar and Shijef had shared. Even allowing for the fact that Shijef had been surly and hostile toward me, with good reason, Stulklirn appeared to me to be smarter than his progenitor. He learned very quickly and patiently worked with our horses so they could get used to his scent.

As had Shijef before him, Stulklirn used the Dreel version of the *circus translatio* to take us back to Cygestolia. We arrived in the grove, and once again I noticed that we were not as tired as we had been when we used the grove to head out. Stulklirn immediately bounded off to explore the forests—he assured us that he would find us—while Aarundel and I rode back to Woodspire.

We found Berengar and Genevera in the central chamber of my suite. They both studied the map upon which the first line had been drawn. Aarundel added the line determined by the new measurements, and Berengar groaned as they intersected in the frozen wastes above Mannkito.

"That means we must take into account an expedition into the Rimefields." He squinted at the map. "Our journey will cover two thousand miles at the very least, with a tenth of that in the ice barrens."

I frowned. "People used to live there when I was alive."

"And they still do, at a bare subsistence level. By the time we make it there, it will be the dead of winter. We will be fighting storms, and there is no way we can carry enough provisions to last us there and back again." He glared at me as if it were my fault where Wasp ended up. "At best we will be in Aurdon this time next year."

I tapped the map near the center of Irtysh. "If we

started here, we'd be looking at five hundred miles or so. Provisions and travel will need to account for less than two months out and two back in the worst case."

Berengar folded his arms. "That would be correct, *if* we could start in Irtysh, but we are over here in Cygestolia. How do we get there?"

Aarundel smiled, so I didn't have to. "A Dreel with a most amazing ability has pledged himself to Neal's service."

"A Dreel?" The delight in Gena's voice brought the smile to my lips that I had denied Berengar. "A Dreel like Shijef?"

I nodded. "His great-great-something-grandson."

Berengar looked at all of us as if we were crazy. "Dreels are myths."

"I'm thinking I was a myth up until a week ago."

Gena bent forward and took a good look at the map. "Neal, did you ever fight a creature up in the Rimefields? A big Man-eating monster?"

I shook my head, then glanced at Aarundel. "I can't remember anything like that."

Aarundel shook his head as well. "We never ventured into the Rimefields. Closest we got was when you fought Shijef in Irtysh."

"Dreels again." Berengar frowned imperiously. "Myths."

Gena tapped the map under the shallow X the two lines had made. "I remember hearing something about an ice-monster living in a smoking ice mountain up here. It eats Men, it is said, and there is a legend about your fighting it, but I think that was cobbled together from other heroic songs from Rzyani sources."

"There's another myth for you, my lord." I smiled carefully at Berengar. "Genevera, does that monster have a name?"

"Bacorzi, Pacorzi . . . Tacorzi perhaps."

Aarundel and I again looked at each other. "Takrakor? Smash down the middle and add the 'zi' for his living in a mountain."

The elder Elf nodded. "Had I thought he still lived, I might have made the connection myself and acted upon it."

I shook my head. "There was no way you could link that myth and Takrakor, and we still might be wrong about it. We won't know until we get there."

"And when you do?"

"I'll ask him politely to give me back my knife, and when he refuses, I'll do to him what I meant to do five hundred years ago."

Chapter 35

New Tricks for an Old Wolf

Early Winter
A.R. 499
The Present

In retrospect Gena saw how it had begun, though had she been asked at the start of the expedition, she would have said there would have been no trouble among the four of them. No one had been designated leader of the group, though she had still seen Berengar in that role, since he had initiated the whole thing. Neal functioned as a guide and adviser, and while she was certain that was how he would have characterized his role, he just naturally asserted himself and gave his opinion when any questions came up.

The Dreel had helped polarize things very quickly because of his devotion to Neal and utter lack of respect for Berengar. And Berengar, while an intelligent and skilled man, had not traveled much in the northern nations and not at all by the *circus translatio*. The exertion of using that route to get from Cygestolia to the grove to the east of Jarudin seriously wore him out. As a result his temper was shorter than usual, and he did not rein it back in.

Neal, on the other hand, seemed to weather travel by

the *circus* better than even she did. She felt embarrassed awakening to the sound of Neal and Stulklirn dumping armloads of wood near the edge of the campsite to feed the fire that kept her warm. "How can you be so full of energy?"

The Man shrugged. "I'm thinking I must have rested a great deal while I was dead."

Gena yawned. "I apologize for awakening you. Had I known . . ."

Neal shook his head. "Now I'm the one who should be apologizing. Someone brings you back from the dead, and you get angry with them? I'm thinking I was more mannerly dealing with the Reithrese emperor in Jarudin than I was with you and Aarundel. Never was one to wake up all cheery, though."

Gena stretched and tossed her blanket across Berengar's feet. She stood and walked over to where Neal squatted. She held her hands out to the fire. "That feels good."

"Something about a fire that warms the body and prompts talk that warms the soul. Many's the friendship welded together over a campfire."

Gena sat down and poked a stick into the fire. "Did you and my grandaunt spend much time talking over a fire?"

Neal thought for a second, and Gena saw sadness flicker over his face. "Once, for a bit, but it didn't last. That was the night that Takrakor and his warriors took your grandfather away. We had more fires on that trip, of course, but we didn't do much talking."

The pain in his voice made her want to hug him, but as she reached out, he withdrew. "Neal, there is no prohibition against our touching."

He gave her a smile, but it died quickly. "I know this, but I fought so long to keep from hugging Larissa, that it's a habit I can't break."

"You could if you tried."

Neal shrugged. "True, but then I'd have to deal with the fact that I'd be hugging the grandniece of the *sylvanesti* I love. To go from living in a tomb to robbing a cradle is a bit much right now."

"Neal, I am only slightly younger than Larissa was when you met her."

"Which means I'm twice your age."

"I do not think the five hundred years you lay dead count against you. Would you deny yourself the charms of a woman just shy a score years?"

Neal seemed to consider that for a moment, then shook his head. "That would be a bit different."

"How so?"

"Being as how I'm an old dog, and succumbing to the charms of a woman is an old trick, I can see myself doing it. Actually being able to touch a *sylvanesti* is a *new* trick."

"You could learn new tricks if you wanted." Gena laid a thick piece of wood on the fire. "I could teach you." Though it came out innocently, she immediately looked up to see how he would interpret her words. *I didn't mean I could teach him about loving a* sylvanesti*—or did I?*

Neal raised an eyebrow, then smiled. "I'm thinking there is one trick you might be able to teach me, if you wouldn't mind."

"Yes?"

He jerked his head toward her baggage. "I saw you packing away some things that Aarundel called flash-drakes. I gather they are some sort of weapon, but I don't recall seeing their like before."

"The Dwarves made them first, and still make the best, but even the Haladina have begun to manufacture them. It is a new weapon, however. These flashdrakes belonged to Durriken." Gena hesitated, instantly afraid of Neal's reaction to what she would say next. "He was my lover, a Man, like yourself. The Haladina murdered him in Aurdon."

Neal did grow a bit distant as she spoke, but remained keenly interested in what she said. "Your grandfather told me of Durriken and how he got the *insigne nuptialis* back. I think I would have liked him."

"Stories about you intrigued Rik quite a bit." Gena stared down at the fire. "He and I were together for three years, then the Haladina took him away from me."

"So Berengar wants to save his family in this, and you're looking to avenge Durriken's death?"

"I guess so. It started as an expedition to help a friend recover Cleaveheart and Wasp, but Rik's murder has made it personal. I carry the flashdrakes because they, and this ring, are all I have to remember him by. The Haladina killed him with the Death of Eight Cuts."

Neal winced. "That is not a nice way to die." He shook his head. "I guess things have changed a great deal, because I can't imagine a *sylvanesti* in the arms of a Haladina."

"Nor can I. The Haladina have taken to setting gems in their teeth to remind themselves of the days of the Reithrese."

Neal looked confused for a moment, then glanced again at her baggage. "So will you show me how to use these flashdrakes?"

She nodded. "We will have to walk away from camp, because they are very loud."

Neal stood and brushed his hands off on the thighs of his breeches. "Stulklirn, will you watch Berengar and make certain he is not harmed while he sleeps?"

The Dreel nodded and crouched down at Berengar's head. "Watch, I will." The creature's feral grin suggested to Gena that the Dreel would have waited an eternity just to see the moment of terror in Berengar's eyes when he awoke and found a Dreel hunched over him.

Neal hefted the saddlebags containing the flashdrakes and led her off on a little path away from the grove. They hiked over a series of leaf-covered hills and descended into a little valley with steep walls that ran roughly twenty-five yards before it curved off to the south. "This should channel the noise away from the grove, I'm thinking."

Gena nodded and cast about for a suitable target. She saw a large mushroom, from which she tore the cap and walked on down the gully. She leaned it up against a tree that had fallen across the ravine, then returned to Neal's side. "That should do."

Neal set the saddlebags down, then took a step back from them. Gena dropped to one knee and opened the one with the flashdrakes. She took them out and handed one to him, then carefully explained and walked through each step of loading her weapon. Neal aped her movements, studying her intently, and asked no question.

Gena found being under his scrutiny both challenging and thrilling. She worked methodically and slowly to load the flashdrake and, in doing so, found the job rather akin to the various ritualized forms of magick she had learned from Larissa. That helped her overcome some of her nervousness and gave her confidence. Neal seemed to appreciate her precision because he worked to imitate her exactly in all she did.

It struck her as being utterly incongruous that she was standing there in Ispar teaching a legend how to operate a weapon that had not come into use until well after his death. That she was even able to speak with him after she had spent her life idolizing him and seeking knowledge about him was unbelievable. That she might have something to offer him, that was the sort of thing of which fantasies were spun.

Finally she drew the flashdrake's talon back and pointed the weapon at the toadstool. "There will be one initial flash, then a larger one and some thunder. Brace yourself."

Neal nodded and she pulled the trigger. The talon struck a spark down into the pan, and the priming powder flared up bright red, then collapsed into a gout of smoke that obscured the target. She held her hand steady, then the pistol charge went off. The thunder from the flashdrake hid any sound of the lead ball hitting the target, but when the smoke cleared, the toadstool was gone, as well as a bit of the tree.

Neal smiled sheepishly, a yard back from where he had been standing. "It *was* loud, wasn't it?"

"Indeed. Come, let's see how I did."

The both of them ran down to where the toadstool had been and laughed as they pulled up short. The fallen tree showed a splintery furrow where the ball had plowed into the wood a bit to the right of the toadstool. The beige target had been knocked from the log by the impact and lay on the ground. Gena picked it up, inspected it, and frowned. "We are shooting a long way off, and I am not that good a shot."

Neal fingered the bullet groove. "Were that ball an arrow and the toadstool a warrior's chest, you'd have skewered his liver. And the way it splintered the wood, I'm thinking armor's of little use."

Gena set the toadstool back in place. "Your turn."

They returned to the saddlebags, and Gena watched as Neal loaded the weapon. The only mistake he almost made was in reaching for the finer-grained priming powder for the primary charge, but when she pointed out the difference, he nodded. "Big grains for the big fire, small grains for the small fire."

"Exactly."

He smiled and cocked the flashdrake. "I'm ready, am I? How do I aim?"

"Close your left eye." She reached up to block it, but he pulled his head aside. "Sorry. Look down the barrel and keep it pointed at your target. At this range the bullet will drop an inch or two. Compensate."

"Done." He smiled like a child playing with a new toy. "Brace yourself."

The talon fell, and in the second before the main charge exploded, Gena noticed how Neal's thickly muscled arm held the heavy flashdrake rock-still. Then the flashdrake vomited fire and smoke, and an earsplitting roar echoed through the forest. As the thick white smoke evaporated, Gena saw no trace of the mushroom's cap.

Neal looked at the smoking flashdrake. "It has quite a jolt to it."

"Rik used to call that 'recoil.' It varies with how much powder you use, and too much can make the flashdrake explode in your hands." Her ears ringing, Gena started to walk down to the target area. "Poor-made imitations of these Dwarven handcannons have been known to kill the person using them."

Neal fell into step beside her. "Slower to use than a bow, but not an arbalest." He stopped as they came to a circle of toadstool fragments, and squatted. Using the gun, he pointed at some of the larger pieces. "Looks like I hit it a bit high and to the left."

"But you hit it on the first shot!" Gena clapped her hands. "You are very good."

"Or very lucky."

"Or," called Berengar from the firing line, "you have

discovered what we did in Aurdon—these things take no skill at all to use. This is why they are restricted from the lower classes."

Neal stood and nodded to Berengar. "Had the Steel Pack had these weapons, we would have swept the Reithrese from the face of Skirren a year or two before the Elven crusade."

"Thank the gods there are few enough of them, and most of those so wretched that they kill those who use them." Berengar dropped his left hand to the hilt of his rapier. "Those flashdrakes require no skill and bring no honor on those who use them."

"Still, they are clearly effective." Neal looked at Gena. "This Durriken of yours must have killed at least two of the Haladina who took him before they killed him."

Gena shook her head and remembered how small Rik had looked stretched out on the table at the Fisher mansion. "He did not shoot his assailants."

Berengar's head came up. "When we found his body, the guns had not even been drawn from the scabbards he had fashioned for them."

Neal's eyebrow rose. "In the time I have slept, the Haladina have become very stealthy, it seems."

"Very." Berengar spat on the ground. "And they have Riveren allies who provide them a safe haven in Aurdon."

"Well, we shall see about that, will we not?" Gena smiled and tried to mediate between the two of them. She headed off any growing argument by agreeing to let Neal practice more with the flashdrakes while she enlisted Berengar in helping her forage for some herbs to spice the gruel she intended to prepare as their meal.

Away from Neal, Berengar could not have been more pleasant or solicitous. He did not shy from her touch and bantered with her effortlessly. He worked to anticipate her needs and very much assumed the leadership role she had expected of him. He did not shy from performing tasks that would have been beneath his station in Aurdon, and some of the camaraderie they had shared on the road returned to their camp.

Gena knew Neal had good reason for his distance—he had become alive again in a world that had passed him by, but she could not help but judge him harshly for it. His inquisitive nature stood him in good stead in adapting, and the varied volume and cadence of the flashdrake reports suggested he had already begun to experiment with the weapons. Still, his willingness and desire to learn about the weaponry of the day mocked his resistance to let down his guard concerning her, and that hurt.

She toyed for a second with the idea of sleeping with Berengar, but she rejected it when she realized she would be doing that to punish Neal. She wondered if, in the same way bringing him back had allowed her to feel superior to Larissa in the realm of magick, seducing Neal would allow her to feel superior to her grandaunt. The instant that question entered her mind, she blushed and felt ashamed. To do such a thing for so petty a reason would dishonor her and mock what Neal and Larissa had shared. While Neal had been dead for five hundred years, to his mind not a day had passed since he died thinking of Larissa.

Neal returned to the camp with the flashdrakes in their scabbards, fastened against the flat of his stomach. "This is how Durriken wore them?"

Gena nodded. "He could draw them quickly and use them while riding."

"While riding?" Neal looked at Berengar. "And you said these required no skill."

"I stand by my statement. Weapons for old men who can no longer use a sword, or in Durriken's case, a small man who made good use of a weapon that extended his reach."

Neal shrugged his way out of the leather harness holding the flashdrakes in place. "I'm thinking I'm not that small, but I don't know if I'm too old to be using this sword."

Berengar smiled effortlessly. "I think it is good you have practiced with the handcannons."

Stulklirn made a rude buzzing noise. "Denman idlespeaks."

Berengar glared at the Dreel. "I have dogs that would not deign to take your scent, much less worry your ragged pelt with tooth."

Stulklirn's eyes brightened and his lips smacked together.

Neal frowned at the Dreel. "Stulklirn, be still. My lord Count, I was thinking I was, that you might honor me by teaching me all that I have yet to learn about swordsmanship. Same as these flashdrakes are new, this rapier you wear was not known in my time. The rapier Aarundel had made for me still isn't familiar. If you would be willing."

Berengar nodded gladly.

Neal smiled broadly. "Shall we pad the blades?"

The count shook his head. "I won't touch you, and I won't let you touch me." He drew his blade with a flourish, then saluted Genevera. "For you, my lady."

Chapter 36

Hatred Fills a Heart of Ice

Early Winter
A.R. 499
My 536th Year
The Present

Being dead for so long must have played hob with my brain, because I should have seen the confrontation with Berengar coming more clearly than I did. I had been brought back to life to help him deal with a situation that he saw as incredibly important. I understood that, but given the magnitude of what I needed to understand about my own situation, his concerns slipped a bit back in line.

I also realized that I had been dealing with him as I would have the Red Tiger. While they looked very much alike, they were not the same person. They shared a drive to accomplish their goals, to be certain, but the Red Tiger had risen from poverty and slavery to revolt against the Reithrese. Berengar came from a noble family and seemed to have an underlying arrogance, which he needed to sustain his mission. As with most people, he saw himself as the hero of his own epic, but his arrogance made him think that others must see him as a hero as well.

His attitude toward the flashdrakes surprised me because I would have thought he was smart enough to see how powerful they were. Actually, he was, but of the two courses of action open to him, he chose the reactionary one. By restricting the handcannons he guaranteed his people would not be able to deal with them. He should have embraced them, learned about them, and learned ways to use and defeat them. An army armed with flashdrakes would be formidable, but knowing their weaknesses would make them vulnerable.

For example, it struck me that these flashdrakes would be singularly useless when a battle was being fought in a rainstorm. Granted, fighting under adverse conditions is never desired, but soldiers can be trained to deal with almost anything. Creating a unit like the Steel Pack that practiced moving and attacking in driving rainstorms would allow him to destroy flashdrakers and win against all sorts of odds.

Arrogance sometimes leads to vanity, and that often causes an overvaluation of honor. I should know because part of my anger at Aarundel and Larissa in using Genevera to bring me back to life revolved around my pride at not having used magick for healing during my career. Vanity, pure and simple. Granted, I had a lot to learn about the world, but being alive definitely beat eternity in a stone house in Cygestolia.

Being brought back from the dead left me with a few questions about myself, which was why I asked Berengar if he would be willing to fence with me. Going into the assault on Alatun, I had seen myself as old and slow and breaking down. The magick that had revived me had not cleared up any old scars, but it might have taken the edge off the damage done by aging. Then again, my attitude slowly turning positive might have done the same thing. Either way, the result was the same—I had no idea how good I was in comparison to the contemporary world.

Berengar appeared ready to go immediately, but I held up a hand and stretched my legs out a little. "Lying in the tomb left me a bit stiff." Joints popped and muscles slowly loosened. I laughed when my right shoulder cracked like a dry twig under heavy tread, Berengar smiled, and Gena winced.

I wish she had not done that. She looked too much like her grandaunt to me, which meant I kept thinking back to times Larissa and I had spent together, trying to remember if I had seen that expression or heard those words before. I did not mind drifting back into memories of Larissa, but coming out of them hurt quite a bit. Whatever resentment I built from that pain I found myself directing toward Genevera—none of which she deserved.

Just as I realized I should not judge Berengar by the Red Tiger, I knew comparing Gena with Larissa was unfair. Genevera was very intelligent, witty, friendly, and beautiful. She compared favorably with her grandaunt, yet because Larissa was untouchable, there remained an aura of mystery around her that held her apart from me. It left her a creature of fantasy, and while I had seen Larissa under similar circumstances to those I was experiencing with Genevera, Gena's approachability helped distance me from her.

The other factor that kept a wall between us was how Berengar acted around Gena. Though she might not have been aware of it, I had seen enough moon-eyed warriors chasing after women in garrison towns to know the look of one smitten. His deference to her, respect of her, and resentment of time she and I spent together told me just how much he thought he loved her. As is true with many honorable men, he hid his intentions so as not to complicate our mission, but I suspected when we returned to Aurium, he would make a clean breast of his feelings.

Suitably stretched out, I drew my rapier from my baggage, raised it in a salute to Gena as had Berengar, then dropped into a low guard. I kept the point of my blade in line with his chest at heart level, with my right hand and blade hilt at waist level, just off my right hip. The blade's balance and slender tapering told me that the thrust was the most important tactic in sword fighting now, but the razored edge on the blade also suggested that it had its uses as well. Even so, the crushing, slashing attacks to which I had become accustomed and in which I had become accomplished were clearly archaic.

I took a quick step forward, extended, and lunged, but Berengar parried me wide, then twisted his wrist and riposted to my chest. He whipped the blade away before it could skewer me, but he was fast and very steady. The parry had been strong, and Berengar recovered from his lunge before I had brought my sword back into a proper guard.

I nodded respectfully to him. "You are very good."

"You did not come at me hard."

"That does not diminish your speed and your skill." I raised my sword and saluted him. "Perhaps you would be willing to instruct me in the current ways of fighting?"

The question surprised him, but after a moment's consideration he consented and my lessons began immediately. He started with forms and guards in that first session, and over the next three weeks we progressed on up to some of the more complicated systems of fighting. The lack of spare rapiers meant we had to use sticks to simulate a second sword when we tried that form, and we likewise had to improvise bucklers from tree bark. Berengar professed a preference for sword and dagger fighting, and I could definitely see that as likely the most common sort of swordplay in an urban setting.

When we fenced, Berengar maintained an edge, and he took great pride in remaining my master at swordplay. While he had taught me everything I knew about this new way of fighting, he had not taught me everything *he* knew. On the other hand, I think I learned a bit more than he expected me to pick up. I knew I had not seen him fight full out, nor had he seen all I had to offer, which made our fencing matches exciting.

From the grove outside Jarudin, Stulklirn had taken us directly to his normal range in Irtysh. Aarundel and I, when Stulklirn joined us, postulated that a Dreel could either use the Elven *circus translatio* or end up in any place he knew well enough to identify inside his mind. We also discovered we did not need the chains to travel when working through a Dreel. In the same way that Shijef had taken us directly from Jammaq to Cygestolia, Stulklirn was able to take us from Jarudin to Irtysh without using any of the circuit groves along the way.

From there we worked almost directly north. We bought more horses and what little supplies we could convince folks to surrender, then headed on our way. People appeared concerned with our traveling toward the Rimefields at this time of year less because of the weather than because Tacorzi was known to extend his range in the winter. Going north during the winter, a number of people asserted, was akin to committing suicide.

While no one would sign on with us as a guide, everyone was willing to share stories about Tacorzi. Descriptions ranged from a pale-blue multitentacled squid-thing that waited in the snow for travelers the way an antlion ambushes its prey, to a ghoul with a legion of skeletal zombies at its beck and call. The latter suited Takrakor better than the former, but we heard about the ice-squid enough that I began to wonder if it was not one of those bone-creatures I had seen the Reithrese use at Alatun.

Ultimately we did not need a guide, because I knew exactly where we were going. I could not have pointed it out on a map, but this close to Tacorzi and Wasp, I just *knew* where we were headed. Of course, knowing the creature laired in the ice caverns at the base of a smoking mountain helped a lot, especially when we crested foothills and saw the snow-clad mountain with a plume of gray smoke smearing the blue sky.

We found the entrance to the ice cavern late in the afternoon, so we pulled back from it and made a camp a considerable distance up in a mountain valley. Not only could I get a sense of Takrakor's presence, but some of the malevolence was leaking through as well. I recalled quite well the last time I faced him, and I doubted five centuries would have diminished his power.

"I think we may have made a mistake, my friends." I looked away from the small fire burning in our little cave as I shared my conclusion. "Takrakor was very deadly the last time we met. We should have had the Consilliarii send a troop of wizards to root him out."

Berengar frowned at that idea. "I hardly think a powerful sorcerer would willfully lair in a hole in the ice. I agree that caution is warranted, but we are not as weak a group as you might think. You and I are formidable warriors, and the Dreel is very strong. Lady Genevera is a magick user of unparalleled skill in my experience. Could not this malevolence you feel be nothing more than his residual hatred of you for killing him?"

"Berengar does make sense on that point, Neal."

"He does, Gena, but then we have to wonder what this Tacorzi is and how Takrakor got here."

Berengar nodded. "I agree, Neal, these are questions we need to answer. Let us reconnoiter the ice cavern tomorrow. If we cannot destroy the creature we find there—if there *is* any creature there—we will retreat and summon more help. With the Dreel we can have more people here in a day or two."

I frowned for a moment because Berengar had advanced the course of action I saw as most logical—if nothing else we had to see what was there. "I agree." I leaned over and pulled the saddlebag with the flashdrakes in it into my lap. "If you do not mind, Gena, I will take these with me tomorrow."

"And I thought you more confident in your abilities with a rapier, Neal." Berengar shook his head. "You do not need those things."

"No disrespect to you as a swordmaster, Berengar, but I will bring these for one very simple reason."

"And that is?"

I smiled. "I had no idea what they were when I first saw them. I'm thinking that if Takrakor is behind the Tacorzi legend, up here he'll not have seen them either. And that means, dishonorable or not, these might be just enough to surprise or distract him so we can get away from him."

The next day dawned bitter cold, with the sky so blue that it might have been an ocean suspended over our heads. No snow had fallen in the night, and the wind had scoured the snowscape down to the hard crust. The snow's frozen skin supported us for a second with each step, then gave way, plunging us knee-deep in snow. We barked our shins on the crust with the next step, repeating the whole cycle with monotonous regularity and fair discomfort.

The crunch of snow under my feet, and the wind's cold

kiss where my scarf and hat left the skin near my eyes open, reminded me of my days as a youth in the Roclaws. As a child, I had always welcomed snow because it transformed the world into a wonderful playground where forts could be built and snowball wars fought. Growing into adulthood, I had seen another side to winter and did not relish the expeditions mounted to find survivors of villages swept away by avalanches. The images of stiff and frozen corpses perfectly preserved danced through my brain, and all too many of them wore my face.

The round tunnel led down through the ice at a fairly sharp angle, but cracks and ripples in the surface made climbing down not as difficult as I might have thought at first. Wearing the flashdrake scabbard over my heavy coat did hinder me somewhat, but the tunnel leveled out quickly enough. It pushed on through blue shadows for a good two hundred yards. Down here, where very little sunlight could penetrate, the walls glowed azure and made our vaporous breaths a light-blue fog.

Down inside the tunnel I felt no movement in the air, which eased the chill only a little. Where my breath plumed up from within the scarf, the vapor managed to freeze on the forelock that had escaped my woolen cap. I had to be careful when blinking my eyes lest they freeze shut as well. Inside my mittens my fingers felt numb, but I kept moving them to keep them limber. Feeling colder than a corpse in my feet, hands, and buttocks, I moved deeper into that blue hell.

I stopped just beyond where the tunnel widened into a huge ice cavern. Though rendered in ice, many of the decorations and much of the architecture came from Jammaq. Columns of ice had been sculpted into bones, and countless tortured faces stared back at me through glassy walls. What I took to be gravel crunched underfoot, but when I looked down, all I could see was the pale ivory of bone fragments.

My companions entered the chamber and had the wisdom to spread out on either side, with Gena and Berengar to my left and Stulklirn to my right. We all stared at the thing lurking in the center of the cavern bowl. It hunched down on a hillock knitted of bones and had bodies in various states of disrepair scattered about it. Unblemished by rot because of the cold, the bodies looked more like dolls that had been rough-used by children at play than once-living creatures.

The thing in the middle—Tacorzi seemed to suit it more than Takrakor—raised its half-fleshed head and gave me a diamond-studded smile. "I knew you would come, Neal." A skeletal hand clicked bony fingers against the hilt of the knife still borne in a harness on its chest. "I knew you had been consigned to the same limbo as had I. Now we will both be free."

It raised the skeletal left arm, and I saw both flesh and tattered muscles dangle like fringe from the limb. The bony hand probed the gaping wound, the ancient, splintered wound, in its chest. "You killed me as I killed you, Neal. Your Elven friends saved you even as my Mistress saved me. I have waited very long for this, very long, very long. . . ."

I studied the charnel house surroundings for a moment. "I think I had the better of the resting places."

"Utility is preferable to comfort." The skeletal creature stared at me as if trying to catalog the differences between us. "Here I nest next to the bosom of my goddess, still her servant despite her cruel judgment of me."

"Your people are gone, and your empire is not even a memory in the minds of Men. You should have given up long ago."

The monster continued to peer at me. "The memories of your despair and pain still please me."

I shivered, and not from the cold. "Why did you do that to me? Why did you rape my brain? Why not take the sword and be done with it?"

Tacorzi's jaw dropped and quivered in a ghoulish imitation of laughter. "Do you not know? *Khlephnaft* must be won in combat or freely given to another. Back then, I could not win it by force of arms, but now I would have no such problem."

As Tacorzi spoke, its lethargy fell away. It heaved itself up and came upright, but not on legs. From the point where its pelvis should have been, I saw only a skeletal body woven of pelvises and leg bones. The creature, its leathery flesh creaking as the body shifted, rose up, and I saw the hillock upon which it had rested was really an enormous skeletal simulacrum of a snake's body.

Worse yet, curving up and over its shoulders, bony tentacles wove back and forth akin to cobras swaying to a minstrel's flute tune. Four of the eight ended in animal skulls that snapped their jaws at us and flashed fangs. Two, a wolf and a polar bear, still maintained part of their pelts. The other two were bare of flesh, and I was certain one was that of a wolf. The other, by Stulklirn's snarled reaction, could have been from a Dreel.

The other four tentacles plunged down into the tangle of bodies lying around Tacorzi's coils. With a harsh snapping sound, they bored into holes in the small of the backs of some corpses. Bodies lurched to their feet. Shambling forward, the zombi quartet oriented on Berengar and Gena. The biting heads turned their attention to Stulklirn.

I shook my mittens free of my hands—the mittens dangled from cords tied to my wrists—and drew my sword. "Leave them, it's me you want and my dagger back that I want."

The half-dead thing shook its head. "*You,* I already know how to kill." He brought his hands up to his face, then slashed them down and away. "I have been a long time in improving the spell. You will die *now*!"

Beginning as a burning spark, the spell he had once before used to destroy me shot out at me. I knew I had to move, had to escape it, but even as I thought about dodging to my right, the spell shifted to track me. As it closed the distance between us, it grew from a spark to a burning cross. I heard it sizzling through the air and actually began to feel cheated out of my second attempt at life.

Suddenly Stulklirn dove in front of me, and the spell hit him full force in the chest. The Dreel howled in pain and fur flashed into an acrid, cloying smoke. As he went down, curling in on himself, I leaped up over his rolling body and slashed the rapier through the tentacle with the bear's head. The skull flew free and shattered on the ground.

Gena gestured at the ragged corpse nearest her, and its threadbare clothes immediately ignited into flame. At once the humanoid body collapsed, and the tentacle reared back as if a viper coiling to strike. The body melted and spread out, a burning mass of putrid rot and old bones, while Tacorzi repeatedly jammed the burning end of the tentacle into the cavern floor to put the fire out.

The scent of burning flesh and Dreel fur assaulted me, bringing to the charnel cavern the scent it should have had from the beginning. Gena readied another spell and cast it at Tacorzi as Berengar sliced another zombi free of its bony lifeline. I beheaded the Dreel tentacle, but the two wolves got my hip and shoulder on the left side. Their assault slackened for a moment as Tacorzi's magick met and exploded Gena's spell, and had I not been wearing thick winter gear, they would have torn me open.

As I curled my left arm around the tentacle biting me at the shoulder and started to cut at Tacorzi with my rapier, I saw Stulklirn roll to his feet. He bellowed a challenge tinged with pain, then raised his paws, crossed them, and slashed them apart in imitation of what Tacorzi had done. A reddish-yellow spark shot from his furred paws and spiraled in at Tacorzi. It struck the monster in a shower of sparks, sending a shudder through Tacorzi's body. A second later I severed the tentacle and it fell to pieces around me.

"Magick I make I can unmake!" Tacorzi cackled. His hands began all manner of arcane motions even as a cruciform design on his chest began to darken and run with rotting flesh. The tentacle Gena had previously burned battered her back against the cavern wall. As she slumped to the floor, one of the zombies managed to jump Berengar, taking him down, while the wolf tentacle gnawing at my hip managed to pull me down.

Stulklirn crushed the wolf skull with one swat of his right paw, then crouched over me. "My magick kill will."

"Not if he unmakes it." I slapped the Dreel on the shoulder. "Circle him. Think of Jarudin."

Casting my sword aside, I stood and began to run at Tacorzi. I assumed the sight of me running unarmed at him would be quite a distraction and limit his ability at concentrating on his unmaking of the quartering spell. His jaw did drop open and his hand motions slackened just a bit, but even his curiosity at my actions did not make him stop his work.

I drew both flashdrakes, cocked the talons, and thrust the handcannons at him. The fleshy half of his face raised an eyebrow, but he saw no threat. I assumed that was because he did not know what they were, but part of me feared he knew it was because, already being dead, he could not be killed again.

I pulled the triggers.

One ball exploded his left hand, spraying finger and wrist bones around before it blew through ribs and shattered the shoulder blade on its way out. The other ball shattered the Reithrese corpse-wizard's jaw. Glittering like dewdrops in sunlight, diamond teeth spun through the air. Knowing how a toothache had destroyed his concentration before, I hoped the horror at having part of his death replayed would cause him all sorts of problems.

Surrounding the both of us, a black, white, and brindle light pattern began and ended in the outline of a Dreel. Dropping the flashdrakes, I grabbed a flailing bone tentacle and heaved on it. Tacorzi spilled forward off his coils. Hauling for all I was worth—despite the sharp pain in shoulder and hip—I pulled Tacorzi along with me as I dove into the Dreel and the world of the Elven *circus translatio*.

I do not know how long it actually took for us to complete the journey to the grove east of Jarudin. We passed through hills and mountains, lakes, towns, and vales, as we flew through that opposite-landscape. I saw no one, as I had before, but my attention remained focused on Tacorzi. I do not know if anyone saw us as a ghost on our journey, but I had no doubt that if someone had, a bard would be singing about the sight soon enough.

At some point during the journey it occurred to me that the premise upon which I had based my plan could have been wrong. Before my death I would have been willing to trust my hunches, but that had gotten me dead once before. If this journey did not kill Tacorzi, I had managed to translocate him from the frozen north to within a day's ride of Jarudin. I had no idea how fast he could travel, configured as he was, but inflicting that sort of danger on the kin of folks I'd known generations before struck me as a poor way to announce my return to the land of the living.

As we arrived in the grove, I realized the one huge mistake I had made. Having dived into the Dreel, I dived out at the other end of the trip. I landed on my left shoulder, sending pain through me, then I rolled and kept rolling. I rolled on out of the grove and in doing so saved my life.

Tacorzi did not land in much better shape than I did, but I was much smaller than he was. As his body came into the grove, it bounced off the ground and slammed into trees on the other side of the grove. That collision sheered limbs from both trees and Tacorzi. Bits and pieces of bones pelted me as they flew out from between the trees. Those that hit me tumbled on after leaving my coat stained with white powder, and a blizzard of bone dust filled the grove itself.

I let things settle for a minute and made certain I had not been hurt. Because I had no indication Tacorzi still lived, I got to my feet and walked back to the grove. A black puddle, looking like the corrupted yolk of a giant egg lay near the edge of the tree circle. Stulklirn walked around the perimeter, shaking white dust from his coat. His fur now bore a white cross on his chest, but he seemed not to have noticed the change.

I shrugged off my coat and massaged my shoulder. "Are you hurt, Stulklirn?"

The Dreel shook his head. "Hurt I am not."

"Are you certain?" I rubbed my chest reflexively. "I know what that spell did to me a long time ago."

"Dreel-friend you are, so know this you may." He pointed at what had once been Takrakor. "The gods made men to kill men. To the Dreel for prey Bok gave sorcerers." He exposed his teeth in a feral grin. "Magick they have, magick we *are*. This is why lifeblack has pooled."

Chapter 37

The Hero as a Man

Early Winter
A.R. 499
The Present

More than the stitch in her side and the throbbing pain on her cheek, Gena felt the cold as she slowly awakened. She found herself slumped in a corner between an ice wall and the cavern floor. The fire her spell had made out of a zombi still guttered a bit, holding the azure shadows at bay, but it produced little heat. She shoved her hands into her mittens again, then found her hat and made sure to tuck the numb tips of her ears beneath the woolen band when she pulled it on.

Even though her toes and parts of her legs felt numb, she was able to move around. Her ribs ached on the right side, and her right eye had already begun to swell half-closed, but she resisted using a diagnostic spell on herself. She knew her injuries were not bad and that the greatest threat to her welfare came from the cold. Her magick could do something to ward off the cold, but if she used all her strength healing herself, she might freeze to death afterward.

She staggered to her feet and felt surprised when the little cry of pain she uttered echoed back to her through the silence. *Am I alone?* Panic rippled through her, but she fought it down. "This is no time to be jumping to any sort of conclusions about anything."

Gena looked first toward where the thing had been. She shivered, but less from the cold than from the memory of what Takrakor had become. She had always used the name Takrakor as something that defined evil in her mind, but Tacorzi superseded the worst. Takrakor, as she had heard in many stories, had been ambitious, and that she could understand. Tacorzi, on the other hand, remained alive while dead, maintained by a hatred for a Man he himself had slain five centuries previously. It was malignant and insane.

She saw neither the creature nor Neal, and that worried her. The Dreel appeared to be gone as well, so she drifted off to her left toward a mound in the midst of a bone-strewn mire. The stink of rotted meat almost overwhelmed her as she approached, but the struggling gasp for breath that emanated from the twisted lump in the center drew her on.

Berengar lay in the midst of what had once been a zombi or two. Viscous black fluids saturated his clothes. Deep down, where great rents had been opened in his clothes to his flesh and beyond, she saw his blood frozen bright red in his wounds. A bone-spear poked through the left leg of his thick leather trousers. One of his ears hung half bitten off, his right shoulder looked dislocated, and his left eye had more red than white in it.

Without a second thought Gena cast a diagnostic spell on him and got some added information. Berengar's nose had been broken, ribs bruised, and one kidney lacerated. She dared not move him because where his blood had not yet clotted, it had frozen, which was likely the only reason he had not yet bled to death from some of the slashes inflicted by the zombies and the flaying whip of a bone tentacle.

She eased herself down onto her knees and concentrated. She mentally listed his injuries and determined for herself which ones were more important and which were less so. Once she had things in a workable order, she set about casting the spells that would bring him as close to functioning as possible without jeopardizing her ability to help them survive in the cold.

Her first spell gently lifted the body from the ground and sealed it in an evergreen cocoon. Brighter bits of green worked along the body, deep within the cocoon, slowly drifting along the cuts and gashes like inchworms. In short order, with a very low energy expenditure on her part, Gena's spell repaired all the holes in Berengar's flesh. She specifically did not have the glowworms leech blood from the bruises, because his body would do that naturally after a number of days. The spell could have done that, but it would have been more expensive in terms of her strength.

The damage to his kidney concerned her the most after making sure he would not leak anymore. As nearly as she could tell, it had been a puncture wound from a zombi weapon. She did not worry so much about blood poisoning from it as she did about making certain that all the little blood vessels were repaired in the organ. The spell she selected for repairing it took more time than the glowworms and cost her far more in terms of energy, but really just employed smaller, smarter versions of the glowworms to do the job.

Once that was taken care of, she used a spell to purge, purify and heighten production of blood. From there she repaired his leg so he could move, put his ear back together, and worked his arm back into the socket. That still left him his bruises, broken nose, ribs, and bloodshot eye, but she had no more strength to use and he had already started to come around.

Berengar winced as he eased himself into a sitting position. "Gena, your face, you have a cut and a bruise."

She nodded. "And your nose has a new bump, and your left eye will swell fully shut in no time."

He tried to laugh, then held his ribs. "I have other injuries, I see."

Gena smiled weakly. "I was able to fix many things, but some will have to heal on their own."

"Where is Neal?"

"I don't know."

"Did he abandon us?"

The disgust in Berengar's voice surprised Gena. "I don't know if he did or not, but I have noticed that Tacorzi is no longer here."

"And the dagger?"

"Gone as well." Gena looked around in the gloom. "Neal's sword and the flashdrakes are on the ground. I cannot tell if the handcannons have been used or not."

The count looked off toward the center of the cavern, then shook his head. "So that thing was a Reithrese?"

She shrugged. "It may once have been. It certainly seemed to know Neal."

"And now he's run off and it's chasing him." Berengar gingerly got to his feet.

"I don't know that Neal ran from the thing." She pointed off toward where Tacorzi had sat. "The flashdrakes are nearer the center than they are the way out of here. Neal and Stulklirn and Tacorzi are just gone."

"I suppose you're right. I think we should collect our things, leave this place, and get back to where we left our supplies. We need fire and food and shelter, none of which we have here." He groaned and wobbled a bit, but managed to stay upright. "Feeling as I do now, I do not believe I want to know what you had to fix."

"Agreed."

Working together, they managed to make the trek from Tacorzi's lair to the cavern in which they had spent the previous evening. Gena made a fire and started melting snow into water for tea while Berengar shucked off his clothes and wrapped himself in blankets. His nose and ribs clearly hurt him, and the bruises on his body were as multicolored as they were oddly shaped, but he bore his wounds stoically. His insistence that she drink and eat before he did marked his concern for her, but he did not protest too much when she volunteered to take the first watch.

"A couple of hours, then you will sleep. Promise me."

Gena did and tossed some more wood onto the fire. She figured their meagre supply would last through the night and into the next day. By then they should be able to travel to more hospitable environs. She smiled and tried to think about more pleasant places to be, both to keep her awake and to keep her mind from wondering if Neal actually had abandoned them. Her efforts failed in both things, and exhausted, she succumbed to sleep before she had a chance to rouse Berengar.

Gena woke with a start when she realized she was sweating. Coming awake, she remembered that she was supposed to be tending the fire. Afraid it had gone out while she dozed, she looked at it and found it burning merrily. That fact and her feeling very warm slowly came together in her sleep-besotted brain. What welded them into a single, coherent thought was seeing Neal squatting across the fire from her.

"How are you, Gena?"

"Hot and sore." She looked from him to Berengar and then over to where Stulklirn lay curled around a huge pile of wood. "Where did that come from?"

"Outside Jarudin."

She shook her head. "But it would take months to get there and back." She glanced at the unconscious Dreel. "Oh."

"We would have been back sooner, but Stulklirn wanted to catch a nap after the initial trip. Gave me time to gather the wood."

"What happened? Where is Tacorzi?"

Neal shrugged as he rubbed his hands together. "Tacorzi is dead."

"How?"

The Man frowned. "Actually, he always was dead, I just let him decay. Walking through the cold, I remembered bodies I'd seen trapped in avalanches and in the mountains by the Reithrese storm. Frozen, they didn't decay. From something Tacorzi said, I assumed he came up here to stop his body from falling apart."

Gena laughed before a twinge in her side stopped her. "His plan didn't work very well."

Neal nodded and gave her a grin that helped ease her pain. "Indeed, he did go to pieces. He built himself up another body the way he did for his brother, but Takrakor only had bones and corpse-crumbs to work with. Anyway, Stulklirn and I dragged him south, and five hundred years of decay caught up with him fast."

"The Dreel is unharmed?" Gena pointed to the white cross on his chest. "He was hit by a very powerful spell."

"Tacorzi meant that spell for me. I guess it didn't affect the Dreel that much."

Gena could tell Neal was being deceptive, but her brain felt too fuzzy to figure out why or where he was hiding something. That conclusion resonated against Berengar's earlier suspicion that they'd been abandoned. She wanted to dismiss her unease instantly—for Neal's return and his thoughtfulness at bringing the wood spoke to his loyalty to his companions—but something stopped her.

Neal tossed another log on the fire, and a shower of sparks obscured him for a moment. "Go back to sleep, Gena. Tomorrow, when we are all set, we will go to Jarudin. I have Wasp, and with it Cleaveheart will once again be mine."

Gena felt much better when she awoke again. Berengar had regained consciousness before she had, and between them, he and Neal had loaded all of their supplies on the horses. While Neal tied Gena's bedroll behind Spirit's saddle, Gena used magick to heal the last of Berengar's injuries, then gratefully partook in a breakfast of tea, traveler's bread, and some currants Neal had brought from the forest outside Jarudin.

The journey through Stulklirn to Jarudin passed so quickly for her that she wondered if she had somehow fallen asleep. She decided she had not, but that her thoughts had moved slowly while her body moved so fast. That was just as well, because she had allowed herself to brood about Neal and the fear his absence had planted in her.

Since before she could remember remembering, her grandfather and grandaunt had sung Neal's praises. She could recall when she became conscious of the fact that Neal was a Man, not an Elf, and that fact made him much more of an exotic and romantic figure in her mind. It made him unique and different and filled her with a desire to know all she could about him. For almost two hundred fifty years, when her studies and travels had allowed it, she had studied Neal and the trail of stories he had left in his wake.

Truths about herself and Neal and their relationship began to dawn on her slowly. She saw that she had viewed him as a hero first and a Man second, which was not surprising, given how her kin had presented Neal to her. In seeing him as a hero, she filled in any gaps in his life, any details she could not learn, with things suitably heroic. His Humanity, which lay at the core of everything he did, became lost behind the legend he had become.

Besides not taking his humanity into account, she realized she had been expecting a lot more from him than he had delivered, and that caused some resentment on her part. She had spent centuries learning about him, dreaming about him, and drawing conclusions about him. In her mind she had played out fantasies and adventures in which they had been able to travel together. She had already decided how he would react to her, and her musings built one on another to fashion a whole relationship that Neal was presently not living up to.

The fact that Neal knew nothing of her imagined relationship with him, and therefore could not react properly to it, had not occurred to her until now. In her fantasies Neal never would have abandoned her. He would have torn Tacorzi apart with his bare hands, then would have tended to her injuries with the same facility he had shown in killing the Reithrese monster. In truth Neal had not abandoned her, but had returned after destroying Tacorzi, yet the fact that he had not done it in the way she would have imagined him doing it left doubt in her mind and room for distrust.

She felt uneasy in allowing herself even a touch of distrust about Neal, but she acknowledged that she had no idea what he was thinking. His initial anger with her made sense, but he calmed down and seemed to accept his place in their quest. At least that was how she saw it, but she wanted to know how *he* saw it. Was he just an adjunct to Berengar's quest, a companion who would facilitate the completion of their mission, or did he have his own agenda? And if he did, what sort of agenda would survive five centuries in the grave?

Her musings ended when they arrived in the grove a day's ride from Jarudin. Her horse's hooves kicked up a lot of bone dust as he trotted on into the circle of trees. She briefly recalled Neal's explanation of what had happened to Tacorzi, which is why she reined her horse away from the black circle within which all the grass had died. She urged her mount on out of the circle, then swung from the saddle. She caught a stirrup with her hand and managed to stay on her feet even though her legs wanted to collapse.

Berengar rode up beside her and looked down with surprise. "Come on, there are still a couple of hours of daylight. We can make headway on the journey to the capital."

Neal came over on Scurra and stopped directly in Berengar's path. "We can leave tomorrow."

"No, the sooner we get there, the sooner we can be in Aurdon with Cleaveheart and end all this. If we delay, more people might die."

Neal hunched forward, resting both hands on the saddle pommel. "Son, if we push on today, *I* will die. I'm tired. I'm stopping." He pointed off to the west. "If you want to ride on to Jarudin, we'll meet you there."

"Fine, give me the dagger."

"I don't think so."

"What?"

Neal straightened back up again, and Gena got the impression he was not as tired as he had made himself out to be. "To you this dagger is nothing but an artifact that is the key to a puzzle you need to solve. To me it's a weapon I've used for years. It's mine, and I'm not giving it over to you just because you want to ride fast to the capital."

Berengar dropped a hand to the hilt of his sword. "You might wish to rethink your decision."

"Unlikely." Neal nodded once, and the Dreel swatted Berengar from his saddle. The count's horse bolted forward as Berengar crashed to the ground. He started to come up, but Stulklirn pressed him back down to the earth with a paw.

"You foul coward!"

Neal laughed. "You are fatigued, my lord Count, and not thinking clearly. Rest with us here and you will see things clearly in the morning."

Gena was pleased to see that Berengar appeared to be in a better humor in the morning. He rose slowly and moved as if a bit achy, then straightened up and walked almost normally when he noticed the Dreel shadowing his every move. He bowed to Gena and Neal, then spoke to them in a solemn voice.

"Please, I beg forgiveness for my actions last night. I . . ." He hesitated as if finding words were not easy. "My family is in jeopardy. I realize now that I had always hoped for a simple solution to all this business, but it has become very complex, from Durriken's death to your resurrection and our journey to the north. We started in the spring and here it is the winter. I want to be back with my family and let them know I have—we have—succeeded in saving them. All this is urgent to me, and I lack perspective."

Neal nodded. "Apology accepted. I understand why you want this to be over soon. Believe me when I tell you that because I started the trouble, I want to see it through to the finish as much as you do."

They breakfasted in silence mostly, then saddled up and headed out. Gena knew she could still use another day of rest, but Berengar's urgency infected her and left her impatient to be gone. Stulklirn led the way and Berengar followed him. Gena and Neal hung back a bit and occasionally lost sight of their companions.

Neal studied the landscape and shook his head. "This looks so much as it was when I first rode here with your grandfather, yet the edges of this forest have been nibbled away. Back then the last half of the journey came within the precincts of the forests." He pointed to the scattered farms and the milling herds dotting the rolling meadows. "No humans in Ispar owned farms—they were all slaves on Reithrese plantations."

"Except the Haladina."

"True, they were mercenaries and were very loyal to the Reithrese."

The wide road leading toward the capital impressed Neal when they started traveling on it. Heading in toward the city, they found the route became more populated, and they passed through a number of small villages that existed solely to serve the traffic in- and outbound from Jarudin. They took a meal in one during the early afternoon, then pushed on hard and reached the capital at dusk.

At Berengar's insistence they rode directly to the Imperial palace and demanded an audience with the emperor. The guards protested, but one of them went off anyway and returned quickly with orders to admit them and escort them to the Reithrese tower.

While other soldiers took their horses away, an even dozen imperial guardsmen marched them into the tower. To Gena the tower seemed unchanged from her earlier visit. At the sight of it Neal grew quiet, and when he crossed the threshold, he pulled his cloak tightly about himself.

Gena gently touched him on the shoulder. "What is wrong?"

He shook his head. "This was never a pleasant place when I was alive, but now it seems so . . . *dead.* I guess a lot of things are beginning to sink in concerning the passage of time. Before I saw this tower this way, I could deny *this* Jarudin was the Jarudin I had known. Now . . ."

"But you saw how much my grandfather and grandmother had changed."

"Yes, but I quickly got past that and was communicating with the people inside their bodies. At their cores they had not changed that much, so I found my old friends therein. I can't explain it."

"You don't have to."

"Thank you."

The guards ushered them into what had been the chapel. All of the dirt and debris had been cleared from it since Gena had last been there. Torches burned atop portable stands, and the emperor himself stood in front of the magickal seal. He looked tired to Gena's eyes, but he executed a bow flawlessly. "Welcome, my guests."

Berengar perfunctorily returned the bow. "We have brought to you Neal Roclawzi. He has come to recover his sword, Cleaveheart."

"Oh, has he?" The emperor looked from Berengar to Neal and back again. "You are trying to tell me this is Neal, Knight-Defender of the Empire."

Neal raised an eyebrow. "I would have thought my term in that office would have expired by now."

"It should have, but Beltran the Great was sentimental and never replaced Neal."

Berengar's nostrils flared. "He *is* Neal. He destroyed Tacorzi to recover the dagger that is the key to this ward."

"*If* that thing is dead, I am in your debt." Hardelwick smiled slyly. "Our gratitude does not, however, extend to giving you Cleaveheart."

"What!" Berengar looked ready to explode, and only Neal's grabbing the back of his tunic stopped him from leaping forward to throttle the emperor. "How can you deny Neal his sword?"

The emperor folded his arms. "I would not deny Neal his sword, but what proof have I that this man is a hero who perished five centuries ago? For all I know, this is some thieving wizard you found who has the expertise necessary to defeat these wards. If we discover the sword Cleaveheart in there, you will be asking me to turn an important piece of imperial history over to you. I have no desire to do that."

"You can't do that!"

"Oh, Berengar, I certainly can. I *am* the emperor, after all."

Neal nodded. "He does have a point."

"Thank goodness one of you sees reason."

Gena frowned. "Forgive me, Highness, but you said you *would* turn the blade over to Neal, and we have told you this *is* Neal. What would it take to convince you that this Man is, in reality, Neal Roclawzi?"

The emperor stroked his jaw with his right hand. "Interesting question, that one."

Neal held up his left hand and showed the back of it to the emperor. "I received this scar in this very chamber." He pointed to the sword frozen in the stone at their feet. "The last Reithrese emperor burned my gauntlet from me, which is how I became scarred and how he died."

Hardelwick waved that story away. "*That* is a common tale, sir."

Gena stepped forward. "You know the stories about Neal. You know them all. Ask him about something no one else knows. Ask him something that only Neal would know."

"You could have instructed him."

"It would have taken more than four months to give him the sort of knowledge that you have of him." Gena smiled carefully. "Besides, I give you my word that this man has not been instructed by me or anyone else in the story of Neal's life."

"The word of an Elf. Your willingness to make an oath like that does count for a great deal." The emperor frowned and crossed his bony arms over his chest. "Very well, I will try this little game."

Neal opened his hands. "I will answer if I can."

"Of that I have no doubt." Hardelwick's eyes glittered wetly in the flickering torchlight. "You killed Tashayul in the Roclaws, yet no tale exists that speaks about how you did it. There is no credible story about your battle with him."

Neal nodded. "It wasn't worth one."

"Tashayul dies and his empire begins to crumble and you say his death was not worth a story?" The emperor frowned. "I would find this hard to believe, but I have heard rumors of how he died. My question is this: what did you use to kill him?"

Neal laughed aloud. "*That* is your question?"

"It is."

Berengar clutched at Neal's left sleeve. "Do you know it? Can you answer it?"

Neal nodded.

The emperor bowed his head. "Your answer, then."

Neal laughed again. "As you wish. To kill Tashayul, I used beavers."

Chapter 38

Bittersweet, the Hero's Reward

Winter
A.R. 499
The Present
My 536th Year

Berengar's grip on my sleeve tightened. "Beavers! Are you insane? Beavers?"

He looked stricken, and Gena suddenly seemed to think I had gone mad. Only the emperor had not changed his expression. "Please, explain your answer."

I nodded and slipped my arm from Berengar's grasp. "I fought against Tashayul when I was sixteen years old, and I had hurt him. I had no idea how badly until years later, but hurt him I had. He left his troops in the field and retreated to Reith for healing. Aarundel and I did not attempt to follow him and headed east instead. Over the next three years we watched as his Reithrese army conquered Centisia, Ispar, Barkol, and Irtysh. That brought him to the Roclaws."

I glanced up unconsciously at Tashayul's image above me. "When he returned to battle, he wore huge, heavy armor and appeared to be almost twice as large as he had been when I fought him. I never saw him outside his armor —which is not unusual, given that I only saw him in battle—and he appeared as deadly as he had been when we fought. He was winning his empire rather easily and had even started the construction on Jarudin so it would be his capital.

"About the only thing Aarundel and I noticed as we wandered before and behind his army, was that he had his best engineers with him rather than off building Jarudin here. They organized work parties that created wonderful wooden bridges, to be replaced with stone bridges as soon as possible. That seemed quite logical because the bridges allowed him to get troops across rivers quickly. We thought that was his reason for building them until we saw one bridge built on the site of a ford where the water was no more than ankle deep."

I frowned. "We went into the Roclaws ahead of his army and made our way to my brother's court. He started organizing, and I set out to do anything possible to slow down the Reithrese advance. Because the mountains are split by passes that have been carved out by rivers, I knew his engineers would have a lot of work. Given that Tashayul appeared to be looking for a spring offensive, I had the late fall and winter to prepare.

"Aarundel, some trappers, and I got ourselves a number of beaver families and transplanted them from down below to some of the higher mountain areas. We induced them to build dams that would catch the winter runoff. That would leave our rivers running low, so the engineers would build bridges meant to handle a lesser flow. They, both the beavers and the engineers, did what we expected, which put the Reithrese where we wanted them."

Walking around toward the marble disk sunk in the floor, I squatted near it. "We opened the highest dam, which poured water down into the next one, and so on. The runoff it had taken two months to collect drained down into the canyons in a matter of three days. Tashayul just happened to be trapped in a canyon when the wall of water hit. In his oversized armor he sank like a stone, and his body was recovered far downstream."

Berengar slipped his superior mask into place. "Then you didn't actually kill him, as the stories say."

"Actually, I did. When we first fought, I'd cut his spine, so the lower part of his body did not work except when magick was used to augment his body. That's why he was so big when he came back—his brother, Takrakor, had created a metal skeleton that he fitted to Tashayul. When a spell was used on it, Tashayul could move normally. Unfortunately for him, Tashayul could do nothing by way of casting magick, so his metal skeleton weighed him down and he drowned. I'd inflicted a wound in our fight that took four years to kill him, which was in keeping with a prophecy that he would die at the hand of someone twenty years old. He did."

Hardelwick stared hard at me, and I met his dark-eyed gaze without flinching. His eyes half-closed, he nodded. "I accept that explanation as the truth."

Gena looked at him. "Does it match the story you had about Tashayul's death?"

I smiled. "He had no story about Tashayul's death. The only people who knew about it were Reithrese, and they were not about to start singing of how their leader drowned. The people of the Roclaws did not celebrate it either, because it was hardly the sort of heroic deed they expected out of me. The Reithrese just pulled back to their imperial borders and waited until a successor to Tashayul had been selected."

The emperor nodded his head to me. "It is true, I was bluffing you. Had someone, say Berengar Fisher here, been impersonating a hero of old, the story told would have been grandly heroic and the sort of thing that would have lived forever in song—as has your duel with the Reithrese emperor in this very room."

I smiled at him. "And if I had told a heroic tale, you would have denied me the sword?"

He shrugged. "And I may still, but you do not yet have it in your possession. If you can defeat the ward, and if the blade is there, then I will have a decision to make."

I nodded and drew Wasp. On my knees I reached out with the blade and touched it to the marble disk. The image shimmered for a moment; then I heard a chorus of voices speaking. One spoke Elven, another Reithrese, and the third Mantongue. That one I understood. "Glory does not lie within. Merely a sword that did win an empire washed in blood. In the name of the common good. Let he who puts hand to hilt, from sacred duty never wilt. An empire won will yet fall if not governed for the good of all."

I hadn't a chance to determine what that meant when I found myself on my feet on burning sands. Across from me I saw a Haladin warrior with his left hand entangled in a *sylvanesti*'s long hair. His right hand raised a hooked dagger, but before he could even think of stabbing it down into her exposed throat, I threw Wasp at him. Five hundred years had done nothing for my ability to throw a knife, or Wasp's ability to be thrown, but it hit the Haladina in the face. I leaped at him, shielding her with my own body as the knife flashed down.

I felt it rake across my back, but I forced the pain from my mind. Grabbing him by the throat and groin, I raised him up, then smashed him down over my right knee, snapping his spine.

His body ran like hot wax through my fingers, and as it puddled out below me, it transformed the desert into a woodland. I heard a strangled cry behind me and whirled. The *sylvanesti* metamorphosed into a Manchild, exhausted and bleeding, who ran along on a dusty game path. Behind him, chasing him, came an Elven warrior with a broad-bladed spear. Spikes and barbs on his armor glinting in the dappled sunlight, the screaming hunter came on and set himself for the thrust that would kill the child.

I found Wasp in my hand as I stepped in to stop the Elf from killing the child. The Elf shifted his spear to target me. I dodged to my right and felt the burning sting of the spear as it sliced into the flesh on my left flank. My left hand closed around the haft of the spear, and I pulled the Elf forward as my right hand brought Wasp up. The dagger pierced the Elf's jaw and jabbed up into and through his mouth. His last curse sprayed me with his blood; then he, too, melted away, and his blood washed the land in red, bringing me to the plains outside Alatun.

I turned to look at the Manchild, but he had again

changed. Dark-haired and slender, with her pale, naked flesh spattered with red mud, I saw a Reithressa stumble along. Her ruby teeth gritted in pain, she scrambled to her feet again, then half slipped in the mud and lay there vulnerable and exhausted.

"To Alatun and victory!" I heard shouted from behind me. As I turned to face this new threat, surprise and shock sent a shudder through me. Racing in at the Reithressa, I saw myself, Cleaveheart in hand. I knew that was not how I had looked at Alatun—at least I hoped it was not—because the man bearing Cleaveheart clearly intended to slaughter the defenseless creature toward which he ran.

Reithrese or not, I had to intervene. I dove and tackled my twin. He went down hard, but kept Cleaveheart in his grasp. I rolled away from him, narrowly avoiding a slash that split open the earth. Blood geysered into the air and poured down over me, all hot and sticky. It revolted me, and I recoiled from the shower; then I saw my analog crawling his way along toward the Reithressa.

Snarling incoherently, I leaped through the gushing wall of blood and landed on his legs. He tried to turn and slash me with the sword, but I blocked his strike, then pounced on his back as he recovered himself. The bloody fountain rained viscous fluid over us, and I took advantage of it. Using my knees to pin his arms, I grabbed his head with both hands and forced his face into a puddle of blood. I held on as he tried to buck me off and twist away, and I continued to hang on until bubbles stopped coming up and his body surrendered.

Then his body melted away, and I knelt there in a bloody lake. The stink of death clung to me, and drying blood threatened to stick my eyes shut. I looked over at where the Reithressa had been, but she had again become a *sylvanesti*. Clothed in robes of the brightest white, she turned toward me and I recognized her. "Larissa?"

A smile slowly spread across her face. "I knew it would be you, Neal. It had to be you. I wish I had been brave enough for it to be the two of us together."

"What are you talking about? You are here, now."

"I will keep my promises to you, Neal, all of them, no matter how much they hurt me, because I would not cause hurt to you." As she spoke, I knew that what I was seeing was a magickal image of her. It could not hear me, it could not reason, and worst of all, it could not explain. All it could do is what Larissa had created it to do when she locked my sword away after my death.

Her image came toward me, hovering above the blood with each step. "Remember that I love you and will always love you, Neal," she said as she extended her right hand toward me. "Never forget me and do forgive me."

I reached up to take her hand in mine, but as my flesh met hers, light flashed and I felt the cool leather and weight of Cleaveheart once again in my hand. As my vision again cleared, I saw the sword with which I had won an empire. An old friend, it fit my hand as if I had never let it slip from my grasp. I smiled and, for a second, felt as I had before I died.

Then a tingle ran up my arm from the sword, and its special magick began to work.

In the same way that Cleaveheart had been more of a traditional Reithrese weapon when Tashayul used it, and then had become a stout broadsword when it passed to me, now it transformed itself again. The cross-hilt threw out tendrils of metal that wove themselves into a fascinatingly intricate basket-hilt. The blade itself stretched and narrowed, with both edges taking on a razor's sheen. The tip narrowed to a needle's point, and the hilt shifted subtly in my hand to provide me the greater control I would need to use it with the techniques I had learned from Berengar.

My circle of vision expanded beyond the sword, and I once again found myself in the old Reithrese chapel in Jarudin. My companions and the emperor, along with the dozen guards beyond them, stared at me intently. I smiled at them, stood, and worked the blade through a simple salute. "May I present Cleaveheart."

Berengar shook his head. "That can't be Cleaveheart. Cleaveheart was a broadsword and this is a rapier." He looked hard at the emperor. "What kind of game are you playing here?"

Hardelwick's expression mixed surprise with delight—the kind of open-faced, open-mouthed smile seen at juggler's shows. "There is no deception, Count Berengar. This is as much of a surprise to me as it is to you. Can you explain this, Man-Who-Would-Be-Neal?"

While I had seen the transformation, I had no idea what they had seen, so I asked.

Gena pointed to the marble circle. "When you touched the dagger to that circle, a solid column of light shot from there to Tashayul's forehead, and it pulled you inside. I saw shadowy movements, but heard nothing and could make no sense of what I saw. Then the light vanished and you were kneeling there with the sword."

I nodded. "This is not the first time this sword has altered its shape. I saw the transformation this time, but I suspect that was just part of a spell that wanted to introduce the changed blade to me. I did not see the change the previous time because it happened during the year between Tashayul's death and my recovery of the blade from Jammaq. This sword is involved with destinies and empires, and appears to change itself to be best suited for the environment in which it is being used."

Berengar smiled. "That is fascinating. Perhaps, as it has become the sort of blade I wield, you should entrust it to me for safekeeping."

"I'm thinking that if I had a wife with whom you danced better than I, you'd not be asking to be keeping her, would you?" I laughed as he shook his head, and the rest joined in. "I'll be keeping Cleaveheart here for the time being, but if you want to continue my fencing lessons, I'd be obliged."

"And I would be honored."

"As will I be if you will consent to be my guests." The emperor bowed to me and I returned the bow. "You realize, of course, that you are still the Knight-Defender of the Empire." Reaching over, he plucked a glove from where it was tucked into the belt of one of his guards and displayed it to me. "As you can see by this brand, we still observe traditions here."

"Then you know I would be honored to be your guest, if that is acceptable to my companions."

Berengar and Gena both nodded their assent. "Highness, you do realize I also have a Dreel in my company?"

Hardelwick's face lit up. "Shijef?"

"His great, great grandson Stulklirn."

"He is welcome as well." The emperor clapped his hands. "In one old diary I read of the feast Beltran intended to throw when you returned from the Reithrese war. As you have consented to return after five hundred years, I think it only fitting I complete his plans—if that is acceptable."

"It is, Highness, provided one thing, I'm thinking."

"Yes?"

I smiled. "I consent as long as you're going to be using food that wasn't put up at the same time I was put down."

Chapter 39

Once More to the City of Gold

Winter
A.R. 499
The Present

Had she been asked to determine which of her companions would have been least enthusiastic with the suggestion of an imperial reception, she would have said Berengar would reject the idea. In fact, the suggestion sparked in him a pleasant attitude that had been rare since they left Jarudin on their way to Cygestolia. It was as if the recovery of Cleaveheart had been the climactic point of the mission and returning it to Aurdon was little more than perfunctory.

Despite his banter with Hardelwick when the offer was made, Neal seemed least at ease with the idea of a celebration. He agreed because there was no way not to agree to the honor—that much seemed clear to her—but she felt he would just as soon have quit the capital as fast as possible. While he seemed happy to have reclaimed his sword from the place where it had been secreted after his death, melancholy took the edge off his normally stout-hearted personality.

The Dreel, whom they found waiting for them in the suite of rooms the emperor gave over to them, appeared to like the capital and greeted the idea of remaining for a day with pleasure. "Capital cats fat be," he reported while smacking his lips.

It took Gena a while to put together her feelings on the idea of the celebration, and they were not crystallized even after a full day spent purchasing suitable clothing for herself and watching Berengar prepare for the feast. She realized she was doing everything she would have done, and, in fact, *had* done, to prepare for similar events in the past, but something seemed wrong in all of it. She found herself getting ready for the feast with the same trepidation with which one might walk across ice of an undetermined thickness. Passage was possible, but each step brought with it fear of disaster and a knowledge that the sound fundaments of the world may be nothing more than eggshell thin.

The palace contained a ballroom that dwarfed the one in the Fisher mansion in Aurdon, and it had been scrubbed clean and brightly lit for the gala. Enough candles burned in that room to set up their own wind currents, and light gleamed from polished gold and silver fixtures, as well as marble statuary and the multicolored floor. Silk streamers and drapes splashed blue and red throughout, and food and drink flowed in abundance.

In spite of the obvious preparations, the room and the people seemed wrong. The room had no life and people moved awkwardly through it. They appeared nervous and studied every little detail as if they were seeing each for the first time. Gena realized, of course, that was likely, which meant the room had been seldom used and, therefore, made everyone uneasy. Had they commonly been called to the room for festivities, they would have been used to it, and even oblivious to some of the more exquisite works of art hung on the walls—pity though that might have been.

The social mix likewise seemed designed to promote awkward and anxious relations. The first circle of guests—Gena thought of them this way because they seemed to cluster together in the northeast corner of the room—were imperial nobles of every rank, sex, and age. Their fine clothes were not new and, while in keeping with the red-and-blue color scheme, attained compliance by the use of scarves, hose, and ribbons that could be added or removed with ease.

Yet that seemed to be the only easy thing about them. Gena watched them interact and found them akin to a pack of dogs sniffing about to determine their correct social status. Clearly in the running for one of the primary positions, Berengar moved among them with a confidence and casual air that suggested he had no doubt as to where he belonged. He deferred to those who were clearly his superiors, by dint of age or wealth, yet remained cordial with those who were obviously beneath him. If he snubbed anyone, it was only someone the others snubbed, reinforcing his right to be there among them by helping exclude those who did not belong.

The second and third circles of guests had been selected by the emperor because of their connections to Neal and his era. Sharp and precise, the officers of the Emperor's Own Steel Pack seemed to take great delight in showing off their martial finery. Each of them wore a branded leather glove on his left hand and snapped to attention when Neal or the emperor passed by. Neal spent a certain amount of time speaking with them, which they seemed to enjoy. From what she heard of the conversations, she assumed that listening intently to old war stories was an acquired skill.

The third circle of guests were the descendants of the people Neal and her grandfather had referred to as "Mountain Men." She knew that the survivors of the group that willingly allowed itself to be trapped in the Hiris mountains had been rewarded with homes in the capital, but from the looks of their descendants, their exaltation had not survived more than a generation or two. All of them appeared to be well mannered, but grossly out of their class at the gathering. Tradesmen mostly, from the looks of their hands, they huddled together in small groups and spoke in low whispers with each other.

Neal spent an inordinate amount of time with those small peasant knots. She stood by him as painfully shy people introduced themselves and told him who their ancestor among the Mountain Men had been. Neal universally greeted them warmly and managed to come up with one anecdote or another concerning their kin. The people graciously excused themselves when he finished, but walked away with warm smiles to meet others of their kind and swap their stories.

She managed to steer Neal aside at one point and pressed a goblet of wine into his hands. "All that talking must make you thirsty."

He nodded wearily and drank a bit. "Wouldn't think it, but after this time I can actually see in them faces I knew."

Gena smiled, then looked down into the dark depths of her own wine. "Are all of those stories true?"

Neal's green eyes narrowed for a moment, then he nodded. "I'm thinking I'm remembering right. Only been about six months to me since I was up in the mountains freezing along with all of their kin. When they give me some details, I can remember most of them. Things have changed, of course, as stories come down through the years. The Mountain Men were all good folks, and I'm thinking they'd be happy that their kin are still living free because of what they did. It would make the sacrifice worth it."

She looked up into his face. "Do you think it was worth it?"

Surprise raised his eyebrows. "I always thought it was worth it. History, at least as reported to me by the Steel Pack and these people, has made the whole fight against the Reithrese into some glorious crusade where all of the people on the correct side of the conflict were rewarded with the spoils of the Reithrese Empire. They have made it into a war of loot, but that wasn't what it was at all. We fought the Reithrese because they denied us freedom and kept us as slaves."

"But knowing that there would be rewards for your actions must not have hurt things."

Neal shook his head emphatically. "We all thought we were going to die, and we were willing to die. If you ask any man or woman here to put a price on his life, you'll find no amount of gold or jewels will suffice. But if you ask the same person if he would be willing to lay down his life so his children and their children will never have to face slavery, there's scarcely one here who would tell you he would not."

He drank a bit as the vehemence behind his words sank into Gena. "You see, Genevera, the Reithrese built an empire to enrich themselves. We liberated an empire to free ourselves. That people became rich and successful after the fact does not mean that we fought our battles because of money. Some of those who were best in battle were likely worst in commerce or agriculture, so they did not benefit from their efforts in the way someone else might have. The point is, though, that we all fought so our futures would not be limited, not so we could limit the futures of others so as to enrich ourselves."

Neal hesitated, then smiled. "Forgive me, I did not mean to lecture you. I . . . it's quite a shock to see what sort of stories survive. We are as removed now from my war as I was from the *Eldsaga.* I wonder now about some of the things I held as truths about Elves because of how the stories were warped."

"But does that matter?"

Neal frowned. "Does it not?"

Gena shrugged. "You managed to look past what the *Eldsaga* said and become friends with my grandfather. You endured incredible abuse at the hands of my people, but you never rejected them. You never struck out against them, you fought for and with them. What you *did,* not what you *thought,* made all the difference."

She pointed to the crowd of Humanity moving toward the walls as the musicians in the northwest corner began to play. "It does not matter if these people think the war was fought for riches or freedom. The fact is that they remain free and they jealously guard their freedom. Berengar's quest to find Cleaveheart and end your domination of his family's destiny is just a small example of how valued freedom has become. The emperor is less a dictator than he is an archivist. That for which you fought lives on."

"Your point is well-taken."

Gena looked out at the couples filling the dance floor. "Would you care to dance?"

Something painful flashed through Neal's eyes before

he forced a smile onto his face. "I am afraid the only Elven dance I know is the *torris*, and I doubt it is seen as suitable for display outside Cygestolia."

"I am well versed in all sorts of the dances found among Men." She reached for his goblet to set it on a table beside hers, but he kept it out of her grasp.

"Please, Genevera, do not take this wrong but"—he looked down—"the last time I danced, it was with Larissa. Yesterday, in recovering the sword, I saw her again. My past and the present are slamming together here, which means that while I would love to dance with you, I would feel awkward doing so."

Gena sensed his withdrawal and decided not to let him get away. "Are you saying, Neal, that you think my grand-aunt would have begrudged me this dance? Are you thinking she would have denied you a chance to dance with her grandniece?"

"No, but . . ."

She snatched away his goblet with her left hand, then took his left hand in her right. "You remember Larissa well, Neal Roclawzi. She would smile to see us like this, and for my part, I want to see if you actually are as good a dancer as she said you were."

One turn on the floor led to another, so the memory of that night's dancing managed to bring a smile to Gena's face even to the point when their journey south had brought them within sight of Aurdon. The emperor had reluctantly allowed them to leave on the promise that Neal would return to Jarudin to help fill in the gaps in the history of how the empire was won. Neal agreed and even allowed the emperor to reinvest him as Knight-Defender of the Empire in a ceremony that included the Steel Pack presenting him with a pair of gloves in which the left hand had been branded with the mountain rune.

A company of the Steel Pack had ridden with them to the borders of Ispar, then turned back before entering Centisian territory. The three weeks spent traveling with them had proved beneficial for keeping Neal's spirits up. The experienced swordsmen among the imperial soldiers took great delight in sparring with Neal and Berengar. While Hardelwick's men were good, and displayed a number of different fencing styles, Neal and Berengar clearly had an edge over all of them. Numerous promises of return matches were shouted back and forth when the Steel Pack departed for the capital.

She found the remaining ten days between the border and Aurdon entertaining. As they rode through territory Berengar knew well, he felt constrained to point out things of interest. His pride in Centisia became evident in his voice and, when they had stopped for breaks, in the way he paced back and forth. Neal tolerated being lectured, but the Dreel took to aping Berengar's strutting in a comical and decidedly unflattering manner, which set Berengar off.

Berengar and Neal began to fence a great deal more earnestly. Berengar still had an edge over Neal, but the gap between them closed quickly. Gena saw more of the unusual and odd moves from the imperial soldiers show up in Neal's repertoire. Berengar managed to counter most all of the ploys Neal used, but he had to work harder at it than he ever had before.

Just outside Aurdon they met a patrol of the Aurdon Rangers. Gena recognized Captain Floris, but had remembered him as a more carefree sort of individual. In the six months since she had last seen him, he had lost weight and had added a scar along his jawline. Even so the Man remained gracious and greeted their party warmly.

"Welcome home, Count Berengar. I am very glad to see you here again. How went your quest?"

Berengar looked over at Neal. "We succeeded. This is Neal Roclawzi and he bears Cleaveheart."

Floris's jaw dropped. "But, but, Neal Roclawzi died five hundred years ago." He shivered. "His ghost has . . ."

"Yes, yes, Floris, this is true. But it is also true that, thanks to Lady Genevera, he lives again." Berengar smiled carefully. "He was told of our plight and has come to set it to rights."

Neal reined Scurra up and offered Floris his hand. "Pleased to meet you, Captain Floris, is it?"

"Yes, sir."

Neal smiled warmly at the soldier and at his men. "A fine group of soldiers you have here, Captain. I gather from what I have been told and your relief at seeing Count Berengar here, that the Haladina have continued to harass caravans coming into Aurdon."

"More than that, sir, they have burned a number of farms. The panic is forcing the price of grain up, which is causing a great deal of unrest in the city." He looked over at Berengar. "Half the Rangers are deployed to guard the warehouses to prevent people from looting them."

"This is most serious, but now we can deal with it appropriately. The treachery that has culminated in this series of events will soon have its own reward." Berengar pointed at one of the soldiers. "Ride back into the city and inform my family that I am returned successful."

Neal frowned. "We could ride on in just as easily as he can. I'm certain Captain Floris has his patrol to continue."

Berengar waved that idea off with a flick of his right hand. "Hardly, he is escorting us into the city. It is his duty and his honor."

"It *is* an honor, my Lord."

Neal shook his head. "I hated parades, and I'd rather be out killing Haladina than riding with us back into Aurium."

"Aur*don*, Neal, it has changed since you were last here." Berengar laughed and started to ride toward the city. "You will find yourself most welcome among my people. Come, we will prepare for a ceremony tomorrow night in which you can undo the curse beneath which you placed us, and true justice can again determine the course of events in Aurdon. And then we will celebrate this new freedom with a festival the like of which you have never seen."

Gena fell in beside Neal as they rode into the city. Floris and Berengar preceded them and the other Rangers rode behind them, but they had enough room from either group to be able to converse without being overheard. A wave of weariness washed over Gena, but she forced it away with a laugh until she saw Neal's dour expression.

"What is the matter? This is almost finished."

Neal shook his head. "Nothing, really, though I should have expected it. I'm thinking that Berengar reminds me of your grandfather when he was in the company of other Elves. On the road we have been of equal importance, all of us. Now, because we are going into his city, he eclipses us."

Gena raised an eyebrow. "I'd not thought Neal Custos Sylvanii would be jealous of anyone."

"Jealous?" Neal frowned, then laughed. "I don't think I'm jealous. I have never wanted what Berengar has."

"You don't find his notoriety vexing?"

"Is that inquiry serious?" Neal watched her carefully, and she sensed she had asked something that lessened her in his eyes. "I have never been one to imagine another person's being praised in any way diminished me. If anything, I can now enjoy an anonymity that eluded me for a long time."

"Forgive me, Custos Sylvanii, I did not mean to presume."

He nodded. "I know." He reached out and touched her lightly on the shoulder, then quickly withdrew his hand. "There is much of your grandaunt in you, and sometimes I forget that you do not know everything she did about me. How she understood me, I do not know, but why, I do."

"Vitamorii."

Neal pounded his right fist against his chest. "She still lives in there, and I'm not of a mind to evict her. But she knew that it would take ambition for me to be jealous of Berengar."

"And you have no ambition."

"Not exactly." His smile returned in full force and made Gena feel better. "It's just that my ambition is to avoid being ambitious."

As they entered the city, Gena watched Neal as he saw what Aurium had become. The shock remained evident on his face throughout the journey. He sat tall in his saddle as he rode through the Haladin district, but the stern expression he had adopted softened when he saw children playing with dogs in the streets. He stood in the stirrups to peer deep into the open market, then waved at the troopers as they rode to their barracks.

Finally they arrived at the Fisher mansion. Berengar dismounted and helped Gena down, then looked up at Neal. "Come, they will want to see you, too."

Neal shook his head. "If you do not mind, my lord, I think I would like to travel through your city. Many are the changes since I was last here."

"I have no objection, Neal, but I would be upset if your sword were to fall into the wrong hands."

Neal nodded and pulled the scabbard with Cleaveheart in it from his belt. He handed it to Gena. "If you will safeguard this as well as your grandaunt did, I will be in your debt."

Gena accepted the weapon, but something in the stiff formality of Neal's tone bothered her. "Are you certain you will not stay with us?"

"Please, I will return and relax here, but this is the first opportunity I have had to be alone in a town. It has been a long time—longer even than you think, really. I just feel a need to hide myself in a crowd."

Berengar nodded and plucked a pouch of coins from Floris's belt. He tossed it to Neal. "Here, this should see to your entertainment without compromising your identity."

Neal deftly caught it. "My thanks, Count Berengar. If you will excuse me."

Gena smiled hopefully at him. "Are you certain you do not want any company?"

"I am certain, thank you." Neal winked at her, but she caught no warmth from the act. He reined his horse around and rode back out through the gate.

Gena watched him go, all the while feeling smaller and smaller inside. A month before, beginning with the dance at the emperor's celebration, she had felt as if they were growing closer. Even on the road they had maintained a new openness, but their arrival in Aurdon appeared to have cut off any further chance to get to know Neal better. If she took what he said to her as the truth, she found herself in competition with her grandaunt, an idea she hated because she knew, ultimately, she would lose in that comparison. Neal idolized Larissa as Gena had once idolized him.

Berengar settled his arm around her shoulder. "Don't worry, Lady Genevera, he will come back."

She looked up at Berengar as they mounted the steps to the front of the mansion. "What makes you so certain of that?"

"It's easy." He nodded at her. "He'll come back because we have his sword."

Chapter 40

Old Weeds Bear Bitter Fruit

Winter
A.R. 499
The Present
My 536th Year

I returned to the Fisher domain rather late in the day, or early, depending upon whether you accounted days by midnight or dawn. Five hundred years had changed Aurdon considerably, and that included a great advance in the brewer's art. Each of the taverns I visited brewed its own ale, and I enjoyed making my survey of their wares. One, an especially crisp, very amber brew lacked the sort of aftertaste I remember from when I was last alive, so I found one more reason to be happy that I had returned to life.

My wanderings had also uncovered for me a number of other reasons to regret my resurrection. Coaxing a full litany of crimes visited by the Fishers upon the Riverens and vice versa had not taken much effort—and it included a complete and detailed chronology of my ghost's intervention in their relations. Of course, I didn't bother to mention I was the Neal who had beset the families so. Despite that omission on my part, I got the distinct impression that keeping track of family fortunes within Aurdon was a sport that amused and delighted a great number of people—especially those with ties to neither clan.

Other things I had learned, things hinted at and rumors whispered, obliquely suggested to me that intrigue rivaled commerce as the primary occupation in Aurdon. Frustrated in their attempts to destroy each other, the Fisher and Riveren families had succeeded in crushing any other merchant house in the city. Normal citizens said they could feel the pressure building to some sort of climax, and already rumors of Berengar's return brought with it speculation ranging from an Elven invasion of the city to mercenaries using flashdrakes to slaughter the citified Haladina wholesale.

I found the room to which the night porter guided me as spartan as it was small, which I really didn't mind. Before my death I had spent months living in a canvas tent, and since then I had fared little better, so the room I had been given appeared opulent. I closed my door and began to shuck my clothes when I heard a light knock from the door leading to the adjoining room.

Bare-chested and barefooted, I opened the door. "Gena. I hope I did not wake you."

Standing there in a long bedgown, with her golden hair gathered into one thick braid, she looked chillingly like her grandaunt had when I reclaimed Cleaveheart. Only Gena's violet eye color marked her as physically different from Larissa, yet in her eyes I saw much more that separated them. The expression on her face told me she had been sleeping, but not well.

"I heard your door close, and I wanted to see if you had survived your peregrinations." She forced a smile on her face and waved a hand through the air between us. "You've been drinking."

I nodded as I backed away from the door and retreated into the room. "That I have, Gena."

"And wenching as well?" She kept her voice light, but I caught a hurt note in her question.

"Wenching, me? In fact, I have not." I shrugged, the ale making the motion sloppier than I wanted. "What woman would be interested in a man old enough to be potting soil?"

"My lord underestimates how well he has been preserved."

"My lady forgets that I remember an Aurium where the Fishers lived in a longhouse with floors of dirt and someone who was likely Berengar's great, great, great, great, great"—I tried to keep track of greats on my fingers, but failed—"grandmother expressed a willingness to lie with me. And I remember Larissa."

I felt my face getting hot and my anger rising, but I could not figure out why, so I tamped the emotion down. "I have not had a chance, in five centuries and more, just to sit in a tavern and watch and listen to people. Traveling with you and Berengar, I have been out of touch with normal people—except at the emperor's festivities and on the road with the Steel Pack."

Gena's face closed down. "I did not mean to anger you."

"I know, and you have not, really." I hesitated, my mouth open, as words lined themselves up in my brain. "It is just that you brought me back to life and reminded me what it was to be Neal Elfward. I needed common folks to remind me what it was like to be the Man I was before I became Neal Elfward."

"But you always were remarkable."

I laughed. "I might have been different, but there was a time when I could see why I had shouldered the responsibilities I had. I had a feel for what normal people wanted and feared. I wanted to recover that."

"Are their fears all that different from those of Berengar or the emperor?"

Something in her voice told me that was not really the question she wanted to ask, but it was the only one she gave me to answer. "They are. The emperor, the Fishers, the Riverens, and all the nobles we met in Jarudin all are removed from the daily terrors of life. The common folk worry about having enough food to eat or enough money to pay their taxes. Berengar worries if a wine has aged enough in a decade to be served to people he wants to impress. The emperor is able to devote all his time to reconstructing the history of the empire, which is a noble pursuit, but well and truly removed from the struggle for existence many people face."

I watched her carefully. "So what is it *you* fear, Genevera?"

She started to answer, then stopped. She folded her arms, then raised her right hand to play with the ring on the silver chain around her neck. "I fear many things, Neal. Tonight I feared that, as your departure mirrored that of Durriken, we would find you as he was found."

"Dead by the Eight Cuts."

"Yes," she whispered hoarsely.

I sensed in her the same pain I had felt in her grandaunt when Aarundel and Marta had been taken away. Then Elven law kept us apart, and even though I wanted immediately to go to Gena and take her in my arms, I hesitated. I took a step forward, then stopped, then started forward again awkwardly.

Her head came up, and she held her left hand out to keep me back. "No, no, I understand your difficulty in reaching out to me. I do, I really do." The ring glittered as she worked it back and forth between thumb and forefinger. "These were the rooms that Berengar had given to Rik and me when . . . before Rik died. This ring is all I have to remember him by."

"That, and the flashdrakes and the memories."

"Yes, and the memories." Tears welled up in her eyes and spilled down over her cheeks, anointing them the way the dew anoints a rose. "And those memories mean I am missing Durriken very much right now—probably as much as you miss my grandaunt. As much as I would like to seek solace in your arms, in a hug, I am afraid it might lead to something that would leave both of us feeling awkward in its wake."

Her soft words sobered me, and I realized that what she was saying was true. As I was a link for her to her past, so she linked me and my past. In her I could find a sense of peace I had not known because of the laws that kept Larissa and me apart. In me she could find a return to the days before Durriken's death and even, perhaps, to the simpler days before she left Cygestolia. We were, each of us, the balm for the other's wounds, but we threatened such complete healing that neither one of us would bear a scar from the experience that had wounded us. And each of us felt that not to have a scar, to remain unmarked, would be to forget and betray people we had dearly loved.

Gena looked past me and shivered. "When Rik died, I felt I had betrayed him by not being there to prevent his death. I am, after all, a sorceress capable of bringing you back from the dead, but I could not do the same for him." She glanced at me and laughed ruefully. "And, of course, in my head I know you were a special case—a combination of circumstances that has no bearing on his situation, yet it eats at me more and more. Even now he lies in the Fisher vault, laid to rest in a place of honor, yet he must be angry with me because I have not done anything to avenge him."

"Would he have wanted vengeance?"

"Yes. No. I don't know." She looked at me imploringly. "He was a man who had once been a slave and who fought for his own freedom. Whoever killed him robbed him of that freedom. I think he would like to be avenged, and after you sever the knot tonight, freeing the Fishers to act against the Riverens and the Haladina, perhaps he will be avenged."

"Your reasoning appears sound." I nodded and held my hand out. "Might I look at that ring?"

She removed it and handed it to me. "Be careful, part of the setting turns and a needle comes out of the rim. He called it a slapdeath ring."

"Even I have heard of them." Following her instructions, I produced the little bit of a needle; along with it came a sweet, cloying scent. "This belonged to Durriken?"

"Lord Orvir, who was Berengar's brother. He died years ago—supposedly while being chased by Haladina or your ghost, depending upon which story you decide to believe." Gena took the ring back from me. "Count Berengar granted Rik the ring and the title so he could legitimately carry the flashdrakes while in Aurdon. I prefer thinking of Rik as he looked the night Berengar gave him this ring, not when they found him."

"I understand and agree with your decision in that matter." I smiled at her in what I hoped was a reassuring manner. "And I would not worry about Durriken's ghost being angry with you. Take it from a man who has been dead—knowing that I was held in the heart of one who loved me was the only thing that made eternity endurable."

That brought a smile to her face. "You are most kind, Neal Custos Sylvanii."

"Kind? I'm thinking I'm only speaking the truth here. You and I know it for the truth, too."

She nodded. "I can but hope you are right."

"Sleep on the idea, Gena, and you will know I am."

She drifted back toward the door to her room. "How will I know?"

I winked at her. "You'll have sweet dreams, and in that way you can be certain."

My dreams were not so sweet, but escaped being nightmares because they happened after the sun had risen. Everything I had learned and suspected and feared all managed to mix together into a surreal battlefield. I stood alone against an army of faceless individuals. Half of them I recognized as having fought and died at my side ages ago. Neither they nor their armor had withstood the test of time at all well, and their keening wail of despair seemed intended to tell me something, but I could not puzzle it out.

The other half of my combatants appeared to be warriors from the era in which I now lived. They bore rapiers that twisted around my parries with the agility of an alley cat and struck with the speed of a viper. When they withdrew, a rank of men carrying flashdrakes stepped forward and triggered volley after volley at me. With each ball that hit me I relived the pain that had given me this scar and that. I realized that in the five centuries since my death, war had become no less savage, but the means for inflicting pain and death had simply become more sophisticated.

Though I only slept fitfully, I did not come fully awake until late in the afternoon. At the foot of my bed I found a suit of clothes laid out for me. Over a white shirt I would be wearing a jacket made of brown brushed leather. The sleeves had been slashed to show off a satiny material the color of emeralds. The trousers, which reached only my knees, had been made out of brown velvet that matched the jacket. The hose matched the emerald of the sleeves, and I had been provided with a pair of brown brushed-leather bootlets that had a triangular profile and no laces to keep them tight on my feet. A similarly shaped hat with a ridiculously long green feather had also been created to complete my outfit, but I'd have sooner worn one of the shoes on my head than anything with that plume.

I washed and dressed myself quickly enough and was surprised by the close fit of the clothes. Though they made me feel considerably younger than I was, and even younger than I appeared to be, I felt only the hat would compromise my masculinity. I cinched my belt tight around my waist and slipped Wasp into the waiting sheath. As I slipped the bracelet I had made so long ago onto my right wrist, I looked for Cleaveheart. I could not find the sword and panicked for a moment before I remembered having entrusted it to Gena the night before.

I knocked on her door and she bade me enter. One step into the room, and any vanity I might have harbored about my appearance vanished. Two women backed away from Gena and giggled at my slack-jawed expression, but they barely existed in my eyes. Never had I seen anyone look as beautiful as Genevera did.

Her golden hair had been brushed out so it shone like silk. It fell to her shoulders and complimented the soft violet of her gown. Cut from satin and gathered here and there with buttons, it draped her in ruffles and frills. Lying taut against her flat stomach, yet flowing out into gathered skirts, the dress confirmed a stateliness and nobility that I had all but missed as we traveled. The gown displayed her bosom to best advantage, and lavender lace gloves hid her delicate hands. Judiciously applied cosmetics molded her inhumanity into an intoxicatingly exotic and seductive snare.

Surprised by her appearance, I wondered how the Genevera I had seen on the trail had been able to blossom into this flower. I knew she had always possessed this sort of beauty, and had easily been as ceremoniously dressed for the emperor's reception, but I had been unable to see her beauty for what it was. Something in my mind prevented me from actually being able to believe what my eyes showed me.

I realized that when I first joined her and Berengar on their quest, in Gena I saw Larissa, and recalling old memories hurt. Then, after Gena had been battered by Tacorzi, I could not imagine her as she stood now. And on the road from Jarudin to Aurdon I had been learning more of the world and trying to integrate my memories of the past with the realities of the present. I had excluded her from that process because I feared having her supplant Larissa in the same way I let changes in the course of a river supplant my old memory of it.

I held my hands open and wide of my body, unable to speak.

She laughed and broke eye contact shyly.

I looked down as well. "Your beauty vindicates the Consilliarii's wisdom in letting your parents and your grandparents bring children into the world."

She nodded her head graciously, then smiled at me. "And you, for a Man who said he was naught but potting soil, are quite handsome. I can understand the Dun Wolf being a legend for more than his prowess in battle."

I laughed. "That being said, I hesitate to ask for my sword."

Gena pointed to the table where the sword lay in its scabbard. I slid the blade and scabbard home at my left hip, then bowed to Gena. "M'lady, if you would do me the honor of allowing me to escort you to the festivities."

"It would be my pleasure."

The two servants cooed and clucked as Gena took my right arm. I stiffened a bit because that meant I could not draw Cleaveheart easily, but to have her on the other side meant we would have the blade between us, and I did not want that. The elder of the two women shooed the younger one over to open the door, and I let Gena precede me from the room.

As she had been at the mansion more than I, she set the pace and direction of our travel. Quickly enough we found ourselves at the head of stairs in the southwest corner of a large and high-ceilinged, rectangular room. Opposite us, along the long western wall, an orchestra had been situated, and played simple and sedate music. The stairs led down to the east, then switched back to the west, which gave all those gathered below us ample time to see us make our way to the room's floor.

The throng below us struck me as just as awkwardly jammed together as the emperor's guests had been. Nearest us I saw Berengar and enough people with similar faces and postures to assume the area at the foot of the stairs was the demense of the Fisher Clan. That meant that the nervous group at the far end of the room were likely Riverens. The people in the middle must have been the richer and more ambitious among Aurdon's population—which meant I did not recognize a single face among them from my journey through the city. The only exception to that rule came in the form of four men who, were they not wearing incredible finery, I would have thought brigands waiting for a signal before robbing the place.

Until we started our descent into the room, a tall, vaguely rectangular lump shrouded in a blue velvet curtain in the middle of the room had attracted a lot of attention. I thought it might be a wardrobe or some similar piece of furniture beneath the cloth, but its presence in the middle of what should have been the dance floor surprised me.

As we entered the room, Genevera doubtless was the cause of so many people looking at us, but the fact that I alone among the people gathered wore a sword did spark conversation. They apparently found me as boorish as they found her enchanting; wearing more than a dagger to a social event such as this was clearly of questionable taste. All of the women who watched Gena through a veil of jealousy likely pitied her for being accompanied by someone like me, while the men probably sympathized with my desire to wear a sword to fend them off when I had her by my side.

Berengar met us at the base of the stairs and bowed deeply. As he straightened up, he signaled the orchestra with his left hand and the music died. His black velvet jacket and trousers had been fashioned similarly to mine, but the slashes in his sleeves showed the same purple satin that had been used to make Genevera's gown. He, too, had eschewed the little cap that had come with my clothes, and he did not wear a sword.

He raised his voice, though he hardly needed to, and addressed everyone in the room. "Friends, relatives, Elders, and distinguished guests, I am most pleased to see you here. This is a night that shall live forever in the history of Aurdon. It is but an echo of a night five centuries ago in which an oath was taken, an oath that defined this city and its nature."

Berengar steered us through the crowd and toward the velvet-hung monolith. "As you all know and have been repeatedly reminded, five centuries ago, before the empire even existed, our city—barely a town then—was torn because of a conflict between two families. Mercenaries, in the service of the Red Tiger, came to Aurium and forged a peace between the Fishers and the Riverens by creating the Knott family."

He reached out and pulled the dark cloth away from what it hid. The curtain puddled at the base of a glass-walled wardrobe with glass doors facing us. In it, above the fanned display of swords that occupied the lower half of the enclosure, hung the sleeves I had knotted together so long ago. Ismere's blue sleeve had faded a bit with age, and Rufus's homespun sleeve had yellowed considerably, but the cloth had not deteriorated as much as I thought it should have. Perhaps the oath I swore that night *did* have some power to it. I did not know, but the revulsion I had felt that night concerning Aurium and the two families came rushing back to me at the sight of the knotted sleeves.

Berengar allowed the buzz running through the crowd to die before he continued. "You all know that I went away from here on an important quest, and I have returned, successful. On the night these sleeves were joined, Neal Roclawzi bound the Fishers and Riverens to work together until Wasp and Cleaveheart sundered the knot you see before you. My quest was to recover those venerable blades so this false alliance could be ended forever."

That brought something of an outburst from the north end of the room, but Berengar ignored whoever had spoken. As the crowd slowly drifted closer, he pointed to me. "This quest was one that took me and my companions from here to Jarudin, Cygestolia, and even to the Rimefields far to the north. Not only did we recover the weapons we needed, but Lady Genevera of Woodspire even brought Neal Roclawzi back to life so he could undo what he had done that night."

I started to speak, but before I could say anything, cries of "Fraud!" erupted among the Riverens. I don't think they intended them as distractions, but merely as an honest expression of their disbelief and outrage at what Berengar had said. After all, if rumors about Berengar's return had begun to spike anxiety among them, then hearing him claim that he had brought Neal Roclawzi back to Aurdon after five centuries in the grave had to seem like the basest and boldest of lies.

Woven amid their shouts, I heard a growl and a scream. As I turned to my left to try to pinpoint their origins, all I saw was a face locked in fury and the naked dagger coming at my back.

Chapter 41

Bright Fruit, Cruel Poison

Winter
A.R. 499
The Present

Gena felt Neal pull roughly away from her before she had a clue anything was wrong. She turned toward him and saw a flash of silver that exploded into bloody crimson as Neal parried a dagger aside with his left forearm. His right fist came around and sounded like an ax chopping wood as it landed square on his assailant's face. The assassin's legs went boneless as blood gushed from his broken nose. He hit the ground, and Neal curled down into a kneeling crouch a second later, clutching his arm against his stomach.

She dropped to her knees beside him. "How badly are you hurt?"

Neal hissed and raised his left arm. The dagger had sliced through the jacket sleeve and had scored a nasty gash on the underside of his forearm. Blood welled up in it and ran down into the sleeve itself. "I've survived worse, but it's always the shallow ones that sting something powerful."

Gena flipped up the hem of her purple gown and tore a strip from one of her white underskirts. "No magick, correct?"

Neal looked at her, then smiled. "Correct." He pulled off the rest of his sleeve and let her bandage the wound. The white bandage quickly reddened, so she produced another tattered bandage from her clothes and wound this one even tighter.

Berengar pounced on the assailant and hauled him to his feet by the scruff of his neck. "Oho, Titus Riveren!" He shook him, and Gena saw the bleeding figure was little more than a boy. Had the blood from his nose not darkened his moustache, she never would have noticed it, because, like his fair eyebrows, it could not be seen against his pale skin. "What treachery is this?"

The dazed boy said nothing coherent, but scarlet bubbles formed on his lips. Blood from his nose ran down over his mouth to his chin, then dripped down to the floor. Had Berengar not held him up, Gena knew the boy would have collapsed again, and she felt sorry for him.

Berengar held him aloft as he might a fox taken after a long hunt. "Everyone here saw this. You all saw a Riveren strike at the man who would tear down the shield behind which they hide. Need any of you any more proof of their baseness and dishonor? Suckling at their mothers' breasts, the Riverens learn to strike at a man's back, so how much worse must they be as adults? And what adult—if he has any concept of responsibility—would use a child as an assassin?"

He released the boy, and Titus pooled in a bony pile at Berengar's feet. The count looked down at Neal and extended his hand to him. "Give me Cleaveheart, and I will strike the blow that will free the Fishers to avenge this assault upon you."

Neal shook his head as he slowly rose. "I'm thinking, Berengar, I've never needed avenging before, and I'm not going to start needing it now."

"Your point is well-taken, Neal." Berengar crossed to the glass cabinet and opened the doors. "There, use Cleaveheart to sunder the knot, then we Fishers will be your allies in destroying the Riverens."

Again Neal shook his head. "If you're thinking the rash act of a child means his family needs killing, then I'm glad the knot exists. And even if Titus there were meant to assassinate me—and since his blade wasn't poisoned, I'm not thinking anyone put him up to this—I've got a question or two I want answered before I throw the Fishers and the Riverens in a pit together."

Berengar stiffened. "Questions can be answered later. Give me the sword and I will sever the knot."

"Hear him out!" shouted someone from the Riveren end of the room.

"The sword, Neal, now! You know not the forces with which you deal."

Gena sensed a hardening in Neal and saw it reflected in the fire flashing through his green eyes. She slowly stood and pulled back away from him, clearing the space between him and Berengar.

Neal's voice rumbled low like the growl of his namesake. "Oh, I'm thinking I have a very good idea of what I'm dealing with. I walked in your city yesterday, and I learned a number of things you'd not be wanting me to know if you had looked at me as more than a way to get your hands on Cleaveheart here."

Berengar's eyes narrowed. "I have no idea what you are talking about."

"No? I think you do, and I think even your family does not know how far you have gone." Neal looked over at the Fishers. "You believed Berengar would be bringing Cleaveheart back to sunder this knot, and when he did that, you knew there would be a war. So you've brought mercenaries into Aurdon. Four companies, at the least, and their captains are here now. You've forgotten that I captained my own mercenary company, so I know the look and understand the language. You may have thought yourselves subtle having them come into town and storing their kits in one of your warehouses, but idle able-bodied men spending Fisher gold attracts attention in the lower reaches of your city."

Neal smiled easily. "Did you also know of a rumor old enough to have grown moss about a secret foundry at Lake Orvir that's making flashdrakes? It's said there's at least ten thousand of the weapons stored there, which is more than enough to equip the mercenaries in your employ. Just the thing an ambitious heir to the imperial throne would need to press his claim and eliminate competition. And with Cleaveheart and the prophecy concerning it, he might even imagine he could retake and reforge the whole of the empire."

Berengar shook his head. "Baseless fantasies of a man whose brain rotted while he lay in his tomb."

"Flight of fancy that might all be, but there are other things I know as facts." Neal glanced over at Gena and she felt her blood run cold. "I know that you had Durriken murdered."

"Preposterous!"

"How do you know, Neal?" Gena stared at the both of them, every kind thought she had ever had about Berengar turning into a barb that skewered her soul. "How can you be certain?"

"Durriken's flashdrakes and Lord Orvir's ring were given to you after Durriken's death by Eight Cuts. Perhaps Haladin culture has changed since my time, but Eight Cuts was reserved for Haladin traitors. Durriken was not Haladin, was he?"

Gena numbly shook her head.

"And even if the Haladina had changed that much, they never would have left his flashdrakes and the ring with him after they killed him. *That* mistake the Reithrese made five centuries ago, and I spotted it then. Berengar has repeated Takrakor's blunder here and now."

Berengar forced a laugh. "Speculation. You offer no link between me and Durriken's death. It would have been just as easy for the Riverens to have killed him, or the Haladina—who were then frightened off before they could loot his body."

Neal shook his head and pointed to the ring lying flat against Gena's chest. "Even when I was young, a slapdeath ring was well-known. Durriken was wearing it and didn't know until too late that your people had come to kill him. He could not use one of the flashdrakes, but he got one man with the ring. *You* may be well liked in Aurdon, Berengar, but your cousin Waldo was not, and many was the person who recounted the tale of his death by food poison at the time of Durriken's demise."

Neal looked the crowd over and shook his head. "I'm thinking, Berengar, that you decided that with Cleaveheart you could win yourself an empire, so you set out to recover the sword. The story about freeing your family from my curse was a convenient dodge, and with her eyes blinded by the desire to avenge Durriken, Lady Genevera missed the clues."

The count stared imperiously down at Neal. "And you did not?"

"Lad, when you go from lustfully looking at her to lustfully looking at my sword, I'm bound to notice."

"You are an old man. Your time is passed. Give me the sword, and I shall let you live out the remainder of your unnatural life in peace."

"I'm thinking, Berengar, that's not possible. You might give me peace, but my conscience would not oblige me." Neal nodded his head toward the cabinet. "You heard Tacorzi—this blade must be given away or won in combat. I will not give it to you."

Berengar smiled easily as he drew a rapier from the rack in the cabinet. "Then I must give it to you, mustn't I?"

Gena saw four men of military bearing move to the forefront of the crowd and edge toward the cabinet. Filtering her fury at having been deceived and betrayed into her magick, she gestured at the cabinet. A purple bolt of lightning launched itself from the palm of her right hand and slammed the doors shut. The energy fanned out and formed a net that sizzled and crackled, filling the air with the scent of ozone.

She met the stares of the four mercenary captains. "This is their fight, unless you foolishly choose to make it *my* fight."

Berengar saluted her. "Bravo, I never wanted interference. You honor me."

"I do nothing of the sort, Berengar." Her eyes sparked with the agonizing fury that knotted her stomach. "You had better pray Neal slays you, because if he does not, I will. And if the job falls to me, the horrors of the *Eldsaga* will be but pleasant memories for you as you die."

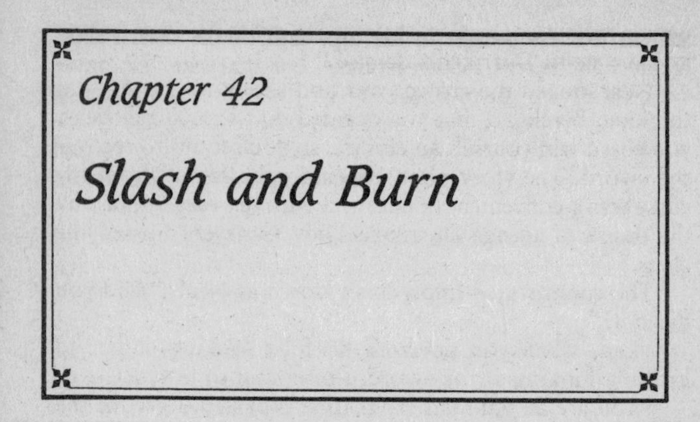

Chapter 42
Slash and Burn

Winter
A.R. 499
The Present
My 536th Year

I let the cold finality of Gena's words sink into me, and I accepted the responsibility of avenging Durriken for her. Likewise I chose to accept preventing the perversion of what we had all fought for so long ago, and I accepted the safeguarding of those who would be maimed and killed if Berengar's dreams of empire became reality. Never before had my reasons for a fight been so clearly drawn. I felt that somehow this battle was more important than any I had ever fought before.

As we set ourselves for combat, I knew it would be child's-play to use Cleaveheart to slash his rapier to bits. I could defeat him in that way, but I chose not to. This was a fight between him and I, between what I was and what he wanted to become. I saw no reason to make his rapier pay for his ambition.

With a whispered hiss Cleaveheart came up and went down in a salute to my foe. He stood slightly taller than I, but carried less weight in his hips and thighs than I did. Technically he was a bigger target, but that size also gave him an advantage in reach. I had discovered, in sparring with smaller foes in the Steel Pack, that reach could decide a fight. I also knew, given his skill and all that I had learned, the inch of reach he may have had over me would matter little.

Berengar saluted me, his blade's razor edges picking up and reflecting the purple lightning playing over the cabinet. He set himself in a low stance, with the tip of his blade pointing at my right eye. I brought Cleaveheart up and targeted his throat. I let the point of my blade circle slowly, making a circuit no larger than a coin. Keeping myself on the balls of my feet, I waited, because I knew that in this place and given his cause, he would have to strike first.

He did not disappoint me. As he slid forward, his point dropped and arrowed in at my right thigh. I snapped my blade down and around to the left, awkwardly inverting the sword in a huge circular parry. I carried his blade back out to my right, then came forward, getting inside his guard. I crashed Cleaveheart's basket-hilt into his face. The blow staggered him and drove him to his knees.

I leaped above the weak return slash, then whipped my blade up and out, catching him on the collarbone. I sliced velvet and the flesh beneath it at his right shoulder. Like my wound I knew it would sting, but it would not hamper him. Dancing back away, I brought my blade back into my guard. "That's *one* cut."

Berengar wiped away blood from his split lip with the back of his left hand. "That makes us even."

"Then I will make you more than even." I waited for him to regain his feet, then I lunged at his belly. He parried me down, hard, and I let my blade go with his move. I cut it back to the right, just missing his knee as he riposted forward and passed his blade between my ribs and right arm. His blade started to come up, seeking the artery running through my armpit. I cocked my wrist, bringing Cleaveheart's point forward in a stabbing motion at his eyes, while swinging my body away from his sword.

His cut missed as he reflexively pulled up short to protect his face. Continuing my spin, I presented my back to him for a tantalizing moment. I knew he had to strike at it, so I cranked my sword down and let it precede me in the spin. My blade picked up Berengar's forehand slash, but the weak block did allow his blade to kiss my right flank and lay open the flesh over my ribs.

Sweat poured fire into the cut, but I did not retreat. As he pulled his sword back for another, heavier cut, I ducked and snapped my blade up. His slash passed over my head as I leaned in toward him and raked my blade obliquely over his stomach. I sliced a cut open on his belly, by his right hip, and that made him yelp. Already low, I rolled back onto my tail and somersaulted back out of his range, then stood.

"That's *two* cuts, Berengar."

He growled out a chuckle. "Again we are even. But we shall not be at the end of this game."

Berengar settled into a guard and wove the point of his blade through a figure-eight pattern. I kept mine circling, but brought my hand up so my hilt remained at shoulder height. My blade pointed at his right knee. I stamped once with my right foot, then feinted at his leg. He brought his blade down and around in a tight circular parry, but I snapped my wrist back. Bringing Cleaveheart back to where it almost touched my right shoulder, I then lashed it forward and razored open a wound on his right flank.

"*Three* cuts."

Berengar fought back fast. He lunged, then withdrew as my parry started. I went to riposte, but his blade extended again in a stop-thrust. I twisted back to my left and avoided being skewered, but only just barely. His point ricocheted off a rib, leaving with a cut beneath my left nipple, and sweat seared into it as well.

As I pulled back, he pressed his attack with short jabs at my legs, groin, and belly. Circling, I managed to fend them off more by moving out of range than by parrying them. Finally he got me on my left hip with a little stab wound. I could have parried it with my free hand, but it would have cost me fingers.

"*Four,* Neal, four," he snarled at me. Another two jabs and he opened a wound on my left shoulder that mirrored the one I had given him. "And that is *five.*"

"Five's not the game." I pulled my left leg back and drove at him. In his pursuit of me he had begun to move more laterally than straight forward, so as I came at him, I had his full body to target. I lunged at his eyes, then ducked beneath his slash-parry and slipped my blade around in a crescent. I cut him on the left breast, leaving his jacket tattered and blood weeping from a flesh wound.

He hissed and wove his silvery blade through a complex pattern that was more show than threat. At best, coming in that high and exploiting his reach advantage, all he could hit was my right shoulder, and he did. His blade bit into the scar Tashayul had left on my shoulder so long before, and I cried out as I retreated away from him.

"There, Neal, that's *six*. Which of us will die marked a traitor?"

"Which indeed, Berengar." I squared myself to him and hunched into a crouch. Sweat stung my eyes and set every cut on my body burning like torches. I shifted my blade so it covered the center of my body, hilt at my navel and bloodied point by my eyes. I breathed in through clenched teeth and took some relief in seeing his chest heave as heavily as mine.

"You are closer than I." His blade started into a knotwork pattern. "Here is *seven*."

For the sake of symmetry I knew he would go for my throat, navel, or right hip, since he was intent on mirroring the pattern of the Haladin ritual. Right hip seemed most likely, and his blade began the journey toward it. I did not move, did not begin my parry until Berengar had committed fully and could not withdraw his attack. In he came, his goal unguarded.

Unguarded and, suddenly, unavailable. I dropped down and pushed off with my left foot. Sliding forward on my knees and twisting beneath his lunge, I got inside and thrust up through his body. Cleaveheart pierced him at the left hip and angled up. It scraped along inside his chest, then bounced off his right shoulder blade and punched out at his right shoulder. Overextended in his futile lunge, his body continued forward and began to fall on me. I shouldered him off to my right, landing him hard on his right flank.

His blade clattered on the marble inlay as it fell from his hand. Cleaveheart, torn from my grasp, rang dully when the hilt hit the floor. Berengar rolled over on his back, his jaw working furiously. Blood bubbled up in his mouth in the place of words and ran down either side of his face. His body shook once, the spine arching, then he lay very still.

His unseeing eyes stared up at the knotted sleeves in the cabinet.

To the south I heard the sound of snapping wood and breaking glass before people started screaming. The crowd parted and I saw Stulklirn shake himself, spraying glass from the shattered remains of the garden doors. Behind me I heard the rustle of Gena's gown, but I held up my empty hands to forestall either one of them coming to my aid.

My gesture also served to still the conversation in the room.

I stood slowly, uncoiling myself like a monster new risen from a long sleep, for that really was what I felt I had become. I let the anger burning inside of me infuse my voice. "Aurdon was a city conceived in evil, and it has not escaped it."

"That's right," shouted a Riveren. "The Fishers accuse us of treachery, but it's their Berengar that was bad."

I skewered him with a stare. "Ah, and you claim the Riverens never did use their influence with the Haladina to bedevil the Fishers? You know you did, and that is just as treacherous."

A Fisher shook a fist at me. "How can you claim to be the judge of what is treachery and what is not when you cheated in this fight?"

I let my shock play over my face. "I cheated?"

"Yes, you were not to the eighth cut when you killed him."

"Only an idiot born of idiots would have assumed I would use a Haladin ritual on someone who was not Haladin."

"Yes, but clearly you meant to do that. You broke the rules!"

"Rules? *Rules!*" I reached over and ripped Cleaveheart from Berengar's body. "Rules are for games. That fight was *not* a game. Berengar's decision to interpret my remarks as implying rules means nothing." I slashed the blade in a vast arc, splattering party-goers from the Fishers to the Riverens and leaving a track of crimson droplets to course down the cabinet's glass. "But, then, that has always been the problem with the Fishers and the Riverens, hasn't it? You always interpret in your *own* way what I have stated clearly in *mine*. This was not a game. None of it, not now, not five hundred years ago, and not during the intervening years. I am not Haladina concerned with Eight Cuts.

"I *am* Neal, and you will finally come to understand what that means."

I pointed to the knotted sleeves. "Five hundred years ago I stood in this place when Aurium was little more than a squalid village. The Fishers and the Riveravens were ready to slaughter each other over what was then a collection of longhouses surrounding a small stone hall. None of you would recognize what you have here in what I saw with my eyes, but by all the gods, you'd recognize your ancestors because they were as petty and shortsighted as all of you are now."

I glanced back at Gena and saw her watching me strangely. I did not know what she was thinking or even if Aarundel had told her about this night's analog, but I hoped she would stay with me and play along with me. I tried to communicate that to her with my eyes, but I did not know if she understood, so I just pushed on.

"That night, so long ago, Lady Genevera's grandfather and Stulklirn's great-great-grandfather stood by me, so it is fitting they are here tonight. Back then we were set to slay all the Fishers and all the Riverens because we knew they could not live in peace with each other. But because there were innocents among them, and because we had a war to fight against the Reithrese, we relented and found a compromise.

"That compromise, clearly, was a mistake." I snarled at all of them. "I have lain in my tomb for five centuries, and the only disturbance of my rest came from here, from Aurdon. Someone plots to kill someone else, so I must intervene. I am forced to act well beyond the time when I should be called upon to do so."

I hesitated as I sorted through the various tales I had heard the day before. "Victor Riveren decides to kill Harald Fisher over a boatload of raw wool, so I have to pitch him down some stairs. Lucretia Fisher plots to poison Deryl Riveren, and I have to force her own draught down her throat. And now, this time, the Riverens are using the Haładina to destroy the Fishers, and the Fishers want to build an empire using Riveren bones as the foundation. This plotting is so widespread, my intervention as a ghost would not suffice. For this I had to come back to *life*!

"This does *not* please me." I nodded to Gena and to Stulklirn. "I have the descendants of my allies at the first visit with me here for a reason. Stulklirn, as Shijef had agreed to do, please make certain no one leaves this room."

Stulklirn stood up to his full height and physically blocked the doors to the garden.

I looked at Gena. "And you, with your magicks, you will be able to slay the old quickly, and I will start with the young."

An older Riveren man pointed at me with a palsied hand. "This is preposterous! You cannot get away with such murder!"

"Can I not?" I stared incredulously at the lot of them. "I am Neal Roclawzi! I am the Knight-Defender of the Empire. I can slay each and every one of you and then simply send a note to the emperor telling him it was necessary. He will forgive me. Moreover, last time I had better things to do than to spend my time killing you foolish people off. Not so, this time.

"You have to remember, I am *five centuries* out of my time. I have no ties, no duties, no one I know, and no one to visit. If I slaughter the lot of you, I can claim your wealth for myself. By the beard of Herin, I was walking in your city yesterday, and I know from talking with the citizens that if I skim you from the top, the people out there will happily proclaim me their lord. With your money and the soldiers you brought to Aurdon, I could even choose to make the emperor abdicate in my favor."

I let myself go. I gestured wildly as I spoke. I fed off their fear and their vanity. I let them imagine their own sins, and I suggested I was there to punish them. I let them know that the doom their ancestors had delayed had returned to swallow them whole.

"The opportunity represented by those knotted sleeves was the *only* alternative your people were offered to death. One by one, piecemeal, you have rejected the bargain struck that night, and you have paid as individuals. You all know it's true, and you have all feared seeing my shade when you plotted and dreamed. Now it is worse because I have been called from the grave and I have with me *now* the blade that longed to drink your blood centuries ago."

"But the Knott family died out," someone pleaded.

"Ah, but my proscription against fighting with each other did not! Are you people stupid? Did you think the deaths of your kin were random events, superstition? When I make an oath, it is not broken. When individuals plotted against each other, I could take one or two lives and be satisfied that my honor had been upheld, but now, *now* you plot to conquer nations. The prize was bigger, the dishonor greater, and the penalty must be commensurately larger!"

Gena's features sharpened into an inhuman mask when she scowled. "You have heard Neal Custos Sylvanii. As he has said, so it will be." She casually gestured backward toward one of the windows in the eastern wall. The wooden lattice holding glass in place exploded in fire, spraying flame and glass out into the darkness. Another magickal spark sailed off through the middle of the conflagration, but I soon lost sight of it. I nodded to her and she smiled most cruelly. "We will need ventilation, for the sanguine aroma from termination will be overwhelming."

"Leave it to a *sylvanesti* to think of these details." I turned toward the assembly. "If the youngest would line up here on my left and the eldest here on my right, we shall begin."

"We can rush them," I heard someone cry, but before I could even begin to think of a counter that would forestall that winning strategy, the sun dawned very bright and very early to the east. It rose fast and shrank as it did, but by the time the fiery sphere had begun to dwindle significantly, a horrible roar and fierce rumbling echoed over the landscape. The ground shook and the chandeliers started swaying back and forth.

I looked from the windows to Gena and back again.

She shook her head, her eyes and voice as strong as they were implacable. "Berengar's weapons' store at Lake Orvir exists no more."

That display of raw power cowed the crowd. They began to shuffle toward the ends of the room I had indicated earlier; then Floris Fisher stepped from the crowd. "I'll be damned if I will let you slay my family. I will fight you, if I must, to prevent it."

I brought my head up and gave him a sidelong glance. "Would you do something even *more* difficult than face me across a sword?"

He came to attention. "I consider the sacrifice of my life nothing if it will save my family."

"I see." I looked over at the Riverens and pointed Cleaveheart at a comely young girl. "You see her?"

"I do."

"She is yours."

Floris shook his head. "I will not murder her to save even my life."

I smiled genuinely at him. "Good, for another Fisher slaying a Riveren would displease me even more than I am displeased now. She is yours to be your wife, to unite your families again."

Floris looked stunned. "But that is what you did last time. You said the penalty had to be greater."

"And so it shall be." I shifted the point of my sword to indicate a raven-haired woman among the Fishers who had been a favorite subject of gossips during my travels. "You are?"

"Martina, my lord."

"Good. Martina, Titus Riveren is now your husband!"

She shook her head adamantly. "He is just a boy."

"Then perhaps you can make him into a Man." I met her dagger stare with a grin. "And perhaps he can make you into something other than a milk-bathing repository of vanity."

That brought a blush to her face and a hearty laugh from the rest of the crowd. Titus looked up from the ground and wiped his face with his sleeve, smearing blood across both.

I looked hard at Martina. "Woman, see to your husband. Now!"

As she reluctantly crossed the floor, I addressed the rest of them. "This is how it shall be from this time forward. Any eligible Fisher will wed a Riveren and vice versa. All families thus united will be known as Knotts. All the wealth of all the families shall be commingled and shared. All business dealings will be held in common between the Fishers and Riverens until there are no more Fishers and Riverens, but only Knotts. That *is* the way it shall be, because I have no desire to return here in five hundred years or a thousand years or ever. If I am forced to, I shall not stay my hand."

I lowered my voice, and the background noise in the room sank appropriately. "Go, call your priests and sanctify these unions. Do it *now*! This second chance at life I give you because *I* have a second life. Let none of you give me cause to return a third time."

Epilogue

Night's Adventure in Aurdon

Winter
A.R. 499
The Present
My 536th Year

Standing in the darkened gardens of the Fisher estate, the cold winter night air leech-sucked warmth from me. The holes in my clothing made that easy, though the bandages over my wounds meant the cold did have to work a bit. Still, the chill did sink into my joints and bones as I leaned on my elbows on the stone balustrade that ringed the garden. Despite the flickering lights in the city below me, the shadows moving through the streets, and the strains of solemn wedding music from the gathering back in the ballroom, nothing felt truly alive to me. It seemed as if I had begun to slip back into my tomb, with my awareness of the outside world slowly evaporating the way light drains from the day at dusk.

A very cynical part of me wanted to believe I actually had been an avenging ghost over the past five hundred years. I wanted to lay claim to the righteous anger I had shown the people back in the mansion. I wanted to shake my head and speak to all the people who had fought for freedom as my allies, complaining to them that our sacrifices had been forgotten because nothing changes and people are no better now than we were then.

I could not do that because I knew it was not true. I did know that the Riverens had forged an alliance with the Haladina as a way to destroy the Fishers without engaging them directly, and they had done this without any intention of seeing the Haladina as true Men. Still, by inviting them into their city, by trading with them, working with them, and learning how they lived, the Riverens demystified the Haladina. The people of Aurdon helped humanize the image of the Haladina. Over time, over generations, that could lead to relations that would mean the Haladina might no longer raid in Centisia.

Only a fool would suggest the change would be easy, but the Elven change toward Men showed the change *could* take place. The Elven change and the change in attitudes toward the Haladina could mean the world would be a better place than the one I had known, or the one I was coming to know now.

I heard the light crunch of gravel and smiled without turning around. "Your destruction of Orvir was very convincing at a time when we needed to be convincing."

Gena came to stand beside me with her arms folded across her chest. "I am pleased you approved."

I shifted to lean on my left forearm and left hip so I could watch her, then shifted a bit to relieve the pressure on the holes I had in me at each point. "You played along well with what I was doing. I had been afraid you would think me crazy."

She smiled, dispelling some of the chill. "My grandfather, in recounting your exploits here the first time, mentioned something called the Codex Mercenarius. I did not know if you planned to actually kill people in there—and I hoped you were not—but I am not certain I would have stopped you if you had."

"Only Berengar needed killing. He was the most ambitious, and not everyone agreed with him and his plans. I suspect he had his brother, Lord Orvir, killed when his lordship discovered the foundry, flashdrakes, and powder-store at his lake estate."

"So Berengar's giving Rik Orvir's ring to prove he had the right to carry his flashdrakes was a joke?"

"I suppose so. I am actually surprised Berengar did not lecture us more on his plans for empire—the ego needed to come up with the sort of plan he did is not one that shies from bragging."

Gena looked out over the city, the light breeze toying with strands of her hair. "He actually did, once, when I pressed him. It seemed like idle conversation at the time—something to make the miles move more quickly as we rode to Jarudin. He was secretive. I had no clue that he wanted Cleaveheart to win an empire before, but now that I think of it, he was always insistent on getting the sword, and not as concerned with finding Wasp."

I shrugged. "I suspected something wrong when I heard the Haladina had not looted your Durriken's body and again when you gave no indication he was a Haladina, yet he was killed with Eight Cuts." My shrug had shifted my weight so my hip hurt, and as I moved to get comfortable, I hit the cut on my left forearm on the balustrade. I turned and sat my rump on the cold stone and frowned. "Even the whispers in the city didn't fully explain everything. What it all came down to was Berengar's desire to get his hands on Cleaveheart."

"I am glad you did not surrender the sword to him." Gena shook her head as I squirmed a bit in getting settled in my new position. "I *could* heal your cuts, you know. I took care of Titus, and I am still able to help you."

I shook my head. "These will make six nice new scars. When I'm old . . ."

Her eyebrow arched.

". . . older, I mean, in body as well as age, these scars will be worth many drinks and meals in some tavern somewhere."

She snorted politely and refrained from laughing. "Are you certain?"

"I've never . . . well, never intentionally had magick reverse the trouble I've gotten myself into. At five hundred and thirty-six I think I am a bit old to change my ways."

"I see." She watched me carefully, her violet eyes picking up an ethereal glow in the backlight from the ballroom. "I think I would apologize again for having saved you, having used magick to heal you, but I am not sorry for having done so."

I shrugged, then winced. "You were not given much choice in the matter."

"Even if I had known, I don't think that would have stopped me." She glanced back at the ballroom and hugged her arms around herself more tightly. "If you had not been here, Berengar would now be leading a mob through the streets of Aurdon, and the streets would be running with Riveren and Haladin blood."

I heard the serious tone in her voice, but still felt compelled to disagree. "Someone else would have stopped him."

"Perhaps, but not so soon. As an Elf, I can still speak with my grandfather and know the horror of the battles fought five centuries ago. In growing up in Cygestolia, I saw the pain caused by the need to destroy the Reithrese. I have seen the faces of warriors haunted by what they did. I know of atrocities and murders, and I know they were terrible. For the people back in the ballroom, the winning of the empire came seventeen generations ago. As you pointed out to me, the truth of what you fought for had been forgotten, and because it had been forgotten, a parody of it would have been played out on the world stage."

"And yet, because I was here and I remembered, it will not be."

She glanced down at the sword hanging by my side. "Unless you decide to win yourself an empire."

I laughed. "Done that, and it wasn't much fun." I winked at her. "Don't know as how I can forgive you for using magick on me, but if you don't want to be sorry for the reason you stated, I'm thinking you have every right to be proud and happy of your choice."

"That's not the only reason I'm not sorry." Her voice caught a bit, and she almost went on to add to her statement, but she stopped and looked out at the city again.

She didn't need to say anything more, because I thought I knew what she was going to say. "There are other reasons not to be sorry, Gena. I, for one, am happy to have seen your grandfather again, and your grandmother, and to have met you."

"You do not have to say that, Neal."

"I'm not. You remind me very much of your grand-aunt."

Gena's hands came down to her sides, and her hands knotted into fists. "I know, and I am sorry."

"Sorry?"

"Because that hurts you because I am not her."

Thoughts and memories I had pushed aside while trying to puzzle out Berengar's game came flooding back into my head. "Larissa and I, we . . . I mean, what we had, we knew, was, uh . . . when we spoke of . . . when she saw you . . ." I stopped and shook my head. "I am not doing this very well."

She looked up at me and choked back tears, but said nothing.

I twisted the bracelet from my right wrist and held it up. "When Larissa gave this to you, what did she say?"

Gena sniffed once, then forced her hands open. "She told me she was going beyond and then handed the bracelet to me. I knew what it was, but I never thought she would give it up. She said, 'I want you to remember, I have chosen you for this. You are my choice.' " Her head came up. "Does that mean something?"

I nodded for a bit until my throat opened enough to let words out. "We knew, as we traveled from Jarudin to Cygestolia for the ceremony involving your father's conception, that we two could never be together. Larissa could not bear the idea that her bloodline and my bloodline would die out. She made me promise that when she found someone for me . . . she wanted our progeny to have a chance at the happiness we could not know."

I took her left hand in mine and slipped the bracelet onto her wrist. "She wanted you to have this, and so do I."

Gena settled it on her arm, then looked up at me. "And she wanted me for you. Do you want that as well?"

"I see the *sylvanesti* have become even more direct over the last five centuries."

We both laughed, but when we stopped, a heavy silence pressed in on me.

I smiled at Gena. "Larissa was very special to me, and you to her. I respect her choice, but I want to respect you as well. I'm thinking that had we not learned a lot about each other on the road, in Jarudin and here, and if there were no attraction between us, we'd not be having this conversation. I am willing to explore the matter further, if you are."

She gave my hand a squeeze. "I am."

I nodded, then winced.

"Pain?"

"In a way. I was just thinking how protective your grandfather was of Larissa. I imagine he's more so of you."

Gena pursed her lips. "I'm thinking you can handle him."

"True enough, I did beat him in Jammaq, and that was when he had *two* eyes."

She stepped close and kissed me, then kissed me again. Her lips tasted sweet, and to my surprise, I didn't wonder if this was what it would have been like to kiss Larissa. Instead I wondered about what it would be like to steal another kiss from Gena.

Settling my arms around her slender waist, I pulled her to me and—scandal though it might have been somewhere in time—kissed her with all the enthusiasm appropriate for a man of my years kissing a *sylvanesti* half my age.

About the Author

Michael A. Stackpole is an award-winning game and computer game designer who was born in 1957 and grew up in Burlington, Vermont. In 1979 he graduated from the University of Vermont with a BA in History. In his career as a game designer he has done work for Flying Buffalo, Inc., Interplay Productions, TSR, Inc., FASA Corp., Hero Games and Game Designers Workshop.

In his spare time he watches far too much television, serves as the Executive Director of the Phoenix Skeptics and plays indoor soccer on the Blue Thunder team. He likes a variety of cuisines including, but not limited to, Mexican, Chinese, Japanese and Thai. While a good cook, he believes in supporting the pizza delivery industry for the good of the economy.

Once a Hero is the fourteenth novel he has written. In the future he plans to write more novels and to start a Twelve-Step program for those who wish to eliminate dangling modifiers from their prose.